# Us

Also by David Nicholls

Starter for Ten

The Understudy

One Day

# Us

## DAVID NICHOLLS

HODDER &
STOUGHTON

First published in Great Britain in 2014 by Hodder & Stoughton
An Hachette UK company

1

Copyright © David Nicholls 2014

A CIP catalogue record for this title is available from the British Library.

Hardback ISBN 978 0 340 89699 0
Trade Paperback ISBN 978 0 340 89700 3

Typeset by Palimpsest Book Production Ltd, Falkirk, Stirlingshire
Printed and bound by Clays Ltd, St Ives plc

Hodder & Stoughton policy is to use papers that are natural, renewable
and recyclable products and made from wood grown in sustainable forests.
The logging and manufacturing processes are expected to conform to the
environmental regulations of the country of origin.

Hodder & Stoughton Ltd
338 Euston Road
London NW1 3BH

www.hodder.co.uk

In memory of my father, Alan Fred Nicholls

Thou only hast taught me that I have a heart – thou only hast thrown a light deep downward and upward into my soul. Thou only hast revealed me to myself; for without thy aid my best knowledge of myself would have been merely to know my own shadow – to watch it flickering on the wall, and mistake its fantasies for my own real actions . . .

Now, dearest, dost thou understand what thou hast done for me? And is it not a somewhat fearful thought, that a few slight circumstances might have prevented us from meeting?

Nathaniel Hawthorne, a letter to Sophia Peabody
4 October 1840

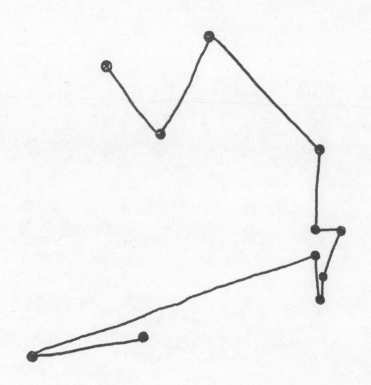

# BOOK ONE

# the grand tour

part one

# ENGLAND

—

The sweet habit of each other had begun to put lines around
her mouth, lines that looked like quotation marks – as if
everything she said had been said before.

Lorrie Moore, *Agnes of Iowa*

# 1. the burglars

Last summer, a short time before my son was due to leave home for college, my wife woke me in the middle of the night.

At first I thought she was shaking me because of burglars. Since moving to the country my wife had developed a tendency to jerk awake at every creak and groan and rustle. I'd try to reassure her. It's the radiators, I'd say; it's the joists contracting or expanding; it's foxes. Yes, foxes taking the laptop, she'd say, foxes taking the keys to the car, and we'd lie and listen some more. There was always the 'panic button' by the side of our bed, but I could never imagine pressing it in case the alarm disturbed someone – say, a burglar for instance.

I am not a particularly courageous man, not physically imposing, but on this particular night I noted the time – a little after four – sighed, yawned and went downstairs. I stepped over our useless dog, padded from room to room, checked windows and doors then climbed the stairs once more.

'Everything's fine,' I said. 'Probably just air in the water pipes.'

'What are you talking about?' said Connie, sitting up now.

'It's fine. No sign of burglars.'

'I didn't say anything about *burglars*. I said I think our marriage has run its course. Douglas, I think I want to leave you.'

I sat for a moment on the edge of our bed.

'Well at least it's not burglars,' I said, though neither of us smiled and we did not get back to sleep that night.

## 2. douglas timothy petersen

Our son Albie would be leaving the family home in October and all too soon afterwards so would my wife. The events seemed so closely linked that I couldn't help thinking that if Albie had flunked his exams and been obliged to retake, we might have had another good year of marriage.

But before I say any more about this and the other events that took place during that particular summer, I should tell you a little about myself and paint some sort of 'portrait in words'. It shouldn't take long. My name is Douglas Petersen and I am fifty-four years old. You see that intriguing final 'e' in the Petersen? I'm told it's the legacy of some Scandinavian heritage, some great-grandfather, though I have never been to and have no interesting stories to tell about Scandinavia. Traditionally, Scandinavians are a fair, hand-some, hearty and uninhibited people and I am none of those things. I am English. My parents, both deceased now, raised me in Ipswich; my father a doctor, my mother a teacher of biology. 'Douglas' came from her nostalgic affection for Douglas Fairbanks, the Hollywood idol, so there's another red herring right there. Attempts have been made over the years to refer to me as 'Doug' or 'Dougie' or 'Doogie'. My sister, Karen, self-proclaimed possessor of the Petersen's sole 'big personality', calls me 'D', 'Big D', 'the D-ster' or 'Professor D' – which, she says, would be my name in prison – but none of these have stuck and I remain Douglas. My middle name, incidentally, is Timothy, but it's not a name that serves anyone particularly well. Douglas Timothy Petersen. I am, by training, a biochemist.

Appearance. My wife, when we first met and felt compelled to talk constantly about each other's faces and personalities and what we *loved* about each other and all of that routine, once told me that I had a 'perfectly fine face' and, seeing my disappointment, quickly added that I had 'really kind eyes', whatever that meant. And it's true, I have a perfectly fine face, eyes that may well be 'kind' but are also the brownest of browns, a reasonable-sized nose and the kind of smile that causes photographs to be thrown away. What can I add? Once, at a dinner party, the conversation turned to 'who would play you in the film of your life?' There was a lot of fun and laughter as comparisons were made to various film stars and television personalities. Connie, my wife, was likened to an obscure European actress, and while she protested – 'she's far too glamorous and beautiful', etc. – I could tell that she was flattered. The game continued, but when it came to my turn a silence fell. Guests sipped their wine and tapped their chins. We all became aware of the background music. It seemed that I resembled no famous or distinctive person in the entire history of the world – meaning, I suppose, that I was either unique or the exact opposite. 'Who wants cheese?' said the host, and we moved quickly on to the relative merits of Corsica versus Sardinia, or something or other.

Anyway. I am fifty-four years old – did I say that? – and have one son, Albie, nicknamed 'Egg', to whom I am devoted but who sometimes regards me with a pure and concentrated disdain, filling me with so much sadness and regret that I can barely speak.

So it's a small family, somewhat meagre, and I think we each of us feel sometimes that it is a little too small, and each wish there was someone else there to absorb some of the blows. Connie and I also had a daughter, Jane, but she died soon after she was born.

## 3. the parabola

There is, I believe, a received notion that, up to a certain point, men get better-looking with age. If so, then I'm beginning my descent of that particular parabola. 'Moisturise!' Connie used to say when we first met, but I was no more likely to do this than tattoo my neck and consequently I now have the complexion of Jabba the Hutt. I've looked foolish in a T-shirt for some years now but, health-wise, I try to keep in shape. I eat carefully to avoid the fate of my father, who died of a heart attack earlier than seemed right. His heart 'basically exploded' said the doctor – with inappropriate relish, I felt – and consequently I jog sporadically and self-consciously, unsure of what to do with my hands. Put them behind my back, perhaps. I used to enjoy playing badminton with Connie, though she had a tendency to giggle and fool about, finding the game 'a bit silly'. It's a common prejudice. Badminton lacks the young-executive swagger of squash or the romance of tennis, but it remains the world's most popular racket sport and its best practitioners are world-class athletes with killer instincts. 'A shuttlecock can travel at up to 220 miles an hour,' I'd tell Connie, as she stood doubled over at the net. 'Stop. Laughing!' 'But it's got *feathers*,' she'd say, 'and I feel embarrassed, swatting at this thing with feathers. It's like we're trying to kill this finch,' and then she'd laugh again.

What else? For my fiftieth birthday Connie bought me a beautiful racing bike that I sometimes ride along the leafy lanes, noting nature's symphony and imagining what a collision with an HGV would do to my body. For my fifty-first, it was running gear, for my fifty-second, an ear- and nasal-hair trimmer, an object that continues both to appal and fascinate me, snickering away deep in my skull like a tiny lawnmower. The subtext of all these gifts was the same: do not stay still, try not to grow old, don't take anything for granted.

Nevertheless, there's no denying it; I am now middle-aged. I sit to put on socks, make a noise when I stand and have developed an unnerving awareness of my prostate gland, like a walnut clenched between my buttocks. I had always been led to believe that ageing was a slow and gradual process, the creep of a glacier. Now I realise that it happens in a rush, like snow falling off a roof.

By contrast, my wife at fifty-two years old seems to me just as attractive as the day I first met her. If I were to say this out loud, she would say, 'Douglas, that's just a line. No one prefers wrinkles, no one prefers grey.' To which I'd reply, 'But none of this is a surprise. I've been expecting to watch you grow older ever since we met. Why should it trouble me? It's the face itself that I love, not that face at twenty-eight or thirty-four or forty-three. It's *that* face.'

Perhaps she would have liked to hear this but I had never got around to saying it out loud. I had always presumed there would be time and now, sitting on the edge of the bed at four a.m., no longer listening out for burglars, it seemed that it might be too late.

'How long have you—?'

'A while now.'

'So when will you—?'

'I don't know. Not any time soon, not until after Albie's left home. After the summer. Autumn, the new year?'

Finally: 'Can I ask why?'

# 4. b.c. and a.c.

For the question, and the ultimate answer, to make sense, some context might be necessary. Instinctively, I feel my life could be divided into two distinct parts – Before Connie and After Connie, and before I turn in detail to what happened that summer, it might be useful to give an account of how we met. This is a love story, after all. Certainly love comes into it.

# 5. the other 'l' word

'Lonely' is a troubling word and not one to be tossed around lightly. It makes people uncomfortable, summoning up as it does all kinds of harsher adjectives, like 'sad' or 'strange'. I have always been well liked, I think, always well regarded and respected, but having few enemies is not the same as having many friends, and there was no denying that I was, if not 'lonely', more solitary than I'd hoped to be at that time.

For most people, their twenties represent some kind of high-water mark of gregariousness, as they embark on adventures in the real world, find a career, lead active and exciting social lives, fall in love, splash around in sex and drugs. I was aware of this going on around me. I knew about the nightclubs and the gallery openings, the gigs and the demonstrations; I noted the hangovers, the same clothes worn to work on consecutive days, the kisses on the tube and the tears in the canteen, but I observed it all as if through reinforced glass. I'm thinking specifically of the late eighties, which, for all their hardship and turmoil, seemed like a rather exciting time. Walls were coming down, both literally and figuratively; the political faces were changing. I hesitate to call it a revolution or portray it as some new dawn – there were wars in Europe and the Middle East, riots and economic turmoil – but there was at least a sense of unpredictability, a sense of change. I remember reading a great deal about a Second Summer of Love in the colour supplements. Too young for the First, I was completing my PhD – on Protein-RNA interactions and protein folding during translation – throughout the Second. 'The only acid in *this* house,' I was fond of saying around the lab, 'is deoxyribonucleic acid' – a joke that never quite got the acclaim it deserved.

Still, as the decade drew to a close things were clearly happening, albeit elsewhere and to other people, and I quietly wondered if a change was due in my life, too, and how I might bring that about.

## 6. drosophila melanogaster

The Berlin Wall was still standing when I moved to Balham. Approaching thirty, I was a doctor of biochemistry living in a small, semi-furnished, heavily mortgaged flat off the High Road, consumed by work and negative equity. I spent weekdays and much of the weekends studying the common fruit fly, Drosophila melanogaster, for my first post-doc, specifically using mutagens in classical forward genetic screens. Those were exciting times in Drosophila studies, developing the tools to read and manipulate the genomes of organisms and, professionally if not personally, this was something of a golden period for me.

I rarely encounter a fruit fly now, outside of a bowl of fruit. These days I work in the private, commercial sector – 'the evil corporation', my son calls it – as Head of Research and Development, a rather grand title but one that means I no longer experience the freedom and excitement of fundamental science. These days my position is organisational, strategical, words like that. We fund university research in order to make the most of academic expertise, innovation and enthusiasm, but everything must be 'translational' now; there must be some practical application. I enjoy the work, am good at it and I still visit labs, but now I am employed to co-ordinate and manage younger people who do the work that I used to do. I am not some corporate monster; I am good at my job and it has brought success and security. But it doesn't thrill me like it used to.

Because it *was* thrilling, to be working all those hours with a small group of committed, impassioned people. Science seemed exhilarating to me then, inspiring and essential. Twenty years on, those experiments on fruit flies would lead to medical innovations that we could never have imagined, but at the time we were motivated by pure curiosity, almost by a sense of play. It was just terrific *fun*, and it would not be an exaggeration to say that I loved my subject.

That's not to say there wasn't a great deal of mundane graft involved, too; computers were temperamental and rudimentary, barely more than unwieldy calculators and considerably less powerful than the phone in my pocket now, and data input was exhausting and laborious. And while the common fruit fly has a great deal in its favour as an experimental organism – fecundity, a short breeding cycle, distinctive morphology – it has little in the way of personality. We kept one as a pet in our lab's insectory, in its own special jar with a tiny rug and doll's house furniture, replacing it at the end of each life cycle. Though it's tricky to sex a fruit fly, we called him/her Bruce. Allow this to stand as the archetypal example of Biochemist Humour.

Such small diversions were necessary because anaesthetising a population of Drosophila, then examining them one by one with a fine brush and a microscope, looking for tiny changes in eye pigmentation or wing shape, is frankly mind-numbing. It's a little like embarking on an immense jigsaw. To begin with you think 'this will be fun' and you put on the radio and make a pot of tea, before realising that there are far too many pieces, nearly all of them sky.

Consequently I was far too tired to go to my sister's party on that Friday night. And not just tired, I was wary too, for a number of good reasons.

## 7. the matchmaker

I was wary of my sister's cooking, which invariably consisted of a tubular pasta and economy cheese, charred black on the surface, with either tinned tuna or lardy mince lurking beneath the molten crust. I was wary because parties, and dinner parties in particular, had always seemed to be a pitiless form of gladiatorial combat, with laurel garlands bestowed to the most witty, successful and attractive, and the corpses of the defeated lying bleeding on the painted floorboards. The pressure to be one's best self in such circumstances I found paralysing, and still do, yet my sister insisted on forcing me into the arena again and again.

'You can't stay at home for the rest of your life, D.'

'I don't stay at home, I'm hardly here . . .'

'Sat in that misery hole, all by yourself.'

'It's not a . . . I'm perfectly happy by myself, Karen.'

'You're not happy! You're not! How can you be happy, D? You're not happy! You are not!'

And it was true that there was not a great deal of glee before that February night, little cause for fireworks or the punching of air. I liked my colleagues, they liked me, but for the most part, I would say goodbye to Security Steve on a Saturday afternoon then not speak until my lips parted with an audible pop on the Monday morning as I greeted him hello. 'Good weekend, Douglas?' he'd ask. 'Oh, quiet, Steve, very quiet.' Still, there was pleasure and satisfaction in my work, a pub quiz once a month, the pint with my colleagues on a Friday night, and if I did occasionally suspect something was missing, well – didn't everyone?

Not my sister. In her mid-twenties Karen was promiscuous in her friendships and ran with what my parents referred to as 'an arty crowd': would-be actors, playwrights and poets, musicians, dancers, glamorous young people pursuing impractical careers, staying up late then meeting for long and emotional cups of tea during all hours of the working day. For my sister, life was one long group hug and it seemed to amuse her in some obscure way to parade me in front of her younger friends. She liked to say that I had skipped youth and leapt straight into middle age, that I had been forty-three in my mother's womb, and it was true, I suppose, that I'd never got the hang of being young. In which case why was she so desperate for me to come along?

'Because there'll be *girls* there—'

'Girls? Girls . . . Yes, I've heard talk of those.'

'One girl in particular—'

'I do know girls, Karen. I have met and spoken to girls.'

'Not like this one. Trust me.'

I sighed. For whatever reason, 'fixing me up with a girlfriend' had become something of an obsession for Karen, and she pursued it with a beguiling mixture of condescension and coercion.

'Do you want to be alone forever? Do you? Hm? Do you?'

'I have no intention of being alone forever.'

'So where are you going to meet someone, D? In your wardrobe? Under the sofa? Are you going to grow them in the lab?'

'I really don't want to have this conversation any more.'

'I'm only saying it because I *love* you!' Love was Karen's alibi for all kinds of aggravating behaviour. 'I'm laying a place for you at the table so if you don't come, the whole evening's ruined!' And with that, she hung up the phone.

## 8. tuna pasta bake

So that evening, in a tiny flat in Tooting, I was pushed by the shoulders into the tiny kitchen where sixteen people sat crammed around a flimsy trestle table designed for pasting wallpaper, one of my sister's notorious pasta bakes smouldering in its centre like a meteorite, smelling of toasted cat food.

'Everyone! This is my lovely brother, Douglas. Be nice to him, he's shy!' My sister liked nothing more than pointing at shy people and bellowing SHY! Hello, hi, hey there Douglas, said my competitors and I contorted myself onto a tiny folding chair between a handsome, hairy man in black tights and a striped vest, and an extremely attractive woman.

'I'm Connie,' she said.

'Pleased to meet you, Connie,' I said, scalpel sharp, and that was how I met my wife.

We sat in silence for a while. I contemplated asking if she'd pass the pasta but then I'd be obliged to eat it, so instead . . .

'What do you do, Connie?'

'Good question,' she said, though it was not. 'I suppose I'm an artist. That's what I studied, anyway, but it always sounds a bit pretentious . . .'

'Not at all,' I replied, and thought, *oh God, an artist*. If she'd said 'cellular biologist' there'd have been no stopping me, but I rarely encountered such people and certainly never at my sister's house. An *artist*. I didn't hate art, not by any means, but I dislike knowing nothing about it.

'So – watercolours or oils?'

She laughed. 'It's a little more complicated than that.'

'Hey, I'm a kind of artist too!' said the handsome man to my left, shouldering his way in. 'A *trapeze* artist!'

I didn't speak much after this. Jake, the fleecy man in vest and tights, was a circus performer who loved both his work and himself, and how could I possibly compete with a man who defied the laws of gravity for a living? Instead I sat quietly and watched her from the corner of my eye, making the following observations:

## 9. seven things about her

1. She had very good hair. Well cut, clean, shiny, an almost artificial black, points brushed forward over her ears ('Points' – is that right?) designed to frame her wonderful face. Describing hairstyles is not my forte, I lack the vocabulary, but there was something of the fifties film star to it, what my mother would call 'a do', yet it was modish and contemporary too. 'Modish' – listen to me! Anyway, I smelt the shampoo

and her scent as I sat down, not because I snuffled around in the nape of her neck like a badger, I knew better than that, but because the table was really very small.

2. Connie listened. For my sister and her friends, 'conversation' really meant taking it in turns to speak, but Connie listened intently to our trapeze artist, her hand on her cheek, her little finger resting in the corner of her mouth. Self-contained, calm, she had a quality of quiet intelligence. The expression she wore was intent but not entirely uncritical or unamused, so that it was impossible to discern if she found something impressive or ridiculous, an attitude that she has maintained throughout the entire course of our marriage.

3. Though I thought her lovely, she was not the most attractive woman at the table. It is traditional, I know, when describing these first encounters with loved ones to suggest that they emitted some special glow; 'her face lit up the room' or 'I could not look away'. In truth, I could and did look away and would say that, in conventional terms at least, she was perhaps the third most beautiful woman in the room. My sister, with her much vaunted 'big personality', liked to surround herself with extremely 'cool' people, but coolness and kindness rarely go together and the fact that these people were often truly appalling, cruel, pretentious or idiotic was, to my sister, a small price to pay for their reflected glamour. So while there were many attractive people there that night, I was very happy to be sitting next to Connie, even if she did not at first sight effervesce, incandesce, luminesce, etc.

4. She had a very appealing voice – low, dry, a little husky, with a noticeable London accent. She has lost this over the years, but in those days there was definitely a slight swallowing of the consonants. Usually this would be an indicator of social background, but not in my sister's circle. One of her cock-er-ney friends spoke as if he ran a whelk stall despite his father

being the Bishop of Bath and Wells. In Connie's case, she asked sincere, intelligent questions, which nevertheless had an undertow of irony and amusement. 'Are the clowns as funny in real life as they are on stage?' – that kind of thing. Her voice had the instinctive cadence of a comedian and she had the gift of being funny without smiling, which I've always envied. On the rare occasions that I tell a joke in public, I grimace like a frightened chimpanzee, but Connie was, is, deadpan. 'So,' she asked, her face a mask, 'when you're flying through the air towards your partner, are you ever tempted, at the very, very last moment, to do this –' and here she raised her thumb to her nose and wiggled her remaining fingers, and I thought this was just terrific.

5. She drank a great deal, refilling her glass before it was empty as if worried the wine might run out. The drink had no discernible effect except perhaps a certain intensity in conversation, as if it required concentration. Connie's drinking seemed quite light-hearted, with a kind of drink-you-under-the-table swagger to it. She seemed like fun.

6. She was extremely stylish. Not expensively or ostentatiously dressed but there was something *right* about her. The fashion of the day placed great emphasis on 'bagginess', giving the impression that the guests around the table were toddlers wearing their parents' T-shirts. Connie, in contrast, was neat and stylish in old clothes (which I have since learnt to call 'vintage') that were tailored and snug and emphasised her – I'm sorry, I apologise, but there really is no way around this – her 'curves'. She was smart, original, both ahead of the crowd and as old-fashioned as a character in a black-and-white film. In contrast, the impression I set out to create, looking back, was no impression at all. My wardrobe at that time ran the gamut from taupe to grey, all the colours of the lichen world, and it's a safe bet that chinos were involved. Anyway, the camouflage worked, because . . .

7. This woman on my right had absolutely no interest in me whatsoever.

## 10. the daring young man on the flying trapeze

And why should she? Jake the trapeze artist was a man who stared death in the face, while most nights I stared television in the face. And this wasn't just any circus, it was *punk* circus, part of the new wave of circus, where chainsaws were juggled and oil drums were set on fire then beaten incessantly. Circus was now sexy; dancing elephants had been replaced by nude contortionists, ultra-violence and, explained Jake, 'a kind of anarchic, post-apocalyptic *Mad Max* aesthetic'.

'You mean the clowns don't drive those cars where the wheels fall off?' asked Connie, her face a stone.

'No! Fuck that, man! These cars *explode*! We're on Clapham Common next week – I'll get you both tickets, you can come along.'

'Oh, we're not together,' she said, a little too quickly. 'We've just met.'

'Ah!' nodded Jake, as if to say 'that makes sense'. There was a momentary pause and to fill the gap, I asked:

'Tell me, do you find, as a trapeze artist, that it's hard to get decent car insurance?'

The percentage varies, but some of the things I say make no sense to me at all. Perhaps I'd meant it as a joke. Perhaps I'd hoped to emulate Connie's laconic tone through raised eyebrow and wry smile. If so, that hadn't come across, because Connie was not laughing but pouring more wine.

'No, because I don't tell 'em,' said Jake with a rebellious swagger, which was all very anarchic but good luck with any future claims, big guy. Having steered the conversation to insurance premiums, I now dolloped out the tuna pasta bake, scalding the back of Connie's hands with fatty strands of molten Cheddar, hot as lava, and as she peeled them off Jake returned to his monologue, stretching across me for more booze. To the extent that I'd ever thought about trapeze artists, I'd always pictured slick, broad Burt Lancaster types, smooth and brilliantined and leotarded. Jake was a wild man, covered in luxuriant body hair the colour of a basketball but still undeniably handsome, strong-featured, a Celtic tattoo encircling his bicep, a tangle of wild red hair gathered into a bun with a greasy scrunchie. When he spoke – and he spoke a great deal – his eyes blazed at Connie, passing straight through me, and I was forced to accept that I was watching a blatant seduction. At a loss, I reached for the rudimentary salad. Doused liberally with malt vinegar and cooking oil, it was my sister's rare culinary gift to make lettuce taste like a bag of chips.

'That moment when you're in mid-air,' said Jake, stretching for the ceiling, 'when you're falling but almost flying, there's nothing like that. You try to hold onto it, but it's . . . transient. It's like trying to hold on to an orgasm. Do you know that feeling?'

'Know it?' deadpanned Connie. 'I'm doing it right now.'

This made me bark with laughter, which in turn attracted a scowl from Jake, and quickly I offered the acrid salad bowl. 'Iceberg lettuce, anyone? Iceberg lettuce?'

## 11. chemicals

The tuna pasta bake was forced down like so much hot clay and Jake's monologue continued well into 'afters', an ironic sherry trifle topped with enough canned cream, Smarties and Jelly Tots to bring about the onset of type 2 diabetes. Connie and Jake were leaning across me now, pheromones misting the air between them, the erotic force field pushing my chair further and further away from the trestle table until I was practically in the hallway with the bicycles and the piles of *Yellow Pages*. At some point, Connie must have noticed this, because she turned to me and asked:

'So, Daniel, what do you do?'

*Daniel* seemed close enough. 'Well, I'm a scientist.'

'Yes, your sister told me. She says you have a PhD. What field?'

'Biochemistry, but at the moment I'm studying Drosophila, the fruit fly.'

'Go on.'

'Go on?'

'Tell me more,' she said. 'Unless it's top secret.'

'No, it's just people don't usually ask for more. Well, how can I . . . okay, we're using chemical agents to induce genetic mutation . . .'

Jake groaned audibly and I felt something brush my cheek as he reached for the wine. For some people, the word 'scientist' suggests either a wild-eyed lunatic or the white-coated lackey of some fanatical organisation, an extra in a Bond film. Clearly this was the way Jake felt.

'*Mutation?*' said Jake, indignantly. 'Why would you mutate a fruit fly? Poor bastard, why not leave it be?'

'Well, there's nothing inherently unnatural about mutation. It's just another word for evolu—'

'I think it's wrong to tamper with nature.' He addressed the table now. 'Pesticides, fungicides, I think they're evil.'

As a hypothesis, this seemed unlikely. 'I'm not sure a chemical compound can be evil in itself. It can be used irresponsibly or foolishly, and sadly that has sometimes been the—'

'My mate, she's got an allotment in Stoke Newington; it's totally organic and her food is beautiful, absolutely beautiful . . .'

'I'm sure. But I don't think they have plagues of locusts in Stoke Newington, or annual drought, or a lack of soil nutrients—'

'Carrots should taste of carrots,' he shouted, a mystifying non sequitur.

'I'm sorry, I don't quite—'

'Chemicals. It's all these chemicals!'

Another non sequitur. 'But . . . everything's a chemical. The carrot itself is made of chemicals, this salad is chemical. This one in particular. You, Jake, you're made up of chemicals.'

Jake looked affronted. 'No I'm not!' he said, and Connie laughed.

'I'm sorry,' I said, 'but you are. You're six major elements, 65 per cent oxygen, 18 per cent carbon, 10 per cent—'

'It's because people try to grow strawberries in the desert. If we all ate local produce, naturally grown without all these chemicals—'

'That sounds wonderful, but if your soil lacks essential nutrients, if your family's starving because of aphids or fungus, then you might be grateful for some of those evil chemicals.' I'm not sure what else I said. I was passionate about my work, felt that it was beneficial and worthwhile, and as well as idealism, jealousy might also have played a part. I'd drunk a little too much and after a long evening of being alternately patronised and ignored, I had not warmed to my rival, who was of the school that thought the solution to disease and hunger lay in longer and better rock concerts.

'There's easily enough food to feed the world, it's just all in the wrong hands.'

'Yes, but that's not the fault of science! That's politics, economics! Science isn't responsible for drought or famine or disease, but those things are happening and that's where scientific research comes in. It's our responsibility to—'

'To give us more DDT? More Thalidomide?' This last blow seemed to please Jake hugely, and he broadcast a handsome grin to his audience, delighted that the misfortunes of others had provided him with a valuable debating point. Those were terrible tragedies, but I didn't remember them being specifically my fault, or my colleagues' – all of them responsible, humane, decent people, all ethically and socially aware. Besides, those instances were anomalies compared to all the extraordinary developments science had given us, and I had a very clear mental image of myself high, high in the shadows of the big top, sawing madly at a rope with a penknife.

'What would happen,' I wondered aloud, 'if you fell from your trapeze, God forbid, and broke your legs and a massive infection set in? Because what I'd love to do, in those circumstances, Jake, what I'd love to do is stand by your bedside with the antibiotics and analgesics just out of reach and say, I know you're in agony but I can't give you these, I'm afraid, because, you know, these are chemicals, created by scientists and I'm very sorry, but I'm afraid I'm going to have to amputate both your legs. Without anaesthetic!'

## 12. silence

I wondered if perhaps I had overplayed my hand. In hoping to sound impassioned I had come across as unhinged. There had been malice in what I'd said, and no one likes malice at a dinner party, not open malice, and certainly not my sister, who was glaring at me with custard dripping from her serving spoon.

'Well, Douglas, let's hope it doesn't come to that,' she said weakly. 'More trifle?'

More distressingly, I was not acquitting myself well in front of Connie. Even though we'd spoken only briefly, I liked this woman very much and wanted to create a good impression. With some trepidation, I glanced to my right, where she remained with her chin in the palm of her hand, her face entirely impassive and unreadable and, to my mind, even lovelier than before as she took her hand from her face, placed it on my arm and smiled.

'I'm so sorry, Douglas, I think I called you Daniel earlier.'

And that – well, *that* was like a light coming on.

## 13. apocalypse

*I think our marriage has run its course*, she said. *I think I want to leave you.*

But I'm aware of having gone off on a tangent and wallowing in happier times. Perhaps I'm casting too rosy a glow. I'm aware that couples tend to embellish 'how we met' folklore with all kinds of detail and significance. We shape and sentimentalise these first encounters into creation myths to reassure ourselves and our offspring that it was somehow 'meant to be', and with that in mind perhaps it's best to pause there for the moment, and return to where we came in – specifically the night, a quarter-century later, when the same intelligent, amusing, attractive woman woke me to say that she thought she might be happier, that her future might be fuller, richer, that all things considered she might feel more 'alive' if she were no longer near me.

'I try to imagine it, us alone here every evening without Albie. Because he's maddening, I know, but he's the reason why we're here, still together . . .'

*Was he the reason? The only reason?*

'. . . and I'm terrified by the idea of him leaving home, Douglas. I'm terrified by the thought of that . . . *hole.*'

*What was the hole? Was I the hole?*

'Why should there be a hole? There won't be a hole.'

'Just the two of us, rattling around in this house . . .'

'We won't rattle around! We'll do things. We'll be busy, we'll work, we'll do things together – we'll, we'll fill the hole.'

'I need a new start, some kind of change of scene.'

'You want to move house? We'll move house.'

'It's not about the house. It's the idea of you and me in each other's pockets forever more. It's like . . . a Beckett play.'

I'd not seen a Beckett play, but presumed this was a bad thing. 'Is it really so . . . horrific to you, Connie, the thought of you and I being alone together? Because I thought we had a good marriage . . .'

'We did, we do. I've been very happy with you, Douglas, very, but the future—'

'Then why would you want to throw that away?'

'I just feel that as a unit, as husband and wife, we did it. We did our best, we can move on, our work is done.'

'It was never work for me.'

'Well, sometimes it was for me. Sometimes it felt like work. Now that Albie's leaving, I want to feel this is the beginning of something new, not the beginning of the end.'

*The beginning of the end.* Was she still talking about me? She made me sound like some kind of apocalypse.

The conversation went on for some time, Connie elated at all this truth-telling, me reeling from it, incoherent, struggling to take it in. How long had she felt like this? Was she really so unhappy, so jaded? I understood her need to 'rediscover herself', but why couldn't she rediscover herself with me around? Because, she said, she felt our work was done.

Our work was done. We had raised a son and he was . . . well, he was healthy. He seemed happy occasionally, when he thought no one was looking. He was popular at school and he had a certain charm, apparently. He was infuriating, of course, and always seemed to be more Connie's son than mine; they'd always been closer, he'd always been on 'her team'. Despite owing his existence to me, I suspected my son felt that his mother could have done better. Even so, was he really the sole purpose and product, the sole work, of twenty years of marriage?

'I thought . . . it had never crossed my mind . . . I'd always imagined . . .' Exhausted, I was having some trouble expressing myself. 'I'd always been under the impression that we were together because we wanted to be together, and because we were happy most of the time. I'd thought that we loved each other. I'd thought . . . clearly I was mistaken, but I was looking forward to us growing old together. Me and you, growing old and dying together.'

Connie turned to me, her head on the pillow, and said, 'Douglas, why would anyone in their right mind look forward to *that*?'

## 14. the axe

It was light outside now, a bright Tuesday in June. Soon we would rise wearily and shower and brush our teeth standing at the sink together, the cataclysm put on hold while we faced the banalities of the day. We'd eat breakfast, shout farewell to Albie, listen to the shuffle and groan that passed for his goodbye. We would hug briefly on the gravel drive—

'I'm not packing any suitcases yet, Douglas. We'll talk more.'

'Okay. We'll talk more.'

—then I would drive off to the office and Connie would head off to the train station and the 0822 to London where she worked three days a week. I would say hello to colleagues and laugh at their jokes, respond to emails, eat a light lunch of salmon and watercress with visiting professors, listen to reports of their progress, nod and nod and all the time:

*I think our marriage has run its course. I think I want to leave you.*

It was like trying to go about my business with an axe embedded in my skull.

# 15. holiday

I managed it, of course, because a public display of despair would have been unprofessional. It wasn't until the final meeting of the day that my demeanour started to falter. I was fidgeting, perspiring, worrying at the keys in my pocket, and before the minutes of the meeting had even been approved I was standing and excusing myself, grabbing my phone, mumbling excuses and hurrying, stumbling towards the door, taking my chair some of the way with me.

Our offices and labs are built around a square laughably called The Piazza, ingeniously designed to receive no sunlight whatsoever. Hostile concrete benches sit on a scrappy lawn which is swampy and saturated in the winter, parched and dusty in the summer, and I paced back and forth across this desolate space in full view of my colleagues, one hand masking my mouth.

'We'll have to cancel the Grand Tour.'

Connie sighed. 'Let's see.'

'We can't go travelling around Europe with this hanging over us. Where's the pleasure in that?'

'I think we should still do it. For Albie's sake.'

'Well, as long as Albie's happy!'

'Douglas. Let's talk about it when I get back from work. I must go now.' Connie works in the education department of a large and famous London museum, liaising on outreach programmes to schools, collaborating with artists on devised work and other duties that I don't quite understand, and I suddenly imagined her in hushed conversation with various colleagues, Roger or Alan or Chris, dapper little Chris with his waistcoat and his little spectacles. *I finally told him, Chris. How did he take it? Not too well. Darling, you did the right thing. At last you can escape The Hole . . .*

'Connie, is there someone else?'

'Oh, Douglas . . .'

'Is that what this is all about? Are you leaving me for someone else?'

She sounded weary. 'We'll talk when we get home. Not in front of Albie, though.'

'You have to tell me now, Connie!'

'It's not to do with anyone else.'

'Is it Chris?'

'I'm sorry?'

'Little Chris, waistcoat Chris!'

She laughed, and I wondered: how is it possible for her to laugh when I have this axe protruding from my skull?

'Douglas, you've met Chris. I'm not insane. There's no one else, certainly not Chris. This is entirely about you and me.'

I wasn't sure whether this made it better or worse.

## 16. pompeii

The fact was I loved my wife to a degree that I found impossible to express, and so rarely did. While I didn't dwell on the notion, I had presumed that we would end our lives together. Of course, this is a largely futile desire because, disasters notwithstanding, someone has to go first. There's a famous artefact at Pompeii – we intended to see it on the Grand Tour we had planned for the summer – of two lovers embracing, 'spooning' I think is the term, their bodies nested like quotation marks as the boiling, poisonous cloud rolled down the slopes of Vesuvius and smothered them in hot ash. Not mummies or fossils as some people think, but a three-dimensional mould of the void left as they decayed. Of course there's no way of knowing that the two figures were husband and wife; they could have been brother and sister, father and daughter, they might have been adulterers.

But to my mind the image suggests only marriage; comfort, intimacy, shelter from the sulphurous storm. Not a very cheery advertisement for married life, but not a bad symbol either. The end was gruesome but at least they were together.

But volcanoes are a rarity in our part of Berkshire. If one of us had to go first, I had hoped in all sincerity that it would be me. I'm aware that this sounds morbid, but it seemed to be the right way round, the sensible way, because, well, my wife had brought me everything I had ever wanted, everything good and worthwhile, and we had been through so much together. To contemplate a life without her; I found it inconceivable. Literally so. I was not able to conceive of it.

And so I decided that it could not be allowed to happen.

part two

# FRANCE

—

'And at home by the fire, whenever you look up there I shall
be – and whenever I look up there will be you.'

Her countenance fell, and she was silent awhile.

Thomas Hardy, *Far From the Madding Crowd*

## 17. note to self

Some guidelines for a successful 'Grand Tour' of Europe:
1. Energy! Never be 'too tired' or 'not in the mood'.
2. Avoid conflict with Albie. Accept light-hearted joshing and do not retaliate with malice or bitter recriminations. Good humour at all times.
3. It is not necessary to be seen to be right about everything, even when that is the case.
4. Be open-minded and willing to try new things. For example, unusual foods from unhygienic kitchens, experimental art, unusual points of view, etc.
5. Be fun. Enjoy light-hearted banter with C and A.
6. Try to relax. Don't dwell on the future for now.
7. Be organised, but –
8. Maintain a sense of fun and spontaneity.
9. At all times be aware of Connie. Listen.
10. Try not to fight with Albie.


## 18. posh inter-railing

The holiday had been Connie's idea. 'A Grand Tour, to prepare you for the adult world, like in the eighteenth century.'

I didn't know much about it either. Connie said that it was once traditional for young men of a certain class and age to embark on a cultural pilgrimage to the continent, following well-established routes and, with the help of local guides, taking in certain ancient sites and works of art before returning to Britain as sophisticated, civilised men of experience. In practice the culture was largely an excuse for drinking and whoring and getting ripped off, arriving home with pillaged artefacts, some bottles of the local booze and venereal disease.

'So why don't I just go to Ibiza?' said Albie.

'Trust me,' said Connie, 'this will be much, much more fun.' We were sitting at the kitchen table on a Sunday morning – this was in happier times, before my wife's announcement – my old *Times Atlas* opened on a map of Western Europe, and there was a kind of glee in Connie that I'd not seen for a while.

'You have to remember this was all in the days before cheap mechanical reproduction, so the Grand Tour was their one chance to see all these masterpieces outside dodgy black-and-white engravings. All the great works of the ancient world and the Renaissance, Chartres Cathedral, the Duomo in Florence, St Mark's Square, the Colosseum. You'd take fencing lessons, cross the Alps, explore the Roman Forum, look down into the crater of Vesuvius and walk the streets of Naples. And yes, you'd drink and whore and get into fights, but you'd come back a *man*.'

'Ibiza it is, then,' said Albie.

'Come on, Egg! Play along,' said Connie. Like an advancing general, she traced her finger across the pages of the atlas. 'Look – we'll start in Paris, do the obvious stops: the Louvre, the Musée d'Orsay, the Monets and the Rodins. We'll train to Amsterdam, see Rembrandt at the Rijksmuseum, the Van Goghs, then find our way – no planes, no cars – across the Alps to Venice, because it's Venice. Back through Padua for the Scrovegni Chapel; Vicenza for Palladio's villas; Verona – Verona's lovely – see *The Last Supper* in Milan; Florence, for the Botticelli in the Uffizi and, well, just for Florence – then Rome! Rome is beautiful. Stop off at Herculaneum and Pompeii and finish up in Naples. Of course, in an ideal world we'd jump back and do the Kunsthistorisches in Vienna, then Berlin, but we'll have to see how your father's holding up.'

I was emptying the dishwasher and confess to being distracted by the low level of rinse aid as well as the ruinous cost of all this travel. But she really did seem very excited by it all, and perhaps it would make a change from our recent family holidays, the three of us restless, bitten and sun-burnt in some expensive villa or fighting for our tiny share of the Mediterranean coast.

Albie remained sceptical. 'So, basically I'm going inter-railing with my mum and dad.'

'That's right, you lucky boy,' said Connie.

'But if it's meant to be this great rite of passage and you're both there, doesn't that sort of defeat the object?'

'No, Egg, because you're going to learn about art. If you were serious about painting in those days, this was your training, your university. Same thing now. You can sketch, take photos, suck it all in. If you want to do it for a living, you have to see these things—'

'A lot of Old Masters, a lot of dead white Europeans.'

'—even if it's just so you've got something to kick against. Besides, Picasso's a dead white European, and you love Picasso.'

'Can we see *Guernica*? I'd love to see *Guernica*.'

'*Guernica*'s in Madrid. We'll do it another time.'

'Or you could just give me the money and I'll go alone!'

'This way it's *educational*,' said Connie.

'This way you get out of bed in the mornings,' I said.

Albie groaned and laid his head on his arms, and Connie took to twisting her finger in the hair at the nape of his neck. They do this, Connie and Albie, grooming each other like primates. 'We'll have fun, too. I'll make sure your father schedules some in.'

'Every fourth day, is that too much?' I returned to the machine. Not just rinse aid, salt too; it was burning through the stuff, and I wondered how I might recalibrate the settings.

'You can still meet girls and get drunk,' said Connie. 'You'll just have to do it with me and your father watching. And pointing.'

Albie sighed and rested his cheek on his fist. 'Ryan and Tom are going backpacking in Colombia.'

'And you can too! Next year.'

'No he can't,' I shouted into the dishwasher. 'Not Colombia.'

'Shut up, Douglas! Egg, sweetheart, this will probably be the last summer holiday we'll have together.'

I looked up, striking my head sharply on the edge of the kitchen unit. The last ever? Was it? Was it really?

'After this, you're on your own,' said Connie. 'But for now let's try and have a nice time this summer, shall we? This one last time?'

Perhaps she'd been planning her escape, even then.

## 19. hissing in fields

When my wife told me that she was going with the turning of the leaves, did my life come to an end? Did I fall to pieces or fail to make it through the days?

Of course there were further sleepless nights, further tears and accusations in the lead-up to the trip, but I had no time for a nervous breakdown. Also, Albie was completing his 'studies' in art and photography, returning exhausted from screen-printing or glazing a jug, and so we were discreet, walking our dog, an ageing Labrador called Mr Jones, some distance away from the house and hissing over his head in fields.

'I can't believe you've sprung this on me!'

'I haven't *sprung* it, I've been feeling this way for years.'

'You haven't said anything.'

'I shouldn't have to.'

'Springing this on me, at this time . . .'

'I'm sorry, I've tried to be as honest as I—'

'I still think we should cancel the Grand Tour . . .'

'Why do we have to?'

'You still want to go? With this hanging over us?'

'I think so—'

'A funeral cortège, backpacking through Italy . . .'

'It needn't be like that. It could be fun.'

'If you want to cancel the hotels you need to say now.'

'I've just told you, I want us to go. Why don't you ever listen to—?'

'Because if you're really trapped in such a living hell—'

'Don't be melodramatic, love, it doesn't help.'

'I don't know why you suggested it if you didn't want to—'

'I did want to, I still do!' She stopped and held my hand. 'Let's put the other decision on hold until the autumn. We'll all go on the trip, we'll have a fantastic time with Albie—'

'And then we'll come back and say goodbye? You won't even have to bother unpacking, you could just chuck your suitcase in a taxi and head off . . .'

At which point she sighed and looped her arm through mine as if nothing were wrong. 'Let's see. Let's see what happens.' And we walked Mr Jones back to the house.


## 20. maps

A route took shape: Paris, Amsterdam, Munich, Verona, Venice, Florence, Rome and Naples. Of course Connie had been to most of these places before, on an epic odyssey of smoking cannabis and kissing local boys, working as a waitress, a tour guide, an au pair in the years before she started art school. In the early days of our relationship, when my work and our puny finances permitted it, we would sometimes take cheap flights to European cities and Connie would spot a bench, a bar or café and lapse into a reverie about the time she and her friends spent a week sleeping on the beach in Crete, or the wild party she had been to in an abandoned factory outside Prague, or the un-named boy she'd fallen madly in love with in Lyon in '84, the Citroën mechanic with his strong hands and broken nose and the smell of engine oil in his hair. I'd find a smile and change the subject, but clearly 'well travelled' meant something different to Connie. Been there, done him, that was our joke. Europe represented first love and sunsets, cheap red wine and breathless fumbling.

I'd had no such rite of passage, partly because of my father, a fierce patriot who raged against the whole world's bloody-minded refusal to knuckle down, learn decent English and live like us. Anything that suggested 'abroad' made him suspicious: olive oil, the metric system, eating outdoors, yoghurt, mime, duvets, pleasure. His xenophobia was not limited to Europe; it was international and knew no borders. When my parents came to London to celebrate my PhD, I made the mistake of brandishing my cosmopolitanism by taking them to a Chinese restaurant in Tooting. Chiang Mai's fulfilled my father's key restaurant criteria in that it was unnervingly cheap and brutally over-lit ('so you can see what you're bloody well eating!') yet I still recall the expression on his face when handed a pair of wooden chopsticks. He pointed them at the waiter, like a switchblade. 'Knife and fork. Knife. And. Fork.'

Of course we argued about this. The Channel Tunnel, he said, was 'like leaving your front door open'. What did he imagine might happen? I asked. A great, marauding horde of toreadors and trattoria waiters and onion-sellers pouring out into Folkestone, Kent? In fairness, my father had lost his own father in Belgium in 1944, and perhaps this provided some deep-seated justification for his hostility, but still, it was irrational in such a rational man. To my father, 'abroad' was a strange, unknowable place where the milk tasted odd and lasted an unnaturally long time.

So I was not well travelled; in fact I barely knew Europe until I met Connie. Wherever we went, she had been there before. Her European map was already dense with red pins signifying stolen rucksacks, missed flights, languorous kissing in ornamental parks, pregnancy scares, fresh oranges off the tree and ouzo for breakfast. On my very first visit to her flat I had glimpsed several photographs stuck to her fridge, new-wave Connie and her art-school friends with gelled perms, blowing kisses at the camera or smoking topless – topless! and with cigarettes! – on a balcony in Sicily.

*My very first visit to her flat.* I'm not even through the door yet. She's still talking to Jake.

## 21. the ejector-seat

After my sister's ironic sherry trifle had been disposed of we were all encouraged to swap places and 'mingle', Connie and Jake vacating their chairs at ejector-seat speed. 'Mingling', it transpired, involved continuing their conversation at a different part of the table, and I watched as the acrobat produced from somewhere, I don't know where – from his tights, perhaps – a small plastic Ziploc bag of dusty sweets which he offered to Connie, who accepted with a nod, almost a shrug of resignation, before passing the bag to my sister and on around the table. They couldn't have been very nice sweets, because everyone was grimacing and washing them down with water. Soon I found myself sitting between two actors on drugs, a position that, a number of peer-reviewed research papers have since confirmed, is precisely the worst place a biochemist can be. One of the actors had been performing excerpts from his one-person show, to my mind one person too many and when the Ziploc bag reached us, he broke off and, shook it underneath my nose. At the end of the table, I caught a glimpse of my sister nodding, nodding, eyes wide in encouragement.

'No thanks,' I said.

'You don't partake?' said the actor, pouting. 'You should! Have a cheeky half, it's lovely.'

'I'm sorry, but the only acid in my house is deoxyribonucleic—'

'Hey, has anyone got any chewing gum?'

I left the table.

Karen intercepted me in her bedroom where I was searching through great piles of overcoats.

'You're going? It's not even ten!'

'I don't really think it's my "scene", Karen.'

'You don't know until you try it.' She was looking terrifically pleased with herself, my sister. Not quite brave enough to rebel in my parents' presence, she enjoyed using me as their proxy. I was simply the nearest old square to hand. 'Why are you so boring, D?'

'Oh, I practise every night.'

'It drives me crazy!'

'Just as well I'm leaving, then.' I had found my coat and was wrapping my scarf around my neck.

'Stay and try it.'

'No.'

'Why not?'

'Because I don't want to, pusher-man! Why are you so keen for me to do something that I don't want to do?'

'Because I think you should try things! It might reveal a new part of your personality.'

'Well, I'm sorry to disappoint you, but this is it. This is everything, this is all there is.'

Karen placed her hand on my chest. 'I think Connie likes you.'

'Oh. Really.'

'In fact she told me so.'

'You are such a liar, Karen.'

'She said she found you very interesting, even all that science stuff. She said it made a change to meet someone who was interested in something other than themselves.'

'I can't find my other glove. There's a glove here somewhere . . .'

'She said she found you very attractive.'

38

I laughed. 'Then the drugs have kicked in.'

'I know! I was as surprised as you.'

'And what makes you think I like her?'

'Your lolling tongue. Also, you'd be insane not to. Everyone loves Connie, she's amazing.'

'If you find my other glove, can you keep it for me please? It looks like . . . well, this one. Obviously.'

Karen blocked my way to the bedroom door, and began unwrapping the scarf from my neck. 'Stay. Just for half an hour. The moment people start touching each other's faces, then you can go.'

## 22. a blurred photo

It did not take long for the 3,4-methylenedioxy-N-methyl-ampthetamine to seep through the bedrock of tuna pasta bake. It was as if an invisible presence were wandering the room, tapping people on the head with a wand that turned them into idiots.

'Let's sit soft!' commanded my sister, eyes goggling, and the guests moved from the kitchen. I put the Pyrex in to soak before being dragged into the tiny living room, which was decked out as a kind of shabby harem with pillows on the floor, candles recklessly tickling the bottom of curtains and the air grey with cigarette smoke. Carole King's *Tapestry* was replaced by something with a tinny snare and choppy piano. The word 'bass' was rhymed with 'face' and soon the dancing began. One of Karen's friends, I noticed, was topless under dungarees.

I was beginning to feel foolish. It was like waiting in a queue for a rollercoaster that I had no intention of riding. Why did I remain, leaning in a corner, making stilted conversation with a dramaturg? My motivation slouched on a beanbag, Jake curled up at her feet like an immense ginger cat. Karen was right; I had liked this girl immediately. I liked her obvious intelligence, the keen attention she directed at people. I liked the humour that played perpetually in the corner of her mouth and smudged eyes. And I found her attractive, of course – her face, her figure . . .

Well, these days, Connie's figure is the subject of perpetual care and a recurring circular argument – *I look awful, no you don't, yes I do, you look wonderful* – an endless rally that I can do nothing to break. She feels, has always felt, that she is too large. You look wonderful to me, I say. She shrugs this away. I look like a blurred photo of myself, she says, I no longer have cheekbones – as if this was what anyone wanted in a face: bones. The truth is I feel the same way about her now as I did back then, which is to say very strongly. We had so little in common and yet she seemed to me to have more wit and grace and *life* in her than anyone in that crowded room, or indeed my world at that time.

So I waited, and eventually she caught my eye and smiled wonderfully, and Jake's eyes followed too. He growled and tried to take her wrist as she stood – a little unsteadily, I noticed. She removed his hand and crossed the room towards me.

I excused myself from the dramaturg.


## 23. magnets

'You're still here!' she said in my ear.

'Just for a while,' I said in hers.

'I wanted to apologise. We didn't really get a chance to speak at dinner. Jake's very interesting, but he doesn't have much of a sense of humour. Or curiosity.'

'No, I noticed.'

'I liked it when you threatened to cut off his legs.'

'Did I do that? I did, didn't I?'

'I was watching your face. You got very eloquent, very passionate. Of course I didn't understand half of what you were saying. I'm completely remedial when it comes to science. I don't know what revolves around what, or why the sky's blue, or the difference between an atom and a molecule. It's embarrassing, really. I took my niece to the seaside last summer and she asked me why the tide came in and out and I told her it was something to do with magnets.'

I laughed. 'Well it's one theory, I suppose.'

She put her hand on my arm. '*Is* it magnets? Please, please tell me it's magnets!'

I was in the process of explaining the influence of the moon's gravitational pull on large bodies of water, when she paused and put her hands on her chest and opened her eyes wide.

'Sorry,' she said, 'I just got a bit of a rush. Are you feeling it yet?'

'The drugs? Oh, I don't really do that kind of thing.'

'Very sensible. Very.'

We looked around the room. The drugs seemed to be having a devastating effect on people's posture, with everyone hunching their shoulders and bobbing their heads in a sort of hyper-tense disco. My sister in particular was scrunched up like a squirrel, sucking her lips inwards in concentration as she shook tiny imaginary maracas.

'Look at them,' said Connie, shaking her head. 'People always say *take this, drink that, you'll lose your inhibitions*. What we need is something that'll give them back. *Here, try this, it'll make you massively sensible*. We'd all have a much better time. Imagine waking up and saying to yourself, "Christ, I was *totally* inhibited last night."'

'Actually, that's exactly what I do say.'

She laughed, for the first time I think. 'Lucky you! Sounds lovely.' There was a brief moment where we did nothing but smile, then: 'It's very loud in here. I need some water. Can we go in the kitchen?'

I noticed Jake, his hooded eyes glaring territorially. 'Actually, I was about to head off home.'

'Douglas,' she said over her shoulder, reaching out her hand, 'you give in *far* too easily,' and I wondered what she meant as I followed her through.

## 24. spatula

In the kitchen I battled with my desire to wipe down all the surfaces.

'Your sister tells me you're some kind of genius.'

'Well, my sister has a low "genius" threshold. She says the same about practically everyone in that room.'

'That's different, though, isn't it? That's talent, and not even talent most of the time. Self-confidence, that's what it is. When she says "genius" she just means they've got a really loud voice. You, you actually know things. Tell me again, about the fruit flies.'

I did my best to explain in layman's terms, while she stood at the sink and drank water from a pint glass in one long gulp, then remained standing with her head thrown back, a good deal of water running the length of her neck.

'. . . then we take the next generation of fruit flies and examine how the chemical agents have altered the . . . are you all right?'

Coming round, she blinked and shook her head a little. 'Me? Yeah, I'm fine, I drank a little too much and now . . .' She sighed and drew her hands down her face. 'Christ, that was a bright idea! I've just broken up with someone, you see.'

'Oh, I'm sorry.'

'No, it was the right thing to do, it was a terrible relationship, it's just . . . it was four years, you know?'

'A long time.'

'Keep talking to me, won't you? Don't go away.'

I had no intention of going away. 'So we look for changes in the fly's pheno—'

'You seeing someone, Douglas?'

'Me? No, not at the moment, not for some time. Pressure of work,' I said, as if this were the reason.

'I knew you were single.'

'Is it really so obvious?'

'No, I mean your sister told me. I think she's been trying to fix us up.'

'Yes. Yes, I'm sorry about that.'

'Don't apologise. Not your fault. She's convinced that I'd be good for you. Or was it the other way around? Either way, nothing's going to happen.'

'Oh.' This struck me as unnecessarily blunt. 'No, well, I suspected that.'

'Sorry, sorry, not because of you – you seem really, really nice – just because, you know, rebound and everything. I'm a bit . . .'

A moment passed. 'I presumed you were interested in—'

'Jake? God, no!'

'It seemed that way at dinner.'

'Did it? I'm sorry, I wanted to talk to you but he just wouldn't stop and – Jake? Really, not for me. Can you imagine that flying through the air towards you, like a great hennaed bear, arms outstretched. I'd keep my hands deep in my pockets, safety net or no safety net.' She poured red wine into the pint glass then gulped it down as if it were lemon barley water. 'If I wanted a self-absorbed egomaniac, I'd call my ex.' She pointed an unsteady finger at me. 'Don't let me call my ex!'

'I won't.'

There was a pause, and she smiled. Lipstick had been replaced by the black stain of the wine, and her dark fringe was now sticky with sweat. Pupils dilated, her eyes were wonderful. She tugged at the front of her dress. 'Is it hot in here, or is it me?'

'It's you,' I said. I had been considering what it would feel like to kiss her, weighing this against what it would feel like to miss the last tube. The kiss felt possible, but it felt un-gentlemanly to take advantage of standards that had been chemically lowered. Which was clearly the case, because now she shivered and smiled and said:

'Please don't misinterpret this, Douglas, but would you mind coming over here and just . . . holding me?'

At which point a fiery ball of hair barrelled low into the kitchen, scooped her up and dangled her over his shoulder. 'Are you hiding from me, little lady?'

'Actually, can you put me down please, Jake?'

'Scuttling away with Doctor Frankenstein . . .' He was shifting her on his shoulder now, as if adjusting a roll of carpet. 'Come and dance with me. Now!'

'Stop it, please!' She seemed embarrassed, upset, her face red.

'Jake, I think you should put her—'

'Here, watch this. Can you do this, Doctor Frankenstein?' And with an ease that would have been admirable if Connie had been willing, he tossed her into the air and caught her on the palms of his hands, his elbows locked so that her head bounced against the lightshade. Her black dress had ridden up and with one hand she tugged it down, the smile on her face fixed and mirthless.

'I said, put. Her. Down!'

I could hardly believe the voice was mine, or indeed the hand that was now at arm's length, brandishing a plastic spatula flecked with tuna pasta bake. Jake glanced at the spatula, then at me, then laughed, rolled Connie down to the ground and with a dainty big-top skip, left the kitchen. 'Prick-tease!' was his parting shot.

'I hope they take away your safety net!' shouted Connie, tugging at her dress's hem. 'Conceited bastard.'

'Are you all right?'

'Me? I'm fine. Thank you.' I followed her glance. The rubber utensil was still in my hand. 'What were you planning to do with that?'

44

'If he didn't put you down, I was going to make him eat something.'

She laughed, rotated her shoulders and put her hand to her neck as if assessing the damage. 'I feel terrible, I have to go outside.'

'I'll come with you.'

'In fact . . .' She put her hand on my arm '. . . more than that, I have to go home.'

'The tubes have stopped running.'

'That's all right, I'll walk.'

'Where do you live?'

'Whitechapel.'

'Whitechapel? That's eight, ten miles away.'

'S'all right, I'd like to. I've got a change of shoes. I'll be fine, it's just . . .' She placed both hands on her chest. 'I need to walk this off and if I'm by myself I'm going to . . . crash into something. Or someone.'

'I'll come with you,' I said.

A moment passed. 'Thank you,' she said. 'I'd like that.'

'I should go and say goodbye.'

'No.' She took my hand. 'Let's make a French exit.'

'What's a French exit?'

'It's when you leave without saying goodbye.'

'I've never heard that before.'

A French exit; no *thank you for having me*, no *I've had a lovely time*. To just walk away, cool and aloof. I wondered if I could.


## 25. mr jones

The morning of departure we awoke at five thirty a.m. and said a fond goodbye to Mr Jones, who was to be cared for by our neighbours, Steph and Mark, for the month-long duration of the Grand Tour. We were always surprised by how much we missed Mr Jones. Even in canine terms he is basically an idiot, perpetually running into trees, falling into ditches, eating daffodils. A 'sense of humour', Connie calls it. Throw Mr Jones a stick and more likely than not he will return with a pair of discarded underpants. Monumentally flatulent, too – weapons-grade. But he is foolish, loyal and affectionate and Connie is entirely devoted to him.

'Bye, old pal, we'll send you a postcard,' she cooed, nuzzling at his neck.

'Don't think there's much point sending a postcard,' I said. 'He'll only eat it.'

Connie sighed deeply. 'I'm not really going to send him a postcard.'

'No, no, I realised that.' We had been wilfully misinterpreting each other's jokes since Connie's warning of departure. It hummed away beneath everything we did, however innocuous. Even saying goodbye to Mr Jones contained the question: who will get custody?

And so we roused Albie, for whom rising before eight a.m. was an infringement of his basic human rights, then took a taxi to Reading and crammed onto a commuter train to Paddington, Albie sleeping en route, or pretending to do so.

Despite my resolutions, we had argued the night before, in this instance about the acoustic guitar that Albie insisted on dragging across Europe – an absurd and impractical affectation, I thought – and there was the usual stomping up the stairs, Connie's familiar sigh, her famous slow head-shake.

'I'm worried he's going to busk,' I said.

'So let him busk! There are worse things a seventeen-year-old can do.'

'I'm worried that he's going to do those, too.'

But it seemed the guitar was as essential as his passport. Needless to say it was I who bundled the case through the turnstiles at the Eurostar terminal, lugged it through security, crammed it into inadequate luggage space on the train as we took our seats where I began swabbing with napkins at the hot coffee now dripping from my wrist. There's a particular grubbiness that comes with travel. You start showered and fresh in clean and comfortable clothes, upbeat and hopeful that this will be like travel in the movies; sunlight flaring on the windows, heads resting on shoulders, laughter and smiles with a lightly jazzy soundtrack. But in reality the grubbiness has set in before you've even cleared security; grime on your collar and cuffs, coffee breath, perspiration running down your back, the luggage too heavy, the distances too far, muddled currency in your pocket, the conversation self-conscious and abrupt, no stillness, no peace.

'So – goodbye England!' I said to fill the gap. 'See you in four weeks!'

'We've not left yet,' said Albie, his first words to me for twelve hours, then produced his Nikon and started taking close-up photographs of the bottom of his shoe.

## 26. albert samuel petersen

Albie is dark, like his mother; his hair black, tangled and long, dangling into his eyes and scratching at the corneas so that I constantly want to lean across to brush it out of the way. Eyes large and brown and wet – 'soulful' is a word that gets bandied about – the dark skin around them the colour of a bruise. He has a long nose, a full, dark mouth and is, by all accounts, an attractive young man. One of Connie's female friends said that he looked like a murderous ruffian in a Caravaggio, a comparison that meant nothing to me until I looked it up. But clearly there is a demand out there for late-Renaissance muggers with scrappy facial hair and consumption, because girls seem drawn to him, feel they can 'really talk' to him, and I've long since given up keeping track of the Rinas and Ninas and Sophies and Sitas for whom surliness, irresponsibility and poor personal hygiene are such irresistible traits.

But he is *cool*, they say, he is deep; people are drawn to him and in this respect, as in all others, he is his mother's son. He is 'not a natural academic', according to his college tutor, 'but he has wonderful *emotional intelligence*', a phrase that made my teeth snap together. Emotional intelligence, the perfect oxymoron! 'How do they test *emotional* intelligence? What qualification does that lead to?' I asked Connie as we drove home. 'Perhaps there's a multiple-choice element. They put you in a room with six people and you have to work out who to hug.'

'It means he has empathy,' she replied dryly. 'It means he has some awareness of and interest in other people's feelings.'

And so it seems the only thing that Albie has taken from my side of the family is my father's skinny height, yet he seems embarrassed and resentful even of this, with his round shoulders and stooped, loping walk, arms dangling, as if unable to manage the weight of his hands. Oh, and smoking, he's taken that from my father, too. In consideration of my views on the subject, he smokes in secret, though it's not a secret that he holds precious, given the number of lighters and Rizla packets he leaves lying around, given the smell of it on his clothing and the burn marks on the window ledge of his filthy bedroom. 'How did they get there, Albie?' I said. 'The swallows? Smoking swallows, with their Duty Free?' at which point he laughed and kicked the door closed. Oh, and as well as the emphysema, cancer and heart disease that he is presumably nurturing in that narrow chest, he suffers from a malaise that requires at least twelve hours of sleep, and yet is singularly incapable of commencing these twelve hours before two a.m.

What else? He is fond of T-shirts with absurdly low-cut v-necks so that his sternum is constantly on display, and he has a habit of withdrawing his arms through the sleeves and jamming his hands into his armpits. He refuses to wear a coat, an absurd affectation, as if coats were somehow 'square' or un-cool, as if there were something 'hip' about hypothermia. What is he rebelling against? Warmth? Comfort? 'Let it go', says Connie, as he strides out into some gale with his rib-cage showing, 'it won't kill him' – but it might, and if it doesn't then the sheer frustration of it all will kill me. Take, for example, the state of his bedroom, a room so filthy that it is effectively a no-go zone, an immense Petri dish of furry toast crusts and lager tins and unthinkable socks that will one day have to be sealed off in concrete like Chernobyl, and this is not just laziness on his part – no, real effort has gone into a situation designed to cause the maximum upset. To me! Not to his mother, but to me, to me, so that it is no longer simply a bedroom, it is a massive act of spite.

And he's a mumbler, a swallower of words. Despite spending the last six years in a perfectly nice part of Berkshire, he speaks in a bored cockney drawl because God forbid anyone should think his father has done well or worked hard, God forbid anyone should think that he's comfortable and cared for and loved, loved equally by both of his parents even if he only seems to desire and require the attentions of one.

In short, my son makes me feel like his step-father.

I have had some experience of unrequited love in the past and that was no picnic, I can tell you. But the unrequited love of one's only living offspring has its own particular slow acid burn.

## 27. helmut newton

But now the train had finally begun to move, and Albie had switched the fearless truth-telling eye of his camera lens from his untied laces to the walls of the tunnels under east London, because you can never have enough pictures of dirty concrete.

'I hope you're going to take lots of pictures of the Eiffel Tower, Egg,' I said, in an affectionate, teasing tone. 'Me and your mother standing in front with our thumbs up?' We demonstrated. 'Or – another tip – I can put my hand out flat like this, so it looks like I'm holding it . . .'

'That's not photography, that's *holiday snaps*.' It seemed the tendency to wilfully misinterpret jokes was contagious. Connie winked at me and squeezed my knee beneath the table.

My son was soon to study photography on a three-year course which we were financing and although my wife, who knew about these things, insisted that he had talent, an 'eye', the fact of it filled me with an anxiety that I fought daily to suppress. At one point he had been intending to study theatre – theatre! – and at least I had managed to nip that in the bud, but now it was photography, the latest of a long series of temporary passions – 'street art', skateboarding, DJ-ing, drumming – the abandoned detritus of which cluttered cellar, attic and garage, alongside the optimistic chemistry set that I had bought and he had tossed aside, the hopeful microscope that had never been unpacked, the dusty box that offered an opportunity to 'Grow Your Own Crystals!'

But there was no denying his enthusiasm. Albie with a camera was something to see, crouching and contorting his long body into a question mark as if playing the role of 'photographer'. Sometimes he fired off frames at arm's length, in what I believe is called 'gangster style', sometimes on tiptoe, back arched like a toreador. Initially I made the mistake of standing and grinning when the camera was produced, but soon realised that he wouldn't actually press the shutter until I'd stepped out of the frame. In fact, in all the thousands of shots that he had taken, many of them loving portraits of his mother – her eyes, her smile – alongside his usual repertoire of wet cardboard boxes and badgers hit by cars, etc., there was not a single photograph of me. Not of my face, anyway, just an extreme close-up of the back of my hand, black and white in heavy contrast, part of a college project that I later discovered was called 'Waste/Decay'.

Albie's passion for photography had been the cause of tension in other ways. I had a printer in my office, a top-of-the-range colour model whose features included glacial speed and shocking running costs. Consequently, I was more than a little annoyed to return from work one day and hear the printer grinding away. Irritably, I examined the top print of a sizeable pile of 8x10s. It seemed to be a high-contrast, minutely detailed black-and-white print of some kind of dark moss and only when I peered more closely did I realise that this was in fact a photograph of a naked female form, shot in profile so to speak. I dropped the photograph, then gingerly examined the shot beneath. In washed-out black and white, it might have passed for some sort of snowy mountain range, were it not for the pale dimpled nipple that crowned the peak. Meanwhile, a third image was rumbling its way out of the machine and from the section that was visible, there seemed every chance that buttocks were emerging.

I called Connie in. 'Have you seen Albie?'

'He's in his room. Why?'

I held up the photographs and predictably, her response was to clasp her hand to her mouth and laugh. 'Oh, Egg. What *have* you been up to?'

'Why can't he just photograph someone's *face* for once?'

'Because he's a seventeen-year-old boy, Douglas. This is what they do.'

'I didn't. I photographed wildlife. Birds and squirrels and iron-age forts.'

'Which is why you're a biochemist and he's a photographer.'

'I wouldn't mind so much, but does he have any idea how much the cartridges cost for this thing?'

Connie, meanwhile, was peering closely at the buttocks. 'My money's on Roxanne Sweet.' She held the photograph to the light. 'I think they're rather good. Of course he's pinched it all off Bill Brandt, but they're not bad.'

'Our son, the pornographer.'

'It's not *pornography*, it's a nude study. If he was painting nudes at a life-drawing class you wouldn't bat an eyelid.' She pinned the print to my office wall. 'Or at least I'd hope you wouldn't. Who knows any more?'

## 28. passion

Soon after, Albie announced his intention to devote his life to a hobby. Why, I asked Connie, could he not study a more practical subject and do the things he enjoyed at weekends and in the evenings, like the rest of us? Because that's not how an arts-based course works, said Connie; he needs to be challenged, to develop his famous 'eye', learn to use his tools. But wouldn't it be cheaper and quicker to just read the manual? I could understand if people still used darkrooms as I had as a young man, but all of that know-how was obsolete, and how could Albie hope to excel in a field where anyone with a phone and a laptop could be broadly proficient? It wasn't even as if he wanted to be a photojournalist or a commercial photographer, taking pictures for newspapers or advertisements or catalogues. He didn't want to photograph models or weddings, athletes, or lions chasing gazelles, photographs that people might pay for, he wanted to be an *artist*, to photograph burnt-out cars and bark, taking pictures at such angles that they didn't look like anything at all. What would he actually *do* for three years, apart from smoke and sleep? And what professional job could he hope for at the end of it?

'Photographer!' said Connie. 'He's going to be a photographer.'

We were pacing around the kitchen, furiously tidying up, by which I mean tidying up, furious. Wine had been drunk and it was late, the end of a long, fraught argument that, as was his way, Albie had provoked then fled from. 'Don't you see?' said Connie, hurling cutlery at the drawer. 'Even if it's hard, he has to try! If he loves it, we have to let him try. Why must you always have to stomp on his dreams?'

'I've got nothing against his dreams as long as they're attainable.'

'But if they're attainable then they're not dreams!'

'And that's why it's a waste of time!' I said. 'The problem with telling people that they can do anything they want to do is that it is objectively, factually inaccurate. Otherwise the whole world would just be ballet dancers and pop stars.'

'He doesn't want to be a pop star, he wants to take photographs.'

'My point still stands. It is simply not true that you can achieve anything if you love it enough – it just isn't. Life has limitations and the sooner he faces up to this fact then the better off he'll be!'

Well, that's what I said. I believed I had my son's best interests at heart. That was why I was so vocal, because I wanted him to have a secure professional life, a good life. Listening up in his bedroom, no doubt he had caught all of my words and none of my intention.

Still, the argument was not my finest moment. I had become shrill and dogmatic but even so I was surprised to discover that Connie was now standing still, wrist pressed to her forehead.

'When did it start, Douglas?' she said, her voice low. 'When did you start to drain the *passion* out of everything?'

## 29. *world of wonder*

'So why did you become a scientist?'

'Because I never really wanted to do anything else.'

'But why . . . I'm sorry, I've forgotten the subject . . . ?'

'Biochemistry, that's my PhD. Literally the chemistry of life. I wanted to know how we work; not just us, all living things.'

'When was this?'

'Eleven, twelve.'

Connie laughed. 'I wanted to be a hairdresser.'

'Well, my mum was a biology teacher, dad was a GP, so it was in the air.'

'But you didn't want to be a doctor?'

'I thought about it, but I wasn't sure about my bedside manner, and the great thing about biochemistry over medicine, my dad said, was that no one ever asked you to look up their bum.'

She laughed, which I found intensely gratifying. Clapham High Street late at night is not the most scenic of routes, and at a little after one in the morning it has its own perils, but I was enjoying talking to her – or talking at her because she was, she said, 'too off her face' to do much but listen. It was a bitterly cold night, and she clung to my arm, for warmth I supposed. She had swapped her high heels for clumpy trainers, and wore a wonderful old black coat with some kind of feathery collar, and I felt intensely proud and protective, and strangely invulnerable too, as we strode past the drunks and muggers, the hens and stags.

'Am I being very boring?'

'Not at all,' she said, her eyelids heavy. 'Keep talking.'

'They used to buy me this magazine, *World of Wonder* or something it was called – my parents wouldn't allow the other ones, the silly ones, *Dandy* or *Whizzer and Chips* or whatever, in the house. So I used to read this terribly dry, old-fashioned magazine and it was full of projects and diagrams and jolly things to do with vinegar and bicarbonate of soda, how to turn a lemon into a battery—'

'You can do that?'

'I have that power.'

'You *are* a genius!'

'Thanks to *World of Wonder*. Fun facts! Did you know caesium has atomic number 55? That sort of thing. Of course at that age you're just like this big sponge, so it all went in, but the bit I loved the best was this cartoon strip, "Lives of the Great Scientists". There was one about Archimedes, I could draw it for you now: Archimedes in his bath, making the connection between volume and density, dancing naked down the street. Or Newton and his apple, or Marie Curie . . . I loved this idea of the sudden beautiful realisation. A light bulb going on, literally for Edison. One individual experiences this flash of insight and suddenly the world is altered fundamentally.'

I hadn't spoken this much for years. I hoped, from Connie's silence, that she was finding me fantastically interesting, but when I looked her eyes were rolled far back into her head.

'Are you all right?'

'I'm sorry. I'm just rushing my tits off.'

'Oh. Okay. Should I stop talking?'

'No, I love it. You're bringing me down, but in a good way. Wow. Your eyes look massive, Douglas. They're taking up your whole face.'

'Okay. So . . . should I keep talking, then?'

'Yes, please. I like listening to your voice. It's like listening to the Shipping Forecast.'

'Boring.'

'Reassuring. Let's keep walking. Tell me more.'

'Anyway, these stories were nonsense for the most part, or hugely over-simplified. Most scientific progress is a slog, and more often than not it stems from a dialogue within a community, lots of people thinking along the same lines and inching forward, rather than these great bolts of lightning. Newton did see the apple fall, but he'd been thinking about gravity well before that. The same with Darwin, he didn't wake up one day and think: natural selection! There'd been years and years of observation, discussion and debate. Good science is slow-moving, methodical, evidence-based. Method. Results. Conclusion. Like my old tutor used to say, "To *assume* makes an *ass* of *u* and *me*!"' Here, rather optimistically, I had hoped she might laugh, but she was staring open-mouthed at her wiggling fingertips. 'Still, I was hooked. It seemed heroic, or at least the kind of heroism I might have access to. Normal boys aspired to be foot-ballers or pop stars or soldiers, and I wanted to be a scientist, because wouldn't it be incredible to have a moment like that? An entirely original idea. A cure, an insight into space and time, a water engine.'

'Anything occurred to you?'

'Not as yet.'

'Well it's still early days!'

'Of course it was all a lot easier in the past. Much easier to make your mark when people still thought the sun revolved around the earth and there were four bodily humours. Not much chance of me making that kind of breakthrough now.'

'Oh no!' she said with real feeling. 'That's not true!'

''Fraid so. Science is a race, you've got to get there first. There's no second prize. Look at Darwin – those ideas were in the air, but he was the first to get his paper published. The only way I could really make a mark now is to be transported back to, say, 1820. I'd jot down some pointers on evolutionary theory. I'd explain to the Royal College of Surgeons exactly why washing your hands is a good idea. I'd invent the combustion engine, the light bulb, the aeroplane, photography, penicillin. If I could get back to 1820, I'd be the greatest scientist the world has ever known, greater than Archimedes or Newton or Pasteur or Einstein. The only obstacle is being a hundred and seventy years too late.'

'Clearly, what you need to do,' she said, 'is invent a time machine.'

'Which is theoretically impossible.'

'There you go again, being negative. If you can make a battery out of a lemon, how hard can it be? I'm sure you could do it.'

'You hardly know me.'

'But I can *tell*. I have a sense. Douglas, some day you are going to do something quite amazing.'

She was very far from sober, of course, but, if only for a moment, I thought she really did believe this of me. Even that it might be true.

## 30. tunnels and bridges

And so we journeyed on, three of us now, in what I chose to take as a companionable silence, sneaking out of London through the back door and surfacing in dreary countryside, all pylons and motorways, a sudden glimpse of a river – the Medway? – crammed with holiday cruisers sulking in the overcast English summer, then more scrappy woodland then the motorway again. Soon enough the guard announced that we were about to enter the Channel Tunnel and the passengers looked obediently to their windows in the hope of seeing – what? Shoals of brightly coloured fish swimming past aquarium glass? A tunnel under the sea is never quite as visually splendid as one hopes, but it is no less an achievement for that. Who designed the Channel Tunnel? No one knows the name. There are no more Brunels or Stephensons, and tunnels, by their very nature, never get the attention of great bridges, but still this was a great feat. I voiced the thought aloud; how tunnels were underrated and it was miraculous, really, to imagine that great mass of rock and water over our heads and yet to feel safe.

'I don't feel safe,' said Albie.

I sat back in my seat. Engineering – why hadn't engineering interested my son?

Out into daylight, a militarised landscape of fences, concrete bunkers and escarpments, then the pleasant, uniform agricultural plain that stretches all the way to Paris. It is, of course, an illusion to imagine that the crossing of arbitrary boundaries on a map should correspond to variations in mood and temperament. A field is a field and a tree is a tree, but nevertheless this could only be France, and the air on the train took on a different quality, or seemed to, as French passengers emanated the satisfaction of returning home, and the rest of us the excitement of being officially 'abroad'.

'Here we are then! France!'

And even Albie couldn't find anything to disagree with there.

I fell asleep, neck cricked, jaw clenched, skull vibrating against glass, then awoke in the early afternoon as we entered the suburbs of Paris, Albie visibly perking up at the sight of graffiti and urban grime. I handed out A4 polypropylene wallets containing itineraries for the North European leg of our trip; hotel addresses, phone numbers and train times; and a loose breakdown of events and activities. 'A guideline, rather than a strict schedule.'

Albie turned the pages back and forth. 'Why isn't this laminated, Dad?'

'Yes, why isn't it laminated?' said Connie.

'Dad's getting sloppy.' My wife and son enjoyed heckling me. It gave them pleasure, so I smiled and played along, confident that they'd be grateful in the end.

Once off the train we felt revived, and I didn't even mind the guitar case clunking against my knees, the coffee corrosion in my stomach and the edginess of that particular station. 'Keep a close eye on your bags,' I warned.

'Any railway station, anywhere in the world,' said Connie to Albie, 'you can guarantee your father will tell you to keep a close eye on your bags.'

Then the sky outside the Gare du Nord opening up, bright and blue, to greet us.

'Are you excited?' I asked my son as he climbed into the taxi.

'I've been to Paris before,' he shrugged. Across the back of the seat, Connie caught my eye and winked and we set off, stopping and starting through the hard, unlovely kernel of the city towards the Seine, Connie and I sandwiching our son, hips pressed closer than we were used to, waiting for the commerce of the Grands Boulevards to give way to the dusty elegance of the Jardin des Tuileries, the lovely and ridiculous Louvre, the bridges across the Seine. Pont de la Concorde? Pont Royal? Unlike London, which has only two or perhaps three decent bridges, every crossing point of the Seine seems wonderful to me, clear views preserved on either side, and Connie and I peered greedily this way and that, following each other's eyes while Albie looked down at his phone.

# 31. on london bridge

We crossed London Bridge a little after two forty-five in the morning. The City was rather different in those years, squatter and less brazen than today, a model village Wall Street and very much alien territory to someone who rarely travelled further east than Tottenham Court Road. Now the place was deserted as if in advance of some impending disaster, and we walked past Monument, down Fenchurch Street, voices clear in the night air, and told the stories that we choose to tell when people are new.

Connie had recovered her powers of speech and told me more about her large, messy family, her mother an ex-hippy, skittish and boozy and emotional, her biological father long absent now, leaving her nothing but his surname. Which was? Moore. Connie Moore – *a terrific name*, I thought, *like a village in Ireland*. Her step-father could not have been more different, a Cypriot businessman who ran a number of questionable kebab shops in Wood Green and Walthamstow, and she was now an anomaly in her family: the arty, smart one. 'I have three half-Cypriot brothers, little bulldogs they are; they all work in the business, and they have no idea what I do. Same as my dad – he'll be watching telly and he'll see a view of the Dales, or we'll be on holiday and he'll see a sunset or an olive tree and he'll say – she slipped into an accent, she has always been very good at accents – '"Connie, you see that? Draw that! Draw it, quick!" Or he tries to commission me. "Draw your mother, she's a beautiful lady, do a painting. I'll pay." To Kemal, that's the supreme achievement of the artist, to draw eyes that look in the same direction.'

'Or hands.'

'Exactly. Hands. If you can fit all the fingers on, you're Titian.'

'Can you draw hands?'

'Nope. I love him, though – Kemal – and my brothers, too. They dote on my mum and she sucks it all up. But I don't see me in any of them, or in her either.'

'What about your father? Your biological—'

She shuddered. 'He left home when I was nine. I'm not really allowed to mention him because it sets my mum off. He was very handsome, I know that. Very charming, a musician. Ran off to Europe. He's . . . out there . . . somewhere.' She gestured towards the east. 'Don't really care,' she said, and shrugged. 'Change the subject. Ask me something else.'

The biographies we give ourselves at such times are never neutral and the image she chose to present was of a rather solitary soul. She was not mawkish or self-pitying, not at all, but with the bravado gone, she seemed less confident, less self-assured, and I felt flattered by her honesty. I loved the conversation that we had that night, especially once she had stopped hallucinating. I had an infinite number of questions and would have been happy for her to recount her life in real time, would have been happy to walk on past Whitechapel and Limehouse into Essex and the estuary and on into the sea if she'd wanted to. And she was curious about me, too, something that I'd not experienced for some time. We talked about our parents and our siblings, our work and friends, our schools and childhoods, the implication being that we would need to know this information for the future.

Of course, after nearly a quarter of a century, the questions about our distant pasts have all been posed and we're left with 'how was your day?' and 'when will you be home?' and 'have you put the bins out?' Our biographies involve each other so intrinsically now that we're both on nearly every page. We know the answers because we were there, and so curiosity becomes hard to maintain; replaced, I suppose, by nostalgia.

## 32. many strange horses in our salty bedroom

In planning our trip I had initially adopted a no-expense-spared attitude, until I calculated the full extent of this expense, at which point I adopted a comfortable-but-no-frills policy. It was this that brought us to the Hotel Bontemps, which may or may not translate as the Good Times Hotel, in the 7th arrondissement. Room 602 was clearly the result of a wager to determine the smallest space into which a double mattress can fit. Brassy and vulgar, the bed frame must have been assembled inside like a ship in a bottle. On closer examination, it also seemed our room was a repository for all of Europe's spare pubic hair.

'All in all, I'd have preferred a chocolate on the pillow,' said Connie, swatting them away.

'Perhaps it's fibres from the carpet,' I suggested hopefully.

'It's everywhere! It's like the chambermaid's come in with a sack and *strewn* it.'

Suddenly weary, I fell backwards onto the bed, and Connie joined me, the covers crackling with static like a Van de Graaf Generator.

'Why did we choose this place again?' said Connie.

'You said it looked quirky on the website. The pictures made you laugh.'

'Not so funny now. Oh God. Sorry.'

'No, it's my fault. I should have looked harder.'

'Not your fault, Douglas.'

'I want everything to be *right*.'

'It's fine. We'll ask them to come and clean again.'

'What's French for pubic hair?'

'I never learnt that. It never came up. Rarely.'

'I'd say, "*Nettoyer tous les cheval intimes, s'il vous plaît.*"'

'*Cheveux. Cheval* means horse.' She took my hand. 'Oh well. We're not going to be here much.'

'It's a place to sleep.'

'Exactly. A place to sleep.'

I sat upright. 'Perhaps we should get going.'

'No, let's close our eyes. Here.'

She took my hand, rested her head on my shoulder, our legs dangling over the edge as if on a riverbank. 'Douglas?'

'Hm?'

'You know the . . . conversation.'

'You want to talk about that now?'

'No, no, I was going to say, we're in Paris, it's a beautiful day, we're all together as a family. Let's not talk about it. Let's wait until after the holiday.'

'Okay. Fine by me.'

And so the condemned man, presented with his final meal, is reminded that at least the cheesecake is delicious.

We dozed. Fifteen minutes later a text from my son in the adjoining room woke us to say that he intended to 'do his own thing' until dinner. We sat up and stretched, brushed our teeth and left. At the reception desk, in French so riddled with errors, guesses and mispronunciation that it was almost a new language, I informed the desk clerk that I was destroyed but there were many strange horses in our salty bedroom, and we walked out into the Paris afternoon.

## 33. *à la recherche du temps perdu*

Connie was still laughing as we crossed from the 7$^{th}$ to the 6$^{th}$ on the sunny side of rue de Grenelle. 'Where on earth did you learn it?'

'I've sort of made it up myself. Why, what's wrong with it?'

'The vocabulary, the accent, the syntax. You always get caught in these *est-ce que* loops. "It is that it is possible that it is that the taxi to the hotel for to take us?"'

'Maybe if I'd studied it, like you . . .'

'I didn't study it! I learnt it from French people.'

'From French boys. From nineteen-year-old French boys.'

'Exactly. I learnt "not so fast" and "I like you but as a friend". I learnt "can I have a cigarette?" and "I promise I will write to you". *Ton cœur brisé se réparera rapidement.*'

'Which means . . . ?'

'Your broken heart will soon mend.'

'Useful.'

'Useful when I was twenty-one. Not so much now,' she said, and the remark lingered a moment as we reached St Germain.

When Connie and I first came here, in the days when we referred to 'dirty weekends' without irony, we were dizzy with Paris, drunk on the beauty of the city, drunk on being there together and also, more often than not, literally drunk. Paris was all so . . . Parisian. I was captivated by the wonderful wrongness of it all – the unfamiliar fonts, the brand names in the supermarket, the dimensions of the bricks and paving stones. Children, really quite small children, speaking fluent French! All that cheese and none of it Cheddar, and nuts in the salad. Look at the chairs in the Jardin du Luxembourg! So much more poised and elegant than the sag and slump of a deckchair.

Baguettes! Or 'French sticks' as I called them then, to Connie's amusement. We carried great armfuls of baguettes home on the plane, laughing as we crammed them into the overhead lockers.

But a branch of The Body Shop is much the same world-wide, and sometimes the Boulevard St Germain seems not that far from Oxford Street. Familiarity, globalisation, cheap travel, mere weariness had diluted our sense of foreign-ness. The city was more familiar than we wanted it to be and, as we walked in silence, it seemed some effort would be required to remind her of the fun we used to have, and could have in the future.

'Pharmacies! What's with all the pharmacies?' I said, in my wry, observational tone. 'How do they all survive? You'd think, from all the pharmacies, they'd be in a constant state of flu. We have phone shops, the French have pharmacies!'

Still she said nothing. Crossing a side street, I noted the gutters were flowing with fast-moving water, sandbags blocking strategic drains. I had always been impressed by this particular innovation in urban hygiene, seemingly unique to Paris. 'It's like they're rinsing out this immense bath,' I said.

'Yes, you say that every time we come here. That thing about pharmacies too.'

Did I? I wasn't aware of having said it before. 'How many times have we been here now, d'you think?'

'I don't know. Five, six.'

'D'you think you could name them all?'

Connie frowned at the thought. Both of our memories were deteriorating, and in recent years the effort required to recall a name or incident felt almost wearyingly physical, like clearing out an attic. Proper nouns were particularly elusive. Adverbs and adjectives would go next, until we were left with pronouns and imperative verbs. Eat! Walk! Sleep now! Eat! We passed a *boulangerie*.

'Look – French sticks!' I said, and nudged her. Connie looked blank. 'When we first came to Paris I said, "let's buy some French sticks" and you laughed and called me provincial. I said that's what my mother used to call them. My dad thought they were barbaric. "It's all crust!"'

'That sounds like your father.'

'The first time you and I came to Paris, we bought about twenty and carried them back on the plane.'

'I remember. You told me off for nibbling at the ends.'

'I'm sure I didn't "tell you off".'

'You said that's what makes them go stale.'

And we were silent again, turning north towards the Seine.

'I wonder what Albie's up to,' said Connie.

'He's asleep, probably.'

'Well that's all right. He's allowed.'

'Either that or he's trying to work out why there are no mouldy mugs on the windowsill. He's probably there now, burning cigarette holes in the curtains. Room service! Bring me three banana skins and an overflowing ashtray . . .'

'Douglas – this is precisely what we came here to avoid.'

'I know. I know.'

And then she slowed and stopped. We were on rue Jacob, standing near a small, somewhat ramshackle hotel.

'Look. It's our hotel,' she said, taking my arm.

'You remember that.'

'That trip, I do. Which room was it?'

'Second floor, on the corner. The yellow curtains. There it is.'

Connie put her head on my shoulder. 'Perhaps we should have gone back to that hotel instead.'

'I thought about it. I thought it would have felt a little strange, with Albie there.'

'No, he'd have liked it. You could have told him the story, he's old enough now.'

## 34. the hotel on rue jacob

It must have been eighteen years ago.

The anniversary of our daughter's birth was fast approaching and, all too soon after, that other anniversary. I knew those days would be hard for Connie. Her grief, I had observed, tended to come in waves, and though the intervals between each crest were increasing, another storm was certainly due.

In my rather strained and bludgeoning way, I had been endeavouring to keep Connie buoyant with a kind of manic chirpiness; the perpetual warbling brightness of a morning DJ, endless loving phone calls from work, constant maudlin pawing and hugging and kisses on the top of her head. Tinny sentiment – Christ, no wonder she was blue – alternating with a private, secret wall-punching rage at the fact that I could do nothing to lift her spirits. Or indeed my own, because didn't I have my own guilt and sadness?

Usually I might have expected her many loyal friends to step in where I had failed, but everywhere we looked babies and toddlers were being brandished, and we both found their proud display almost unbearable. In turn our presence seemed to make the new parents self-conscious and embarrassed. Connie had always been greatly loved, always popular and funny, but her unhappiness – people seemed affronted by it, especially when it quashed their own joy and pride. And so without any discussion we had withdrawn to our little world to sit quietly by ourselves. Walked, worked. Watched television in the evenings. Drank a little too much, perhaps, and for the wrong reason.

Of course, I had considered that another child might be the answer. Connie, I knew, longed to be pregnant again, and though

66

we were fond and affectionate and, in some ways, closer that we'd been before, things were not easy. The stresses and strains of 'trying for a baby' have been rehearsed many, many times. In the shadow of what had happened – well, I won't go into the details except to say that anger, guilt and grief are poor aphrodisiacs and our sex life, once perfectly happy, had taken on a rather dogged and dutiful air. It was not so much fun any more. Nothing was.

Paris, then. Perhaps Paris in the spring might be the answer. Hackneyed, I know, and I wince now to recall the lengths I went to in order to make that trip perfect; the first-class travel, the flowers and champagne ready in the hotel room, the chi-chi and expensive bistro I had reserved – all this in a largely pre-internet world where arranging such excursions involved PhD levels of research and nerve-shredding phone calls in a language that, as we've established, I neither spoke nor understood.

But the city was beautiful in early May, absurdly so, and we walked the streets in our best clothes and felt as if we were in a film. We spent the afternoon in the Rodin Museum, returned to the hotel and drank champagne while crammed into the tiny bathtub, then went woozily to dinner at a restaurant that I had previously reconnoitred, French but not cartoonishly so, tasteful, quiet. I don't remember all that we said, but I do remember what we ate: a chicken with truffles under the skin that tasted like nothing we'd ever eaten before and wine, chosen purely by luck with a blind jabbing motion, that was so delicious as to be almost another drink entirely. Still in that corny film, we held hands across the table and then we went back to our hotel room on rue Jacob and made love.

Afterwards, on the edge of sleep, I was startled to notice that Connie was crying. The combination of sex and tears is a disconcerting one, and I asked, had I done something wrong?

'There's nothing to be sorry for,' she said, and, turning, I could see that she was laughing too. 'Quite the opposite.'

'What's funny?'

'Douglas, I think we've done it. In fact, I know we have.'

'Done what? What have we done?'

'I'm pregnant. I know it.'

'I know it too,' I said, and we lay there and laughed.

Of course, I should point out that there was no way of 'knowing' this. In fact, at that precise moment, it probably wasn't even true, as the gametes take some time to make contact and form the zygote. Connie's 'sense' of conception was an example of 'confirmation bias' – a desire to favour the evidence that confirms what we wish to believe. Many women claim to 'know' for sure that they are pregnant after sex. When, as in most cases, it transpires that they're not, they immediately forget their prior certainty. In the rare cases that they're right, they see this as confirmation of some supernatural or sixth sense. Hence confirmation bias.

Nevertheless, two weeks later a pregnancy test confirmed what we both already 'knew', and thirty-seven weeks after that Albert Samuel Petersen was welcomed into our world and chased our blues away.

## 35. the little ray of sunshine

- For crying out loud, Albie!
- Why is it a problem?
- But why don't you want to come with us?
- I want to do my own thing!
- But I've booked the table for three people!
- They won't mind. Go with Mum. Stare into each other's eyes, whatever.
- What will you do?
- Walk around, take photos. I might go and listen to some music.

- Well, shall we come with you?
- No, Dad, that is not a good idea. It's the opposite of a good idea.
- But wasn't the point, wasn't the whole point of this trip that we spend some time together as a family?
- We spend loads of time together, every day!
- Not in Paris!
- How's Paris different from home?
- Well, if I have to answer that . . . Do you have any idea how much this trip is costing?
- Actually, if you remember, I wanted to go to Ibiza.
- You're not going to Ibiza.
- Okay, tell me how much this is costing, then. How much, tell me?
- It doesn't matter how much.
- Well it obviously does, seeing as you keep bringing it up. Tell me how much, divide it by three, I can owe it to you.
- I don't mind how much, I just wanted – we wanted to spend time as a family.
- You can see me tomorrow. Christ, Dad!
- Albie!
- I'll see you in the morning.
- Fine. All right. See you in the morning. No lie-ins. Eight thirty sharp, or we'll have to queue.
- Dad, I promise you, at no point during this holiday will I relax.
- Goodnight, Albie.
- *Au revoir. A bientôt.* And Dad?
- What?
- I'm going to need some money.

## 36. tripadvisor

The restaurant where we'd eaten the famous chicken was closed for the annual exodus of the Parisians to the gîtes of the Loire, the Luberon, the Midi-Pyrénées. I've always had a grudging admiration for the chutzpah of this mass evacuation, a little like being invited to dinner only to find the hosts have gone out and left a tray of sandwiches. Instead we went to a local bistro that was so 'Parisian' that it resembled a set from a situation comedy; wine bottles barely visible under cascades of candle wax, canned Piaf, no inch of wall without a poster for Gauloises or Perrier.

'*Pour moi, je voudrais pâté et puis l'onglet et aussi l'épinard. Et ma femme voudrait le salade et le morue, s'il vous plaît.*'

'The beef, and the cod for madame. Certainly, sir.' The waiter left.

'When I speak in French, why does everyone reply in English?'

'I think it's because they suspect that you're not a native French speaker.'

'But *how do they know?*'

'It's a mystery to me,' she laughed.

'In the War, if I dropped behind enemy lines, how long before they cottoned on to the fact that I was English?'

'I suspect before the parachute opened.'

'Whereas you—'

'I'd roam the country, undetected, blowing up bridges.'

'Seducing young mechanics from the Citroën garage.'

She shook her head. 'You have a distorted impression of my past. It wasn't like that. Not entirely. And even when it was, it wasn't much fun. I wasn't very happy back then.'

'So when did you become happy?'

'Douglas,' she said, taking my hand by the fingertips, 'don't fish.'

Thankfully we were now of an age where we no longer felt obliged to maintain a constant stream of conversation. In between courses, Connie read her novel and I consulted the guidebook to confirm the opening times and ticketing arrangements for the Louvre, and suggested some restaurants for the following day's lunch and supper.

'We could just walk out and find somewhere,' she said. 'We could be spontaneous.' Connie disapproved of guidebooks, always had. 'Why would you want to have the same experience as everyone else? Why join the herd?' And it was true that there was a preponderance of English and American voices amongst the customers around us, a sense from the staff that they were giving us what we wanted and expected.

But the food, when it came, was fine, with that excessive use of butter and salt that makes restaurant cooking so delicious, and we drank a little more wine than we should have, and enough cognac for me to forget, temporarily, my wife's desire to move on. In fact, we were positively light-hearted by the time we made it back to the tiny room and, with the mild surprise that tended to accompany the act these days, we made love.

Other people's sex lives are a little like other people's holidays: you're glad that they had fun but you weren't there and don't necessarily want to see the photos. At our age too much detail leads to a certain amount of mental whistling and staring at shoes, and there's also the problem of vocabulary. Scientific terms, though clinically accurate, don't really convey the heady dark intensity, etc., etc. and I'd like to avoid simile or metaphor – valley, orchid, garden, that kind of thing. Certainly I have no intention of using a whole load of swear words. So I won't go into detail, except to say that it worked out pretty well for all concerned, with that pleasant sense of self-satisfaction, as if we'd discovered that we were still capable of performing a forward roll. Afterwards we lay in a tangle of limbs.

'A tangle of limbs'. Where did I get that from? Perhaps one of the novels that Connie encourages me to read. *They fell asleep in a tangle of limbs.* 'Like a pair of honeymooners,' said Connie, her face very close, laughing in that way she has, eyes wrinkling, grinning, and I was suddenly hit by a wave of unspeakable sadness.

'This has always been all right, hasn't it?'

'What?'

'This. . . side of our relationship.'

'It has. You know that. Why?'

'I just realised, one night we're going to do this for the last time, that's all.'

'Oh, Douglas,' she laughed and pressed her face into the pillow. 'Well, that's taken all the fun out of it.'

'The thought just occurred to me.'

'Douglas, everyone has that eventually.'

'I know. But this'll be a little sooner than anticipated.'

She kissed me, sliding her hand behind my neck in that way she has. 'You don't need to worry. I'm pretty sure that wasn't quite the last time.'

'Well that's something, I suppose.'

'I'll tell you when it's the last time. I'll toll a bell. I'll wear a shroud and we'll play a slow funeral march.' We kissed. 'I promise, when it's the last time, you will know.'


## 37. first time

The first time we made love was a very different kettle of fish. Again, I won't get into specifics, but if I had to use a single word to sum it up, the word would be 'terrific', and though Connie would undoubtedly find a better word, I like to think she would agree. Which might surprise people, I suppose. I don't want to blow my own trumpet, but I've always been better at that kind of thing than others might expect. I'm keen, for one thing, and at that time I had also been playing a great deal of badminton, so was in pretty good shape. Also, it's important to remember that Connie was still under the influence of certain artificial stimulants, and I'm prepared to accept that was also a factor. There was Chemistry between us, if you like. I once pointed out to Connie that she wouldn't have taken me home if she'd been sober. Rather than deny it, she laughed. 'You're probably right,' she said. 'Another reason to Just Say No.'

We arrived at the unassuming terraced house behind Whitechapel Road just before four in the morning. Apparently this area has since become fashionable, and perhaps Connie and her friends planted that seed, but at the time this was uncharted territory for someone like me. We were a long way from the All Bar Ones and Pizza Expresses of Hammersmith, Putney and Battersea, the somewhat suburban boroughs where many of my friends and colleagues lived.

'It's mainly Bangladeshi, with a little bit of old East End. I love it. It's what the city used to be, before the yuppies moved in.' She opened the door. Was I meant to come in?

'Well . . . I'd better be off, I suppose,' I said with a shrug, and Connie laughed.

'It's nearly four!'

'I thought I'd walk.'

'Back to Balham? Don't be daft, come in.'

'There'll be a night bus, I'm sure. If I can get to Trafalgar Square, I can change and get the N77 . . .'

'For Christ's sake, Douglas,' she laughed. 'For a PhD, you're extremely dim.'

'I didn't want to assume anything.'

'To assume,' she said, 'makes an ass of u and me.' Then she leant forward, put her hand behind my neck and kissed me with some force. And that – that was terrific too.

## 38. lime, vodka, chewing gum

The house was an organised mess. 'Curated' is the word Connie would use, with every inch of wall covered with reproductions, postcards, posters for bands and clubs, photographs and sketches. The furniture was what might be called 'eclectic': a church pew, school chairs, an immense pale leather G Plan sofa partially buried beneath discarded clothes, magazines, books, newspapers. I saw a violin, a bass guitar, a stuffed fox.

'I'm having vodka!' shouted Connie from the kitchen – I didn't dare to wonder what the kitchen was like – 'But there's no ice. Would you like vodka?'

'Just a small one,' I replied. She entered with the drinks and I noticed that she had reapplied lipstick somewhere along the way, and that made my heart sing too.

'As you can see, the cleaners have just been.'

I took my glass. 'There's fresh lime in this.'

'I know! Sophisticated,' she said, biting the slice. 'Club Tropicana.'

'Are any of these paintings yours?'

'No, I keep those safely locked away.'

'I'd love to see something. Your work.'

'Maybe tomorrow.'

*Tomorrow?*

'Where's Fran?' She had told me all about Fran, her house-mate, who, like all housemates through the ages, was 'completely mad'.

'She's at her boyfriend's.'

'Oh. Okay.'

'It's just you and me.'

'Okay. And how are you feeling?'

'A little better. I'm sorry for freaking out like that. I shouldn't have taken that pill, it was a bad idea. But I appreciate you staying with me. I needed . . . a calming presence.'

'And now?'

'Now, now I feel . . . perfectly fine.'

We smiled. 'So,' I said, 'am I sleeping in Fran's bed?'

'Good God, I bloody hope not.' She took my hand and we kissed again. She tasted of lime and chewing gum. In fact the gum was still in her mouth, which would have thrown me at any other time.

'Sorry, that is disgusting,' she laughed, removing it, 'us kicking that around in there.'

'Don't mind,' I said.

She stuck the gum on the doorframe. I felt her hand on my back, found my hand on her thigh, on top of the dress then beneath it. I stopped to catch my breath. 'I thought you said nothing was going to happen?'

'I changed my mind. You changed it for me.'

'Was it because of the lemon battery thing?' I said, and she laughed while we kissed. Oh yes, I was quite the wisecracker.

'My bedroom's a disaster area,' she said, breaking away. 'Literally and figuratively.'

'I don't care,' I said, and followed her upstairs.

Do I sound uncharacteristically suave in all of this? Do I sound aloof, nonchalant? The truth is that my heart felt like a fist trying to punch its way through my rib-cage – not from the excitement of it all, though it was thrilling, but from a sense that finally, finally something good was about to happen to me. I felt the proximity of change, and I had wanted more than anything for something in my life to change. Is it still possible to feel like that, I wonder? Or does it only happen to us once?

## 39. a brief history of art

Cave paintings. Clay then bronze statues. Then for about 1,400 years, people painted nothing except bold but rudimentary pictures of either the Virgin Mary and Child or the Crucifixion. Some bright spark realised that things in the distance looked smaller and the pictures of the Virgin Mary and the Crucifixion improved hugely. Suddenly everyone was very good at hands and facial expression and now the statues were in marble. Fat cherubs started appearing, while elsewhere there was a craze for domestic interiors and women standing by windows doing needlework. Dead pheasants and bunches of grapes and lots of detail. Cherubs disappeared and instead there were fanciful, idealised landscapes, then portraits of aristocrats on horseback, then huge canvases of battles and shipwrecks. Then it was back to women lying on sofas or getting out of the bath, murkier this time, less detailed, then a great many wine bottles and apples, then ballet dancers. Paintings developed a certain splodginess – critical term – so that they barely resembled what they were meant to be. Someone signed a urinal, and it all went mad. Neat squares of primary colour were followed by great blocks of emulsion, then soup cans, then someone picked up a video camera, someone else poured concrete, and the whole thing became hopelessly fractured into a kind of confusing, anything-goes free for all.

## 40. the philistine

Such was my understanding of the history of art – its 'narrative', I ought to call it – until I met my wife. It is barely more sophisticated now, though I've picked up a few things along the way, enough to get by, so that my art appreciation is almost on a par with my French. In the early days of our relationship Connie was quite evangelical and bought me several books, second-hand editions because we were in our happy-but-poor phase. Gombrich's *The Story of Art* was one, *The Shock of the New* another, given specifically to stop me tutting at modern art. Well, in the first flush of love, if someone tells you to read something then you damn well read it, and they're terrific books, both of them, though I've retained almost nothing of their contents. Perhaps I should have given Connie a basic primer in organic chemistry in return, but she never expressed an interest.

Still – and I'd hesitate to confess this to Connie, though I think she knows – I've always felt a little at a loss with art, as if a piece of me is missing, or was never there. I can appreciate draughtsmanship and deft choice of colour, I understand the social and historical context, but despite all my best efforts my responses seem to me fundamentally shallow. I don't quite know what to say or, indeed, feel. In portraiture I look for people that I recognise – 'Look, it's Uncle Tony' – or for the faces of film stars. The Madame Tussaud's school of art appreciation. In realist works I look for detail; 'Look at the eyelashes!' I say, in idiotic admiration at the fineness of the brush. 'Look at the reflection in his eye!' In abstract art I look for colour – 'I love the blue' – as if the works of Rothko and Mondrian were little more than immense paint charts. I understand the superficial thrill of seeing the object in the flesh, so to speak; the sightseeing approach that lumps together the Grand Canyon, the Taj Mahal and the Sistine Chapel as items to tick off. I understand rarity and uniqueness, the 'how much?' school of criticism.

And of course I can see beauty. In my work, I see it all the time: the symmetrical cleavage of a fertilised frog egg, the stained stem cells of a zebrafish embryo or an electron micrograph of *Arabidopsis*, the thale cress flower; and I can see the same forms and patterns, the same pleasing proportion and symmetry in paintings. But are they the right paintings? Do I have taste? Am I missing something? It's subjective, of course, and there are no right answers, but in a gallery I always have that feeling that the security guards are waiting to bundle me out of the door.

My wife and son have few such insecurities. Certainly they weren't on display in the Italian gallery of the Louvre, where Albie and Connie were playing that game of seeing who could stare at a painting the longest. In this case it was a fresco by Botticelli, cracked and faded and a lovely thing, but was there really so much to see? I waited while they drank it all in, the brush strokes, the interplay of light and dark, all the things I'd missed. Eventually there was movement, and we strolled on past endless varieties of crucifixions and nativities, assorted martyrs whipped or pierced with arrows, a nonchalant saint with a sword embedded in his head, a scene of Mary – it's usually Mary – recoiling from an angel that had left a vapour trail behind him. 'Braccesco, apparently,' I said. 'Jet-powered angel!' as if it meant something, and we moved on.

We passed a terrific battle scene by someone called Uccello, soldiers clustered together into a black porcupine, the cracks and tears on the canvas adding to its grandeur in a strange kind of way. Then in the grand central corridor my eye was drawn to a portrait of a bearded man whose face, on closer inspection, was composed of apples, mushrooms, grapes, a pumpkin, his nose a fat ripe pear. '*L'Automne* by Arcimboldo. Look, Albie, his face is made up of fruit and vegetables!'

'Kitsch,' said Albie, presenting with his eyes the award for Most Banal Remark Ever Made in an Art Gallery. Perhaps this was why those museum audio-guides had become so popular; a reassuring voice in your ear, telling you what to think and feel. *Look to your left, take note, please observe*; how terrific it would be to carry that voice with you always, out of the museum and throughout all of life.

We moved on. There was a lovely fuzzy da Vinci, as if seen through smeary spectacles, of two women cooing over baby Jesus, but this didn't seem to interest Connie and Albie, and I couldn't help but notice that the more famous and familiar a work of art, the less time they spent looking at it. Certainly they had no interest in the *Mona Lisa*, the Hard Rock Cafe of Renaissance art, hanging regally between signs that warned of pickpockets in an immense, high-ceilinged room while other neglected canvases glared. Even early in the day a crowd had gathered, and were posing with that particular 'can't believe it!' smile that people have when their arm is around a celebrity's shoulder. 'Albie! Albie, can you take a photo of me and your mum . . .' I said, but they'd already snubbed the Giaconda in favour of a small canvas on the other side of the *Mona Lisa*'s wall – a murky Titian, in the shadows both literally and figuratively, of two large, naked women giving a recorder concert. They stared and stared and I wondered, what was I meant to take from this? What were they seeing? Once again I was struck by the power of great art to make me feel excluded.

Back in the main corridor, Albie paused before a little portrait by Piero della Francesca, then produced a small, expensive leather-bound sketchbook and began copying it in charcoal, and my heart sank. There may well be a scientific paper to be written on why walking in an art gallery is so much more exhausting than, say, climbing Helvellyn. My guess is that it is something to do with the energy required to hold muscles in tension, combined with the mental exertion of wondering what to say. Whatever the reason, I sank exhausted onto the leather couch and watched Connie instead, the way her skirt stretched across her bottom, the movement of her hands, her neck as she raised her eyes to a canvas. That was art, right there. That was beauty.

She looked at me, smiled and crossed the room, touched her cheek against mine. 'Tired, old man? That'll be last night.'

'Too much art. I wish I knew which ones to look at.'

'Thumbs up, thumbs down?'

'I wish they'd just point out the good ones.'

'Maybe the "good ones" aren't the same for everyone.'

'I never know what to say.'

'You don't have to say anything. Just respond. Feel.'

She pulled me to my feet and we hiked on through this vast, regal storeroom, past ancient glass, marble and bronze, into the French nineteenth century.

## 41. art appreciation

Sexual nostalgia is a vice best indulged in private, but suffice to say that our first weekend together was quite an eye-opener. Those February days were dark and squally and we were reluctant to leave the little house in Whitechapel. Certainly there was no question of my going to the lab on Saturday, and instead we slept, watched films and talked, hurrying out at night to pick up Indian takeaway from a restaurant where Connie was well known and greeted by the entire staff, who showered us with complimentary poppadums and those little tubs of raw onion that no one really wants.

'And who is this handsome young man?' asked the head waiter.

'He's my hostage,' said Connie. 'He keeps trying to make a run for it, but I won't let him get away.'

'It's true,' I said, then, while she ordered, wrote 'Help me!' on a napkin and held it up, and they all laughed, Connie too, and I felt immense warmth and affection, and also a little envy, for the vibrancy of someone else's life.

Sunday morning had a melancholy air, like the last day of a wonderful holiday, and we stepped out to the corner shop for newspapers and bacon, then sought refuge in her bed. Of course it wasn't all sex, sex, sex, though largely it was. There was conversation, too, and Connie played me her favourite records, and she slept a great deal, at seemingly random times of day and night, and in those hours I would extricate myself from the mess of blankets, bedspreads and quilts, and explore.

The bedroom was murky and under-lit, the skirting boards concealed behind hundreds of books: volumes of fine art, vintage *Rupert* annuals, classic novels and reference works. Her clothes hung on a bare rail – no wardrobe – an arrangement that struck me as almost unspeakably cool, and I secretly longed to work my way through the rail, insisting that she try things on. There were portfolios containing her pictures, too, and although she had banned me from examining these, I untied the ribbons and took a look while she slept.

They were portraits, mainly, some stylised with facial features slightly askew, some more realistic, the contours drawn on to the skin with fine ink lines, like a three-dimensional graph. Eyes downcast, faces turned towards the floor. Her work was more accessible than I had expected, conventional even, and though I found them rather gloomy, I liked them very, very much. But then I'd have liked a shopping list as long as it was her shopping list.

Downstairs, the living room was stylishly ramshackle and scrappy, as if a great deal of thought had gone into the huge pile of children's board games, the Chinese restaurant sign, the ancient filing cabinets and seventies bric-a-brac. Mustard thick-pile carpet gave way to the sticky tiles of the kitchen, dominated by an immense jukebox containing the same mystifying mix of 'good' and 'bad' taste: obscure electronic and punk bands muddled in with seventies novelty records, songs by Frank Zappa, Tom Waits and Talking Heads alongside ABBA and AC/DC and the Jackson 5.

Clearly I was out of my depth. Irony, was that the difference? My own cultural tastes were fairly unsophisticated but at least they were sincere, and how was I to tell the good kind of bad taste from the bad kind of bad taste? How did one listen to a piece of music ironically? How did one adjust one's ears? An

ABBA album in my hands would be a source of derision, in Connie's a sign of cool, and yet it was still the same verse-chorus-verse. Was the vinyl imbued with different qualities, depending on who played it? I had, for instance, been a long-time advocate of the music of Billy Joel, particularly his early- to middle-period albums, and this had been the cause of some mockery from the hipper, edgier biochemists. Bland, they called him, middle-of-the-road and safe. Yet here on Connie's jukebox was Barry Manilow, a far less sophisticated artist. What did Connie do to 'Mandy' that somehow rendered it 'cool'?

The same applied to décor. The paraphernalia that gave Connie and her flatmate art-school credibility – the medical school skeleton, parts of mannequins, the stuffed animals – would have made me look like a serial killer. I dreaded the day that Connie would see my Balham flat – the flat-pack furniture and bare magnolia walls, the comatose yucca plant, the all-too-prominent television. Yet I also dreaded the idea that she might not make it that far.

## 42. *cartes postales*

Of course, she'd be mortified to be reminded of all this. Ironic bad taste is harder to pull off in a comfortable family home, where a phone that looks like a lobster is unlikely to raise much of a smile. That baton has been passed to Albie, forever on the lookout for interesting road signs or the disembodied heads of dolls.

What they both still share, though, is a fetish for postcards. Albie has plastered his bedroom with them, like very expensive wallpaper, and so we dutifully found ourselves in the Louvre gift shop, both of them compiling great stacks of *cartes postales*. I tried to join in the game, selecting a card from the racks, *The Raft of the Medusa* by Géricault, a painting that I'd enjoyed seeing in the flesh, so to speak, because of its fantastic drama. It hung in 'Large French Paintings', alongside canvases the size of a family home, depicting battles in the ancient world, cities in flame, the coronation of Napoleon, the retreat from Moscow; the Ridley Scott school of art, full of effects, strong lighting and a cast of thousands. The three of us had stood before the immense *Medusa*; 'I wonder how long it took to paint . . .' and 'Look at this man here. He's in trouble!' and 'I wonder how we'd manage in that situation?' were my observations. I showed the postcard to Albie, the power of the image somewhat diminished at 4x6 inches, and he shrugged and gave me his pile of chosen cards, and Connie's too, and off I went to pay for them.

## 43. postcards

In Whitechapel, postcards covered the whole of the kitchen wall, two or three thick at some points, jumbled in with Polaroids of her art-school friends. There were a lot of punk-ish girls posing with cigarettes, but I was also struck by the number of handsome young men on display, usually with Connie or Fran draped adoringly around them, pouting and blowing kisses. Men in army fatigues or paint-stained overalls; men with eccentric facial hair; intimidating, unsmiling men, and one in particular, a shaven-headed thug with very blue eyes, a cigarette dangling from his mouth and a bottle of beer in his hand. An action-movie mercenary staring at the camera while Connie clung to him or kissed the top of his stubbled head or pressed her cheek to his; impossible to ignore the infatuation in her, awful to see it too.

'I should probably take those down,' she said, behind me.

'Is that . . . ?'

'That's Angelo. My ex.' *Angelo*. Even his name was a blow. How could a Douglas compete with an Angelo? 'He's very handsome.'

'He is. He's also not important to me any more. Like I said, I'm going to take them down.' With a little tug she tore the most prominent photo from the wall and placed it in the pocket of her dressing gown. Not in the bin, but in her breast pocket, next to – well, her breast.

There was a moment's silence. We had made it to Sunday afternoon, a time of the week that always threatens to tip over into an almost unbearable gloom, and I wanted very much to leave on a positive note. 'Perhaps I'd better go.'

'The hostage is escaping.'

'If I make a run for it, will you stop me?'

'I don't know. Do you want to be stopped?'

'I wouldn't mind.'

'Okay,' she said. 'Then let's go back to bed.'


## 44. romantic comedy behaviour

Excruciating, isn't it? But that was how we spoke to each other once upon a time. It was a new voice for me. Something had changed and I had no doubt, as I finally stumbled from the house on Sunday night, aching and comically dishevelled, heading back to Balham on empty trains, that I was in love with Connie Moore.

This was by no means a cause for celebration. It had sometimes puzzled me why falling in love should be regarded as some wondrous event, accompanied by soaring strings, when it so often ended in humiliation, despair or acts of awful cruelty. Given my past experience, the theme from *Jaws* would have been more fitting, the violins from *Psycho*.

Of course I had been involved in two or three 'serious' relationships, each lasting slightly longer than the shelf-life of a half-dozen eggs, but while there had been moments of happiness and affection, no hearts had been set aflame as yet. And yes, I had 'dated' too, a series of unsuccessful job interviews for a post I didn't really want, the meetings largely taking place in cinemas because there would be less obligation to speak. Often I was home by a quarter to ten, queasy from a large bag of Maltesers. Love and desire played little part in these dates. Embarrassment and self-consciousness were the key emotions, discomfort increasing exponentially at each encounter until one or other of us cracked and blurted out a standard-form 'let's be friends', after which we'd part, sometimes at a brisk run. As to romantic love, the real thing, I had been stricken once before, but reminiscing about Liza Godwin was like expecting the *Titanic*'s captain to fondly recall the iceberg.

We met on our first day at university, where she was studying modern languages, and were immediately great friends, inseparable, right up until I committed the error of making a pass at a sherry party that had got out of hand. She responded to my attempted kiss by ducking, quite low, bending from the knees and hurrying away, like someone avoiding the blades of a helicopter. This cooled our friendship and soon I was resorting to notes and letters posted under the door of her room in our halls of residence. Once a mutual pleasure, our proximity became so problematic to Liza that she moved to different accommodation, and I would telephone her there, late at night, not entirely sober, because what could be more charming and devil-may-care, what could melt a woman's heart like a deranged phone call after midnight?

To her credit, Liza remained sympathetic and understanding of my feelings, right up until the point where several members of the rugby team suggested that I might consider 'backing off' for a while. Their intervention removed all ambiguity and, in the battle between love and violence, violence won. I never spoke to Liza Godwin again. Still, I'm afraid I took it all very badly. I hesitate to use the word 'overdose'. A disregard for the safety guidelines would be more accurate. The aspirins were soluble and the volume of water required to dissolve, I think, five of them, was considerable and meant that I woke up with a desperate need for the bathroom and a perfectly clear head. Looking back, it all seems very uncharacteristic; embarrassing, too, my one moment of adolescent melodrama. What was I hoping to achieve? It was hardly a 'cry for help'; I would have been embarrassed to make that much noise. 'A cough for help', perhaps that was what it was. A clearing of the throat.

So there was good reason to fear a recurrence of a condition whose symptoms were insomnia, dizziness and confusion followed by depression and a broken heart. As the Northern Line train rattled into Balham, the doubts were already crowding in. It wasn't even as if Connie's decision had been the product of a rational mind, and the passion she had felt at three a.m. seemed unlikely to survive until the following Thursday, our second date, when we would be sober and self-conscious. Then there was Angelo to contend with, lurking even now in the pocket of her dressing gown nearest to her breast. Nothing could be taken for granted. Winning Connie Moore, keeping Connie Moore would be a challenge that would continue right up until an afternoon in Paris . . .

## 45. *pelouse interdite*

. . . where we slept off our lunch in the Jardin du Luxembourg, a park so elegant and groomed that I always half expect to be asked to remove my shoes. Lying on the grass is only permitted in a cramped strip at its southern end, sunbathers clinging to it as if to the hull of an overturned cruise ship. Our mouths were sticky from red wine and salty duck and we took it in turns to quench our thirsts with briny sparkling water that had long since ceased to sparkle.

'How do French people do it?'

'Do what?' Connie's head was resting on the pillow of my stomach.

'Drink wine at lunchtime. I feel like I've been anaesthetised.'

'I don't know if they do any more. I think that's just us tourists.'

To our left, four Italian language students were hunched over Chinese takeaway in plastic trays, the syrup and vinegar smell hanging in the hot, still air. To our right, three skinny Russian boys were listening to Slavic hip-hop on the speaker of their mobile phone, running their hands over their shaved heads and intermittently howling like wolves.

'City of Proust,' sighed Connie, 'the city of Truffaut and Piaf.'

'You are having a nice time, aren't you?'

'Very much so.' She reached behind her, searching for my hand, but the effort was too great and her arm dropped back.

'You think Albie's happy?'

'Posing around Paris at his father's expense? Of course he is. Remember it's against his principles to show happiness.'

'Where does he keep disappearing off to all the time?'

'Maybe he has friends here.'

'Which friends? He doesn't have friends in France.'

'Friends means something different now to what it meant in our day.'

'In what way?'

'Well, he goes online and writes, "hey, I'm in Paris" and someone else says, "I'm in Paris too!" or someone says, "my friend lives in Paris, you should meet up." And so he does.'

'Sounds terrifying.'

'I know. All those new people, all that spontaneity.'

'It was hard enough having a pen-pal.'

She rolled on to her front, latching on to something new. 'Douglas, you had a pen-pal?'

'Günther from Düsseldorf. He came to stay, but it wasn't a success. Couldn't eat my mother's food. He was visibly wasting away, and I was terrified we'd get in trouble for sending back this malnourished child. In the end my father practically tied him to a chair until he'd eaten his liver and onions.'

'Such golden memories you have. Did you get invited to Düsseldorf?'

'No, strangely enough!'

'You should find the address, track him down.'

'Maybe I will. Did you have a pen-pal?'

'French girl. Elodie. She wore an unnecessary bra and taught me how to roll cigarettes.'

'So it *was* educational.' Connie turned again, and closed her eyes.

'It would be nice to bump into him, though,' I said. 'Every now and then.'

'Günther?'

'Our son.'

'We're seeing him tonight. I've fixed it. Now let me sleep.'

We dozed to the lulling sound of Russian hip-hop in which, interestingly, only the profanities remained in English, presumably so as to offend the widest possible international audience. In the late afternoon, sitting and yawning, Connie suggested we rent bicycles. Still a little drunk, we rode the municipal machines, unwieldy as wheelbarrows, along whichever street we liked the look of.

'Where are we going?'

'We're deliberately getting lost!' she shouted. 'No guidebooks, no maps allowed.'

And despite being too foggy to ride a heavy bicycle on the wrong side of the road, I adopted a devil-may-care, freewheeling attitude, knees clipping wing mirrors, ignoring the waved fists of the taxi-drivers as I smiled, smiled, smiled.

## 46. françois truffaut

The warm feelings continued into the evening. Connie had spotted an open-air cinema screen in an urban park not far from Place d'Italie and decided that we would go and watch a movie there. A stolen bedcover from the Good Times Hotel was our picnic blanket; there was rosé wine, bread and cheese, the evening was warm and clear. Even Albie seemed pleased to be there.

'Will it be in French?' he asked, as we established our base in front of the screen.

'Albie, don't worry, you'll understand. Trust me.'

The film was called *Les Quatre Cents Coups*, or *The 400 Blows*, and I recommend it. My own taste in cinema tends towards the thriller or science-fiction/fantasy genres, but despite the lack of actual blows it was very entertaining. The film concerns the misadventures of an intelligent but irresponsible young man called Antoine who ends up in trouble with the law. His amiable father, who is being betrayed by the mother, loses patience with young Antoine, and the boy is sent to a sort of borstal. Escaping, he runs towards the sea – he has never seen the sea before – and then, well, the film just stops with the young man looking into the camera in a challenging, almost accusatory way.

In plot terms it was no *Bourne Identity* but I found myself enjoying it nonetheless. It was a film about poetry, rebellion, the elation and confusion of youth – not *my* youth necessarily, other people's youth – and it had a profound effect on Albie, who was so engaged in the film that he temporarily forgot to drink excessively, and knelt erect with his hands placed on his thighs in a pose that I'd last seen on the gym mats at his primary school.

The sky darkened and the projection came into sharper focus, swallows darting across the screen like specks on the celluloid – or perhaps they were bats, or both – and Albie sat there, identifying violently with the character despite, I think it's fair to say, having had a pretty stable childhood. Every now and then I turned to see his profile flashing white in the light of the monochrome screen, and I found myself feeling a terrific fondness for him, for both of them, for us, the Petersens, a little pulse of love and affection, a conviction that our marriage, our family, was not so bad, was better than most, and that we would survive.

Anyway, it was all very atmospheric and congenial and all too soon it was over. The final image froze, Antoine Doinel was giving us that look from the screen, and Albie was rubbing his cheeks with the heels of his hands as if cramming the tears back into his eyes.

'That,' he declared, 'was the greatest fucking film I have ever seen in my life.'

'Albie, is that language really necessary?' I said.

'And the photography was amazing!'

'Yes, I liked the photography too,' I chipped in hopefully, but Albie and his mother were deep in an embrace, Albie squeezing her as they both laughed, and then he was running off into the summer night and Connie and I, too drunk to risk the bicycles again, held hands and walked home through the 13th, the 5th, the 6th, the 7th, love's young dream.

## 47. the intrinsic difficulty of the second date

Despite my PhD, the intricate algorithm of what to do on a second date had entirely defeated me. Each restaurant seemed either too formal and ostentatious or too casual and downmarket. It was late February, so too cold for Hyde Park, and my usual preferred option, the cinema, wasn't right either. We wouldn't be able to talk at the cinema. I wouldn't be able to see her.

We arranged to meet on the campus quad outside the laboratory where I was working on my post-doc. Since leaving art school, Connie had been employed four days a week at a commercial gallery in St James's. She had railed against the place – the lousy art, the customers with more money than taste – but it enabled her to pay the rent while she worked on her own paintings in the small east London studio she shared with friends – a collective was the term they used – each of them waiting for their break-through. As a career plan, it all sounded hopelessly unstructured to me, but the St James gallery at least meant she could pay her rent and eat. In a stammering phone call, I had instructed her on the bus routes open to her, the precise workings of the 19, the 22, the 38. 'Douglas, I grew up in London,' she had told me, 'I know how to catch the bus. I'll see you at six thirty.' By six twenty-two I was beneath the clock tower, staring at the latest *Biochemist*, eyes sliding across the page without gaining purchase, still staring at six forty, hearing her before I saw her; the tap-tap of high heels was not a common sound on this part of the campus.

In our digital age we now have the electronic means to summon up a face more or less at will. Back then faces were like phone numbers; you tried to memorise the important ones. But my mental snapshots of the previous weekend had begun to fade. Chaste and sober on a squally, gun-metal weekday, would I be disappointed?

Not a chance. The reality, when I saw her, far exceeded my memories: the wonderful face framed by the raised collar of a long black overcoat; some sort of old-fashioned dress beneath it, rust red; carefully made-up; dark eyes, lips to match her dress. The scampi platter at the Rat and Parrot had ceased to be an option.

We kissed a little awkwardly, an earlobe for me, hair for her. 'You look very glamorous.'

'This? Oh, I have to wear this for work,' she said, as if to say *this isn't meant for you*; eight seconds gone and already a botched kiss, an imagined slight. The evening stretched before us like a tightrope across some vast canyon.  To mark the importance of the occasion, I was wearing my best jacket, raffish chocolate brown corduroy, and a knitted tie, dark plum. Her hand travelled to the knot and adjusted it.

'Very nice. Good God, you actually have a pen in your top pocket.'

'As a scientist, I have to. It's my uniform.'

She smiled. 'Is this where you work?'

'Over there, in the lab.'

'And the fruit flies?'

'They're inside. Do you want to come and see?'

'Am I allowed? I always assumed all labs were top secret.'

'Only in films.'

She grabbed my arms with both hands. 'Then I have to see the fruit flies!'


## 48. insectory

She stared at the clouds of flies, her face close to the muslin, quite bewitched. It was as if I'd taken her to the unicorn enclosure.

'Why fruit flies? Why not ants or beetles or stick insects?'

Whether her interest was genuine, exaggerated or feigned, I couldn't say. Perhaps she viewed the insectory as some kind of art installation; I know such things exist. Whatever the reason, 'why fruit flies?' was the kind of question that I longed to hear, and I explained about the fast breeding, the low upkeep, the conspicuous phenotypes.

'Which are . . . ?'

'Observable characteristics, traits, manifestations of the genotype and the environment. In fruit flies, shorter wings, eye pigmentation, changes in the genital architecture.'

'"Genital architecture". That's the name of my band.'

'It means that you can see indications of mutation in a very short time. Fruit flies are evolution in action. That's why we love them.'

'Evolution in action. And what do you do when you want to examine their genital architecture? Please, please don't tell me you kill them all?'

'Usually we knock them unconscious.'

'With tiny truncheons?'

'With carbon dioxide. Then after a while they stumble back onto their feet and get on with having sex.'

'My typical weekend.'

A moment passed.

'So can I keep one? I want . . .' She pressed a finger to the glass '. . . that one there.'

'They're not goldfish at the fairground. They're tools of science.'

'But look – they really like me!'

'Perhaps it's because you smell of old bananas!' Another moment passed. 'You don't smell of old bananas. I'm sorry, I don't know why I said you smelt of old bananas.'

She looked over her shoulder and smiled, and I introduced her to Bruce, our pet fruit fly, to show that it was not only the art-school crowd who knew how to have a good time.

## 49. caution

The tour continued. I showed her the cold room, where we remarked on how cold it was, and the 37-degree room.

'Why 37 degrees?'

'Because it's the temperature inside the human body. This is what it feels like to be inside someone.'

'Sexy,' said Connie, deadpan, and we moved on. I showed her dry ice, I showed her the centrifuge in action. Through a microscope we looked at cross sections of the tongue of a rat that had been infected with parasitic worms. Oh yes, it was quite a date, and I began to note the amused faces of my colleagues working late as usual, mouths open, eyebrows raised at this lovely woman peering into flasks and test tubes. I gave her some Petri dishes, to mix her paints in.

When she'd seen enough we went, at her suggestion, to a tiny Eastern European restaurant that I had walked past many times without ever imagining I might enter. Faded, dimly lit, it was like stepping into a sepia photograph. A hunched and ancient waiter took our coats and showed us to a booth. At Connie's suggestion, we drank vodka from small, thick glasses, then ate velvety soup a shade of burgundy, delicious dense dumplings and pancakes and syrupy red wine and sat side by side in the corner of the almost empty room, and soon we were fuzzy-headed and happy and even almost at ease. Rain outside, steam on the windows, an electric-bar fire blazing; it was wonderful.

'You know what I envy about science? The certainty. You don't have to worry about taste or fashion, or wait for inspiration or for your luck to change. There's a . . . methodology – is that a science word? Anyway, the point is you can just work hard, chisel away and eventually you'll get it right.'

'Except it's not quite as easy as that. Besides, you work hard.'

She shrugged and waved her hand. 'Well, I used to.'

'I saw some of your pictures. I thought they were amazing.'

She frowned. 'When did you see them?'

'Last weekend. While you were asleep. They were beautiful.'

'Then they were probably my flatmate's.'

'No, they were yours. Hers I didn't like at all.'

'Fran is very successful. She sells a lot.'

'Well, I don't know why.'

'She's very talented, and she's my friend.'

'Of course, but I still loved yours. I thought they were very . . .' I searched for some artistic term. 'Beautiful. I mean, I don't really know much about art—'

'But you know what you like?'

'Exactly. Also, you can draw terrific hands.'

She smiled, looked at her own hand, splayed the fingers and then placed it over mine. 'Let's not talk about art. Or fruit flies.'

'Okay.'

'How about last weekend instead? What happened, I mean.'

'Fine,' I said and thought, *here it is, the bolt gun.* 'What did you want to say?'

'I don't know. Or rather, I thought I did.'

94

'Go on.'

She hesitated. 'You go first.'

I thought a moment. 'Okay. It's very simple. I had an amazing time. I loved meeting you. It was fun. I'd like to do it again.'

'That's it?'

'That's all.' It was by no means all, but I didn't want to alarm her. 'You?'

'I thought . . . I thought the same. I had a *happy* time, unusually. You were very sweet. No, that's wrong, I don't mean that, I mean you were thoughtful and interesting and I liked sleeping with you too. Very much. It was fun. Your sister was right – you were what I needed.'

I had found myself in this situation often enough to recognise the imminent arrival of a 'but' . . .

'But I don't have a very good track record with relationships. I don't associate them with happiness, certainly not the last one.'

'Angelo?'

'Exactly. Angelo. He wasn't very nice to me and he's made me . . . I suppose, I want to be . . . cautious. I want to proceed with caution.'

'But you want to proceed?'

'With caution.'

'With caution. Which means?'

She considered for a moment, biting her lip, then leant forward. 'Which means that if we got the bill right now and went outside, if we found a taxi and went home to your bed, then I'd be very happy.'

Then she kissed me.

. . .

. . .

. . .

. . .

. . .

'Waiter!'

## 50. the wild party in room 603

The party started at a time you might reasonably expect most parties to stop, the usual treble and bass boom-tsk of electronic music soon replaced by a low-frequency oom-pah oom-pah with a distinctive comb-and-paper buzz.

'Is that . . . an accordion?'

'Uh-huh,' mumbled Connie.

'Albie doesn't play the accordion.'

'Then he has an accordionist in his room.'

'Oh, good grief.'

Now the asthmatic chug resolved into four familiar stabbing minor chords, played in rotation, accompanied by much foot-stomping and thigh-slapping percussion, provided by my son.

'What is this song? I know this song.'

'I think it's "Smells Like Teen Spirit".'

'It's what?'

'Listen!'

And sure enough, it was.

When – if – I thought of accordionists, the word suggested an olive-skinned male wearing a Breton top. But here, Nirvana's howl to youthful alienation was bellowed by a primal female voice, a kind of soulful town crier, with Albie now accompanying her on percussive guitar, his chord changes always just a little way behind.

'I think they call it jamming,' I said.

'As in jamming your fingers in your ears,' said Connie.

Resigning myself to a long night, I turned on the light and reached for my book, a history of World War II, while Connie sandwiched her head between two foam pillows and assumed a horizontal brace position. The accordion, like the bagpipes, is part of the select group of instruments that people are paid to stop playing, but for the next forty-five minutes my son's mysterious guest pushed at the musical limits of the squeezebox, regaling much of the fifth, sixth and seventh floors of the Good Times Hotel with, amongst others, a boisterous 'Satisfaction', a sprightly 'Losing My Religion' and a version of 'Purple Rain' so long and repetitive that it seemed to stretch the very fabric of time. **'We are enjoying the concert, Albie,'** I texted, **'but it's a little late'.** I pressed send and waited for the message to be received.

I heard the bleep of a text arriving on the other side of the wall. A pause, and then 'Moondance' sung by emphysemic wasps.

'Perhaps he didn't read my text.'

'Hm.'

'Perhaps I should call reception and complain. What's French for "remove the accordionist from room 603"?'

'Hm.'

'Seems a bit disloyal, though, complaining about my own son.'

'Hasn't stopped you in the past.'

'Or shall I just knock on the—?'

'Douglas, I don't care what you do as long as you stop talking!'

'Hey! I'm not the one with the accordion!'

'Sometimes I think an accordion would be preferable.'

'What does that mean?!'

'It doesn't mean— It's two thirty, just . . .'

And then the noise stopped.

'Thank you, God!' said Connie. 'Now, let's go to sleep.'

But the irritation lingered and we lay beneath its cloud, contemplating other nights we had spent like this, dwelling on a moment's unkindness, impatience or thoughtlessness. *I think our marriage has run its course. I think I want to leave you.*

And then a jolt, like a bass drum behind our heads, followed by the particular, insistent thump-thump-thump of a headboard banging against a wall.

'They're jamming,' I said.

'Oh, Albie.' Connie laughed, her forearm across her eyes. 'That's just perfect.'

## 51. the rock accordionist

We met the beguiling musician the next morning in the hotel's gloomy basement breakfast room. Uncharacteristically for Albie, they were up before us, though it was hard to see the girl's face at first, clamped as it was to Albie with the tenacity of a lamprey eel. I cleared my throat, and they peeled apart.

'Hello! You must be Douglas and Connie! Christ, look at you, Connie, you're gorgeous! No wonder your son is so hot, you're a be-auty.' Her voice was gravelly, Antipodean. She took my hand. 'And you're a very beautiful man too, Dougie! Ha! We were just having some breakfast, the breakfast here is a-mazing. And it's all free!'

'Well, not exactly *free* . . .'

'Here – let me move Steve out of the way.' Steve, it seemed, was the name of her accordion. Steve had his very own chair, where he sat toothily grinning. 'Come on, Steve, let poor Mr Petersen sit down, he looks wasted.'

'We enjoyed your concert last night.'

'Aw, thank you!' She smiled, then used her fingers to arrange her features into a clown's sad face. 'Or did you not really mean that?'

'You play very well,' said Connie. 'We'd have enjoyed it more before midnight.'

'Oh no! I'm so sorry. No wonder you look fucked, Mr Petersen. You'll have to come and see me play at a reasonable hour.'

'You're actually playing a concert?' said Connie, with a hint of incredulity.

'Well, *concert*'s a big word. Only outside the Pompidou.'

'You're a busker?'

'I prefer "street performer", but yes!'

I don't *think* my face fell, I tried not to let it, but it's true that I was wary of any activity prefixed with the word 'street'. Street art, street food, street theatre, in all cases 'street' preceding something better carried on indoors.

'She does an amazing "Purple Rain",' mumbled Albie, who was slumped diagonally across the banquette like the victim of a vampire.

'Oh we know, Albie, we know,' said Connie, regarding the accordionist through narrowed eyes. The girl, meanwhile, was scooping the contents of many tiny jars of jam into a croissant. 'I hate these little jars, don't you? *So* shitty for the environment. And *so* frustrating!' she said before cramming her entire tongue into one.

'I'm sorry, we didn't quite get your—'

'Cat. As in the hat!' She patted the black velour bowler that she wore at the back of her head.

'And are you Australian, Cat?'

Albie tutted. 'She's from *New Zealand*!'

'Same thing!' She gave a loud bark of a laugh. 'You guys better get some breakfast in you, before I eat it all. Race you!'

## 52. on practical ethics in the breakfast buffet system

Over the years, at conferences and seminars, I've had some experience of the breakfast buffet system and have noticed that when confronted with a table of ostensibly 'free' food, some people behave with moderation and some as if they've never tasted bacon before. Cat was of the group that believes that 'eat as much as you like' is a gauntlet thrown down. She stood at the juice dispenser, pouring a glass then downing it, pouring a glass then downing it; juice-hanging, I call it and I wondered, why not just open the tap and lie beneath it? I smiled at the waiter who shook his head slowly in return, and it occurred to me that if management made the connection between last night's accordion workout and the woman now piling a great mound of strawberries and grapefruit segments into her bowl, then we might be in very real trouble.

We shuffled along the counter. 'So what brings you to the Eternal City, Cat?'

'Paris isn't the Eternal City,' said Connie. 'The Eternal City is Rome.'

'And it's not eternal,' said Albie, 'it just feels like it.'

Cat laughed and wiped juice from her mouth. 'I don't live here, I'm just passing through. I've been bumming round Europe ever since college, living here, living there. Today it's Paris, tomorrow Prague, Palermo, Amsterdam – who knows!'

'Yes, we're the same,' I said.

'Except we have a laminated itinerary,' said Connie, examining the empty grapefruit container.

'It's not laminated. What I mean is, we're going to Amsterdam tomorrow.'

'Lucky you! I love the 'Dam, though I always end up doing something I regret, if you know what I mean. Party town!' She was filling a second plate now, balancing it on her forearm like a pro and focusing on proteins and carbohydrates. Lifting the visor on the bacon tray, she inhaled the meaty vapour with eyes closed. 'I'm a strict vegetarian with the exception of cured meats,' she said, loading dripping coils of the stuff onto a plate already overflowing with cheese, smoked salmon, brioche, croissants . . .

'That's certainly quite a breakfast you've got there!' I said, smile fixed.

'I know! Albie and me've worked up quite an appetite,' and she gave a low, dirty laugh and snapped at his buttock with the bacon tongs while Albie grinned sheepishly at his plate. 'Anyway,' she said, 'most of this is for later on.'

That, to my mind, was crossing a line. The buffet was not a picnic-making facility nor a come-one-come-all larder. I had resolved to be nice to Albie's new friends and their eccentricities, but this was theft, plain and simple, and when a banana followed a jar of honey into the capacious pockets of her velvet shorts I felt that I could restrain myself no more.

'Don't you think maybe you should put some of that back, Cat?' I said, light-heartedly.

'Beg pardon?'

'The fruit, the jars of honey. You only need one, two at the most.'

'Dad!' said Albie. 'I can't believe you'd say that!'

'Well, I just think it's a bit excessive . . .'

'Awk-ward!' trilled Cat in an operatic falsetto.

'She's not eating it all now.'

'Which is exactly my point, Albie.'

'No, fair enough, fair point – here, here . . .' And Cat began tossing jars and fruit and croissants back on to the table willy-nilly.

'No, no, take what you've got, I just think maybe don't put stuff in your pockets—'

'See what I mean, Cat?' said Albie, gesturing towards me with an open hand.

'Albie . . .'

'I told you, this is what he's like!'

'Albie! Enough. Sit.' This was Connie, with her sternest face. Albie knew well enough not to argue, and we returned to the table, took our seats and listened to Cat . . .

## 53. the cat in the hat

. . . how she loved New Zealand, how beautiful it was but how she'd grown up in a boring suburb of Auckland, so dull and middle-class, mile upon mile of identical houses. Nothing ever happened there – or rather, things did happen there, terrible things, but no one ever talked about them, they just closed their eyes and carried on with their dull, conventional, boring lives and waited for death.

'Sounds like where we live,' said Albie.

Connie sighed. 'I challenge you, Albie, to name one terrible thing that's happened to you in your whole life. Just one. Cat, poor Albie here is scarred because we didn't let him have Coco Pops back in 2004.'

'You don't know everything about me, Mum!'

'Well, I do as a matter of fact.'

'No, you don't!' Albie protested, looking betrayed. 'And since when were you this great defender of home, Mum? You said you hated it too.'

Had she? Connie, moving on, said, 'Cat, my son is posturing for your benefit. Carry on. You were saying.'

Cat was ramming salami inside a baguette with a dirty thumb. 'Anyway, my dad, who's a complete and utter *bastard*, insisted that I study *engineering* at the uni, which was a complete waste of time . . .'

Albie was grinning at me but I declined to meet his eye and poured more coffee. 'Well, not a complete waste of time,' I said.

'It is if you hate it. I wanted to experience things, see things.'

'So what did you study instead?'

'Ventriloquism.' She held a marmalade jar to her ear and a small voice said, *help me! help me!* 'That got me into puppetry and improv and I joined this street theatre group, operating these giant marionettes, and we just hit the road, travelled all over Europe, had a wild time until they all wimped out and went home to their little jobs and little houses and dull, predictable little lives. So I carried on, travelling solo. Love it! Haven't seen my parents now for four years.'

'Oh Cat, that's terrible,' said Connie.

'It's not terrible! It's been amazing for me. No roots, no rent, meeting the most incredible people. I can live wherever I want now. Except Portugal. I'm not allowed into Portugal, for reasons which I am not at liberty to divulge . . .'

'But what about your parents?'

'I send my mum postcards. I phone her twice a year, Christmas and birthday. She knows I'm fine.'

'Hers or yours?' said Connie.

'I'm sorry?'

'You said you phone her Christmas and birthday. D'you phone her on *her* birthday or *your* birthday?'

The question seemed to puzzle Cat. '*My* birthday, of course,' she said, and Connie nodded.

'And your father?' I asked.

'My father can go screw himself,' she said proudly, popping the bread into her mouth, and I noted how Albie could barely contain his admiration.

'That seems a little harsh.'

'Not if you met him. If you met him, it's a grrr-eat review!' She laughed her laugh again, the kind you see in films to denote madness and the waiter's stare got a little harder. Despite my best efforts, I was finding it difficult to warm to Cat. She was somewhat older than Albie, which made me feel absurdly defensive of him, and her skin had a chafed look, as if it had been scoured with some sort of abrasive – my son's face, presumably. There were panda smudges around her eyes and a red smear around her mouth, again attributable to my son, and high arched eyebrows that seemed drawn on. What did she remind me of? When I first arrived at university I attended a fancy-dress screening of *The Rocky Horror Picture Show* with the aforementioned Liza Godwin, which remains one of the most wearying evenings of enforced wackiness that I have ever writhed through in my life. The things I did for love! I am not a religious man but I vividly remember sitting in my seat wearing a pair of Liza

Godwin's torn tights, with a lipsticked rictus grin on my face, praying, please, God, if you do exist, let me not do 'The Time Warp' again.

And yes, there was something of that *Rocky Horror* quality to Cat, and perhaps this appealed to our son, his hand on the small of her back, her fingers exploring the torn knees of his jeans. It was all rather disturbing, and I must confess a certain relief when she said:

'Okay, you good people, it was a pleasure to encounter you. You've got a fine young man here!' She slapped his thigh for emphasis.

'Yes, we're aware of that,' said Connie.

'Enjoy the sights! Young man, escort me to the door – I don't want the buffet police to wrestle me to the floor and strip-search me!' There was a guffaw and the scrape of a chair as she hoisted the accordion called Steve from his seat and squashed her bowler hat down on to her curls. A high trill from Steve, and they were gone.

We sat in the kind of silence that follows a collision, until Connie said, 'Never trust a woman in a bowler hat.'

We laughed, enjoying the sweet marital pleasure of shared dislike. '"Mum, Dad, I'd like you to meet the woman I intend to marry."'

'Douglas, don't even joke about it.'

'Well I liked her.'

'Is that why you told her to put her breakfast back?' giggled Connie.

'Was that too much, d'you think?'

'For once, Douglas, I say no.'

'So what do you think he sees in her? I think it's the laugh.'

'I don't think it's *just* the laugh. I think sex might have something to do with it too. Oh, Albie,' she sighed, and a look of awful sadness came across her face. 'Douglas,' she said, her head on my shoulder, 'our boy's all grown-up now.'

## 54. oversharing, undersharing

I had hoped the three of us would spend our last day in Paris together, but Connie felt tired and insisted, rather snappily, that she'd like just one minute to herself if that was all right, just one single minute if that wasn't against the law. With just each other for company, my son and I had a tendency to panic, but we steeled ourselves and set out for the Musée d'Orsay.

The weather had turned, the city humid beneath low, dense cloud. 'Storm later,' I said.

Nothing from Albie.

'We liked Cat,' I said.

'Dad, you don't have to pretend, because I don't care.'

'We did, we did! We thought she was very interesting. Challenging.' A short distance, silence, then:

'D'you think you'll stay in touch?'

Albie wrinkled his nose. We had not spent a great deal of time discussing affairs of the heart, my son and I. There were friends – Connie's friends, mainly – who had conversations of startling frankness with their children, constantly hunkering down on baggy sofas to confer on relationships, sex, drugs, emotional and mental health, taking every available opportunity to parade around naked, because isn't that what teenage kids really want? Evidence of time's decay brandished at eye-level? While I found this approach smug and contrived, I also accepted that there was room for improvement on my part, a certain reticence that I should do my best to overcome. The nearest my own father came to 'opening up' about relationships was a selection of National Health leaflets on sexually transmitted diseases that he left fanned out on my pillow, a parting gift before I left for university and all the information I would ever need on the workings of the human heart. My mother changed the television channel every time two people kissed. Both had passed through the permissive 1960s untouched. It might as well have been the 1860s. How my sister and I ever came to be, I've frankly no idea.

But wasn't emotional openness something I'd intended to work on? Perhaps this was an opportunity to chat about the turmoil of these teenage years, and in turn I could confide some of the ups and downs of married life. With this in mind, I took a short detour to rue Jacob, the hotel where Connie and I had stayed eighteen years ago, and I paused and held Albie's arm.

'You see this hotel?'

'Yes.'

'That window, up there? Corner of the second floor, the one with the yellow curtains?'

'What about it?'

I placed my hand on his shoulder. 'That, Albert Samuel Petersen, is the bedroom where you were conceived!'

Perhaps it was too much too soon. I'd hoped that there might be something rather poetic about it, seeing the exact place where sperm and egg had fused and he had blinked into existence. Part of me thought that he might find it amusing, imagining his parents as their younger selves, so different from our current, less carefree incarnations. I'd hoped that he might even be touched by my nostalgia for his creation in an act of love that, in my memory at least, had been freighted with emotion and care.

Perhaps I hadn't thought it through.

'*What?*'

'Right there. In that room. That is where *you* came to be.'

His face shrivelled into a mask of disgust. 'Now there's an image I will never get out of my head.'

'Well, how else do you think it happened, Albie?'

'I know it *happened*, I just don't want to be forced to *think* about it!'

'I thought you'd like to know. I thought that you'd be . . .'

He began to walk on. 'Why are you being like this?'

'Like what?'

'Saying all this stuff. It's very weird, Dad.'

'It's not weird, it's a friendly conversation.'

'We're not friends. You're my father.'

'That doesn't mean . . . adults, then. We're both adults now, I thought we could talk like adults too.'

'Yeah, well thanks for oversharing, Dad.'

We walked on and I considered the concept of 'oversharing', and what undersharing might be, and whether it was ever possible to settle on something in between.

## 55. *épater le bourgeois*

Soon we were at the Musée d'Orsay, standing in the extraordinary concourse of the old converted train station. 'Look at that incredible clock!' I said, in my awed voice. Albie, too cool for awe, walked on and began to take in the paintings. I like the Impressionists, which I know is not a particularly fashionable line to take, but Albie was making a great show of his indifference, as if it were me who'd painted the poplar trees, the young girls seated at the piano.

Then suddenly we found something more to his taste: *L'Origine du Monde* by Gustave Courbet. The style and techniques were the same that you might see applied to ballet dancers or a bowl of fruit, but here the subject was the splayed legs of a woman, her face beyond the frame. It was a disconcerting picture, explicit and unflinching, and I did not love it. Generally speaking I dislike being shocked. Not because I'm a prude, but because it all seems so juvenile and easily achieved. 'Where *do* they get their ideas?' I said, glancing at it and moving on.

But Albie clearly wasn't going to miss an opportunity to make me uncomfortable, and he stopped and stared and stared. Determined not to seem priggish, I doubled back and returned to his side.

'Now *that* is oversharing!' I said.

Nothing.

'It's quite confrontational, isn't it?' I said. Albie sniffed and tilted his head, as if that made a difference. 'Amazing to think it was painted in 1866.'

'Why? You think naked women were different back then?' He was walking up and peering at the canvas now, so close that I thought the security guard might intervene.

'No, I just mean that we tend to think of the past as inherently conservative. It's interesting to note that outrage is not a late-twentieth-century invention.' This was *good*, I thought. It sounded like the kind of thing Connie might say, but Albie only scowled.

'I don't think it's outrageous. I think it's beautiful.'

'Me too,' I said, though without conviction. 'Great picture. Terrific.' I latched on to the caption once again. '*The Origins of the World*.' When I'm nervous I tend to read things out – captions, signage, often more than once. '*The Origins of the World*. Witty title,' and I expelled air sharply through my nose to show just how damned hysterical I found it. 'I wonder what the model thought of it. I wonder if she came round to look at the canvas and said, "Gustave, it's like looking in a mirror!"'

But Albie had already produced his sketchbook from his bag, because it wasn't enough to stare at this anonymous woman's private parts, clearly he was going to have to sketch them, too.

'Meet you in the gift shop,' I said, and left him there, madly cross-hatching and shading in.

## 56. the comfort zone

Then, on our final night in Paris we all went to a Vietnamese restaurant, but I had to leave early because I was injured by my soup.

I have always had a poor record with heavily spiced food, believing, not unreasonably, that if a substance burns my fingers I shouldn't put it in my stomach. Of course Albie loves fiery food, thinking that it reflects his tempestuous personality or politics or something. As for Connie, her mood had improved a little since the great breakfast-buffet farrago, but she was wearying of bistros. 'I swear, if I see another duck leg, I shall scream.' Albie suggested Vietnamese, and wasn't I meant to be trying new things and leaving my so-called 'comfort zone'? So at Albie's suggestion we set off in our wobbly convoy of bicycles to a Vietnamese restaurant in Montparnasse.

'"*Authentiquement épicé*"!' Albie read approvingly in the menu. 'Which basically means "bloody hot"!'

I ordered some sort of beef soup, specifying '*pas trop chaud, s'il vous plaît*', but the bowl, when it arrived, was so heavily dosed with small vicious red chillis that I wondered if perhaps it was some sort of practical joke. Perhaps Albie had put them up to it, perhaps the chefs' faces were pressed to the little round window, chuckling away. Either way I was having to drink a great deal of beer to cool my palate.

'Too much for you, Dad?' he grinned.

'Just a little.' I ordered one more beer.

'You see?' grinned Connie. 'Anything that isn't boiled meat in gravy . . .'

'That's not true, Connie, you know it's not,' I said, a little snappily perhaps. 'As a matter of fact, it's delicious.'

And then it wasn't delicious anymore. I had been attempting to avoid the chillies by sieving the soup through my teeth, but something must have slipped through, because my mouth was suddenly ablaze. I drained the beer and, in slamming the glass down, flipped the large ceramic spoon from the broth, catapulting a ladleful into my right eye. So heavily dosed with lime juice and chilli was this broth that I was momentarily blinded, scrabbling around the table for a napkin, grabbing one that had been discarded by Albie and was smeared with the chilli sauce from his spare ribs, which I then proceeded to rub into the affected eye and, somehow, the unaffected eye too. If he hadn't been laughing no doubt Albie would have warned me, but tears were pouring down my face now, and Albie and Connie's amusement had turned to embarrassment and concern as I stumbled blindly to the bathroom, bumping into several diners, stumbling through a beaded curtain into first the ladies' – *desolé! desolé!* – then the gentlemen's toilets and finally locating the world's smallest and most impractical handbasin, into which I attempted to squeeze my head, scraping my forehead with the tap and pouring first scalding hot, then cold water into my eye. I stood there, spine twisted, with the water jetting uncomfortably onto my eyeball, then into my mouth which was now mercifully numb, with a chemical throb that recalled the removal of an impacted molar some years ago.

I stayed like this for some time.

Eventually I stood and examined my reflection, my shirt soaked and clinging to my chest, my forehead bleeding, my tongue swollen and lips apparently rouged, my right eye sealed tight. I peeled the lid back, the sclera heavily veined and the colour of tomato soup. Peering at the ceiling, I noted that some sort of scratch, like a hair on a camera lens, had appeared at the edge of my vision, dancing around and out of sight as I attempted to examine it further. A scar. *This*, I thought, *is why we have comfort zones, because they are comfortable. What can possibly be gained by leaving them?*

As I returned to the table, Albie and Connie regarded me with the solemn faces that precede bouts of hilarity. When the laughter broke, I attempted to join in, because I wanted to be fun rather than a figure of it. I had prepared a line to this end: 'You see? This is why we wear protective goggles in the lab,' I said, though the joke didn't really land.

'You look as if you've been tied to a chair and beaten,' said Connie.

'I'm fine. Fine!' I said, smiling, smiling as I pushed the bowl away. 'Here, you have it.'

'I think the food here is amazing.'

'Well, I'm pleased,' I said, 'but personally I prefer food that doesn't actually injure you.'

Connie sighed. 'It hasn't *injured* you, Douglas.'

'It has! It has actually scarred my cornea. From now on every time I look at a plain white surface I'll see that soup.' This set them off again, and suddenly I'd had enough. Wasn't I trying? Wasn't I doing my best, making an effort? I drained a beer, my third or fourth I think, scraping my chair as I stood to go.

'Actually, I'm going to walk back to the hotel.'

'Douglas,' said Connie, her hand on my arm, 'don't be like that.'

'No, you'll be far happier by yourselves. Here . . .' I was tugging money from my wallet now, belligerently tossing notes on to the table in a way that I'd seen in films. 'That ought to cover it. Amsterdam train's at nine fifteen, so early start. Please don't be late.'

'Douglas, sit down, wait for us, please—'

'I need some fresh air. Goodnight. Goodnight. I'll find my own way home.'

## 57. *je suis désolé mais je suis perdu*

I got lost, of course. The sinister black slab of the Montparnasse Tower was behind, then in front of me, to my left and right, hopping around, and now the back streets had opened out into an avenue, wide and dull and unpopulated, an elegant dual carriageway that would lead me eventually to the *Périphérique*. I was walking towards a motorway, soaked through with beer, soup, water and sweat, drunk and blinded in one eye, neither loveable nor full of love, full of nothing but irritation and frustration and self-pity, and lost, quite lost, in this idiotic city. City of Light. City of Bloody, Bloody Light.

I had not dared to dwell on the idea, but when we'd set out I had imagined that this trip might in some way repair our relationship, perhaps even lead to a change of heart on Connie's part. I *think* I want to leave you, she'd said, and didn't 'think' imply some doubt, the possibility of persuasion? Perhaps the newness of our surroundings would recall when we were new to each other. But it was absurd to think a city could make a difference, absurd to think oil paintings and marble statues and stained glass could make that change. Place had nothing to do with it.

Now I saw the great gilded dome of Les Invalides against the purple sky, the searchlights on the Eiffel Tower swooping as if hunting down a fugitive. The air had taken on that charged quality that precedes a summer storm and I realised I was still some distance from the hotel. They'd be in bed now, quite happily asleep, my family. The family I was about to lose, if I'd not lost them already, and I trudged on down that long, dull deserted avenue, wondering why it was inevitable that my plans should fail.

I turned right at the Musée Rodin. Through a gap in the wall, a sculpture of five men stood in a huddle, wailing and moaning in various attitudes of despair, and this seemed like an apt spot to rest. I settled on the kerb. My phone was ringing – Connie, of course. I considered not answering but I've never been able to ignore Connie's call.

'Hello.'

'Where are you, Douglas?'

'I seem to be outside the Rodin Museum.'

'What on earth are you doing there?'

'Seeing an exhibition.'

'It's one in the morning.'

'I got a little lost, that's all.'

'I expected you to be waiting at the hotel.'

'I'll be back soon. Go to sleep.'

'I can't sleep without you here.'

'Nor with me, it would seem.'

'No. No, that's right. It's . . . a dilemma.'

A moment passed.

'I got a little . . . het up. I apologise,' I said.

'No, I do. I know you and Albie like to wind each other up, but I shouldn't join in.'

'Let's talk no more about it. Amsterdam tomorrow.'

'Fresh start.'

'Exactly. Fresh start.'

'Well. Hurry back. There's going to be a storm.'

'I won't be long. Try to get some—'

'We do love you, you know. We don't always show it, I'm aware of that. But we do.'

I took a deep breath. 'Well. As I said, I'll be back soon.'

'Great. Hurry back.'

'Bye.'

'Bye.'

'Bye.'

I sat for a moment, then hauled myself to my feet and quickened my pace, determined to beat the imminent rain. Amsterdam tomorrow. Perhaps Amsterdam would be different. Perhaps everything would go right in Amsterdam.

part three

# THE LOW COUNTRIES

—

I do not know what I may appear to the world, but to myself
I seem to have been only like a boy playing on the sea-shore,
and diverting myself in now and then finding a smoother
pebble or a prettier shell than ordinary, whilst the great ocean
of truth lay all undiscovered before me.

Isaac Newton

## 58. *an experiment on a bird in the air pump*

But oh, the joy of it, the joy and bliss and thrill of each consecutive day, so unlike anything I had experienced before. It was dizzying, really, to be in love at last. Because this was the first time, I knew that now. Everything else had been a misdiagnosis – infatuation, obsession perhaps, but an entirely different condition to this. This was bliss; this was transformative.

The transformation began even before our second date. I had for some time been living the wrong sort of life and my drab flat in Balham was a reflection of this. The bare magnolia walls, the flat-pack furniture, the dusty paper lightshades and 100-watt bulbs. A woman as cool as Connie Moore would not stand for this. It would all have to go, to be replaced by . . . well, I wasn't entirely sure, but I had twenty-four hours to decide. And so the night before our date I left the lab early, took the bus to Trafalgar Square and went to the National Gallery gift shop to bulk-buy art.

I bought postcards of works by Titian and Van Gogh, Monet and Rembrandt, posters of Seurat's *Bathers at Asnières* and da Vinci's *Virgin and Child*. I bought reproductions of Van Gogh's *Sunflowers* and, by way of contrast, Joseph Wright of Derby's *An Experiment on a Bird in the Air Pump*, a rather ghoulish Enlightenment painting of a man suffocating a cockatoo, but one that neatly fused our interests in art and science. Sprinting up Regent Street to the department stores, I bought clip-frames and cushions – my very first cushions – and little rugs and throws (was that a term? Throws?) and decent wine glasses, new underwear and socks and, in a further fit of optimism, new bedding: plain and stylish rather than the graph-paper design my mother had bought me in the mid-eighties. In toiletries, I bought razors, lotions and balms. I bought scruffing lotion without knowing what scruffing was, I bought floss and mouthwash, soaps and gels that smelt of cinnamon, sandalwood, cedar and pine, a whole arboretum of scents. I spent a fortune and then took it all home in a cab – a black cab! – because there wasn't room on the bus for the brand new me.

Back in Balham I spent the evening distributing this new me around the flat, contriving as far as possible to give the impression that this was how I had always lived. I scattered books and threw the throws. I arranged fresh fruit in my new fruit bowl, discarded the sad yucca and the desiccated succulents and replaced them with flowers – fresh cut flowers! Tulips, I think – and contrived a vase out of a 500 ml Pyrex conical flask that I had liberated from the laboratory . . . cheap *and* amusing, too! Now if – if – she ever set foot in my flat, she would mistake me for someone else entirely; a bachelor of quiet good taste and simple needs, self-contained and self-assured, a man of the world who owned Van Gogh prints and cushions and smelt of trees. In cinema comedies there's sometimes a scene where the central character has to frantically assemble a disguise, and this evening had that air about it. If the wig was slightly askew, the moustache peeling away from the lip, the price tag still on the fruit bowl, if the disguise was ill-fitting and held in place by Velcro, well, I'd fix that when I could.

## 59. *sunflowers*

And sure enough, the inspection came the morning after the successful second date. Making tea, I watched through the door as Connie pulled on an old T-shirt – oh, God, the sight of that – took a fresh apple from the bowl, examined it and padded around the flat, the apple gripped between her teeth as she pulled out album sleeves, peered at the spines of books and cassettes and videotapes, examined the postcards tacked oh-so-casually to the new cork noticeboard, the framed prints on the wall.

'There's a picture here of a man suffocating a cockatoo.'

david nicholls

'Joseph Wright of Derby!' I shouted, as if this were a quiz. '*An Experiment on a Bird in the Air Pump.*'

'And you really love Van Gogh!' she shouted through to the kitchen.

Did I? Should I? Was that a good thing? Had I overdone the Van Gogh? I thought everyone liked Van Gogh, but did that make Van Gogh a bad thing? I pressed the moustache back on to my lip.

'I love him,' I called back. 'Don't you?'

'I do. Not this one, though.' Then, Connie, I will take it down. 'And Billy Joel, too. There's a lot of Billy Joel.'

'The early albums are terrific!' I yelped, but by the time I carried tea through – loose-leaf Earl Grey in simple white china, milk in a new jug – she had disappeared. Perhaps *Sunflowers* had caused her to leap out of the window. I heard the shower running and stood stupidly in the middle of the floor, tea cooling on a tray, for somewhere between eight and twelve minutes, wondering if I could go in, if I had earnt that right. Eventually she opened the door of the bathroom, winding a new towel around her, her hair wet, her face scrubbed plain. Or perhaps she'd scruffed. Either way, she was beautiful. 'I've made you some tea,' I said and held out the tea that I had made her.

'You have more toiletries than almost any man I've ever met.'

'Well, you know.'

'You know the strangest thing about them? They're all brand new.'

I had no answer to this, though thankfully it didn't matter because we were kissing now, apple and mint on her breath.

'Put the tray down, maybe?'

'Good idea,' I said, and we fell back on to the sofa. 'It's not so terrible here, is it?'

'No, I like it. I like the order. It's so clean! In my flat you can't cross the room without stepping on an old kebab or someone's face. But here's so . . . neat.'

'So I've passed the inspection?'

'For the moment,' she said. 'There's always room for improvement.'

Which is exactly what she set out to do.

## 60. *pygmalion*

I'm inclined to think that, after a certain age, our tastes, instincts and inclinations harden like concrete. But I was young or at least younger then, and more willing and malleable, and with Connie, I was happy Plasticine.

Over the following weeks, then months, she began a thorough process of cultural education in the art galleries, theatres and cinemas of London. Connie had not been considered 'academic' enough to go to university and occasionally seemed insecure about this fact, though goodness knows what she thought she'd been missing. Certainly, where culture was concerned, she had a twenty-seven-year head start on me. Art, film, fiction, music; she seemed to have seen and read and listened to pretty much everything, with the passion and clear, uncluttered mind of the autodidact.

Music, for instance. My father liked British light classical and traditional jazz, and the soundtrack to my childhood was 'The Dam Busters March', then 'When the Saints Go Marching In' then 'The Dam Busters March' again. He liked a 'good beat', a 'good tune' and on Saturday afternoons would sit and guard the stereo, album cover in one hand, cigarette in the other, tapping his toe erratically and staring into the eyes of Acker Bilk. Watching him enjoy music was like seeing him wear a paper hat at Christmas; it looked uncomfortable. I wished he'd take it off. As for my mother, her proud boast was that she could do without music entirely. They were the last people in Britain to be genuinely horrified by the Beatles. Listening to Wings' *Greatest Hits* at a reasonable volume was the closest I came to punkish rebellion.

Connie, on the other hand, was uncomfortable in a room

without music. Her father, the vanished Mr Moore, had been a musician, and had left behind only his collection of LPs; old blues albums, reggae, baroque cello, birdsong recordings, Stax and Motown, Brahms symphonies, bebop and doo-wop, Connie would play them to me at every opportunity. She used songs rather like some people – Connie, for instance – used alcohol or drugs; to manipulate her emotions, raise her spirits or inspire. In Whitechapel she would pour immense cocktails, put on some obscure, ancient crackling disc and nod and dance and sing and I'd be enthusiastic too, or enthusiastically feign it. Someone once defined music as organised sound, and much of this sound seemed very badly organised indeed. If I asked, 'Who is this singing?' she'd turn to me open-mouthed.

'You don't know this?'

'I don't.'

'How can you not know this track, Douglas?' They were 'tracks', not songs.

'That's why I'm asking!'

'What have you been doing all your life, what have you been listening to?'

'I told you, I've never really been that into music.'

'But how can you not like music? That's the same as not liking food! Or sex!'

'I do like it, I just don't know as much as you.'

'You know,' she would say, kissing me, 'you are extremely lucky that I came along.'

And I was. I was extremely lucky.


# 61. contemporary dance forum

My cultural education was not confined to music, but extended all the way to contemporary dance, a form that I found entirely impenetrable, entirely opaque. There seemed to be no language for it. What was I meant to say? 'I liked the way they threw themselves against the wall'?

'It's not about what you liked and didn't like,' Connie would reply, 'it's about what it made you feel.' More often than not, it made me feel foolish and conventional. The same applied to theatre, which had always seemed to me like a funereal form of television; since the time of the Greeks, had anyone ever left a play saying, 'I just wished it were longer!' Clearly I'd been going to the wrong shows. We saw plays in tiny rooms above pubs and promenaded around vast warehouses, saw a blood-soaked *Midsummer Night's Dream* set in an abattoir, a pornographic *Private Lives*, and I was never bored. How could I be? It was a rare night in the theatre that didn't involve someone brandishing a dildo, and over time I became inured, or at least learnt to disguise my shock, because if this was a cultural education, it was also a form of audition. I wanted to like what Connie liked because I wanted Connie to like me. So things were no longer 'wacky'. Now they were 'avant-garde'.

In fairness, I enjoyed a great many of the cultural events, particularly the movies ('films' we called them now), which were very different to the escapist fare I had previously favoured, and rarely featured interstellar drive, a serial killer on the loose or bombs counting down to zero. Now we went to the cinema to read. Little independent cinemas that sold coffee and carrot cake and showed foreign films about cruelty, poverty and grief; occasional nudity, frequent brutality. Why, I wondered, did people seek out portrayals of the very experiences that, in real life, would send them mad with despair? Shouldn't art be an escape, a laugh, a comfort, a thrill? No, said Connie, exposure brought understanding. Only by confronting the worst traumas of life could you comprehend them and face them down, and off we'd trot to watch another play about man's inhumanity to man. On which subject, we also went to gigs – it amused Connie to hear me say the word 'gig' – and I'd do my best to jump around and make some noise when told to do so.

The opera, too. Connie had a friend who worked at the opera

– of course she did – and we'd get cheap tickets to see Verdi, Puccini, Handel, Mozart. I loved those evenings, often more than Connie, and if the director had transposed the action of *Così fan tutte* to a Wolverhampton dole office, I could still close my eyes, reach for her hand and listen to that wonderfully organised sound.

Do I sound like a philistine? Unsophisticated and uncouth? Perhaps I was, but for every gritty four-hour film about Gulag life, there was another that was stylish, intelligent and affecting in ways that were rarely found in the multiplex. Even the dance was beautiful in its way, and I was grateful. My wife educated me; a common phenomenon, I think, and one that is rarely or only begrudgingly acknowledged by the husbands that I know. As a scientist, I had sometimes been sceptical and resentful of the great claims made for The Arts – widened horizons, broadened minds, freed imagination – but if culture was improving then yes, I was improved. And yes, I know, Hitler loved the opera too, but I still felt strongly that my life had been altered in some indefinable way. I hesitate to use the word 'soul'. Certainly life felt richer, but was this due to contemporary dance or the person by my side?

I'm troubled by the past tense. *Connie was, Connie once, Connie used to.* In the early days of our relationship, we made a vow: we would never be too tired to go out, we would always 'make an effort', but this was one of those solemn vows we were destined to break. Perhaps there were simply fewer things she wanted to show me, but we gradually became less adventurous after we married, after we left London, after we became parents. Inevitably, I suppose; you can't go on dates for twenty-four years, it's not practical. And who would want to go to a gig now? What would we eat, where would we sit, what would we do with our hands? We could always do something else instead. Go to Paris, go to Amsterdam.

But I still listen to Mozart, alone in my car rather than high up in the gods with Connie at my side. Selected highlights, greatest hits. I have a fine in-car stereo system, top-of-the-range, but still the music is barely audible above the roar of the air-conditioning and rush hour on the A34. Over-familiar, the music has become a kind of audio-Valium, background music rather than something I listen to actively and attentively. A gin and tonic after a long day. A shame, I think, because while each note remains the same, I used to hear them differently. It used to sound better.

## 62. new beginnings in belgium

But wasn't this exciting? A new day and new beginnings in a brand new part of the world? The train from Paris would take us to Amsterdam in a little over three hours, hopscotching over Brussels, Antwerp and Rotterdam. Connie pointed out that we'd be bypassing Bruegels and Mondrians, a notorious altarpiece in Ghent, the picturesque city of Bruges, but the Rijksmuseum lay ahead and I was still entranced by European train travel, the ability to board a train in Paris and get off in Zurich, Cologne or Barcelona.

'Miraculous, really, isn't it? Croissant for breakfast, cheese toastie for lunch,' I said, boarding the 0916 at the Gare du Nord.

'Goodbye, Paris! Or should that be *au revoir*?' I said, as the train pulled out into the sunlight.

'According to the map on my phone, we are in Belgium . . . now!' I said, as we crossed the border.

It's a terrible habit but a silence in a contained space makes me anxious, and so I tug and tug at the conversation as if struggling to start a lawnmower.

'My first time in Belgium! Hello, Belgium,' I said, tugging away, yank, yank, yank.

'The wifi on this train is useless,' said Albie, but I smiled and looked out of the window. I had decided to shake off last night's ennui and enjoy myself by sheer effort of will.

My high spirits were in contrast to the landscape, which was, for the most part, industrialised farmland interspersed with neat little towns, the church spires like push-pins punctuating the map. Last night's storm had kept me awake and I was still a little queasy from the beer, but the swelling in my eye had eased and soon we'd be in Amsterdam, a city that I'd always thought of as civilised and, unlike Paris, easygoing. Perhaps some of that 'laid-back' quality would rub off on us. I reclined my seat. 'I love this rolling stock,' I said. 'Why is continental rolling stock so much more comfortable?'

'You're full of fascinating observations,' said Connie, laying down her novel with a sigh. 'Why are you so full of beans?'

'I'm excited, that's all. Travelling through Belgium with my family. It's exciting to me.'

'Well, read your book,' she said, 'or we'll push you off the train.' They returned to their novels. Connie was reading something called *A Sport and a Pastime* by James Salter. On the cover, a hunched naked woman bathed at an impractical sink in black and white, while the back cover description claimed the novel was 'sensual and evocative, a tour-de-force of erotic realism'. 'Erotic realism' sounded like a contradiction in terms to me, but it boded well for the hotel in Amsterdam. Albie, meanwhile, was reading *L'Etranger* by Albert Camus, which in English was the title of Billy Joel's fifth studio album, though I doubted the two were connected. The book was a gift from Connie, who had presented Albie with a selection of novels in translation by European authors, many of whom had consecutive Ws, Zs and Vs in their names. It was an intimidating reading list, I thought, and Albie clearly felt so too, as he was making heavy work of *L'Etranger*. Even so, with regard to fiction, he was still a better student than I.

## 63. aspects of the novel

In the early days of our relationship, on a trip to Greece I think it was, I neglected to take a book on to the plane. It was not a mistake I would make again.

'What are you going to do for two hours?'

'I've got some journals, work stuff. I've got the guidebook.'

'But you haven't got a novel to read?'

'I've just never really been that bothered about fiction,' I said. She shook her head. 'I've always wondered who those freaks are who don't read novels. And it's you! Freak.' She smiled through all this, but I still sensed an incremental slip, a loosening of my grip on her affections, as if I'd casually confessed to some racial bigotry. Can I really love a man who doesn't see the point of made-up stories, a man who would rather find out about the real world around him? Since then I've learnt never to sit down on any form of public transport without a book of some sort in my hand. If it's a novel, then chances are it will have been provided by Connie, and will have won some award but won't be too complicated. The literary equivalent, I suppose, of my father's 'a good beat, a good tune'.

And I do read a great deal of non-fiction, which has always seemed to me a better use of words than the made-up conver-sations of people who have never existed. Academic papers aside, I read the more advanced popular-science and economics books and, like many men of my generation, I enjoy military history, my 'Fascism-on-the-march books', as Connie calls them. I'm not sure why we should be drawn to this material. Perhaps it's because we like to imagine ourselves in the cataclysmic situ-ations that our fathers and grandfathers faced, to imagine how we'd behave when tested, whether we would show our true colours and what they would be. Follow or lead, resist or collabo-rate? I expressed this theory to Connie once and she laughed and said that I was a textbook collaborator. 'Delighted to meet you, Herr Gruppenführer!' she had said, rubbing her hands together obsequiously. 'If there's anything you need . . .' and then she laughed some more. Connie knew me better than anyone alive, but I did feel strongly that she had misjudged me in this respect. It might not be immediately apparent, but I was

Resistance through and through. I just hadn't had a chance to prove it yet.

## 64. the ardennes offensive

As the train rolled on to Brussels I reached for my own book, a dense but engaging history of World War II. The date was March '44, and plans were well under way for Operation Overlord. 'Good God,' I said, and placed the book back down.

'What is it now?' said Connie, somewhat impatient.

'I just realised, a little in that direction is the Ardennes.'

'What's special about the Ardennes?' said Albie.

'The Ardennes,' I said, 'is where your great-grandfather died. Here . . .'

I flicked towards the centre of the book and a map of the Ardennes Offensive. 'We're about here. The battle was over there.' I indicated the red and blue arrows on the map, so unrepresentative of the flesh and blood to which they corresponded. 'This was "the Bulge", a last-ditch German counterattack against the US forces, a terrible battle, one of the worst, in the forest in the dead of winter. A sort of awful final convulsion. Germans and Americans mostly, but a thousand or so British got tangled up too, your great-grandfather among them. Bloody destruction, as bad as D-Day, just half an hour that way.' I pointed east. Albie peered out of the window as if looking for some evidence, pillars of smoke or Stukas screaming out of the sun, but saw only farmland, ripe and placid and serene. He shrugged, as if I was making this all up.

'I have his campaign medals in my desk drawer. You used to ask to see them, Albie, when you were little. D'you remember? He's buried out there too, a little place called Hotton. My dad only went to the cemetery once, when he was a little boy. After he retired I offered to take him again – do you remember, Connie? – but he didn't want to get his passport renewed. I remember thinking how sad that was, only seeing your father's grave once. He said he didn't want to get sentimental about it.'

I had become unusually voluble and a little emotional, too. I'd never been particularly nostalgic about family history and had little knowledge of all but the lowest branches of the family tree, but wasn't this interesting? Our family heritage, our small role in history. Terence Petersen had fought in El Alamein, in Normandy too. As our only child, Albie would inherit his campaign medals. Shouldn't he at least acknowledge their significance and the sacrifice of his forebears? Yet Albie seemed primarily interested in checking the signal on his mobile phone. My own father, had I behaved like this, would have knocked it out of my hand.

'Perhaps I should have gone there anyway,' I continued. 'Perhaps we should all have gone. Got off at Brussels and hired a car. Why didn't I think of this before?'

'We'll go some other time,' said Connie, who had closed her book now and was watching me with some concern. 'Would anyone like some coffee?'

But I had heard the distant rumble of an argument and now wanted the storm to break. 'Would you be interested in that, Egg? Would you want to come along?' I knew that he would not, but I wanted to hear him say it.

He shrugged. 'Maybe.'

'You don't seem very interested.'

He ruffled his hair with both hands. 'It's history. I never knew anyone involved.'

'Nor did I, but still . . .'

'Waterloo is over there, the Somme is back in that direction; we probably had Petersens there, Moores too.'

'It was *my* grandfather.'

'But you said yourself, you never even knew him. I don't even remember granddad. I'm sorry, but I can't make an emotional connection to stuff that happened all that time ago.'

*Emotional connection*, what an idiotic phrase. 'It was only seventy years, Albie. Two generations ago there were Nazis in Paris and Amsterdam. Albie's a very Jewish-sounding name—'

'Okay, this is a very gloomy conversation,' said Connie, unnaturally bright. 'Who wants coffee?'

'At the very least you could have been called up for service. Do you ever wonder what that would have been like? Standing terrified in a forest in Belgium in the dead of winter, like my grandfather? No wifi signal there, Albie!'

'Can both of you lower your voices, please? And change the subject?'

I had merely raised my voice to be heard above the ambient noise of the train, it was Albie who was shouting. 'Why are you making me out to be ignorant?' I know all this, I know what happened. I know, I'm just not. . . obsessed with the Second World War. I'm sorry, but I'm not. We've moved on.'

'We? We?'

'We've moved on, we don't see it everywhere. We don't look at a map and see these . . . arrows everywhere. That's okay, isn't it? Isn't that healthy? To move on and be European, instead of reading endless books about it and wallowing in it?'

'I don't wallow, I—'

'Well I'm sorry, Dad, but I'm not nostalgic for tank battles in the woods and I'm not going to pretend to care about things that don't mean anything to me.'

Don't mean anything? This was my father's father. My dad grew up without a dad. Perhaps Albie thought that this was a perfectly acceptable, even desirable, state of affairs but, still, to be so aloof and dismissive, it seemed . . . disloyal, unmanly. I love my son, I hope that is abundantly clear, but at that particular moment I found I wanted to bounce his head smartly off the window.

Instead I waited a moment, then said, 'Well, frankly, I think that's a shitty attitude.' Which, in the silence that followed, seemed scarcely less violent.

## 65. switzerland

Alternative points of view are more easily appreciated from a distance. Time allows us to zoom out and see things more objectively, less emotionally, and recalling the conversation it's clear that I overreacted. But despite being born some fifteen years after its end, the War overshadowed every aspect of my childhood: toys, comics, music, light entertainment, politics, it was in everything. Goodness knows how this must have felt to my parents, to have seen the traumas and terrors of their early youth re-enacted in situation comedies and playground games. Certainly, they didn't seem overly sensitive or scarred. Nazis were one of the few things that my father found amusing. If the thought of his father's loss upset him then he concealed it, as he concealed all strong feelings, anger aside.

My son, by contrast, was of a generation that no longer thought of countries in terms of Allied or Axis, or judged people on the basis of their grandparents' allegiances. Outside of first-person shoot-'em-ups, the War never crossed Albie's mind and maybe this *was* healthy. Maybe this was progress.

But it didn't feel like progress on the train. It seemed like disrespect, ignorance and complacency and I told him so, and in response he tossed his book onto the table, muttered beneath his breath, clambered over Connie into the aisle and away.

We waited for the other passengers to return to their newspapers. 'Are you all right?' she said quietly, with the intonation of 'are you mad?'

'I'm perfectly fine, thank you.'

We travelled on in silence for two or three kilometres, before I said, 'So clearly, that was all my fault.'

'Not entirely. About eighty-twenty.'

'No need to ask in whose favour.'

Another two kilometres slipped by. She picked up her book, though the pages didn't turn. Fields, warehouses, more fields, the backs of houses. I said, 'By which I mean you might sometimes support me in these arguments.'

'I do,' said Connie, 'if you're right.'

'I can't recall a single instance—'

'Douglas, I'm neutral. I'm Switzerland.'

'Really? Because it's clear to me where your allegiances—'

'I don't have "allegiances". It's not a war! Though Christ knows it feels like it sometimes.'

We passed through Brussels, though I could not now tell you much about it. In a park to the left I caught a glimpse of the Atomium, the stainless-steel structure built for the World's Fair, a fifties version of our present day and something I'd have liked to see. But I couldn't bear to mention it, and could only manage:

'I found his attitude upsetting.'

'Fine, I understand,' said Connie, her hand on my forearm now. 'But he's young and you sound so . . . *pompous*, Douglas. You sound like some old duffer calling for National Service to be reintroduced. In fact, you know who you sound like? You sound like your dad!'

I'd not heard this before. I had never expected to hear it and I would need time to take it in, but Connie continued:

'Why can you never let things go? You just pick and pick away at them, at Albie. I know not everything is easy at the moment, Christ knows it's not easy for me either, but you're up, you're down, you're manic, chattering away, or you're storming out. It's . . . hard, it's very hard.' In a lower voice. 'That's why I'm asking again: are you feeling all right? You must be honest. Can you do this journey or shall we all go home?'

## 66. peace talks

I found him as we entered Antwerp, sitting on a high stool in the buffet car eating a small tub of Pringles. His eyes, I noted, were a little red.

'There you are!'

'Here I am.'

'I've walked all the way from Brussels! I thought you'd got off.'

'Well, I'm here.'

'Bit early in the day for Pringles, isn't it?'

Albie sighed, and I decided to let the point go. 'It's an emotive subject, war.'

'Yeah. I know.'

'I think I lost my temper.'

He upended the tub into his mouth.

'Your mother thinks I should apologise.'

'And you've got to do what Mum says.'

'No, I want to. I want to apologise.'

'S'okay. It's done now.' He licked his fingertip and started swabbing the bottom of the tub.

'So are you coming back, Egg?'

'In a bit.'

'Okay. Okay. Excited about Amsterdam?'

He shrugged. 'Can't wait.'

'No. Me neither. Me neither. Well . . .' I placed a hand on his shoulder and took it off again. 'See you in a bit.'

'Dad?'

'Albie?'

'I would come with you, to the War Cemetery, if you really wanted. There's just other places I'd rather go first.'

'All right,' I said. 'I'll bear that in mind.' I looked around me for some way to cement the truce. 'D'you want anything else to eat? They have those waffles. Or a Kinder Bueno?'

'No, because I'm not six.'

'No. Right,' I said, and returned to my seat.

And that, pretty much, was everything that happened to us in Belgium.


## 67. grachtengordel

I had visited before, once with Connie and on conferences too, so my experience was somewhat selective, but even so, Amsterdam's reputation as a city of sin always seemed something of an anomaly to me, as if one were to discover the presence of an immense crack-den in the centre of Cheltenham Spa. Both faces of the city, genteel and disreputable, were in evidence as we rumbled our suitcases along the lanes that zigzagged west from the Centraal station towards Keizersgracht; fine, tall seventeenth-century townhouses, glimpses of interior-designed living rooms and copper-panned kitchens, a little gift shop selling notepads and candles, a bikini-clad prostitute on the early shift drinking tea from a mug in a pink light, a baker's, a café filled with stoned skateboarders, a shop selling fixed-wheel bicycles. Amsterdam was the trendy dad of European cities; an architect, perhaps, barefoot and unshaven. Hey, guys, I told you, call me Tony! says Amsterdam to his kids, and pours everyone a beer.

We crossed the bridge at Herenstraat. 'Our hotel is in the Grachtengordel, which we're entering now. Grachtengordel, literally, the girdle of canals!' I was a little out of breath but keen to maintain an educational element to our visit. 'It looks wonderful on a map, this series of concentric circles like the growth rings on a tree trunk. Or horseshoes, nesting horseshoes . . .' But Albie wasn't listening; he was too distracted, eyes casting here and there.

'My God, Albie,' said Connie, 'it's a hipster's paradise.'

We laughed at this, though I'd be hard-pressed to define a hipster, unless it referred to the pretty girls in large, unnecessary spectacles and vintage dresses, sitting high on rickety bicycles. Why do the youth of other cities always seem so attractive? Did the Dutch walk the streets of Guildford or Basingstoke and think, my God, just *look* at these people? Perhaps not, but Albie was certainly agog in Amsterdam. For all its grace and elegance, I suspected that Paris had been a little hard and severe for Albie. But here, here was a city that he could work with. The question, as in any trip to Amsterdam, was how long before sex and drugs raised their complicated heads?

A little under eight minutes, it transpired.

## 68. sex dungeon

The hotel, which advertised itself as 'boutique' and had seemed perfectly pleasant on the website, had been decked out to resemble a top-of-the-range bordello. Our receptionist, an attractive and courteous transvestite, greeted us with the news that Connie and I had been upgraded to the honeymoon suite – the 'irony suite', I thought – and directed us down corridors lined variously with black silk, satin and PVC, past large-scale prints of a corseted dominatrix sitting astride a flustered panther, a pop-art tongue prodding a pair of cherries to no useful end and a concerned Japanese lady encumbered by a complex series of knotted ropes. 'She,' said Connie, 'is going to get pins and needles.'

'Dad,' asked Albie, 'have you booked us into a sex hotel?' and they began to laugh convulsively as I fumbled with the key to our room – which, I noticed, was called the 'Venus in Furs' suite, while Albie was in 'Delta of Venus' next door.

'It's not a sex hotel, it's "boutique"!' I insisted.

'Douglas,' said Connie, tapping the print of the bound Japanese lady, 'is that a half hitch or a bowline?' I did not answer, though it was a bowline.

The honeymoon suite was the colour of a kidney. It smelt of lilies and some kind of citrus disinfectant and was dominated by an immense four-poster from which the canopy was missing, leading me to wonder what function the posts served, since they had no structural purpose. Black sheets, hot-pink bolsters, purple cushions and crimson pillows were piled in the absurd Himalayan ranges that now seem to be *de rigueur*, but in this case were presumably there to create a kind of pornographic soft-play area. In stark contrast to all the mahogany and velvet, a huge off-white Bakelite contraption stood adjacent to the bed on a raised dais, like the kind of specialised bath you'd find in an old people's home.

'What is *that*?' said Connie, still giggling.

'Our very own Jacuzzi!' I pressed one of the worn buttons on the control panel and the tub was lit from below by pink and green lights. Another button and the thing began to churn and grind like a hovercraft. 'Just like our honeymoon,' I shouted over the roar.

Connie was quite hysterical now, as was Albie, entering through the adjoining door to laugh at our room. 'You can really pick a hotel, Dad.'

I was feeling defensive. I had made the booking, and the hotel was meant to be a treat, but I did my best to remain good-humoured. 'How's your room, Egg? Dare I ask?'

'It's like sleeping in a vagina.'

'Albie! Please . . .'

'There's a massive picture of lesbians kissing over my bed. They're freaking me out.'

'We have this masterpiece,' and Connie indicated a large tinted canvas of a spiky-haired lady fellating some fluorescent tube lighting. 'I don't know much about art, but I know what I like.'

'She's going to get a shock, licking that,' I said.

'Isn't it outrageous?' said Connie. 'So seedy. I feel like I want to wipe everything down with a damp J-cloth.'

'Look,' I said. 'Tea-making facilities.'

'Kinky. I wonder what the breakfast buffet's going to be like?' said Albie.

'Oysters,' said Connie, 'and great trays of cocaine.'

'Well, I like it,' I said. 'It's boutique!' and I did my best to laugh along.

When everyone had calmed down, we stepped out to a pleasant café in the Noordermarkt, and sat in the square beneath the handsome church there. We ate cheese toasties and drank small glasses of delicious beer, trying out our Dutch accents, an accent like no other in the world. 'It's a little bit cockney, a little bit sing-song,' said Connie. 'And the "S"s have a "sh" sound to them. '"Sho – welcome to our shex hotel. If you require anything – handcuffsh, a courshe of penischillin . . ."'

'No one talks like that,' I said, though it wasn't bad.

'Nonshenshe. It'sh perfect.'

'You sound like Sean Connery.'

'Because, Egg, that's exactly how it sounds – it's a Germanic cockney Sean Connery.' And perhaps it was the beer at lunchtime, or the sun on our faces, or the charm of that particular corner, but it was as if the Petersens had decided that we liked Amsterdam very much, that it would suit us very well, after all, as a family.

## 69. the night visitor

Until then I really only knew the city in winter, in the rain. It had been raining on our first trip here, in November, nine months or so after we had first met, yet still very much during our prolonged probationary period. Connie had been endeavouring to incorporate me into her social life, with the caution usually reserved for releasing zoo animals into the wild. As part of the programme, we had gone to Amsterdam with Genevieve and Tyler, two friends from her college who had recently married. As artists, I'd presumed they'd be keen to see the Rembrandts and Vermeers, but they seemed much more interested in nodding their heads in various coffeehouses. Smoking cannabis held little appeal for me. I did my bit, but one puff of Purple Haze – or Cherry Bomb or Laughing Buddha – instilled a degree of anxiety and paranoia that was remarkable even for me. Certainly I felt no desire to giggle as the blood drained from my face and the dread took hold. I decided to leave them to it, and spent a solitary afternoon in the Anne Frank House instead.

This was shortly before Connie and I began to co-habit and my nostalgia for that first spring and summer remains undimmed. We saw each other every day, but kept separate flats, separate family and friends and social lives. There were those cultural excursions, of course, but if Connie felt the need to 'have a late one' with her art-school pals, or go to a nightclub where things might 'get messy', whatever that meant, then I would suggest she go alone. She rarely fought to persuade me. Sometimes I found myself wishing that she'd fight a little harder, but I did not protest. Once the party was over she'd always come and see me at two or three or four in the morning. She had a key by then – what a happy day that was, cutting that key for her – and she'd let herself in and climb wordlessly into my bed, body warm, make-up smeared, breath smelling strongly of wine and toothpaste and 'social' cigarettes, and she would fold herself into me. Sometimes we would make love, at other times she would twitch and fidget and sweat, a restlessness that I put down to alcohol or some kind of drug use, though I knew better than to preach or pry. If she could not sleep we would talk a little, with Connie doing her best to sound sober.

'Good party?'

'The usual. You didn't miss anything.'

'Who was there?'

'People. Go back to sleep.'

'Was Angelo there?'

'Don't think so. He might have been, somewhere. We didn't talk very much.'

Which didn't make sense, if you thought about it.

'And do you still love him?'

Of course I refrained from asking this latter question, despite it being foremost in my mind, because I valued sleep too much. Most people entering a relationship carry with them a dossier sub-divided into infatuations, flirtations, grand amours, first loves and sexual affairs. Compared to my sheet of lined A4, Connie possessed a three-drawered filing cabinet of the things, but I had no desire to flick through the faces. After all, she was here, wasn't she? At two and three and four in the morning, all through that wonderful first spring, that glorious first summer.

But there was no escaping Angelo. She had once believed, she said, that they were soul-mates, until it transpired that he had many other soul-mates dotted around London. Quite apart from the flagrant infidelity, his other offences were legion. He had undermined her confidence, jeered at her work, made remarks about her looks, her weight, screamed at her in public places, thrown things, even stolen money from her. There had been a mercifully brief allusion to him being 'a bit dark in the bedroom' and certainly there had been physical fights, which shocked and angered me, though she insisted she had 'given as good as she got'. He was a drinker, an addict, unreliable, belligerent, child-ishly provocative, rude. 'Intense', she said. In short, he was every-thing that I was not. So what possible appeal could he hold for her now? All that was student stuff, she said. Besides, Angelo had a new girlfriend anyway, beautiful and cool and they had so many friends in common, they were bound to bump into each other, weren't they? No real harm done, nothing to worry about. I would meet him too, some day soon.

## 70. corduroy

And so it came to pass, at the wedding of Genevieve and Tyler, one of those ferociously unconventional affairs – the bride and groom entering the reception on a motorbike, I recall and, for their first dance, pogo-ing wildly to French punk. No white marquee for Genevieve and Tyler. The party was held in a soon-to-be-demolished prosthetic limb factory on the Blackwall Tunnel Approach, and was a good deal edgier and more nihilistic than the weddings I'd been used to. I'd never seen quite so many angular people in one industrial space before, all under thirty – no jolly aunts in hats here – all enjoying a buffet of ironic kebabs. I'd taken a gamble on a new corduroy suit, and the heavy fabric on a warm September day, combined with a certain self-consciousness on my part, was causing me to perspire to a quite startling degree. Beneath the jacket, dark circles of sweat had formed. My contortions beneath the hand-dryer had had little effect, and so now I stood perspiring as I watched Connie talk to beautiful people.

I think I can honestly say that I've never met a biochemist that I didn't like. My friends and colleagues might not have been particularly glamorous but they were open, generous, funny, kind, modest. Welcoming. Connie's clan was a different proposition. Noisy, cynical, overly concerned with the appearance of things, and on the few occasions I had visited her shared studio – a garage, really, in Hackney – or went to private views, I had felt awkward and excluded, loitering at the edge like a dog tied up outside a shop. I had wanted to be involved in Connie's work, to show interest and enthusiasm because she really was a wonderful painter. But being with her artist friends drew attention to differences that I was keen to play down.

They weren't all monsters, of course. Artists are an eccentric temperamental bunch, with habits that would earn them short shrift in most labs, but that's to be expected. Some of them were, and remain, good friends, and several of them did make an effort at social events. But as soon as conversation turned to 'what are you working on?' they would suddenly need to 'go for a wee'. And so I stood there at the wedding, the human diuretic, in a puddle of malarial sweat.

'Look at you, man! You need a salt tablet,' said Fran, Connie's old housemate. I was unsure of Fran's true feelings for me, and remain so even now that she is Albie's godmother. She has always had the particular gift of hugging and shoving away at the same time, like repelling magnets pushed together. Here she stepped back and brushed her cigarette ash off my arm. 'Why don't you take this off?'

'I can't now.'

She started tugging at the jacket buttons. 'Come on, take it off!'

'I can't, my shirt's too wet.'

'Ah, I get it.' She placed a finger on my sternum and leant all her weight on it. 'You, my friend, are caught in a vicious circle.'

'Exactly. It's a vicious circle.'

'Ahhhh,' she said, rubbing my arm. 'Connie's lovely, lovely, funny, lovely boyfriend. You make her so happy, don't you, Dougie? You look after her, you do, you really do. And she deserves it, after all the bullshit she's been through!'

'Where is she, by the way?'

'She's over by the DJ, talking to Angelo.'

And there he was, leaning over her, his arms braced on either side as if preventing her escape. In fairness, she didn't seem too keen to leave, laughing as she was, touching her hair, her face. I picked up two bottles of beer and approached. In honour of this very special day, Angelo had ironed his mechanic's overalls and shaved his head, and he ran both hands over his scalp as he followed Connie's look and watched me approach.

'Angelo, this is Douglas.'

'Wotcha, Douglas.'

'Pleased to meet you, Angelo.' Keen to avoid awkwardness or rancour, I had decided to adopt an amiable, amused demeanour, pointedly relaxed, but he took both my hands, which were encumbered with beer bottles, and pulled me close. Angelo was my height but distinctly broader, his eyes unblinking, very blue, a little crazed – the much-vaunted 'intensity', I suppose, turning our conversation into a staring competition.

'What's up, my friend? Are you nervous?' he said as I looked away.

'No, not at all. Why would I be?'

'Because you're sweating like a bastard.'

'Yes, I know. It's this jacket. Bad choice, I'm afraid.'

He was holding my lapels now. 'Corduroy. From the French, "cord du roi", cloth of the king.'

'I didn't know that.'

'Well, I've taught you something. A noble fabric, very regal. And it's always good to hear your trousers when you walk, so people know you're coming. Means you can't sneak up on people and BOO.'

I jumped and he laughed. 'Angelo,' said Connie. I was aware of being bested by this man, and of hating him with a venom that I found new and invigorating.

'Clearly Connie's a lucky lady,' he continued. 'Lucky to be shot of yours truly, at least. I presume she's mentioned me.'

'No. No,' I said. 'I don't think so.'

Angelo grinned and reached for the knot of my tie. 'Here, you're coming undone.'

'Angelo, leave it, please,' said Connie, a hand on his arm. Angelo stepped back and laughed.

'Well, we should hang out, yeah? The four of us. That's my girlfriend, over there, Su-Lin,' and he indicated a girl out on the factory floor, dancing in her bra and a deerstalker hat. 'Here

. . .' and he mopped my forehead with a greasy napkin, tucked it in my top pocket and loped off, howling.

'He's really drunk,' said Connie. 'He gets a bit manic when he's drunk.'

'Well I liked him. I liked him a *lot*.'

'Douglas . . .'

'I like the way he doesn't blink, it's very attractive.'

'Don't start, please.'

'What?'

'The rutting-stag thing. He was a big part of my life, a long, long time ago. The important word is *was*, he *was* – past tense. He was what I needed at that time in my life.'

'And what do you need at this time in your life?'

'I'm not even going to answer that.' She took my hand. 'Come on. Let's go up to the roof and dry you out.'


## 71. firsts

The early days of any relationship are punctuated with a series of firsts – first sight, first words, first laugh, first kiss, first nudity, etc., with these shared landmarks becoming more widely spaced and innocuous as days turn to years, until eventually you're left with first visit to a National Trust property or some such.

We had our first major argument that night, a significant landmark in any relationship, but upsetting nonetheless because everything up to that point had been, well, bliss. I've made that point, I think. Just bliss.

As usual, Connie had been drinking – we had both been drinking – and was dancing now with no clear intention of ever stopping. She was always an exceptional dancer, did I mention that? Self-contained, rather aloof. She had a particular face when she danced, intent and inward-looking. Lips parted, eyelids heavy. Frankly, there was something rather sensual about it. At a family wedding, I was once told by my sister that I danced like someone wrestling with a bout of diarrhoea, clenched and anxious, and so I had chosen not to light up any dance-floors since. Instead I leant against the wall and ran through a mental list of all the things I wished I'd said to Angelo. He was still there, of course, dancing with a champagne bottle in his hand and Su-Lin riding on his back.

It was time for me to go home. I crossed the floor to Connie.

'I think I might head home,' I shouted, over the clanging music.

She steadied herself with her hand on my forearm. 'Okay,' she said. Her make-up was smeared, her hair sticking to her forehead, dark patches on her dress.

'D'you want to come with me?'

'No,' she said, and pressed her cheek to mine. 'You go.'

And I should have gone, right then, and waited for her at home. Instead . . .

'You know, just one time, you might at least try to persuade me.'

She looked puzzled. 'Okay. Stay. Please.'

'I don't want to stay. I'm not talking to anyone. I'm bored. I want to go.'

She shrugged. 'So go. I don't see what the problem is.'

I shook my head and began to walk away. She followed. 'Douglas, if you don't tell me what's wrong, I'll have to guess.'

'Sometimes I think you're happier when I'm not around.'

'How can you say that! That's not true.'

'So why do we never go out with your friends?'

'We're here, aren't we?'

'But not together. You bring me here then walk away.'

'You're the one who wants to leave!'

'But you're not exactly desperate for me to stay.'

'Douglas, you're an individual. Go if you want, we're not joined at the hip.'

'Because God forbid we should be that close!'

She tried to laugh. 'I'm sorry, I don't understand – are you angry because I'm having fun? Is it because Angelo's here? Don't walk away, explain it.'

We were in a concrete stairwell now, storming down the flights past furtive guests kissing or smoking or doing goodness knows what. 'Why do you never introduce me to your friends?'

'I do! Don't I?'

'Not if you can help it. When we do go out it's just you and me.'

'Okay then, because you wouldn't enjoy it. You don't want to go clubbing or stay up all night, you're too worried about work so I don't invite you.'

'You think I'd spoil the fun.'

'I think you wouldn't have fun, which means I wouldn't have fun.'

'I think there's another reason.'

'Go on then.'

'I think you're embarrassed by me sometimes.'

'Douglas, that's ridiculous. I love you, why would I be embarrassed by you? Don't I come home to you every night?'

'When there's no one else around.'

'And isn't that better? Just the two of us? Don't you love that? Because I do! I fucking treasure it, and I thought you did too.'

'I do! I do.'

We found ourselves out on the street, a wasteland really, the buildings in various stages of demolition. On the roof of the factory above us, there was laughter and music. Faces peered down. Perhaps Angelo was watching us too, down here amongst the breezeblocks and paving slabs, our argument losing its momentum and starting to seem foolish.

'Do you want me to come round later?' she said.

'No. Not tonight.'

'So do you want me to come right now?'

'No, you have your fun. I'm sorry if I got in your way.'

'Douglas . . .'

I began to walk away. The sky was darkening. Summer was over, autumn on the way. It was the last good day of the year and I felt, for the first time since we had met, the old inexpressible sadness of life without her.

'Douglas?'

I turned.

'You're going the wrong way. The train's in that direction.'

She was right, but I was too proud to go back past her and it was only as I wandered through the rubble, clambering over fences pursued by Alsatians, hugging the crash barriers of dual carriageways as lorries stormed by, hopelessly lost, that I realised our first argument had masked another first.

She had told me that she loved me.

It was the first time anyone had said the words without some qualifying clause. Had I imagined it? I didn't think so. No, it had definitely been there. I might have clicked my heels with joy, the first person to have done so on the Blackwall Tunnel Approach, but I had bodged the moment, so tangled up in petulance and self-pity, so befuddled with jealousy and alcohol that I'd not even bothered to acknowledge it. I stopped and looked about me, trying to get my bearings, then began to walk back the way I'd come.

For such a large building, the factory was proving quite elusive and after half an hour of wandering through the wasteland, I'd begun to think that I would be too late, that the reception would be over. Just as I was about to give up and find the nearest tube, I saw three bursts of light in the night sky, the sound booming after. Fireworks, a rocket exploding over the factory like a rescue flare. I turned and ran towards it.

They were playing ironic slow songs now; it was 'Three Times a Lady' as I walked in, if I recall. Connie was sitting alone on the opposite side of the dance-floor, elbows on her knees. I walked towards her and saw her smile then frown in quick succession, and before she could speak I said:

'I'm sorry. I'm an idiot.'

'You are, sometimes.'

'And I apologise. I'm trying not to be.'

'Try harder,' she said, then stood and our arms were around each other. 'How could you think those things, Douglas?'

'I don't know, I get . . . nervous. You're not going anywhere, are you?'

'I wasn't planning to, no.'

We kissed, and after a while I said, 'You too, by the way.'

'You too what?'

'I love you too.'

'Well,' she said. 'I'm glad that's settled.'

The following January, some eleven months after we had met, I drove Connie in a hired van from Whitechapel to Balham, checking the rear-view mirror as if looking for pursuers, with the hope and the intention that she would never leave my side again.

## 72. erotic realism

We passed an uneventful night in our honeymoon suite. On our return from an early supper in a Jordaan café, I filled up the Jacuzzi in the hope that Connie might join me. 'Let's fire this baby up!' I said, and clambered in. But the sensation was rather like being thrown into the propellers of the Portsmouth to Cherbourg ferry, and the noise disturbed Connie, who had got into bed early to read.

'Care to join me?' I bellowed coquettishly.

'No, you have fun,' she said.

'I'm setting it to turbo!' The roar of jet engines. 'IT'S VERY RELAXING!'

'Douglas, turn it off! I'm trying to read,' snapped Connie and returned to her book. Despite the pleasant day, we had not quite shaken off the scene on the train and I reflected, not for the first time, how our arguments seemed to have a longer half-life these days. Like colds and hangovers, they took an age to shake off and the reconciliation, if it came at all, didn't have quite the same decisiveness that it once had. I climbed from the infernal machine, we set about jettisoning the great piles of velvet pillows and silk cushions, and closed our eyes. The next day was the Rijksmuseum, and I would need my wits about me.

## 73. saskia van uylenburgh

For a feeling of true righteousness and invulnerability, there's nothing quite like riding a bicycle in Amsterdam. The traditional power relationship with the car is reversed and you're part of a tribe of overwhelming numbers, sitting high in the peloton, looking down on the bonnets of those foolish or weak enough ' to drive. Here people cycled with a reckless swagger, talking on the phone, eating breakfast, and on a bright, beautiful August day, our bicycles purring and rattling down Herengracht to the Golden Corner, there seemed no better place to be.

To the right, the Rijksmuseum. There is, I suppose, no set template for a national museum, but even so, I was struck by – not its plainness, but its lack of pretension. No columns or white marble, no Classical aspirations, none of the Louvre's palatial splendour but a kind of municipal functionality; a fine train station or an ambitious town hall.

Inside, the central atrium was immense and luminous and I felt – we all felt, I think – a renewed enthusiasm for the Tour. Even Albie, red-eyed and smoky-smelling from last night's unspecified adventure, was enlivened by it all. 'S'nice,' he said exultantly, and we strode on to the galleries.

That was a good morning. At occasional moments, Connie

even took my hand, a gesture that I associate with either youth or senility, but which here seemed to signify that I was forgiven. We went from room to room with the same glacial slowness I'd experienced at the Louvre, but I didn't mind this time. As well as art, there was an immense model galleon the size of a family car, glass cases full of ferocious weapons and, in the Gallery of Honour, the most extraordinary room of paintings. I am, as I think I mentioned, no art critic, but what was striking about Dutch art was how familiar and domestic it all felt. No Greek or Roman gods here, no crucifixions or Madonnas. Kitchens, back gardens, alleyways, piano practice, letters written and received, oysters that seemed wet to the touch, milk captured in mid-flow so accurately that you could almost taste it. Yet there was nothing banal or drab about any of it. There was pride, joy even, in the everyday scenes and portraits of real personalities, flawed and vain, muddled and silly. Pudgy and coarse-featured, the older Rembrandt was not a handsome man and in *Self-portrait as the Apostle Paul,* he looked frankly knackered, eyebrows raised and ruined face crumpled with a weariness that I recognised all too well. Recognition was not something I had felt in front of the saints, gods and monsters of the Louvre, splendid though they were. This was great art and the postcard bill was going to be immense.

In an imposing dark blue room the three of us sat, elbow to elbow, in front of *The Night Watch,* which, my guidebook said, was probably the fourth most famous painting in the world. 'What do you think are the top three?' I asked, but no one wanted to play that game, so I looked at the painting instead. There was a lot going on. It had, as my father would say, a good beat, a good tune, and I pointed out all the little details – the funny expressions, the jokes, the gun going off accidentally – that I'd picked up from the guidebook, in case Albie missed them. 'Did you know,' I said, 'that Rembrandt never gave it that name? The scene isn't really happening at night. The old varnish darkened and made it gloomy. Hence *The Night Watch*.'

'You're full of interesting facts,' said Connie.

'Did you know the painting contains a self-portrait of Rembrandt? He's right at the back, peeking over that man's shoulder.'

'Why not put the guidebook down now, Douglas?'

'If I had one criticism to make of it—'

'Oh. This'll be good,' said Albie. 'Dad's got notes.'

'If I had one criticism it would be the little girl in gold.' In a shaft of light, a little to the left of centre, a girl of eight or nine is beautifully dressed in exquisite robes with, somewhat anomalously, a chicken tied to her belt. 'I'd say, "Rembrandt, listen, I love the painting, but you might want to take one more look at the little girl with the chicken. She looks really, really old. She's got the face of a fifty-year-old woman, it's quite disconcerting and it draws attention from the centre of the—"'

'That's Saskia.'

'Who's Saskia?' said Albie.

'Rembrandt's wife. He used her as the female model for lots of his paintings. He was devoted to her. So they say.'

'Oh. Really?' There had been nothing about this in the guidebook. 'D'you think she thought it a bit strange?'

'Maybe. Perhaps she would have liked it, her husband imagining her youth, before he met her. Anyway, she probably never saw it. She died while he was painting it.'

This all seemed very unlikely to me. 'So, either he painted it while she was dying . . .'

'Or he painted her face from memory.'

'His older wife dressed as a young girl.'

'In loving memory of her. As a tribute, after she'd gone.'

And I didn't quite know what to make of this, except perhaps to note that artists in general really are very strange.

## 74. the real amsterdam

We didn't leave the museum until early afternoon, exhausted but inspired and with our schedule still in good shape. Sitting in the Museumplein, I identified several local lunch options, but Albie seemed engaged in some electronic conversation, giggling over the screen of his phone for reasons that became clear as I felt two fingers jab into my spine.

'Don't move, Petersen! Buffet police! We have reason to suspect you're carrying a concealed pain au chocolat.'

'Cat! Well, what a surprise!' said Connie, a little tightly. 'Albie, you trickster.' Albie was grinning in an unlovable way, delighted at the playing out of his brilliant little joke.

'I followed you – all the way from Paris! Hope I didn't freak you out there, Mr P., it's just Albie told me where you were and I couldn't resist. Come here, you beautiful boy!' and here she grabbed our son's face with both hands and gave him a smacking kiss that echoed across the park. 'How's the 'Dam? Are you having a wild time? Isn't it an amazing city?'

'We're having a very nice time, thank you—'

'Yeah, Albie told me you've checked him in to some kinky knocking-shop. Sounds hysterical.'

'It's not kinky,' I said patiently, 'it's boutique.'

'So what have you done, where have you been, what are you going to do? Tell me everything!'

'The flower market, cycling around the canals. We're going to the Van Gogh Museum tomorrow, and a canal cruise if we have time.'

'That's all the pretty-pretty tourist stuff – you need to see the *other* Amsterdam. We should all hang out! What are you doing right now?'

I felt, instinctively, that my itinerary was under threat. 'Actually, we're going to the Anne Frank House, then the Rembrandt House Museum.'

'Well, we don't *have* to,' said Connie. 'We can go tomorrow.'

'Why don't you guys go without us?' said Albie, hopefully. Clearly the idea of the four of us 'hanging out' was as unlikely and awkward to Albie as it was to me. 'Me and Cat want to go and explore.'

'I really want to take you to the Anne Frank House, Albie. I think you should see it.'

'I'm too tired to do much more, Douglas,' said Connie treacherously. 'Perhaps we should go tomorrow morning?'

'No! No, it's the Van Gogh Museum tomorrow. We're leaving in the afternoon.'

'Wouldn't you rather see the *real* Amsterdam?'

No, Cat, dammit, no! I had no desire to see the real Amsterdam. We had reality back in Berkshire, that's not why we were here; we had no interest in the way things really were. A perfectly co-ordinated schedule of sightseeing was unravelling before my eyes. 'If we don't go to the Anne Frank House today, the whole plan falls apart.' I felt myself getting shrill.

'Let us at least grab some lunch and chill out though, yeah? I've got a bike, and I know this amazing vegetarian buffet in De Pijp . . .'

## 75. eat as much as you can bear

Chickpeas like little balls of limestone. Some kind of bland, spongy curd cheese. Spinach like the algae on a Chinese beach, cold okra like a bucket of slugs. Necrotic avocado, sandy couscous, flaccid courgettes in a green-grey water sauce made from water. Kidney beans! Just plain cold kidney beans, exquisitely emptied from the can.

'Isn't it incredible? Who needs meat!' said Cat who, the last time I saw her, had been stuffing her rucksack with bacon like some crazed taxidermist.

'We ate a lot of meat in Paris. A lot,' said Connie, shifting allegiance in the most audacious way.

'I hope you didn't eat foie gras,' warned Cat, one finger pointed in my face.

'No, just duck, steak, duck, pâté, duck, steak . . .'

'And it was all delicious, I thought.'

'Dad won't eat anything *unless* it's got a face.'

'I don't think I heard anyone complain at the time.'

'It's very hard to get top-notch veggies in Paris. Kind of bungs you up after a while, though, doesn't it?' said Cat, puffing out her cheeks. 'Especially with all those baguettes. At least this bread has got some goodness in it.' The bread was rubbery and dense like window putty, and sprinkled with the contents of the baker's dustpan. 'I'm going in again! Who's coming for more delicious veggies?' and off Cat and Albie hopped to the buffet bar, where the tea-lights beneath silver hoppers kept the food pleasingly tepid.

I returned to my plate with a sigh. 'There is nothing here that, if you threw it against a wall, wouldn't stick and slide down very slowly.'

'Except the bread,' laughed Connie.

'The bread would ricochet off and take out an eye.'

'Well, you did say you wanted to try new things.'

'I only want to try new things that I know I'm going to like,' I said, and Connie laughed. 'Does she only ever eat from buffets, I wonder?'

'Leave her alone. I like her.'

'Really? You've changed your tune.'

'She's fine when she calms down. And look at them. It's sweet.' Over at the buffet, they stood shoulder to shoulder, trying to choose between norovirus and listeria. 'Young love. Were we once like that, Douglas, I wonder?'

'It's three fifteen. If we're going to get to the Anne Frank House we need to go now.'

'Douglas, can we leave it be? Even the Gestapo didn't want to get there this much.'

'Connie!'

'We're spending time with Albie, doing what he wants to do. Isn't that what you wanted?'

And so we polished off our watery curd, paid and mounted our bikes and spent the afternoon touring the outer rings of Amsterdam, Cat pointing out the amazing little bars, the squats where she'd stayed, the skateboard parks and huge estates and street markets. In truth much of it was perfectly nice and it was interesting, I suppose, to see where the Moroccan population lived, the Surinamese and the Turks. But as we looped back towards the centre, another destination became clear.

'And this,' said Cat, 'is my favourite coffee shop!'

It was inevitable, I suppose. Ever since we'd arrived in Amsterdam, Albie had been glancing sideways at these places in the same way that he once regarded toy shops. Now, standing outside the Nice Café, he was looking at the ground, grinning.

'It's a really blissful, vibey little place, dead friendly,' reassured Cat. 'I know the bud-tender, he'll look after us.'

'Oh, I don't think so, Cat.'

'Come on, Mr P. When in Rome . . .'

'No, thank you. It's really not for me.'

'How do you know if you've never tried it?' said Albie, the exact rationale I once used to get him to eat cabbage.

'I have tried it; of course I've tried it, Albie. I was young once!'

'I think I missed that bit,' said Connie.

'When I was with you, Connie, as a matter of fact, and Genevieve and Tyler. I pulled a massive whitey, if you recall.'

'"Massive whitey",' sniggered Albie.

'Mr P., you dark horse. Why not give it another go?'

'No, thank you, Cat.'

'Okay, Dad's out,' said Albie, barely bothering to hide his relief.

'How about you, Mrs P.?' said Cat, and all eyes turned to Connie.

'Mum?' said Albie.

Connie weighed up her options.

'Okay,' she said, 'sounds good,' and off she went to park her bicycle.


## 76. water in the wine

At various points during Albie's teenage years I had found myself in these situations, confronting the kind of 'life dilemma' that pads out the weekend newspapers. What is the correct parental response to shoplifting, the unsuitable friend picked up at the playground, the smell of alcohol or tobacco on teenage breath, the money disappearing from the dresser, the esoteric search history on the family computer? How much water in the wine? Should a girlfriend be allowed to stay the night, what is the policy on locked doors, on bad language, bad behaviour, bad diet? In recent years these dilemmas had come thick and fast and I had found them quite bewildering. Why had we not been issued with a clear set of guidelines? Had I caused my own parents all this ethical writhing? I was sure I had not. The most illicit act of my teenage years was to sometimes watch ITV. Yet here we were again, the latest instalment of this perpetual radio phone-in. I stood along-side Connie as she chained her bike. 'Are you sure you want to do this?'

'Quite sure, thank you, Douglas.'

'And you really think you should be encouraging him?'

'I'm not encouraging him, I'm just not being a hypocrite about it. Look at him! He's with a girl in Amsterdam, he's a teenager. Frankly, I'd be more worried if he didn't want to do it.'

'You don't have to sanction it, though.'

'How am I *sanctioning* it, Douglas?'

'By joining in!'

'I'm keeping a gentle eye on him. Also, as a matter of fact, I quite fancy a smoke.'

'You do? Really?'

'Is that really so strange? Really, Douglas?'

Cat and Albie were watching us now. 'Fine. Fine. But if he drops out to become a bud-tender, then it's your responsibility.'

'He won't become a *bud-tender*.'

'I'm going to leave you to it.'

'You don't have to.'

'I think you'll have more fun without me.'

'Okay,' she shrugged, 'we'll see you later,' and I thought, once more, *you know, just one time, you might at least try to persuade me*.

We walked back to the expectant party. 'I'm leaving, your mother is staying.'

Albie pulled his fist down and hissed, 'Yessssss!' at this best of all possible outcomes.

'Just don't eat the space cookies,' I said. 'There's no way to control the dosage.'

'Truth. Sound counsel, Mr P.,' said Cat, patting my arm. 'Words to live by.'

'I'll see you back at the hotel, for supper maybe,' said Connie, pressing a cheek against mine, and off they went to the Nice Café.

## 77. a great ocean of care

I was certainly in no mood for the Anne Frank House now. Without Albie there seemed little point, and while the Rembrandt House Museum was atmospheric and informative, particularly on the extraordinary technical demands and innovations of seventeenth-century engraving, I found myself distracted and ill at ease.

Because it was all very jolly, wasn't it, all very cool, sitting around and getting stoned all afternoon with your mum? What a lark, what memories to share! But I wanted my son to have ambition, I wanted him to have drive and energy and a fine, fierce mind. I wanted him to look out into the world with curiosity and intelligence, not with the awful solipsism and silliness of the stoned. Irrespective of the medical risks, the memory loss and apathy and psychosis, the possibility of addiction or exposure to hard drugs, what was this idiotic obsession with chilling out? I wasn't aware of having been relaxed at any time in my entire life; that was just the way things were, and was it really so bad? To be taut as a wire, on the ball, conscious of the dangers around you – wasn't that to be admired?

Such were my thoughts as I bicycled back and forth along the city's eastern canals, which were more utilitarian, less picturesque than those in the Grachtengordel. Oh, no doubt they were all having a fine time, self-lobotomising in the Nice Café. No doubt they were flopping about on beanbags in that idiotic fug, eating banana bread and giggling at the colour blue or mocking that funny old square and his fear of new experiences. But why couldn't they recognise my reservation for what it was; not narrow-mindedness, not conservatism or caution but *care*, a huge amount of care, an ocean of it. I disapproved because I cared. Why wasn't that apparent?

I found myself falling out of love with Amsterdam. For a start, there were far too many bicycles. The whole thing had got completely out of hand, the bridges and streets and lampposts choked with them like they were some alien weed. Many of them were decrepit anyway and I began to fantasise how, if I were mayor of Amsterdam, I would instigate a cull of the bloody things; a strict one person, one bike policy. Anything abandoned,

anything not roadworthy to be removed with bolt-cutters if necessary and melted down. In fact, in my sour frame of mind I began
to get quite carried away with the idea. I'd take them all on, the
cyclists of Amsterdam, with their inadequate lighting and one-
handed riding, their high saddles and sanctimonious air. I'd be
like Caligula, ruthless, fearless. I'd build a bonfire. Yes, melt
down the bikes, the bloody, bloody bikes!

## 78. de wallen

I found myself in the red light district.

I don't wish to sound defensive about the fact, but there was
a Chinese restaurant that I was eager to return to. Connie and
I had been there many years ago and I had it in mind to eat a
whole Peking duck as revenge for all that okra. It was early
evening, still warm and bright, and there was a sort of happy
hour vibe as stags and hens, self-conscious couples and a gang
of bikers overflowed from bars onto the bridge that crossed the
canal. The ladies in the red-curtained booths waved and smiled
at me like old friends as I tried to find a place to park my bicycle
in the absurdly congested tangle of scrap iron and rubber, and
found myself surrounded by the wretched things, untangling
pedals from chains and handlebars from brake cables, kicking
down my bike stand, contorting between the frames to lock the
thing. Then, as I stood and extricated myself, I tapped the bicycle
to my left with my hip, just a little nudge and, in a kind of
strange, almost hallucinatory slow-motion, watched as the tiny
movement sent the bicycle crashing into the next, then the next,
then the next, then the next, a chain reaction passing from bike
to bike like an ingenious and ambitious domino run, kinetic
energy building through four, five, six bikes before it reached the
huddle of vintage motorcycles. There were four of them, immaculate, polished things, parked just outside the bar where their

owners were drinking, so that they'd be safe. So that they would come to no harm.

There was a loud scraping noise as the brake handle of the last bicycle slashed its mark deep into the shiny red petrol tank of the first motorbike, then the crash as they too tumbled to the ground, one, two, three, four, then silence. Very strange, to hear silence in a crowded city street. Eerie, almost, though it didn't last for long. Someone laughed. 'Oh, *shit*,' said someone else. From the bikers' bar – I noted here that it was called 'Valhalla' – there came a roar as a group of immense red-faced men pushed through the crowd towards the beloved bikes that now lay, wheels spinning, in a pile of polished chrome.

All of this took a matter of perhaps ten seconds, and absurdly I wondered if I might still be able to walk away. After all, it wasn't exactly my fault. It was gravity, it was the bike, it was a chain reaction, nothing to do with me. Perhaps if I just walked away, perhaps if I whistled as I walked, as in a cartoon, no one would notice.

But I was standing alone at the precise centre of a great circle of destruction, and soon the men were barrelling towards me, the four of them like the fingers in a fist, hatred in their eyes. The Dutch accent didn't seem so affable now, it seemed harsh and guttural as they quickly formed a circle around me, hands gripping my shoulder as if steadying me for a punch that I knew would surely come. The man with his nose touching mine was blond as a Viking, with a face like a cheap cut of meat, missing teeth – never a good sign – and beer on his breath. 'No speak Dutch,' I repeated idiotically, 'no speak Dutch,' on the basis that bad English is more easily understood than the good kind. But it's possible to spot swearing in almost any language and now four other hands were grabbing my arms, walking me – carrying me – through the crowd that had now gathered to watch the sport. Three motorcycles were hauled upright and inspected, but the nearest bike lay on its side in a way that seemed suggestive of a dying horse, the owner crouching beside the beloved creature, keening quietly, rubbing his thumb over the horrible scar on the highly polished fuel tank. Unusually for a Dutchman, he seemed to speak fairly limited English, because the only words I could pick up were 'You pay, you pay,' then, as he grew in linguistic confidence, 'you pay big'.

'I didn't do it!'

'Your bike did it.'

'Not my bike. My bike over there,' and I gestured across the devastation to where my bike stood, immaculately vertical. There was, I suppose, an interesting debate to be had here about causality and the notion of 'fault', intention and chance, but it might save time if I simply reached for my wallet. I had never re-sprayed a motorcycle. How much might that cost?

I began negotiations. 'I can give you . . . eighty euros.' This made them laugh in an unpleasant way, and an immense paw took my wallet and started searching through the folds and pouches. 'Excuse me – could you give that back?'

'No, my friend,' said the blond man. 'We are going to the bank!'

'Give him back his money!' said a voice to one side, and looking over my shoulder I saw that a woman was pushing her way through the crowd, a large black woman with improbably blonde hair, tying her dressing gown over what appeared to be some sort of white fishnet body-stocking. 'Here,' she said, snatching my wallet and returning it to me, 'this is yours. You hold this until I say.'

There was, at this point, a certain amount of shouting in Dutch, the woman jabbing her finger into the lead biker's chest – her nails were extravagantly long, curved and painted – then throwing her shoulders back and pushing her chest towards him, using it as one might a riot shield, while pointing at me and gesturing up and down. She shouted something, causing the crowd to laugh and the biker to shrug defensively, then suddenly she changed her tone and tack, flirting with the man instead, her arms draped over his shoulders. He laughed and pinched his nose in thought. Looked me up and down. I seemed to be the subject of some sort of negotiation.

'How much in your wallet?' said the lady who, I surmised from the body-stocking, was either a prostitute or very outgoing. Would she be coming to the bank too? Perhaps she wasn't my ally after all. Perhaps they were all going to rob me and toss me in the canal. 'About two hundred and fifty euros,' I said, defensively.

'Give me one hundred fifty.' She beckoned with two fingers of her hand. I hesitated, and she spoke fast and low. 'Give it to me and you might live.'

I handed over the money, which she packed into a tight ball and stuffed into the biker's fist. Then, before he'd had a chance to count it, she took my arm and pushed her way through the crowd towards a flight of stairs. Behind us, the bikers were protesting loudly: 'You pay more! More!' But the lady gestured dismissively, hissed something about the police, and I was bustled up the steps of the townhouse, through a red-lit doorway.

## 79. paul newman

My saviour's name was Regina – though that may have been a pseudonym – and she was terrifically nice.

'What is your name, my new friend?'

'Paul,' I said, then with an awful inevitability, 'Newman. I'm Paul Newman.' I'm not sure where my pseudonym came from. It lacked the ring of plausibility, and probably wasn't even necessary. After all, I hadn't done anything wrong. But too late; for the time being I was Paul Newman.

'Hello, Paul Newman. Come . . .'

I took a seat on a sort of vinyl platform. The bedroom, if bedroom is the right word, contained a sink and a rudimentary shower and was lit in a deep red, and I thought for a moment what a terrific place it would be for developing photographs. A cheap fan blew ineffectually, a kettle sat in the corner. There was a microwave, and a powerful smell of some chemical approximation of coconut. 'I watched the whole thing from the window. You are a very unlucky man, Paul Newman,' she said, and laughed. 'They were big guys. I think they might have killed you, or at least emptied your bank.'

'What did you tell him?'

'I told him to claim on insurance. He has insurance, that is what insurance is for! You are shaking.' She illustrated with juddering hands. 'Would you like some tea?'

'Tea would be lovely. Thank you.' While we waited for the kettle to boil I became very aware of her bare bottom, which was large, dimpled and never more than half a metre from my face. I turned to the window onto the street, intrigued to see the booth from this point of view, and noted that she had exactly the same swivelling office chair that I'd once had in my lab, though I didn't point this out. Instead I turned to the TV.

'Ah, I see that you have *Downton Abbey* here too!'

Regina shrugged. 'You want to watch something else?' she said, and indicated a small pile of pornographic DVDs.

'No, no. *Downton*'s fine.' Without asking, she stirred two sugars into the tea and passed me my mug, and I noticed that my hands were indeed shaking. I used my left palm as a saucer. At a loss for conversation, I asked, 'So – have you been working here long?'

Regina told me that she had been doing this for six or seven years. Her parents were Nigerian, but she had been born in Amsterdam and had started working here through a friend. The winter was depressing and it was hard to pay the rent on the little booth without the tourists around, but she had some regular customers that she could rely on. Summer, on the other hand, was too busy, too much, and she shook her head woefully. 'Stag nights!' she said, and wagged a finger at me as if I had been organising them all. Apparently a lot of men required drink to get their courage up, then found themselves unable to perform. 'They still have to pay, of course!' she said, pointing a finger with some menace and I laughed and nodded and agreed that this was only fair. I asked if she knew her colleagues and she said they were mainly friendly, though some girls had been tricked into coming here from Russia and Eastern Europe, and this made Regina sad and angry. 'They think they're going to be dancers, can you believe that? Dancers! Like the world needs all these dancers!'

After a moment, she said, 'What do you do, Paul Newman?'

'Insurance,' I said, giddy on my whimsical flight of fancy. 'I'm on holiday here with my wife and son.'

'I have a son too,' she said.

'Mine's seventeen.'

'Mine's only five.'

'Five is a lovely age,' I said, which I've always thought an idiotic remark. When do ages stop being 'lovely'? 'Five's lovely, but fifty-four's a bastard' – that should be the follow-up. Anyway, Regina's five-year-old son, it transpired, lived in Antwerp with his grandparents because she didn't want any of them seeing her at work, and at this point the little room took on a sombre air and we sat in silence for a minute or so, watching events below stairs at Downton and contemplating the anxieties of parenthood.

But all in all, it was an interesting and informative conversation, not one I'd expected to have that evening and I did feel we'd made some sort of connection. But I was also aware of eating into her time and also that she was practically naked, and so I stood and reached for my wallet.

'Regina, you've been really kind, but we've been talking for a while so I really want to pay you something . . .'

'Okay,' she shrugged. 'It's fifty for complete service.'

'Oh, no. No, no, no. I don't need a complete service.'

'Okay, Paul Newman, you tell me what you do need?'

'I don't need anything! I'm here with my family.'

She shrugged again, and took the mug from my hand. 'Everyone has a family.'

'No, we're here for the Rijksmuseum.'

'Yes,' she laughed, 'I hear that a lot.'

'My wife's off with my son. The only reason I'm here at all is because I was looking for a Chinese restaurant.' This made her laugh even more. 'Please, don't laugh at me, Regina, it's true. I was just looking for somewhere to . . . I just wanted to find . . .' And I imagine that at this point some kind of delayed shock kicked in, combined with the stresses and strains of the last few days, because for some reason I seemed to be crying in absurd, jagged gasps, hunched over on the vinyl bench, one hand pressed across my eyes, like a mask.

I wish I could report here that Regina told me to put my money away and held me to her warm, soft breast and soothed my brow, the kind of thing that would happen in an arty film or novel. Two lost souls meeting, or some such nonsense. But in real life lost souls don't meet, they just wander about and I think, in all honesty, she was as embarrassed as I was. A nervous breakdown in a red-lit booth was a breach in etiquette, and there was a palpable briskness as Regina took the remaining hundred euros, stood and opened the door.

'Goodbye, Paul Newman,' she said, her hand on my shoulder. 'Go and find your family.'

## 80. mellow times

In the Mellow Times Café they played Bob Marley's *Greatest Hits*, which even I would have rejected as a little obvious. My bud-tender, a tall boy called Tomas with a patchy beard and a flute-y, lisping voice, asked me what I wanted, and I asked for something that would simultaneously calm me down and cheer me up, not too strong; did such a brand exist? Seemingly it did; he gave me something called Pineapple Gold and, like a good GP, advised me not to combine it with alcohol, though it was too late for that advice as I had already been to several bars.

Back in the honeymoon suite, I pulled out my phone and noted a series of texts from Connie that I imagined represented a spiral of lunacy:

**Where are you?**

**Call me!!!**

**It fun here!! Join us**

**come have fun**

**u ok hun?**

**funny old man callme!!!**

**love you loads**

But even that last message failed to cheer me. 'I love you' is an interesting phrase, in that apparently small alterations – taking away the 'I', adding a word like 'lots' or 'loads' – render it meaningless. I opened the windows wide, set the Jacuzzi to massage, placed my 'gear' in a saucer on the edge and climbed in.

I wish I could report some psychedelic odyssey. Instead, I felt the same sense of overheated melancholy that I usually associate with three p.m. on Boxing Day. Good God, did people really go to prison for this? My head hummed with the unpleasant throbbing one feels in a bath that's too hot, a sensation amplified by the fact that I *was* in a bath that was too hot, bubbling and churning like some terrible casserole. The drug was failing to bring about the amnesia I craved. I was, if anything, even more painfully aware of the failure of my best hopes. Despite my efforts, or perhaps because of them, the Petersens were stumbling. If there had been two of us, or four of us, perhaps there might have been some balance. But together we had the grace of a three-legged dog, hobbling from place to place.

By now I was feeling rather ill. The bedroom smelt like a burning spice rack and it was a non-smoking room, too, adding to my paranoia. My heart was beating far too fast and I became convinced that it would pop like my father's and I would expire like a rock star, on the floor of an Amsterdam sex hotel after three beers and two puffs of a very mild joint. One hand on my chest, still soaking wet, I stumbled into our absurd bed and waited beneath damp sheets for Connie to come home.

She returned at three a.m., just as she had that first summer. It had been my firm intention to sulk but she was dopily affectionate, settling her head on my shoulder. Her hair smelt smoky, there was an unfamiliar spirit on her breath and a slight, not unpleasant smell of sweat.

'Oh my God,' she murmured. 'What a night.'

'Was it fun?'

'In a teenage kind of way. We went to see bands! Did you get my texts? We missed you. Where were you?'

'I met a prostitute. Called Regina. Then I OD'ed in the Jacuzzi.'

She laughed. 'Oh, is that right?'

'Where's Albie?'

'He's next door. I think he brought some friends back.' And sure enough, through the door of our adjoining rooms could be heard the sound of laughter, and an accordion playing 'Brown-Eyed Girl'.

## 81. exposed floorboards

From now on there would be no more returns at three or four in the morning. Now we went to bed and woke together, stood at the sink and brushed our teeth, shaping the habits and tics, the gestures and dances of a life together, beginning the process by which things that are thrilling and new become familiar, scuffed and well loved. Specifically . . .

Connie always dozes when the alarm goes off whereas I am already awake. Connie puts her bra on before any of her other clothes, I work on the lower half then proceed upwards. Connie

likes a manual toothbrush, I swear by electric. Connie talks on
the phone for hours, I am brief and to the point. Connie carves
a roast chicken like a surgeon, I make excellent stews. Connie
is late for flights, whereas I like to be there the requisite two
hours before departure, because why would they ask if they
didn't mean it? Connie has a facility for mimicry and dancing,
I do not. Connie dislikes mugs but rarely uses a saucer with a
teacup, habitually burns toast, hates having her ears touched or
whispered into, licks jam off her knife, chews ice-cubes and
sometimes, shockingly to me, eats raw bacon off the chopping
board. Connie likes gritty award-winning dramas, old musicals
and berating politicians on the news. I like documentaries about
extreme weather conditions. She dislikes tulips and roses, cauliflower and swede, and eats tomatoes as if they were apples,
wiping the juice from her chin with her thumb. She paints her
toenails in front of the TV on Sunday nights, each leg raised in
turn in a wonderful way, sheds a startling amount of hair into
the plughole yet never removes it, has a terrifying dent in her
scalp which she calls her 'metal plate' from a childhood mishap
on a diving board, a surprising number of black fillings in her
teeth, a raised mole on her left shoulder, two piercings in each
ear. She leaves a certain smell on her pillow, prefers red wine to
white, thinks chocolate is overrated, and has an infinite capacity
for sleep, could sleep standing up if she chose. We made these
discoveries each day, then stood and undressed on opposite sides
of the bed in which we made love 90, then 80, then 70 per cent
of our nights. We witnessed all the petty maladies, the stomach
upsets and chest infections, the gnarled toenails, the ingrowing
hairs, boils and rashes that took the gleam off the person we
had first presented. No matter, no panic, these things happen,
and instead we shopped for food together, pushing the trolley
a little self-consciously at first, trying on this domesticity. We
had what we ironically referred to as our 'drinks cabinet' and
brought back lurid liqueurs when we travelled abroad. We argued

over tea, Connie favouring fragrant, vaguely medicinal brews over regular tea-bags. We argued once again when she destroyed my fridge by defrosting the freezer section with a screwdriver, then again about the efficacy of Chinese medicine, and once more about furniture, as my perfectly decent sofa-bed was removed and replaced with Connie's smoky, baggy velvet affair. My fitted carpets, chosen for their hard-wearing neutrality – 'office carpets', she called them – were torn up. We painted the floorboards together, as young couples must.

There were other changes, too. Connie was, in those days, ferociously untidy. She isn't like that now and I suppose it's one of the ways in which I've managed to change her, but in those days she used to leave a trail of pen lids, sweet-wrappers, hair slides and grips and pins, elastic bands, pieces of costume jewellery, the backs of earrings, packets of tissues, a single piece of gum wrapped in foil, small change from around the world. It was not unusual for her to reach into the pocket of a capacious coat for keys and to pull out a small wrench, a stolen ashtray, a desiccated apple-core or the stone of a mango. Books were left face down on the toilet cistern, discarded clothes were pushed into a corner like fallen leaves. She liked to 'leave dishes to soak', an act of self-deception that I've always abhorred.

But, for the most part, I didn't mind. Light travels differently in a room that contains another person; it reflects and refracts so that even when she was silent or sleeping I knew that she was there. I loved the evidence of her past presence, and the promise of her return, the way she changed the smell of that gloomy little flat. I had been unhappy there, but that was in the past. It felt like being cured of some debilitating disease, and I was jubilant. 'Domestic bliss' – the pairing of those words made perfect sense to me. I don't mean to strike an inappropriate note, but few things have ever made me happier in my life than the sight of Connie's underwear drying on my radiator.

## 82. kilburn

London changed, too. The city that had always seemed somewhat mean and grey, ineptly conceived, impractical and dour, became renewed. Connie was a Londoner and knew it like a cabbie. Street markets and drinking dens, Chinese, Turkish, Thai shops and restaurants and greasy spoons. It was like discovering that the somewhat dreary house in which you've grown up has one hundred further rooms, each leading off the other, each full of strangeness or beauty or noise. The city where I lived made sense because Connie Moore was in it.

After eighteen months together we sold my Balham flat, scraped our savings into a pile, somehow acquired a joint mortgage and bought a place that would feel like ours. North of the river this time, a top-floor flat in Kilburn, larger, lighter, better for parties – not criteria that had ever troubled me before – with a small but pleasant spare room. The purpose of this room was vague. Perhaps people could stay over, or perhaps Connie could start painting again – she had not painted for a while, despite my encouragement, but had given up her share of the studio and was working full time in the St James gallery. Artists, she said, had a few years after college in which to make an impression and she felt this hadn't happened. She still sold paintings, but less frequently, and she did not replace them with new work. Well, never mind, perhaps now she would have the space she needed. 'And this . . .' said Connie to Fran, swinging open the door, 'is the nursery!' and they both laughed for some time.

We pulled up the carpets there too, and threw a housewarming party, the first party I had ever thrown. My friends from the lab eyed her friends from the arts like rival gangs at a teenage disco,

but there were cocktails, and one of Connie's musician friends
DJ-ed and soon there was dancing – dancing, in my own home!
– the two clans emulsifying after a vigorous shake. At midnight
the neighbours came up to complain. Connie pressed drinks into
their hands and told them to change out of their pyjamas and
soon they were dancing too. 'You see this?' said my sister Karen,
drunk and self-satisfied, her arms tight around the necks of
Connie and me. 'This was my idea!' She squeezed a little tighter.
'Just imagine, D, if you'd stayed at home that night. Imagine!'

When the last guest had finally left we made strong coffee
and stood at the sink washing glasses together in the late-summer
dawn, the windows wide open onto the roofs of north-west
London. Begrudgingly, I had to admit there was a great deal to
thank my sister for. Though not my field, I was familiar with
the notion of alternative realities, but was not used to occupying
the one I liked the best.

## 83. two single beds, pushed together

So much changed during those years that it became impossible
to conceal the truth from my parents, and so one Easter we drove
east. Connie was an undeservedly confident driver and owned a
battle-scarred old Volvo with moss growing in the window frames
and a forest floor of crisp packets, cracked cassette cases and old
A-to-Zs. She drove with a kind of belligerent sloppiness, changing
the music more often than she changed gear, so that tensions
were already quite high as we pulled up outside my family home,
Victorian red-brick, lawn neat, gravel raked.

I had met Connie's family many times. It was impossible not
to, given their closeness, and generally we got on very well. Her
half-brothers would gather around me at family events, calling
me 'Professor' and urging me to visit various north-east London
takeaways, insisting, 'Anything you want, on the house.' Kemal,

her step-father, thought me 'a true gent', and a far better proposition than the hooligans she usually brought home. Only Shirley,
Connie's mother, remained sceptical. 'How's Angelo?' she would
ask. 'What's Angelo up to? Have you seen Angelo?' 'It's because
Angelo used to flirt with her,' Connie explained. It was never
suggested that I should flirt, too.

Arriving at my parents', I wondered whether Connie might
flirt with my father and perhaps draw him out of his spiked
shell. Was that worth a try? Curtains twitched as we pulled up.
My father's hand raised at the window, my mother at the front
door. Hello, would you mind taking your shoes off?

Connie was completely charming, of course, but I'd always
been led to believe that one talked to parents in the same polite,
over-enunciated tone used for customs officials and police officers,
conversation kept within tight parameters. What a lovely home,
we've brought you some flowers, no more wine for me! Connie,
however, made a great show of not altering her tone at all,
simply talking to them like normal people.

But they weren't normal people, they were my parents. Connie
was charming and bright, but my father smelt the artiness on her
and it made him anxious. My mother was bemused. Who was
this attractive, glamorous, outspoken creature, holding hands with
her son? 'She's very vivacious,' she whispered as the kettle boiled.
It was as if I'd turned up wearing an immense fur coat. Separate
rooms would have been too draconian, but despite there being a
perfectly good double bed, we were shown into the spare room
with two singles, my mother holding open the door as if to say,
'Here it is, your den of filth and shame.' Connie was never one
to shy away from a fight, and I imagined my parents in the dining
room below, staring at the ceiling, cigarettes suspended halfway
to their mouths at the sound of Connie and me pushing the beds
together, giggling. Teenage rebellion, at the age of thirty-three.

The revolution continued at dinner. Despite smoking like a
pair of burning tyres, my parents were rather reserved about

alcohol and kept their sparse selection of ancient bottles in the garden shed with the spiders. Sherry was for trifles; brandy was for shock. Alcohol loosened inhibitions, and inhibitions were worn tight here. When it became clear that my parents were not going to open the bottle we had brought with us, that it would join the miniature of whisky and the curdled advocaat at the end of the garden, Connie made a great show of 'popping out for some more wine', returning in the car with two bottles and, it transpired later, a small bottle of vodka concealed in her coat.

I wish I could say the alcohol made things go with a swing. Over a dinner of fatty pork, talk somehow turned to immigration policy because, famously, nothing brings people together like the subject of immigration. We had all been drinking now, Connie and my father in particular, and my mother had asked a question about the relative racial mix of Kilburn in comparison with Balham. Were there still a lot of Irish there, as opposed to West Indians or Pakistanis? The implication being, I suppose, that the Irish were in some way 'not so bad'. Connie had replied, in moderate tones, that there were all kinds of communities there, that often when people said Pakistani they meant Bangladeshi, which was like confusing Italy with Spain, and that the racial mix was part of the excitement and pleasure of living in London. But did she feel safe at night? asked my father.

It is probably not necessary to transcribe the argument that followed. In their defence, my parents' views were widely held, but they were expressed with inappropriate anger, my father's curled finger tapping an invisible window pane with every spurious 'fact!', and soon Connie was shouting, 'My step-father is Turkish Cypriot, should he go home? My half-brothers, they're half English, half Cypriot. What about my mum, she's English, Irish, French, but she's married to one of them – should she have to go, too?'

'Maybe we should change the subject?' I suggested.

'No, we will not!' said Connie emphatically. 'Why do you always want to change the subject?'

And so we went on. The insinuation on Connie's part – perhaps she even stated it outright – was that my parents were provincial bigots. The contention on my parents' part was that Connie was 'not in the real world', that she was not waiting for a council house with her three kids, that she was unlikely to lose her job in some swanky art gallery to somebody who had just got off the boat from Poland. 'You don't get the boat from Poland,' said Connie, petulantly, 'you *fly*.'

There was a pause, and we all looked at our congealed dinner.

'You're very quiet,' said my mother, in hurt tones.

'Well,' I said, 'I agree with Connie.'

For the most part I did agree with Connie. But if Connie had been arguing for a moon made entirely of cheese, I would have agreed with her too. I was going to be on her side from now on, and my parents saw this, and were saddened by it, I think. But what choice did I have? In a fight you side with the people you love. That is just how it is.

## 84. immense wristwatches

The three gentlemen at breakfast were large and self-confident: a Dutchman, an American and a Russian. They were well-dressed, teak-tanned, expense-account men, reeking of cologne, the kind of men who let other people shave them, the kind of men you find on yachts. With their immense wristwatches, they were a different breed, and our party of four seemed rather grey and muted in comparison. Connie and I had slept badly, Cat and Albie not at all, and they were still drunk or stoned or some combination of the two. If they reeked of beer and spirits, I reeked of disapproval. A reckoning was due between Albie and me. There had been complaints from the hotel staff about last night's party, and I was waiting for an opportunity to announce that no, I would not be paying for the contents of the mini-bar and no, I was not happy that we had missed the best part of our final morning in Amsterdam due to hangovers. And so the seven of us sat in the gloomy subterranean breakfast room, at tables too close together, consuming acrid coffee and the kind of croissants that come in cellophane wrappers while the businessmen boomed away.

'People talk about manufacturing costs,' the handsome American was saying, 'and we're not stupid, we see that as a factor, but where's the benefit if we're left with a shitty product?' He was no older than thirty, blue-chinned, muscular beneath a tailored shirt. 'Our current manufacturers, we're sending 10 to 15 per cent back as faulty or under par.'

'It is a false economy,' said the nodding Dutchman, slighter and less confident, some sort of middle-man or facilitator. Perhaps there was a business conference in town, a trade fair of some kind.

'Precisely. A false economy. What you offer us, and this is why we're pursuing this so hard, is consistency, efficiency, transportation links . . .'

'Reliability . . .' said the Russian.

'It is a win-win situation,' said the Dutchman, who seemed to have a business idiom for every circumstance. They continued in that rather brash tone, and I attempted to bring our own conversation back to check-out times, the storage of luggage, the importance of intelligent packing. We were heading to Munich by sleeper train that evening, then across the Alps to Verona, Vicenza, Padua and Venice, a journey that had seemed rich with romance when I had made the reservations, but now seemed fraught with danger.

Yet Albie and Cat seemed transfixed by the men to our right, exchanging eye-rolls and little shakes of the head and derisive little huffs and tuts at all this talk of timescales and profit margins and brands. 'Take this model . . .' said the American, and a glossy brochure made its way across the table, close enough for us to see.

The brochure illustrated a gun, some sort of assault rifle, and it was one of many glossy documents among the coffee cups. We were close enough to reach across and grab one, and for a moment I thought Albie might do just that. Here was the gun in loving close-up, here was the gun dismantled, cradled in a mercenary's arms. I'm no expert on combat weapons, but it looked like rather an absurd object to me. Embellished with telescopic sights and spare magazine clips and jumper-snagging bayonets, it looked like the kind of gun a teenage boy would draw – a space rifle. Indeed, there was discussion about the specialised leisure and hunting sectors, the accessories they'd buy, the gadgets and gizmos. *That's interesting*, I thought, *they're weapons manufacturers*, and I drank the last of my coffee. 'Well, Cat,' I said, 'I'm afraid it's time to say goodbye!'

But nobody was listening to me. They were too busy staring, doing their best to radiate disapproval. Cat was craning her neck towards them, shoulders thrown back, eyes wide, street-theatre style. Bad enough that these men were capitalists, but to be discussing such a trade in public, in daylight, in voices loud enough to make our coffee cups shake?

'Well, the museum opens at ten!' I said, and began to stand.

'You are here on holiday?' said the Dutchman, unable to ignore the stares.

'Just two days, unfortunately!' I said, neutrally enough I thought. 'Come on, everyone. We've still got to check out.'

And now Albie pushed his chair noisily away, stood and planted both hands firmly on their table. 'The bathroom's over there,' he said, in a clearer voice than I was used to hearing.

The American adjusted his shoulders. 'And why would we need the bathroom, son?'

'To wash all that blood off your hands,' said Albie, and then several things happened at once, not all of them entirely clear to me. I recall that the American stood, placing one hand behind Albie's neck, pressing his face towards the open palm of his other hand, saying, 'Where? Show me the blood, son! Where?' I saw Connie hanging off the American's arm, calling him an arsehole, attempting to pull his hand away, a coffee cup spilling, the Dutchman gesturing at me angrily – why couldn't you mind your own business? – the waiter crossing quickly, amused and then alarmed, the big Russian laughing at it all until Cat stood too, took a glass of orange juice and poured it onto a brochure, then another, then another, until it began to pool on the glossy pages and then cascade into the Russian's lap and he too stood, revealing his great size just like in a slapstick comedy, at which Cat started to laugh herself, a theatrical cackling, quite maddening, which caused the Russian to start calling her a stupid bitch, a stupid mad bitch, all of which made her laugh even more.

At least that is what I recall. It was not quite a brawl, no punches were thrown, it was more a tangle of reaches and grabs, jeers and sneers, ugly in the extreme and pointless too, I felt. As to my own behaviour, I had intended to play the role of peacemaker, disentangling arms and appealing for calm. That was my intention, to calm the situation, and at some point I wrapped my arms around Albie, holding him back but inciden-tally allowing the American to shove his shoulder – not hard, just a demeaning little jab. I held on to Albie tight, pulling him away, doing my best to separate the parties and proceed with the day that I had planned for my family. As I say, it was all a blur. What was undeniable, though, because everyone remem-bered it afterwards, was that at some point I had dragged Albie away and used the words:

'I'd like to apologise for my son.'

# 85. sunflowers again

Albie did not come to the Van Gogh Museum. Connie nearly didn't make it either, so sullen and angry was she that morning, riding her bike with head-down fury, barely bothering with hand signals.

We stood in front of *Sunflowers*, one of several versions Van Gogh painted, and I was reminded of the print I'd had on my wall. 'Do you remember? In the Balham flat? I bought it to impress you.' But she was not in the mood for nostalgia, and all my other observations about the thickness of the paint on the canvas and the rich palette of colours made not a mark on the impenetrable shell of my wife's contempt. She was even too angry to buy postcards. So much for the soothing power of great art.

Sure enough, the explosion came as we stepped outside.

'You know what you should have done? When that guy went for Albie? You should have punched him in the nose, not held Albie's arms so he could hit him.'

'He didn't hit him, it was a little shove.'

'Makes no difference.'

'Albie started it! He was being obnoxious, he was showing off.'

'Makes no difference, Douglas.'

'You think that would have helped? That guy would have knocked me flat! Would that have helped the situation, me getting beaten up in front of everyone? Is that what you'd have preferred?'

'Yes! Yes, that man would have broken your nose and split your lip and I'd have wanted to *kiss* you, Douglas, because you'd have stood up to someone for the sake of your son! Instead, you simper away: "We're having a lovely time here, just two days unfortunately".'

'It was a fatuous argument in the first place! Good God, what are you, nine years old? So they make guns! You don't think we need guns? The police, the army? You don't think someone has to manufacture them? It's the politics of primary school to shout abuse at people going about their lawful business, even if you disapprove . . .'

'Douglas, you have an incredible capacity for missing the point. Will you listen to me, just for once? The debate does not matter. It's not about the issues. Albie might have been naïve or ridiculous or pompous or all of those things, but you *apologised*. You said you were embarrassed by him. You took the side of a bunch of arms-dealers! Bloody bastard arms-dealers against your son – *our* son – and that was wrong, it was the wrong thing to do, because in a fight you side with the people you love. That's just how it is.'

## 86. daydreams of near disaster

When I first began to feel my son slipping away from me – I think perhaps he was nine or ten when I first felt the wriggling of his fingers in my manic grip – I found myself indulging in a particular fantasy. I'm aware that it sounds perverse, but what I hoped for at that time was some accident, some near disaster, so that I could be as heroic as the occasion demanded, and show the strength of my devotion.

In the Everglades of Florida, Albie is bitten by a snake that finds its way into his shoe, and I suck the venom from his filthy heel. Hiking in Snowdonia a sudden storm descends, Albie slips and breaks his ankle and I carry him through fog and rain to safety. A freak wave sweeps Albie off the Cobb at Lyme Regis and, without hesitation, without even thinking about taking my car keys and phone and placing them somewhere safe, I leap into the pounding surf, dive and dive again beneath the grey waters until I find him and carry him to the shore. It transpires that Albie needs a kidney. My kidney is a perfect match – be my guest, please. Take two! If ever he were in danger, I had no doubt about my instinctive courage and loyalty.

Yet put me in a little breakfast room in an Amsterdam hotel . . .

I would apologise, that's what I'd do. I would take him some-where quiet and explain, that I was tired, that I had not slept all night, and perhaps he had not noticed but there were certain tensions between his mother and me and that consequently I was a little on edge, but that I loved him hugely and couldn't we now move on, both literally and figuratively? The train to Munich was in two hours. We'd be in Italy in two days' time.

But when I returned to the hotel, I found Connie leaning on the reception desk, the heels of her hands pressed to teary eyes. Without looking up, she slid the letter towards me, written in Albie's scrawling hand on the back page of my itinerary.

*Mum, Dad,*

*Well, that was fun!*

*I appreciate the effort and all the money but I don't think the Grand Tour is working out. I feel like I'm being got at all the time, which isn't much of a holiday for me, surprise surprise, so I'm heading off and leaving you to get at each other instead. At least now you'll be able to stick to your schedule, Dad!*

*I don't know where I'm going. I might stay with Cat or I might not. I've taken my passport from your room and also a little money – don't worry, Dad, I'll pay you back, and for the mini-bar too. Put it on the bill.*

*Please don't try to email, text or phone. I'll be back in touch when the time is right. Until then I just need some time to clear my head and think certain things through.*

*Mum, don't worry. And Dad, I'm sorry if I disappoint you.*

*See you whenever,*
*Albie*

part four

# GERMANY

—

Surely you have to succeed, if you give everything you have.

Penelope Fitzgerald, *The Bookshop*

## 87. couchette

We had taken a sleeper train once before, to Inverness then on to a cycling holiday in Skye, the autumn of our second year.

The trip had been a birthday surprise; meet me at such and such a time, bring your passport and a swimming costume, the kind of larky spree that was new to me. If Connie was disappointed to discover that she would need neither passport nor swimming costume then she didn't show it, and we laughed a lot, I recall, in the tiny couchette of the train from Euston. In the films of my childhood, sleeper trains were shorthand for a kind of suave sauciness. In reality, like saunas and Jacuzzis, sleeping compartments are not nearly the sensual playground we're led to believe and this is another way in which fiction lies to us. The real experience can easily be simulated by paying two hundred pounds to make love in a locked wardrobe on the back of a fast-moving flatbed truck. Nevertheless, we persevered despite a great deal of giggling and cramp, and somewhere between Preston and Carlisle there was a mishap with birth control.

This was something about which we'd always been quite fastidious, and while neither of us panicked, we both were forced to contemplate the theoretical notion of parenthood, of how that might feel, what it might look like. We thought about it as we cycled across a squally Skye, we thought about it while lying whisky-breath'd in soft, strange beds in various B&Bs, we thought about it while peering at Ordnance Survey maps in search of shelter from the latest downpour. We even joked about it, that if it was a girl we would call her Carlisle, if it was a boy, Preston, and we found the idea . . . unhorrific. 'Pregnancy scare' is the traditional phrase and yet we weren't scared in the least, and this, too, felt like another milestone.

On our return journey to London, we squeezed into a bunk the size of a large cot and Connie revealed that she was not pregnant after all.

'Well, that's good news,' I said. Then, 'Is it?'

She exhaled, then turned and lay with her hand across her forehead. 'I don't know. I think it is. It always was in the past. I actually feel a little disappointed, to be honest.'

'Me too,' I said, and we lay in silence for a while in our shared berth, taking in the implications of this.

'That doesn't mean we should start trying, full on. Not yet.'

'No, but if it happens . . .'

'Exactly. If it happens – are you okay?'

'Just cramp.' In truth I could no longer feel my legs, but didn't want to move away just yet.

'For what it's worth . . .' she said.

'Go on.'

'For what it's worth, I think we'd be quite good at it. Being parents, I mean.'

'Yes, so do I,' I said. 'So do I.'

And I returned to my own bunk, sure in the knowledge that she was at least half right.


## 88. couchette 2

We didn't speak much on the sleeper train to Munich. We lay very still, stacked on shelves, in off-white cubicles of moulded plastic, wipe-clean, with ample sockets for recharging appliances. It was all very smooth and functional, but the hum of the air-conditioning and the blackness outside the window contributed to the impression that we were new inmates in some intergalactic prison cell.

We could have flown to Italy, of course, but I wanted us – the three of us – to at least touch on Germany and Austria, and wouldn't it be more fun, more romantic, to be a red dot sliding across that great land-locked central mass? Playing cards and drinking wine in our reasonably priced pre-booked couchette while Albie strummed his guitar and read Camus next door, then waking refreshed in Munich, a city new to all of us. There were Raphaels and Dürers at the Alte Pinakothek, Monets and Cézannes at the Neue, there was a famous Bruegel, a Turner – Connie loved Turner. We would go to the beer gardens with Albie, sit in the August sun and feel light-headed with lager and meat. Munich was going to be wonderful.

But now Albie was gone, lost in Europe with a lunatic accordionist, and we two stumbled on in a daze of concern on her part, and guilt on mine. While Connie lay on the top bunk pretending to read, I stared out of the window.

'He'll probably have a much better time without us,' I said, not for the first time. Not for the first time, there was no reply. 'Perhaps I should call him anyway.'

'What for?'

'I've told you. To apologise, chat. To check he's all right.'

'Let's just . . . let's just leave it be, Douglas. Yes?' She switched off her light and the train moved on. Somewhere out there lay Düsseldorf, Dortmund, Wuppertal and Cologne, the German industrial heartland, the mighty Rhine, but all I could see were the lights on the Autobahn.

## 89. margaret petersen

My mother died shortly after our return from Skye, the first time a grave had opened up in my road of life. Another landmark, I suppose.

It seemed that she suffered a stroke while sitting quietly at her desk during a biology class, and it took her ever-obedient pupils some time to respond and raise the alarm. My father rushed to the hospital only to discover that a further stroke had killed her while she lay on a trolley awaiting diagnosis. I arrived two hours later and watched as he responded with quite startling rage; at the bloody pupils who had remained stupidly in their seats, at the bloody teachers and hospital staff, at whoever was meant to be in charge of this whole life and death business. My mother's death was 'bloody stupid', he said – she had been two bloody years away from retirement! Grief manifested itself as fury then indignation, as if there had been an administrative error, as if someone somewhere had fouled up and got the order of things wrong and he would have to pay the price by continuing to live on, alone. Men, alone; it just wasn't right.

I also grieved, and to a degree that surprised me, because it would be a distortion to claim that my mother and I were particularly close or affectionate. There had been moments, of course. She had always been a great nature-lover, and she'd soften in the country, become hearty and good-humoured, identifying the trees and birds with little trace of her classroom manner, offering me her arm, telling stories. Back at home, though, she was a reserved and rather conservative woman. Observing other mothers at the school gates, I wondered why she wasn't warmer, brighter, a corrective to my father's sternness. But then perhaps that was their secret. Perhaps they were a perfect match, like a pair of drumsticks.

Yet there seemed to be no easy correlation between the awful grief I felt at her death and our closeness – or lack of it – in life, and it occurred to me that perhaps grief is as much regret for what we have never had as sorrow for what we have lost. As consolation, I had Connie now, who was a wonder throughout all of this, from that first emergency phone call through the arrangements and preparations, the funeral, the packing away of clothes, trips to the charity shop, the mournful administration of bank accounts and wills, the sale of a house now too big, the purchase of a little flat for Dad. Though Connie and my mother had never got on, had fought openly on more than one occasion, she recognised the irrelevance of this and was present and respectful; affectionate but not cloying or melodramatic or indulgent. A good nurse.

My mother was buried on a December morning, my parents' house – now my father's house – cold and dark when we returned and pushed the single beds together once again. Connie took off her funeral dress and we lay beneath the covers holding hands, knowing that there would be three more of these funerals along the way, four if her errant father ever resurfaced, and we would get through them together.

'I hope you don't die before me,' I said, which was mawkish I know, but permissible in those circumstances.

'I'll do my best,' she replied.

Anyway, the weeks passed, the sympathy and condolences were offered and accepted, the salty tingling sensation behind the eyes ceased and over time I lost that special status that the bereaved acquire, was returned to my civilian state and we continued on our way together.

Twenty years later, Connie's step-father remains in good health, her natural father too for all we know. Shirley, Connie's mother, shows every sign of being immortal, a living testament to the life-giving properties of tiny hand-rolled cigarettes and rum. Smoked and pickled, it appears she will go on forever and perhaps Connie won't need me after all.

## 90. thank you and goodbye

In Munich I got the hotel exactly right for once; a pleasant little family-run place near the Viktualienmarkt, comfortable, unpretentious, quaint but not kitsch. An elderly lady of the type that gets eaten by wolves was there to open the door for us.

'What about our other guest? Mr Albie . . . ?'

I felt Connie stiffen next to me.

'Our son. He couldn't make it, I'm afraid.' Couldn't stand it, couldn't bear it. *I'd like to apologise for my son . . .*

'I am sorry to hear that,' said the lady, frowning sympatheti-cally. 'And I am sorry that we cannot refund at such late notice.'

'*Danke schön,*' I said, though I don't know why. *Danke schön* and *auf Wiedersehen* were the only words of German I knew, and so I was doomed to spend our time here thanking then leaving.

Even though official check-in was not for several hours we were shown to our room, which was pleasant in a Brothers Grimm way, over-filled with rustic Bavarian furniture of a kind I hoped Connie would like, old and rather sinister. But she hadn't slept well on the train and so lay down on the immense bed, curling up her body in that girlish manner that she still has sometimes. 'Very thin pillows in Germany,' I observed, but she had closed her eyes so I sat in a rocking chair, poured some water and read up about Bruegel. The rim of the glass smelt rather musty, but apart from that, everything else was tip-top.

## 91. *the land of cockaigne*

There are an awful lot of Brueg(h)els, a mystifying array of Jans and Pieters, Elders and Youngers, and matters are not helped by their lack of flair when it came to picking Christian names.

But of the dynasty, Bruegel the Elder – note the missing 'h' – is the original and best. There are only forty-five paintings or so in existence and one of the most famous is in the imposing Alte Pinakothek, which we visited that afternoon. There were plenty of pleasant Jans and Pieters along the way, vases of flowers and country fairs full of tiny detail, the kind of paintings that make fine jigsaws, but the Bruegel with no 'h' was something else entirely, hanging with little fanfare in an unprepossessing room.

*Das Schlaraffenland* depicts a mythical 'land of milk and honey'
– a roof tiled with pies, a fence made of sausages and, in the
foreground, three bloated men: a soldier, a farmer and some sort
of clerk or student, surrounded by half-eaten food, trouser flaps
undone, too stuffed and bloated to work. It's one of those
'disturbing' pictures – a live pig running around with a knife in
its back, a boiled egg with little legs, that kind of thing – and I
knew enough about art to spot an allegory when I saw one.

'Eat smaller portions.'

'I'm sorry?' said Connie.

'The meaning. If you live in a land where the roofs are made
of pies, learn to pace yourself. He should have called it *Carbs
at Lunch*.'

'Douglas, I want to go home.'

'What about the Museum of Modern Art?'

'Not to the hotel. Home to England. I want to go back there
now.'

'Oh. Oh, I see.' I kept my eyes fixed on the painting. 'They're
dropping like flies!'

'Shall we . . . shall we sit down somewhere?'

We walked into a larger room – crucifixions, Adam and Eve
– and sat some way apart on a leather bench, the presence of
the museum guard adding to the mood of a particularly difficult
prison visit.

'I know what you were hoping. You thought maybe if things
went well, we might still have a future. You were hoping to
change my mind, and I want you to know that I'd love to be
able to change my mind too. I'd love to know for certain if I
could be happy with you. But this isn't making me happy, this
trip. It's . . . too hard, and it's not a holiday if you feel chained
to someone's ankle. I need some space to think. I want to go
home.'

I smiled through the most terrible disappointment. 'You can't
abandon the Grand Tour, Connie!'

'You can keep going if you want.'

'I can't go on without you. Where's the fun in that?'

'So come back with me.'

'What will we tell people?'

'Do we have to tell them anything?'

'We're back from holiday twelve days early because our son has run away! It's humiliating.'

'We'll . . . pretend we got food poisoning, or some aunt died. We'll say Albie went off to meet friends, do his own thing. Or we'll stay at home and close the curtains, hide, pretend we're still travelling.'

'We won't have any photographs of Venice or Rome . . .'

She laughed. 'Never in the history of the human race has anyone asked to see those photos.'

'I didn't want them for other people. I wanted them for us.'

'So . . . maybe we'll tell people the truth.'

'That you couldn't stand another minute here with me.'

She slid along the bench and pressed her shoulder against mine. 'That's not the truth.'

'What is, then?'

She shrugged. 'The truth is that maybe this wasn't the best time to be in each other's pockets.'

'It was your idea.'

'It was, but that was before . . . I'm sorry – you've arranged it all, I appreciate the effort, but it's also . . . well, an effort. It's too much to take in. It's too confusing.'

'We won't get any money back, everything's pre-booked.'

'Maybe money's not the most important thing at the moment, Douglas.'

'Fine. Fine, I'll look into flights.'

'There's a plane to Heathrow at ten fifteen tomorrow. We'll be home by lunchtime.'

## 92. *schweinshaxe mit kartoffelknödel*

And so passed our last day in Europe together.

We walked the remaining rooms of the gallery but, without Albie to educate, the Grand Tour seemed redundant now. Our eyes skimmed over Dürers, Raphaels and Rembrandts, but nothing registered and there was nothing to say. Before long we returned to the hotel and while Connie packed and read, I walked the streets.

Munich was a strange combination of grandly ceremonial and boisterously beery, like a drunken general, and we might all have had fun here together, I suppose, on a balmy August night. Instead I went alone to a vast beer hall near the Viktualienmarkt where, to the accompaniment of a Bavarian brass band, I tried to raise my spirits by ordering a lager the size of a torso and a roasted ham hock. As with much in life, the first taste was delicious, but soon the meat took on the quality of a gruesome anatomy lesson as I became aware of the muscle groups, the sinews, bone and cartilage. I pushed the thing away, defeated, drained the pail of beer and stumbled back to our hotel bed where I awoke a little after two in the morning, smelling of ham, a half-crazed desiccated husk . . .

## 93. the fire extinguisher

. . . because what had I given Connie, after all? The benefits for me were clear, but throughout our time together I had seen the question flicker across the faces of friends and waiters, family and taxi-drivers: what's in it for her? What does she see that so many others have missed?

It was a question that I was unwilling to ask her myself, in case she frowned and had no answer. I believed – because she had told me so – that I offered her some kind of alternative to the men she had known before. I was not vain, bad-tempered, unreliable, temperamental, I had no drug or alcohol issues, I would not steal from her or cheat on her, I was not married, bisexual or manic-depressive. In short, I lacked all the qualities that, from her teens into her late twenties, she had found irresistible. I was unlikely to suggest that we smoke crack, and though this seemed to me a fairly basic, entry-level requirement in a partner, it was at least one I could fulfil. Point one in my favour: I was not a psychopath.

It was also clear to everyone that I loved her to a quite ridiculous degree, though devotion is not always an appealing characteristic, as I knew from experience. Then there was our sex life, which, as I have mentioned, I think was always more than satisfactory.

She had always been interested in my work. Despite its frustrations, I retained my belief in scientific endeavour and I think she admired me for this. Connie always said I was at my most attractive when I talked about my work, and she'd encourage me to describe it long after she'd ceased to comprehend the subject matter. 'The lights come on,' she said. As the nature of my employment changed those lights flickered somewhat, but initially she valued the many differences between us – art and science, sensibility and sense – because after all, who wants to fall in love with their own reflection?

More practically, I was practical; adept at basic plumbing and carpentry and even electrical wiring, and only once was I thrown across the kitchen. I could walk into a room and spot a load-bearing wall; I was a meticulous and thorough decorator, always sugar-soaping, rubbing down, always rinsing out my brushes. As our finances melded, I was diligent and thorough in ensuring everything was in place: pensions, ISAs, insurance. I planned our holidays with military care, maintained the car, bled the radiators, reset the clocks in spring and autumn. While there was breath in my body, she would never lack sufficient AA batteries. Perhaps these achievements sound drab and pedestrian, but they were in stark contrast to the flaky, self-absorbed aesthetes she had known before. There was a sort of mild masculinity to it all that, for Connie, was both new and comforting.

More thrillingly, I was extremely reliable in a crisis – changing a tyre on the hard shoulder of the M3 at night and in the rain, aiding an epileptic on the Northern Line while others sat and gawped; everyday heroism of a very minor sort. Walking on the street I always took care to be nearest to the kerb and though she laughed at this, she liked it too. Being with me, said Connie, was like carrying a large, old-fashioned fire extinguisher around with her at all times, and I took satisfaction in this.

What else? I think I offered my wife a way out of a lifestyle she could no longer sustain. The Connie Moore I'd met had been a party girl, always dancing on tables, and I think I offered her a hand down to the floor. She gave up the notion of making a living as an artist, for a while at least, and took to working in the gallery full time. It must have been hard, I suppose, promoting the work of others rather than producing her own, but her talent would still be there, she could always go back to it once we were settled, once her style of painting came back into fashion. In the meantime we still had fun, terrific fun, and there were dinners with friends and many late nights. But there were fewer hangovers, fewer dawn regrets, fewer mystery bruises. I was the safest of harbours, but I do want to emphasise that I could be fun, too. Not in a large group perhaps, but when the pressure was off, when it was just the two of us, I don't think there was anywhere we'd rather have been.

A great deal of stress is placed on the importance of humour in the modern relationship. Everything will be all right, we are led to believe, as long as you can make each other laugh, rendering a successful marriage as, in effect, fifty years of improv. To someone who felt in need of fresh new material, as I did during that long, dehydrated night of the soul, this was a cause for concern. I had always enjoyed making Connie laugh, it was satisfying and reassuring because laughter, I suppose, relies on surprise and it's good to surprise. But like a fading athlete, my response times had slowed and now it was not unusual for me to find the perfect witty comeback to remarks made several years ago. Consequently I had been resorting to old tricks, old stories, and I sometimes felt that Connie had spent the first three years laughing at my jokes and the next twenty-one sighing at them. Somewhere along the way I had mislaid my sense of humour and was now only capable of puns, which are not the same thing at all. 'I fear the wurst!' The joke had occurred to me in the beer hall, and I wondered if I might use it over breakfast. I would offer her a pale sausage, and when she refused I'd say, 'The trouble with you, Connie, is that you always fear the wurst!' It was a good joke, though perhaps not enough in itself to save our marriage.

Yet undeniably there had once been a time when I made Connie laugh constantly, and when I became a father I had hoped to develop this amusing persona further. I pictured myself as a kind of Roald Dahl figure, eccentric and wise, conjuring up characters and stories out of air, our children dangling off me, their faces bright with laughter, delight and love. I never quite achieved this, I don't know why; perhaps it was because of what happened to our daughter. Certainly that changed me, changed both of us. Life seemed a little heavier after that.

Anyway, I don't think Albie ever appreciated my lighter side. I did my best but my manner was queasy and self-conscious, like a children's entertainer who knows his act is failing. I could remove the top of my thumb and put it back again but unless a child is particularly witless, this material wears pretty thin. And Albie had never been witless. When I put on funny voices to read a story, he became visibly embarrassed. In fact, when I thought about it, it was hard to recall if I had ever made my son laugh through something other than personal injury, and I sometimes wished Connie would tell him, 'You might not appreciate this, Egg, but once upon a time your father used to make me laugh so much, *so* much, we'd talk all night and laugh until we cried. Once upon a time.'

Now, I feared the wurst.


## 94. soft mints

Sadly we left before breakfast and took an early taxi through the sleeping city to Munich Airport, about which there is little to say. Picture an airport.

I dreaded England. Like a failed football team returning from some nine-nil humiliation, we sat in the departure lounge, quite unable to speak or even raise our eyes. *I'd like to apologise for my son.* Forever I would carry with me the sight of his face, the shock and shame, as if I had slapped him, which in a way I had. And it was here, I suppose, that the football team analogy broke down. We weren't a team. I was the goalie who had let in all nine goals.

Would I go back to the office nearly two weeks early? What would they say? Would they sense it? This man's holiday was so bad that it destroyed his family! They fled, actually fled; one in Holland, one in Germany. Even if I didn't go to work, even if Connie and I stayed at home with the curtains drawn, we would be tormented by the absence of Albie. As I remarked more than once, he might be having a perfectly civilised time. He had a passport, a phone, access to money, Camus and a highly sexed girlfriend; in some ways it was an enviable situation. But without knowing for sure, with those words still between us, it was impossible not to squirm with anxiety. *Apologise for my son*. Was he in some crack-den in Berlin? Drunk on a branch line in the Czech Republic, stoned in a squat in Rotterdam, beaten up in an alley in Madrid? Would he return in September, October, Christmas, at all? What about college? Would he abandon the education he had fought for, albeit rather feebly? What if Europe simply . . . swallowed him up?

I could no longer sit still. 'I'm going to go for a stroll,' I said.

'Now?'

'There's plenty of time.'

'I'll see you at the gate,' she shrugged. 'Take your bag.'

There's a certain optimism in going for a walk in airports. What on earth do we expect to find – something new and enchanting? I strolled off to see what a German newsagents looked like and, having discovered that it looked like a British newsagents, was about to purchase some Soft Mints with the last of my loose euros when my phone rang.

I scrabbled in my pocket. Perhaps it was Albie. The display indicated a +39 number – Spain, Italy?

'Signor Petersen?'

'*Oui, c'est moi*,' I said, disorientated.

'*Buongiorno*, I'm calling from the Pensione Albertini, about your reservation?'

'*Ja, ja*,' I said, jamming a finger into my other ear.

'I have done my best, but I'm afraid that I cannot bring your reservation forward at such short notice. My apologies.'

'My reservation?'

'Your change of plans. You are now arriving in Venice tomorrow night?'

'No, no, not at all. Not for three, four days yet.' That was our plan, a train across the Alps then one night each in Verona, Vicenza, Padua then on to Venice. 'When did he, I mean *I*, when did I call?'

'Perhaps fifteen minutes ago.'

'By telephone?'

Pause for the lunatic. '*Sì. . .*'

'My reservation was for one single and one double room. Which did I ask to rearrange?'

'The double room.'

'For tomorrow?'

'*Sì*, tomorrow. But we spoke about this just fifteen minutes —'

'Did I by any chance say where I was calling from?'

'I don't understand . . .'

'And you're sure it was a Signor Petersen?'

'*Sì.*'

Albie! It must have been Albie calling, tampering with my itinerary, trying to use our hotel reservation to save money. They were on their way to Venice after all.

'Well, *grazie mille* for trying.'

'So we will in fact see you in Venice in four days' time as we had previously arranged?'

'*Sì, sì, sì.* In four days.'

'Splendid.'

'You've been very helpful. *Auf Wiedersehen! Ciao!*'

I was some way from the newsagents now, the Soft Mints warming in my grip, unpaid for. A fugitive! I checked the departure board. Boarding commencing. Checked my pockets. Phone, passport, wallet, all I would need. In my hand luggage, a phone charger, a book, a tablet computer and a history of the Second World War. I stepped back onto the concourse, saw Connie, saw some stairs leading to a raised balcony above the lounge. I climbed the stairs and watched her, unseen.

I watched her for fifteen minutes as departure time approached, eating my way through the contraband Soft Mints, a real bandito. I watched her quite, quite full of love, despite her palpable irritation and impatience at my absence, and I came to a decision.

I would not lose my wife and son.

If the notion was unacceptable to me, I would not accept it.

I would not return to England now and spend our last summer slowly dismantling our home, watching Connie separating herself from me, dividing us in two and making plans for a future that did not include me. I refused to live in a house where everything I saw or touched – Mr Jones the dog, the bedside radio, the pictures on the wall, the cups from which we drank our morning tea – would soon be allocated, mine or hers. We had been through too much together, and it was not acceptable, and neither was it acceptable to have my son wandering the continent in the belief that I was ashamed of him. It could not, would not be allowed to happen.

I finished the stolen mints. There's a saying, cited in popular song, that if you love someone you must set them free. Well, that's just nonsense. If you love someone, you bind them to you with heavy metal chains.

## 95. final call for the heathrow flight . . .

Connie was standing now, anxiously looking for me, left and right, no doubt thinking, *this is strange, this isn't like him at all, always there two hours before departure, laptop in a separate tray, liquids and gels in a Ziploc bag.* Well, not any more, my love! The new me dialled her number, watched as she groped in her handbag, found the phone, glared at the screen, picked up . . .

'Douglas, where the hell are you? The gate is closing in five—'

'I'm not catching the flight.'

'Where are you, Douglas?'

'I'm in a taxi. In fact I've already left the airport. I'm not going back to England.'

'Douglas, don't be ridiculous, they're calling our names—'

'Then get on the plane without me. Make sure you tell them I'm not coming, I don't want to inconvenience anyone.'

'I'm not getting on the plane without you, that's insane.'

'Listen to me, Connie, please? I can't come back until I've put things right. I'm going to find Albie first, and apologise face to face, and then I'm going to bring him home.'

'Douglas, you have no idea where he is!'

'Then I'll find him.'

'How can you find him? He could be anywhere in Europe by now, anywhere in the world . . .'

'I'll find a way. I'm a scientist, remember? Method. Results. Conclusion.'

I watched her now as she lowered herself back into the seat. 'Douglas, if you're doing this to . . . prove something . . . to me . . . well, it's very touching, but it's not really the point.'

'I love you, Connie.'

She spanned her forehead with her hand. 'I love you too, Douglas, but you're tired, you've been under a lot of strain, and I don't think you're thinking straight . . .'

'Please don't try and talk me out of this. I'm going to go on alone.'

A moment passed, and she stood. 'Are you sure that's what you want?'

'I am.'

'What will I tell people?'

'I don't care.'

'Will you at least call me?'

'When I've found him. Not before.'

'Can I talk you out of this?'

'No, you can't.'

'All right. All right, if that's what you want.'

'I'm afraid you'll have to carry the suitcase. Get taxis, won't you?'

'But what will you wear?'

'I've got my wallet and my toothbrush. I'll buy myself clothes along the way.'

Her head lolled backwards; in distress, perhaps, at the thought of me buying my own clothes. 'Okay. If you're sure. Buy nice things. Look after yourself.' She put her hand to her eyes. 'Don't fall to pieces, will you?'

'I won't. Connie, I'm sorry we won't see Venice together again.'

'I'm sorry too.'

'I'll send postcards, though.'

'Please do.'

'Kiss Mr Jones for me. Or shake his paw.'

'I will.'

'Don't let him sleep on the bed.'

'I wouldn't dream of it.'

'Seriously, because if he gets into the habit—'

'Douglas. I won't.'

'I love you, Connie. Did I say that?'

'You mentioned it in passing.'

'I'm sorry if I've let you down.'

'Douglas, you have never—'

'I won't let you down again.'

She said nothing.

'You'd better catch your flight now,' I said.

'Yes. I'd better. Gate . . . ?'

'Gate 17.'

'Gate 17.' She shouldered her bag and began to walk.

'You've forgotten your book,' I said. 'It's on the chair.'

'Thank you,' she said, picked it up, then hesitated a moment. It didn't take her long to search me out on the balcony above. She raised her hand and I raised mine back.

'I'll see you when I see you,' I said.

But she had already hung up. I watched Connie walk away and then I set off to save my son, whether he needed it or not.

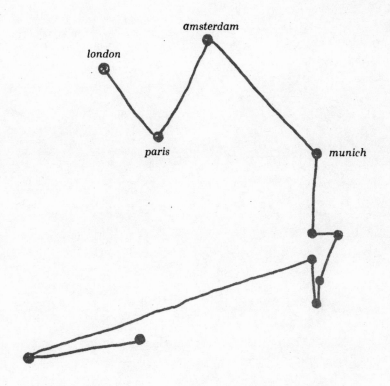

BOOK TWO

# the renaissance

part five

# VENICE AND THE VENETO

—

Sometimes she went so far as to wish that she should find herself in a difficult position, so that she might have the pleasure of being as heroic as the occasion demanded.

Henry James, *The Portrait of a Lady*

## 96. proposal

In Venice I proposed to Connie.

Not the most original scenario, I know. In fact, there was nothing much original in our trip that February, the third anniversary of our meeting. We entered the city by water taxi on a bright, crisp day, nestling in seats of burgundy leather as we bounced across the lagoon, then standing wind-whipped on deck as the city appeared and two thoughts battled in my head: was anything in the world more beautiful, and was anything in the world more expensive? This was my Venetian state of mind; awe versus anxiety, like browsing in a wonderful antiques shop where signs constantly remind you that breakages must be paid for.

And so we did what tourists do in Venice in the winter. We sheltered from the rain and when the sun came out drank bitter hot chocolate in chilly squares of quite staggering grace and beauty, and sipped Bellinis in dim, expensive bars, bracing ourselves for the bill. 'It's a tax on beauty,' said Connie, doling out the notes. 'If it were cheap here, nobody would ever leave.'

She knew the city well, of course. The trick in Venice, she said, is to see St Mark's once, then bounce off it to the outer edges. The trick is to be spontaneous, curious, to get lost. Instinctively, I resisted the notion of getting lost. For accomplished and enthusiastic map-readers like myself, Venice offered untold challenges and I spent a great deal of time tracing our route until Connie snatched the map, lifted my chin with her finger and commanded that I look up for once and appreciate the beautiful gloom of the place.

This was what surprised me most about Venice: just how sombre it could be; all those tourists taking snaps and thinking about death. Venice was my first experience of Italy, so where were the floury-handed mammas and tousle-headed rascals that I'd been led to expect? Instead this was a city of closed doors, its besieged citizens narrow-eyed and resentful – understandably so – of the endless waves of visitors even in winter, like house-guests who will not take the hint and go. Even the festivals were gloomy; the Venetian idea of a good time was for everyone to dress up as skeletons. Perhaps it was a legacy of the plague, the silence or the shadows, the dark canals or the absence of green spaces, but walking the deserted alleys and rainswept esplanades, I found the melancholy quite overwhelming, yet also weirdly pleasurable. I don't think I've ever been as simultaneously sad and happy in my life.

Perhaps this ambiguity did not make it the best spot to propose marriage. Too late for doubt, though; the engagement ring was packed, concealed in the finger of a glove, the restaurant table booked. We had spent a light-hearted morning on the cemetery island of San Michele, Connie posing in her overcoat and taking photographs of tombs, then marching arm in arm from Cannaregio to Dorsoduro, ducking into under-lit churches and gloomy court-yards along the way, and all the time I wondered: should I kneel when I ask her? Would that be amusing or embarrassing for us both? Would she prefer a simple 'Will you marry me?' The formal, period-drama feel of 'Would you give me the honour of becoming my wife?' The laid-back 'Hey, let's get married!'? We returned to the hotel, dressed up and strode out and had a wonderful dinner of tuna carpaccio and grilled fish, my hand travelling intermittently to the ring – antique silver, single diamond – in my suit jacket. 'Indigestion?' asked Connie. 'Heartburn,' I replied. There was beau-tiful *gelato*, some kind of almond digestifs and then out we walked, our heads spinning, into a crisp bright night. 'Let's stroll to La Salute!' I suggested casually and there, with the great marble church flaring like magnesium in the moonlight and St Mark's Square illuminated across the Grand Canal, I reached into my jacket, retrieved the ring and asked Connie, 'Will you be my wife?'

Think how romantic it would have been if she'd said yes. Instead she laughed, swore, frowned, bit her lip, hugged me, swore, kissed me, laughed and swore and said 'Can I think about it?' Which was reasonable enough, I suppose. Few decisions are more life-altering. Even so, I couldn't help wondering why it had come as such a surprise. Love led to marriage, and weren't we in love?

Thankfully the 'Yes' did come, though not until some months later. So while the question was 'popped' in the moonlight by the Grand Canal, it was answered at the delicatessen counter of the Sainsbury's on Kilburn High Road. Perhaps it was my choice of olives that swung it. Either way, there was much jubilation and relief over the cured meats and cheeses, and a tearful and emotional check-out.

Perhaps I should have taken Connie back there, to Kilburn Sainsbury's. I'm sure we could have made it that far at least.

## 97. hannibal

But I am leaping backwards and forwards simultaneously. I'm still in Germany where, after watching my wife walk away, I scrambled into a taxi, returned to Munich and the scrappy chaos of the Hauptbahnhof, dabbing at the touchscreen of a ticket machine and hurling myself onto the late-morning train across the Alps to Venice via Innsbruck, changing at Verona, with just a shoulder-bag and passport, quite the Jason Bourne.

The train compartment, too, was of the kind favoured by spies and assassins and that journey only got more exciting as the train left the suburbs, crossed a wide green plain towards the mountains then suddenly, within the space of a few hundred metres it seemed, we were in the Alps. As someone born and raised in Ipswich, I have never been complacent about mountains, and I found the Alps extraordinary. Peaks like hounds' incisors, vertigo-inducing plunges, the kind of landscape that might have been imagined by a deity or an ambitious CGI-effects supervisor. Good God, I murmured to myself and instinctively took a photograph on my phone, the kind of desultory, mediocre photograph that is never seen by anyone and serves no purpose, and I thought of my son, and how, had a falling meteor lopped the top off the highest peak, he would still not have raised his camera.

After Innsbruck, the terrain became even more spectacular. It was by no means a wilderness – there were supermarkets, factories, petrol stations – but even in high summer there seemed to be something lunatic about people living and working in such a terrain, never mind building a railway through it. The train skirted another escarpment, the valley falling away beneath us to meadows of the same lime green as the model railway landscapes I'd built too far into my teens. I thought of Connie, of how she would be getting home soon, saying hello to Mr Jones, opening mail, throwing wide the windows to renew the air, breaking the seal on the empty, stale fridge, loading the washing machine, and I thought of how much I wished she could see all of this.

But awe is a hard emotion to sustain for hours on end and soon it all became rather boring. In the buffet, I ate a croissant with pastrami and mozzarella which, gastronomically speaking, covered all the bases. Back in my compartment I dozed, waking to find that Brenner had become Brennero. The church spires changed, the mountains softened into hills, pines gave way to endless vineyards. Germany and Austria were now far behind and I was in the Italian Alps and, before too long, in Verona.

## 98. ...where we set our scene

A lovely city, russet brown and dusty rose and baking in the August afternoon. So keen was I to catch my quarry that I had only allowed myself a two-hour window here, stomping across beautiful piazzas and over mediaeval bridges, ticking them off the list – an appalling way to see a city, really, a betrayal of our original intent when planning the Grand Tour. No matter – there were more important things than culture now. I noted the fine Roman amphitheatre, third largest in the world – tick – saw the Torre dei Lamberti, the market on the Piazza delle Erbe, ornate Piazza dei Signori – tick, tick, tick. Marching along a marble-paved shopping street, I followed the crowd through an alleyway into a packed, cacophonous courtyard beneath a stone balcony – Juliet's balcony, supposedly. It looked as if it had been glued to the wall, and sure enough my guidebook informed me with a sniff that it was only built in 1935, though given that Juliet was a fictional character, this seemed to be missing the point. 'Romeo, Romeo, wherefore art thou, Romeo!' shouted wags from around the globe. In the heat of mid-afternoon the courtyard was a literal tourist trap, but I watched dutifully as perspiring visitors took it in turns to pose with a kitsch-y bronze statue of Shakespeare's heroine, her right breast worn grey from a million hands. Fondling her breast brought good luck, apparently. A Japanese gentleman nudged my arm and mimed a camera, international sign language for 'do you want me to take your picture?', but I struggled to imagine that a photograph of me squeezing the breast of a bronze statue would be anything other than soul-crushing and so politely declined, pushing my way towards the exit, pausing only to read the graffiti'd wall, layer upon layer of *Simone 4 Veronica, Olly + Kerstin, Marco e Carlotta*. I could have added to it, I suppose: *Connie and Douglas 4ever. Je t'aime*, I read, *ti amo, ik hou van je*, the declarations so densely inscribed as to resemble a Jackson Pollock.

Jackson Pollock. 'You see, Connie? I'm learning,' I said out loud. '*Ik hou van je.*'

## 99. ferrovia

The only way to arrive in Venice is an early-morning water taxi across the lagoon. I arrived by train at night with the backpackers and the students who tumbled, thrilled and dazed, out of the strange and rather elegant railway station, a low-ceilinged marble slab like the kind of coffee table that you crack your shins on. I had found the city's last remaining room in a remote, unpromising *pensione* in Castello and decided to walk that considerable distance, striding along the still-bustling Strada Nova, peering into youthful faces in case Albie was already here. Venice in high summer was a new experience for me and I noted the humid air and the brackish, ammonia smell of the canals before realising with some embarrassment that the stagnant odour was coming from me. Somewhere between Munich and Venice I had come to smell like a canal, and I resolved to address this in the comfort of my hotel room.

But for the first time my orienteering failed me, the *fonda-mentas*, *rivas*, *salitas* and *salizzadas* sending me in circles, and it wasn't until after midnight that I arrived at the Pensione Bellini, a cramped and crumbling building in the shadow of the Arsenale.

There's something furtive and indecent about arriving at a hotel after midnight, and the resentful and suspicious night manager directed me up many flights of stairs to an attic room the size of a double bed, containing a single bed. Through the thin wall I could hear the hotel's boiler gurgle and then roar into life. I peered into the mirror in the glare of the bare bulb. The heat and humidity were Amazonian and rubbing the skin on my perspiring forehead produced a grey scurf like the debris from a pencil eraser, the accumulated grime of seven nations. I had not shaved since Paris, barely slept since Amsterdam, not changed my clothes since Munich. Verona's sun had glazed my nose, and only my nose, to a flowerpot red, while the skin beneath my eyes was blue-grey with exhaustion. I looked haggard, there was no denying it, like a hostage about to record a video message. To Albie's eyes I would look frankly alarming but I was too worn out to remedy this now, even to make the journey to the shared bathroom in the hall. Instead I scraped at my armpits with plastic soap and brown water from the tiny sink, rinsed my fusty clothes and lay them like seaweed on the window ledge, collapsed onto the sagging mattress and, to the roar and gurgle of hotel plumbing, fell instantly asleep.

## 100. an experiment with mice

Imagine, if you will, a scale model of Venice. Not a huge city by any means, not much larger than Reading, but more intricate and with clearer boundaries. Now imagine two figures, also to scale, turning left and right at random in that maze for twelve hours like mice in, well, a maze. The maze is not regular; wide streets and immense squares alternate with narrow alleys and bridges that act as funnels. Allowing for constant movement over, say, fourteen hours, what is the probability of the two figures coming within sight of each other?

I'm not a statistician, but instinctively I knew the chances were small. They were by no means inconceivable, however, and I would be aided by the fact that footfall in Venice tends to correspond to certain well-trodden paths, from the Ferrovia to St Mark's, from St Mark's to the Pescheria, to the Accademia, back to the Ferrovia. Much as we'd like to imagine ourselves free-spirited explorers, visitors walk around Venice in the same way that we walk around a supermarket, an airport or an art gallery, channelled by all kinds of factors, conscious and unconscious; should I walk down this dark, urine-stinking alley or towards that charming little bakery? Studies have been made of this sort of behaviour. We think we have independence and imagination, but we have no more freedom to roam than trams on rails.

So the labyrinth was smaller than it first appeared, and factor in the assumption that I was probably looking for two people, that they were unlikely to be constantly on the move and that the sound of an accordion would be hard to ignore, and I felt mildly confident that I could find them. In fact, I don't mind admitting that I was rather excited about the project as I settled down to a two-star Italian breakfast of sponge cake, orange squash and the world's hardest pineapple. My mission had an element of espionage to it, and I was enjoying planning my route with a water-soluble felt-tip pen on the very same laminated map that I'd brought along all those years ago, allowing me to annotate then wipe it clean at the end of each day.

'That is a very good system you have there,' said the room's sole other occupant, a smiling woman, German, Scandinavian perhaps.

'Thank you,' I replied. I had barely opened my mouth in twenty-four hours and my own voice sounded unfamiliar.

'If ever a city demanded a map, it's this one,' she said.

I smiled, not wishing to be rude. 'It is important not to skimp on a good-quality map,' I said, intriguingly.

She sipped her tea. 'Do you know the city well?'

'I've been here once before. More than twenty years ago now.'

'It must have changed enormously since then,' she said.

'No, it's pretty much the— oh, I see. Yes, beyond recognition! All these new buildings!' It had been a good joke on her part, and I thought perhaps I could run with it, riff on the idea in some way. 'In those days, the streets weren't even flooded!' was the best that I could do, but she looked confused, and so I slipped the much-scrutinised map, a stolen banana and a sachet of dried toast from the buffet into my bag and left. Oh yes, Cat, I was quite the outlaw now.

But first I would need to equip myself. As island-dwellers, Venetians face limited choices in menswear, but I bought three pairs of identical socks, three pairs of underwear, three T-shirts in pale blue, grey and white and, for evening wear, two button-down shirts and a thin jumper in case of a chill. To protect my vulnerable scalp from the sun, I bought a baseball cap, the most neutral I could find and the first I had ever owned, though perhaps it wouldn't be necessary in the shady canyons of San Paolo and Santa Croce. Because I would be walking for most of the day, I bought some rather natty running shoes in moulded plastic, absurd outsized things that promised to mould themselves to my feet in a very space-age way. I bought some moistened toilet tissue and a single bottle of water that I would refill. Returning to the Pensione Bellini, I organised my purchases and caught sight of myself in the mirror once again.

Sleep had repaired some of the damage. I still had not shaved, and now sported the beginnings of a rather fetching beard, flecked with white and grey, the kind Hollywood actors grow when required to appear less handsome than they are. I rather liked it. I looked . . . unfamiliar. I put on my new sunglasses, pulled down the baseball cap and hit the canals.

## 101. the shape of time

Imagine time as a long strip of paper.

This is not the shape of time, of course. Time has no shape, being a dimension or conceivably a direction or vector, but imagine for the purposes of the metaphor that time can be represented as a long strip of paper, or a roll of celluloid, perhaps. And imagine that you are able to make two cuts in the strip, joining those ends to form a continuous loop. This strip of paper can be as long or as short as you wish, but that loop will roll forever.

For me, the first snip of the scissors is easily apparent and comes about halfway across London Bridge on the night I first met Connie Moore. But the second cut is harder, and is that not the case for everyone? The edges of unhappiness are usually a little more blurred and graded than those of joy. Nevertheless, I find my scissors hovering, hovering . . .

But not just yet. We aren't even married yet.

## 102. learning to say 'wife'

We married, and that was fun. We had been guests at so many weddings, Connie and I, that it had sometimes felt that we had been attending a three-year part-time course in wedding management. Both of us were clear about what we didn't want, and that was a fuss. We'd have a city wedding, registry office then a meal in our local Italian restaurant with close family and good friends. It would be small but stylish. Connie would be responsible for the guest list, the readings, the décor, the menu, music and entertainment. I would be responsible for turning up.

And making a speech, of course. In the run-up to the wedding, I went over the text again and again, putting more effort into that speech than almost any piece of prose since my PhD on protein-RNA interactions, though it's arguable as to which contained the better jokes. Because I wanted everything down word for word in 14-point Arial, I had been obliged to transcribe my emotions several months before experiencing them. I predicted that she would be beautiful, that I would feel happy and proud – no, never happier, never more proud than when standing next to her, and certainly these predictions did come true. She was spectacular that day, dressed like an old-fashioned film star, in a rather tight-fitting low-cut black dress, an ironic antidote to traditional virginal white. In later years, she'd regret the choice. 'What was I thinking?' she would say. 'I look like a prostitute in a Fellini film,' but for the record I thought she looked wonderful. Certainly I was happy and proud, grateful and relieved. An underrated emotion, I think, relief. No one presents a bouquet with the words, 'I've never been more relieved in my life'. But then I had never expected to marry at all, and to be marrying *this* woman . . .

During the short service, Connie's friend Fran read a poem

by T. S. Eliot which sounded very nice but which I would challenge anyone to put into good plain English, and my sister gave a fraught rendition of the Beatles' 'In My Life' on an electric keyboard, smiling bravely through a torrent of tears and mucus that might have been appropriate had Connie and I recently perished in a plane crash, but which seemed so ghoulish in our presence that Connie got the giggles, then passed them on to me. To distract myself I stole a glimpse at my father, who sat with elbows on knees, pinching the bridge of his nose as if attempting to stem a nosebleed.

Then the 'I do's, the exchange of rings, the posing for photographs. I enjoyed it all, but weddings turn the bride and groom into performers and we were, I think, both a little self-conscious with each other that day, neither of us used to being the centre of attention. In the photographs I look sheepish, preoccupied, as if I've been shoved onto the stage from my place in the wings. We look happy, of course, and in love, however that manifests in photos, but one always hopes that wedding-day conversation between bride and groom will consist only of endearments, a perpetual 'you complete me', and there were taxis and seating plans and sound systems to organise, and of course the speeches too. My sister had volunteered, quite early on, to be my 'best man', and delivered a boastful speech that focused on how all our present and future happiness had been her idea, and how we could never possibly repay our vast debt and should not even try. Kemal, Connie's stepfather, made an amusing speech that returned, again and again, to my wife's figure to uncomfortable effect, and then it was my turn.

I told some of the stories that I've related here, about our first meeting, about Jake the trapeze artist, about Connie saying yes at the delicatessen counter of Kilburn Sainsbury's. I am not a natural raconteur but there was a decent amount of laughter, as well as some muttering and shushing from the table containing Connie's art-school friends.

Because Angelo was there, did I mention that? In the months

before the wedding, there had been some debate about his presence, but it would have seemed paranoid and conventional on my part to banish all her former boyfriends, not to mention that it would have halved the guest list. So here was good old Angelo, drinking heavily and providing, I imagined, a sardonic commentary on the event. To Angelo's gang, I was clearly something of a Yoko Ono figure. Never mind. I focused my thoughts on my wife. 'Wife' – how strange that sounded. Would I ever get used to it? I brought the speech to a sentimental but sincere conclusion, kissed my wife – that word again – and raised a glass in her honour.

We danced to Ella Fitzgerald's recording of 'Night and Day', Connie's choice. My only specification had been that our first dance shouldn't be anything too fast or wild, so we rotated slowly like a child's mobile. It can't have been much of a spectacle, because after the first few revolutions, Connie started to improvise ducks and spins that left us momentarily tangled, to laughter from the guests. Then we cut the cake, we circulated, and occasionally my eyes would scan the room over the shoulder of a colleague or an uncle, searching out Connie, and we'd smile or pull a face or just grin at each other. My *wife*. I had a wife.

My father, looking slighter since my mother's death, left early. I had offered to find a hotel for the night, an indulgence that appalled him. Hotels, he thought, were for royalty and fools. 'I have a perfectly good bed at home. I can't sleep in strange beds anyway,' he said. Now he was keen to catch the Ipswich train 'in case your sister starts to sing again'. We laughed, and he placed one hand on my shoulder. 'Well done,' he said, as if I'd passed my driving test. 'Thanks, Dad. Bye.'

'Well done,' was Angelo's phrase too, as he maliciously embraced me then brushed the cigarette ash off my shoulder. 'Well done, mate. You won. Treat her well, yeah? Connie's a great girl. She's golden.' I agreed that she was golden, and thanked him. My sister, ever the keen-eyed critic of other people's work, hung off my neck, drunk and emotional and gave me her feedback. 'Great speech, D,' she said, 'but you forgot to tell Connie how gorgeous she is.' Had I forgotten? I didn't think I had. I thought I'd made it perfectly clear.

And then, a little after midnight, exhausted and wine-mouthed we were in a cab, heading to a smart hotel in Mayfair, our one concession to luxury. We didn't make love that night, though I'm reassured that this is not uncommon among newly married couples. Instead we lay facing each other, champagne and toothpaste on our breath.

'Hello, husband.'

'Hello, wife.'

'Feel different?'

'Not particularly. You? Suddenly feel jaded? Trapped, confined? Oppressed?'

'Let me see . . .' She rotated her shoulders, flexed her wrists. 'No, no I don't think so. Early days, though.'

'I love you.'

'I love you too.'

Was it the happiest day of our lives? Probably not, if only because the truly happy days tend not to involve so much organisation, are rarely so public or so expensive. The happy ones sneak up, unexpected. But to me at least, it felt like the culmination of many happy days, and the first of many more. Everything was still the same and yet not quite the same, and in the moments before sleep I felt the kind of trepidation that I still feel the night before a long, complicated journey. Everything is in place, tickets, reservations and foreign currency, passports laid out on the table in the hall. If we are at our best at all times, or at least endeavour to be so, there is no reason why everyone shouldn't have a wonderful time.

Still, what if something goes wrong along the way? What if the plane's engines fail, or I lose control of the car? What if it rains?

## 103. *il pesce*

Viewed from above, Venice resembles a broad-bodied fish with a gaping mouth, a bream or perch perhaps, with the Grand Canal as its intestinal tract. My route began at the fish's tail, the eastern tip of the city, Castello, the old docks, long straight terraces of the loveliest workers' houses in Europe. Then back along the northern shore, the dorsal fin, through Cannaregio, where the streets had a sunnier, almost coastal aspect. Through the Ghetto to the train station then down the main tourist drag, which felt like a drag, tourists queuing to squeeze over the Rialto Bridge. *How many masks did one city need?* I wondered, shuffling along another lightless shopping street, so that arriving in St Mark's Square felt like coming up for air, so bright and immense that no crowd of tourists could fill it, though they were trying now. By the Grand Canal – the fish's swim bladder, I suppose – I took a moment to rest. That morning I had seen adenoidal guitarists, 'Dance of the Sugar Plum Fairy' performed on the rims of wine glasses, a startlingly inept juggler whose routine consisted of dropping things, but fewer acts than I'd expected. Searching for the terms 'busker' and 'Venice' on my phone revealed that the city was considered hostile territory. The internet was alive with angry and resentful living statues who had been bustled into motion by assiduous *polizia municipale*. A permit was required, and I was sure Cat was too wild and free-spirited to submit to Italian bureaucracy. I would be searching for a guerrilla accordionist, someone who hit fast, hit hard and disappeared into the crowd. No time to rest, then. For energy I ate my bruised banana and pushed on, shuffling through the crowds towards the Fenice theatre, where a busker in Pierrot costume sang a warbling '*La donna è mobile*'. Tired now; it was too much, too many people. I burrowed south, hurrying past West

African men selling handbags and on to Dorsoduro, the belly of the fish.

## 104. the macadamia

After all that ancient stone, there was something pleasingly light and temporary about the wooden Accademia Bridge, and I took a moment to look east to the entrance of the Grand Canal, taking in the view. A strange phrase that, 'taking in', implying as it does some sustenance or retention. While I could admire the elegance and proportion of the scene, I was primarily aware of the mass of tourism around me, and also of the extraordinary confidence of the Venetian architects in allowing their finest buildings to teeter at the water's edge. What about damp? What about flooding? Wouldn't it make sense to have a little lawn or garden as a sort of buffer zone between the house and all that water? But then it wouldn't be Venice, said Connie's voice in my head. Then it would be Staines.

I walked on and heard another voice. 'How is that map working out for you?' In foreign cities, I assume that anyone speaking to me wants money, and so I continued some way before turning and seeing the lady from the *pensione*'s breakfast room. I doubled back.

'It's serving me very well. You're queuing for the Accademia?' I asked, somewhat idiotically given that she was queuing for the Accademia.

'Accademia,' she said.

'I'm sorry?'

'*Acca*demia, not Ac*cade*mia. The desk clerk in the hotel corrected my pronunciation. First and third syllable. It's *Acca*demia. Like the nut.'

'Sorry, which nut?'

'The macadamia nut.'

'No, you mean the ma*cada*mia nut!' I said.

I'm not sure the written word captures the full splendour of this comeback. I was so pleased that I found myself making a little whining noise in the back of my throat, and the woman smiled at the first nut-pronunciation joke in human history. It seemed unlikely that either of us could top the remark, so, 'Enjoy the gallery!' I said. 'See you at breakfast!' she replied, and on I strode towards Campo Santa Margherita, where I gorged on a slab of pizza, greasy and delicious, and a litre of chilled sparkling water, then on, belching privately, to the exhaust fumes and bluster of Piazzale Roma in the fish's mouth. Head to tail had taken me a little under three hours.

But it was the body of the fish, San Paolo and Santa Croce, that defeated me, the blind alleys and dog-legs and compass-defying switchbacks. My map was useless here, and finding myself alone in a cool, exquisite courtyard, my response was not 'what grace, what beauty' but 'what a pointless waste of time'. After an hour of dispirited wandering, I struck south to the open promenade of the Zattere, the fish's pelvic fin. On floating pontoons the tourists were eating *gelati* but I was behind schedule now, and in very low spirits by the time I approached La Salute, where I slumped on the marble steps near the spot where I had proposed to Connie on a winter's night, twenty-two years ago. Now a young busker stood there, Albie's age, singing an Oasis song, written before he was born, the words learnt phonetically and stripped of their consonants.

*'Un mayee, ure gonna be uh-un uh safe mee . . .'*

I missed my wife and wondered how long she would remain so. I missed my son and despaired of ever finding him and bringing him home. I pressed the heels of my hands into the sockets of my eyes.

*'An afer awwww, ure my wunnerwaw.'*

Then I picked up my backpack, caught the vaporetto back to the tip of the fish's tail, did the same thing all over again, and then once more.

## 105. the plateau

When I was a child, this is how I imagined married life to be.

The day after the wedding, you begin to walk hand in hand across this great wide plateau and in the distance ahead there are scattered obstacles, but there are also pleasures, little oases, if you like – the children that you will have and who will grow healthy, loving and strong, the grandchildren, Christmas mornings, holidays, financial security, success at work. Failures, too, but nothing that will kill you. So there are ups and downs, undulations on the plain, but for the most part you can see what's coming up ahead and you walk towards it, the two of you hand in hand for thirty, forty, fifty years, until one of you slides over the edge and the other one follows soon after. Looking up from the viewpoint of a child, that was how marriage seemed.

Well I can tell you now that married life is not a plateau, not at all. There are ravines and great jagged peaks and hidden crevasses that send the both of you scrabbling into darkness. Then there are dull, parched stretches that you feel will never end, and much of the journey is in fraught silence, and sometimes you can't see the other person at all, sometimes they drift off very far away from you, quite out of sight, and the journey is hard. It is just very, very, very hard.

Six months after our wedding, my wife had an affair.

## 106. the guy at work

I'm not sure how much I can say about the affair, because I wasn't there. Infidelity is much easier to discuss from the participants' point of view. They have the looks and smiles and secret touches, the beating hearts, the thrill and the guilt. The betrayed know nothing of this, we're just fulfilling our responsibilities in happy ignorance until we stroll into the plate glass.

Neither can I offer an intriguingly tangled web of hints, clues and gradual realisations. There were no mysterious phone calls, no mislaid credit-card slips for restaurants that I'd never been to, no detective work on my part at all. I found out because Connie told me, and had she not confessed I would not have found out. She told me without preamble on a Saturday morning, resting her head against the cupboard because she didn't know what to do.

'What to do?' I said.

'What to do next.'

'About what?'

'About Angus.'

'Angus?'

'Angus, my friend, the guy at work.'

Apparently there was a guy at work – he was always a 'guy', which irritated me – an artist who had recently exhibited at the gallery where she now worked full time. Working late, they had drunk a little wine and kissed, and she had thought about that kiss a lot, and so had this Angus, this *guy*, and the following week they had gone to a hotel.

'A hotel? I don't understand, you're here every night, you're always here! When did you—'

'One afternoon. Two weeks ago. Christ, Douglas, have you really suspected nothing? Have you really not seen the change?'

I had not. Perhaps I was unobservant, or insensitive, or complacent. We had not made love as frequently as before but that was hardly unusual. Wasn't this marriage's oldest joke? We were meant to be trying for a baby but if we had lost some of our initial zeal for that project, was that really a surprise? And yes, there had been moments where Connie had seemed a little distant, uncommunicative, distracted, times when we shuffled around the kitchen sink together like colleagues on a morning tea break, times when I fell asleep to the sound of her uneven breathing instead of asking what was wrong. But I was working very hard in those days, extremely hard, through the night sometimes in order to complete one project while securing funding for the next, and there were limitless demands on my time and my attention.

Well, she had my attention now. I am not an especially passionate man. Months, years go by without me raising my voice, and I think people sometimes misinterpret this as docility. But when I do lose my composure – well, a fitting analogy would be the difference between kinetic and potential energy, between the flow of a river and a dam that's about to burst. Good God, the memory of that awful weekend; the shouting and the tears and the punched walls, the awful circular argument. Why had she done it? Was it because she loved him? No, not really. Did she still love me? Yes, of course she did. Then why? Was it because she loved him? No, not really and so on and so on late into the night. The neighbours complained, but not because of the dancing this time. By the second day the shock and rage had dissipated somewhat, and we were staggering from room to room, insensible and incoherent. We left the house and walked along the Regent's Canal, somewhere new to be unhappy. Why had she done it? Was she bored? No, or only occasionally. Unhappy? No, or only sometimes. She some-times wanted, she said, to feel younger, wanted something new. Change. Then did she want the marriage to continue? Yes, abso-lutely yes! Did she still want children? Yes! Children with me? Yes, more than anything. Then why had she . . . ?

By Sunday night we were exhausted. Those two days were like some awful fever and I suppose we hoped, by the end of it, that the danger had passed. Nevertheless I insisted that Connie sleep elsewhere, dispatching her to Fran's, because wasn't this the convention? The suitcase, the waiting taxi? I did not want to see or hear from her until she'd made her choice.

But no sooner had the taxi pulled away than I wanted to run after it and wave it down. Because I had a terror that once banished, she might never return.

## 107. phone call from connie

'Did I wake you?'

'A little bit.'

'I don't think you can wake someone a little bit, can you?'

'I mean I was just dozing off. There's a time difference, you know.'

'Of one hour, Douglas! I'm sorry, do you want to go back to sleep?'

'No, no, I want to talk to you.' I levered myself further up the swampy bed. Eleven o'clock.

'I know I wasn't meant to call you, but—'

'Connie, is there news?'

'No news. I take it you've not found him yet.'

'No, but I will.'

'How do you *know*, Douglas?'

'I have my methods.'

She sighed. 'I'm still texting him once a day. Nothing melo-dramatic. Just "please call, we miss you".' There was an artifi-cial precision to her voice that suggested she had been drinking, the vocal equivalent of walking in a straight line for a policeman. 'I've told him we're both in England. Not a word back, Douglas.'

'That doesn't mean he's not okay. It just means that he's still punishing me.'

'Us, Douglas, both of us.'

'You've done nothing wrong. It's me.' She did not contradict me. 'If you do hear anything, don't tell him I'm here. Ask him where he is but don't say I'm looking.'

'I've checked his email, his Facebook account too. Not a word.'

'How can you check those? I thought he kept that private.'

Connie laughed. 'Please, Douglas. I am his mother.'

'Where are you now?' I asked.

'On the sofa. Trying to read.'

'Anyone know you're home?'

'Only the neighbours. I'm lying low. How's the hotel?'

'A little bleak, a little damp. You remember that old fish tank that Albie refused to clean? It smells like that.' Down the line, I heard her smile. 'The mattress sort of sucks you in.'

'What's that noise?'

'That's the hotel boiler. It's okay, it only happens whenever anyone runs a tap.'

'Oh, Douglas, come home.'

'I'm fine, really.' A brief pause. 'How's our stupid dog?'

'He's not stupid, he's complicated. And he's fine. Happy I'm back.'

'How's the weather?'

'Rainy. How is it in Venice?'

'Hot. Humid.'

'It's funny, I can only ever think of Venice in the winter.'

'Yes. Me too.'

'I'm sorry not to be there.'

'You could fly out?'

'I don't think so.'

'I found our spot today. Where I proposed to you. You remember?'

'It rings a bell.'

'I didn't seek it out. It wasn't a pilgrimage, it was on my route.'

'That's fine. I'm sorry I wasn't there with you.'

'Yes, we could have laid a wreath.'

'Douglas—'

'I'm kidding. It's, whadyacallit, dark humour.' Some time passed. 'You don't regret it, do you?'

'What?'

'Saying yes.'

'I don't think I did say yes, did I?'

'Well, eventually you did. After I'd worn you down.'

'I did. And I haven't regretted it for a moment. Don't let's talk about it now. I only phoned to say I miss you.'

'I'm glad. And now I must go to sleep.'

'And Douglas? I appreciate what you're doing. I think it's a little mad, but it's . . . admirable. I love you.'

'Are we still saying that?'

'Only if it's true.'

'Well then, I love you too.'

## 108. aching

I did not fall asleep until six, then woke at seven to discover that my knee joints had ossified. My hips ached as if I'd been struck by a car, so it took me some time and a great deal of groaning and sighing to clamber from the sucking maw of my mattress and sit on the edge of the bed. I had sweated feverishly in the night, the bedding now damp enough to propagate cress, and I drained the bedside glass of water and stumbled, hunched, to the tiny sink to drink again and again. On examination, my feet were monstrous, as moist, pale and bony as a vacuum-packed pig's trotter. Angry water-filled blisters had formed at heel and toe. Clearly it was absurd to think that I could walk the same circuit three times today, or even once. I would have to rethink my plans, find key thoroughfares and lie in wait. The Rialto, the Accademia Bridge, the western entrance to St Mark's – surely Albie would funnel through there at some point. I stuck useless plasters to the worst of the corns and blisters, descended with a robot's gait to the breakfast room, filled bowls with tinned peaches and dusty muesli and lowered myself carefully into a chair.

'Ow . . . ow . . . ow.'

'So, did you succeed?' said the woman.

'Succeed?'

'In seeing all of Venice in one day?'

'I think so. Which is why I can't move my legs. How was the . . . *Acca*demia? Did I say that right?'

'Beautifully. I didn't go in the end. Coach parties arrived before me and I hate peering over people's shoulders. There were just too many tourists. Me included, of course.'

'The tourist's paradox: how to find somewhere that's free of people exactly like us.'

'Though of course, like every tourist, I think of myself as a *traveller*.' We smiled at each other. 'Perhaps I was naïve, but I really wasn't prepared for the crowds.'

'Yes, I've only ever been here in winter.'

'Perhaps August was a mistake. Verona was the same.'

'Very busy.'

'You were in Verona too?'

'Only for two hours. I was changing trains.'

She exhaled and shook her head. 'I made the mistake of seeing Juliet's balcony. I don't think I've ever been more depressed in my life.'

'Me too! I felt the same way.'

'I practically wanted to hurl myself off it.' I laughed and, encouraged, she leant forward. 'You're on the way to . . . ?'

*I'm looking for my estranged son.*

'I'm not sure yet. I'm . . . following my nose.'

We lapsed into silence for a moment. Then . . .

'I feel foolish shouting across the room like this,' she said. 'Do you mind if I join you?'

'Not in the least,' I said, folding my map to make room.

## 109. freja kristensen

I suppose this was why some people travelled, to meet new people, though this has always been a vexed area for me. Conversation, the gradual unveiling of oneself, one's quirks and characteristics, opinions and beliefs; what a fraught and awkward business that is. Connie had always been the gregarious one, and I was inclined to let her meet new people on my behalf. But this woman was sitting diagonally opposite me now, and I had little alternative but to offer my hand.

'I'm Douglas. As in the fir.' A weak joke, I know, but one that might have special resonance for a Scandinavian.

'My name is Freja, but I'm afraid I can't think of a pun to go with that.'

'How about Deep-fat Freja!' I said in time to hear the voice inside my head scream, 'No!' We fell into a somewhat shocked silence and, in a panic, I was obliged to comment on her breakfast.

'Cheese for breakfast – I've always thought that was a very European thing, cheese and salami.'

'You don't have that in England?'

'No. To eat cheese at breakfast would be quite taboo. Likewise the cucumber and tomato have no place on our morning table.' Good God. *Talk normally, you bloody fool.*

'Though in fairness, you can hardly call this cheese.' She dangled the pale, perspiring square between finger and thumb. 'At home we have this same material tiling my bathroom floor.'

'There appear to be chocolate chips in my muesli.'

'The world has gone mad!'

'It's not the greatest hotel in Venice, is it?'

Freja laughed. 'I thought it would be fun to travel on a budget, but roughing it is always more enjoyable in theory than in practice.' *Roughing it*; she spoke very good English. 'I was told my room had air-conditioning but it sounds like a helicopter landing. Yet without it I wake each morning and have to peel the wet sheets off me.'

There seemed to be something slightly lewd about this revelation, so I moved on. 'Where are you from, Freja?'

'Copenhagen.'

'You speak wonderful English.'

'Do I?' she said, smiling.

'You speak better English than my son!' I said, the kind of pointless jibe that had brought me here in the first place.

'Thank you. I wish I could pretend it was because I read a lot of Jane Austen, but mainly it comes from bad television. Cop shows, detectives. By the age of nine, every schoolchild in Denmark knows the English for 'we've found another body, superintendent'. And pop songs, too – you're bombarded from an early age, the same all over Scandinavia.' She shrugged. 'Absurd, really, that I speak better English than Swedish. But knowing me, knowing you, there is nothing we can do!'

'I wish I could reply in Danish.'

'Don't feel too bad. We've long given up hoping that the world will take lessons.'

'My wife enjoys very much your television programmes.' *It'll be herring and Lego next*, I thought, and wondered if it was a particularly British, no, English trait, to grab at clichés like this.

'Our gift to the world.' She smiled and pushed her chair back. 'Douglas, against my better judgement I am going to get more of this disgusting fruit juice. Can I get you something? They have cake . . .'

'No, thank you.'

I watched her go. *My wife enjoys very much your television programmes*. The mangled syntax was back, and why was I straining to mention Connie? Certainly I had no desire to deny her existence, but neither was there any reason to hang a 'married' sign around my neck – except, I suppose, from an awareness that Freja was a very attractive woman. Fifty or so, I guessed, with flattish features and a pleasant, healthy glow suggestive of black bread and swims in icy lakes. Clear skin, the veins close to the surface on her cheeks. Laughter lines around very blue eyes, dark hair that might well have been dyed – it was a slightly unreal dark brown, like Cherry Blossom shoe polish. She smiled over her shoulder and I found myself sitting straighter and running my tongue over my teeth.

'So,' she said on her return, 'are you travelling alone?'

'I am. For the moment. I'm hoping to meet up with my son in a day or two,' I replied, which was true, if not quite the whole story. 'You?'

'Yes, I'm alone. I've just got divorced.'

'I'm sorry to hear that.'

'It was best for both of us.' She shrugged and laughed. 'That's what people say, isn't it? Where is your wife? She's not travelling with you?'

'She's back in England. She had to go home early. A family thing.'

'And you didn't want to go with her?'

Here my imagination failed me. 'No. No.'

'Do you like travelling alone?'

'This is only my third day.'

'For me it's my second week.'

'And how is it?'

She considered for a moment. 'I thought Italy would cheer me up. I thought I would walk all day through little mediaeval streets and sit every night with a book in a little restaurant and eat a modest meal with one glass of wine before retiring to bed. It seemed so *nice* in my imagination. But usually I'm given the table by the bathrooms, the waiters keep asking if I'm expecting someone and I find myself fixing this very relaxed smile to let everyone know I'm all right.' She demonstrated a tight grin that I recognised at once.

'In Berlin I once went to the zoo by myself,' I said. 'That was a mistake.'

Freja laughed and put her hand to her mouth. 'But *why?*'

'I was on a conference, and I heard it was a great zoo, so . . .'

'I've been to the theatre alone,' said Freja. 'The cinema I think is okay, but the theatre feels . . . awkward.' We smiled at this and continued a light-hearted riff about places one should never go alone. Paintballing! A rollercoaster! Trampolining! The circus, we decided, was the worst. *One ticket for the circus, please! No, just the one. One adult, yes.* By the end we were quite hysterical. 'I feel better,' she said, wiping her eyes. 'Now the table for one doesn't seem so bad.'

'Last night I was so exhausted I ate a sandwich in my room with my head out of the window, so there wouldn't be crumbs.'

'Congratulations!' She handed me the sugar bowl with mock formality. 'You win today's international loneliness award.'

'Thank you, thank you!' I said, accepting the trophy and acknowledging the applause then, feeling a little foolish, placing the sugar bowl down. 'And now I must go.' I attempted to stand, groaning and steadying myself on the edge of the table. 'Christ, I'm like some ancient old . . .'

'Goodness, what have you done to yourself?'

'I overdid it yesterday. I walked completely around Venice, three times.'

'Why on earth would you do such a thing? Surely there's no pleasure in that.'

'Not after the first time, no.'

'So why?'

'I'm looking for . . . it's a long story, I'd rather—'

'I'm sorry, I'm prying.'

'No, no, not at all. But I must get going.'

'Well, if you need a break . . .'

I stopped and turned. 'I don't know how you feel about visiting art galleries on your own,' she said, 'but I prefer not to.'

'Um . . .'

'I'm going to the Accademia first thing this morning. It opens at eight thirty. It's really not far. We can walk around very slowly, sit on benches. If you'd like.'

Might I find Albie there? Would he really be queuing at opening time for a museum of Venetian art? Unlikely, but would it really be so bad to devote an hour or so to the Grand Tour?

'I'll meet you back here in fifteen minutes.'

And so Freja and I walked out along the Riva degli Schiavoni, which was still cool and quiet in the morning sun, and I found myself hoping, perversely, that I would not bump into my son.

## 110. seeing art with other people

Freja and I liked the Accademia very much. There was a sense of the art belonging to a city that, on the evidence of many of the canvases, had barely changed in seven hundred years. Crisp and vivid Bellinis; exquisite, bright Carpaccios; and, in one room, an immense Veronese the size of an advertising hoarding, three great arches swarming with figures, twenty, thirty of them all distinctly individualised and dressed in anachronistic Venetian garb, with a biblically robed Christ at the centre, preparing to eat, somewhat unconventionally, what looked like a terrific leg of lamb.

'*The Feast in the House of Levi,*' said Freja, consulting the caption on the wall and stepping unwittingly into my trap.

'That's what Veronese ultimately called it, but in fact it was originally *The Last Supper*. The Inquisition didn't like the picture, they thought it was irreverent – all these people, bustling around, Germans, children, dogs, black people. You see that cat, under the table by Christ's feet? They thought it was blasphemous. So instead of painting out the animals and the dwarves, Veronese

234

simply changed the title. Not a Last Supper, but *The Feast in the House of Levi.*'

Freja looked me up and down. I realise this is a cliché, but her eyes really did scan up then down. 'You know a great deal about art,' she said.

I shrugged modestly. 'My wife's the expert. I've just picked up a thing or two along the way.' . . . *from the internet*, I should have said. *My expertise lies entirely in looking things up*, but I kept my counsel and strolled on, hands locked professorially behind my back.

'So what do you do?'

'I'm a scientist, a biochemist by training. Nothing to do with art, I'm afraid. You?'

'A dentist, so to me biochemistry sounds fascinating. Dentistry is also not very artistic.'

'But necessary!'

'I suppose so, but there's not much room for free expression.'

'You have terrific teeth,' I said, somewhat idiotically.

'Well, I've learnt that as soon as you say you're a dentist, people start peering into your mouth. I suppose they want to see if you practise what you preach.'

'"Practise what you preach" – you see? Your English is incredible.'

'You mean I know a lot of clichés?'

'Not clichés. Idioms. You're very idiomatic.'

'So much praise!'

'I'm sorry.'

'No, I don't mind. Why would I mind?'

In the final gallery we found a terrific mural by Carpaccio, occupying a whole room and telling the legend of the life of St Ursula in comic-book form. If I knew anything about Renaissance art, it was that stories of saints rarely end well. In this case, the virtuous Ursula says goodbye to her betrothed and leaves Britain to go on a pilgrimage with 10,000 virgin followers, but they're all beheaded by the Huns in Cologne. In one canvas, an arrow is fired point blank into Ursula's chest, and I wondered what message could be drawn from that?

'The moral is, don't go to Cologne,' said Freja.

'I went to a conference in Cologne. I thought it was a charming city.'

'But were any of you virgins?'

'Well, we were all biochemists so, yes – almost certainly.'

She stepped closer to the canvas, tilting her head. 'Poor St Ursula. Poor ten thousand virgins. Still, it's a comfort, I suppose, to know that someone is having a worse holiday than you.'

For all the gore of the final frames, it was a wonderful painting, full of colour and life and strange, imaginary cities under cobalt blue skies, with that precise perspective that is so conspicuous in early-Renaissance art, as if they had all been issued with really terrific geometry sets. 'I don't want to sound conceited, but I'm pretty sure that, if I'd been around in the early Renaissance, I could have come up with the theory of perspective.'

'Yes!' said Freja, grabbing my forearm. 'I've always wondered, why did no one pick up on that before? "Listen, everyone! I've just realised, when things are far away they appear smaller."'

I laughed, then remembered my new guise as an art historian. 'Of course it's a little more complicated than that.'

'Of course, of course.'

'I love Carpaccio's version of England.'

'Yes,' said Freja, 'it just so happens to look exactly like Venice.'

'I suppose, if you'd spent your life in Venice, you might very well expect everywhere to look like Venice.'

'Why would you wish for anything else?'

And then we were out in the clean blue light of the morning, our surroundings seeming somehow refreshed and made vivid now that we had seen them on old canvases. Those strange top-heavy chimneys were still there, the same accentuated geometry of the buildings and fruit-bowl hues of pink and orange and peachy yellow, the forced perspective of the eastward view from the top of the Accademia Bridge. We took it in.

'What a place,' said Freja. 'It shouldn't be here, and yet here it is.'

'There's a nice café on Santa Margherita,' I said. 'If you're not in a hurry.'

## III. ponte dei pugni

We headed west. Freja had been separated for two years, divorced for six months. 'The usual story. It hardly bears repetition. He had an affair, and then I had a silly affair to punish him for his affair, and then he had another affair, like some ridiculous poker game. Except that he fell in love with his lover and I did not. To begin with it was awful, a catastrophe. Chaotic and shocking and sad. We had built this business together – we were in the same surgery every day – and all through the day there would be arguments and rows and accusations. Believe me, no one wants to see their dentist cry, not while they're working. Can you imagine? Tears plopping into your mouth while this hysterical woman is wielding a drill. And of course the children were so furious with us both.'

'How many children?'

'Two, both girls. But they had already left home for university, so perhaps things could have been worse.'

'And do you think that was a factor in the break-up?' I said, adopting a casual tone.

'That they'd left home?'

'And that your work was somehow . . . complete?'

Freja shrugged. 'For him, perhaps. Not for me. I loved our family, I was proud of us; it never occurred to me to think of it as work. My husband used to send me crazy, of course, but that was beside the point. The point was we were married and we would be together until we died.' She was silent for a moment. 'So it was awful to begin with, screaming and shouting and tears, and the girls went a little off the rails. But then you're lying in the wreckage – to continue the metaphor – you're lying in the wreckage and you reach down and feel for your legs, they're still there, and both your arms and your skull is in one piece. You can see and hear and realise you can still stand up. And that's what you do. You stand up and you catch your breath and you stagger away. I'm talking a lot. It is because I have said nothing but "*grazie*" and "a table for one" for the last three weeks.'

'I don't mind. Really.'

We were out of the dark alleys now, into Campo San Barnaba, the church front bright and elegant and unadorned.

'I haven't seen this square. I like it a lot,' said Freja, and as her tour guide I felt rather proud.

'You must see this,' I said, the expert once again. On the bridge at the far side of the square, four white marble footprints were inlaid deep into the stonework. 'It's a fighting bridge. If you had a dispute with someone, you settled it here. A sort of public boxing ring. The footprints were where the fight started.'

'You're a real local historian, Douglas.'

'I read the guidebooks. It sends my wife crazy. She's always telling me to put the book away and look up. Look up!'

We placed our feet in the marble indentations. 'Perhaps I should have brought my husband here,' she said.

'Do you get on now?'

'As well as you can with someone you've hated. It is "amicable" – is that the word? Amicable,' she said and raised her fists.

## 112. winter music

At the Caffè Rosso our coffees were extruded from an immense brass contraption that hissed and steamed like the boiler of a locomotive. We took them outside to the sunny terrace of that wonderful square, with its lopped-off *campanile* at the western end, snipped through cleanly as if by giant scissors.

'What happened to the church tower?'

'I've no idea.'

'Douglas, I thought you would have an interesting story. I thought you knew everything.'

'I didn't have time to look it up. Sorry.'

There was an expectant silence. Freja had confided in me, and it was my turn now to offer up some explanation as to why a dishevelled man in middle age was circling Venice in a teenager's trainers. Instead I found my attention drawn to the young violinist who had begun to play across the square, mournful music in a minor key. Bach, I guessed. If I ever find a piece of music depressing beyond belief, I assume that it is Bach.

'So, Douglas. You and your wife, are you together or separated?'

I lowered my coffee cup, opened and then closed my mouth.

'I hope you don't mind my asking,' said Freja. 'I have been boring you all this time about my life, I thought you might like an opportunity to bore me in return.'

'That's only fair. And I'd tell you if I knew. We're in a . . . transitional state. By which I mean we're physically apart, but still together. The process has not . . . we're in flux. I'm not explaining this very well, am I?'

'You mean you haven't yet decided if you want to stay together.'

'Oh, no. I've decided. She hasn't.'

'I see. At least I think I see. Do you mean that—?'

'Freja, I hope you won't mind, I realise you've been very open, and I'm not being coy. But my reason for being here, here in Venice, it's more complicated than . . . it's not entirely . . . what I mean is, I'd prefer to keep it to myself. Does that make sense?'

'Of course. I apologise.'

'No need. Please don't.'

We listened to the violinist for a while as he performed elaborate trills and variations on the same repeating sequence of
minor chords. He was a young man in scuffed shoes and an
untucked shirt, with that rather unworldly air that musicians
sometimes share with scientists and mathematicians. I wondered,
perhaps Albie might have taken to the violin instead of the
guitar. Perhaps we should have pushed him in that direction.

'He's very good,' said Freja, 'but I find this music far too sad,'
and I too felt saddened, and chastised. 'It's winter music,' she
added.

*I'd like to apologise for my son.* I had lost sight of my purpose
and forgotten why I was here. I had become distracted by an
absurd and irrelevant flirtation. All these sideways glances, these
confidences, this pathetic affectation of culture and sophistica-
tion – I was making myself ridiculous. I should leave.

'Of all the ones I've seen, I like this square the most,' said
Freja. 'I've been trying to understand what makes it different
and I think it's the trees. In Venice I don't miss the cars at all,
but I do miss the colour green.'

'I must go,' I said, standing abruptly.

'Oh. Oh, really?'

'Yes, yes I have to, I'm behind schedule, I must . . . start
walking.'

'Perhaps I could walk with you.'

'No, I really need to cover some ground. It's hard to explain.'
My heart was racing suddenly; too much coffee perhaps, or fear.
'The fact is, Freja, my son has gone missing. That makes it sound
as if he's been abducted; he hasn't, he's run away and I have a
theory that he's here in Venice and I have to find him. So . . .'

'I see. That's awful, I'm sorry, that must be a worry for you.'

'It is. I apologise.'

'Why do British people apologise for being in distress? It isn't
your fault.'

'But it is! It is! That's the whole bloody point!' I was leafing through my wallet now, panic rising. 'I'm sorry, I only have twenty euros.'

'I'll pay.'

'No, I'd like to pay. Here, take it.'

'Douglas, please sit down.'

'No, no I must keep going—'

'Two minutes will not make a difference.'

'Here, take the twenty—'

'Douglas, I'm leaving tomorrow morning.'

'That's fine, I don't want any change, but I really must—'

'Douglas, I said I'm leaving. Venice. I probably won't see you again.'

'Oh. I see. You are? I'm sorry, I . . .' Perhaps I should have sat down at this point, but I continued to stand. 'Well, it was very nice to meet you, Freja,' I said and offered my hand.

'And you,' she said, taking it with little enthusiasm. 'Good luck. I hope you find whatever it is you're looking for.'

But I was already running away.


## 113. the serpentine

We were different after the affair.

Not unhappy, but more formal, on our best behaviour. As Connie became quiet and withdrawn so I became overly attentive, like a waiter who constantly asks how you're finding the food. How was your day? What would you like to do tonight, what shall we eat, what shall we watch? But pretending that nothing has changed is a change in itself. The fact remained that one of us had wronged, one of us had been wronged, and my determination to overlook this fact had turned me into a particularly unctuous and ingratiating parole officer.

There had been conditions for her return, a certain 'laying down of the law', but nothing too onerous or unreasonable. Of course, she would not see or speak to this 'guy' again. We would try to be more open and honest about our dissatisfactions and irritations. We would go out together more, talk more, be kinder to each other and, for my part, I would endeavour not to refer to the infidelity. It would not be forgotten – how could it be? But neither would it be wielded as a weapon or a negotiating tool, or a justification for infidelity on my part, a condition that I happily accepted.

More importantly we decided that we would commit whole-heartedly to the project of starting a family and, sure enough, within a few months of almost breaking up, I received a telephone call.

'Have you had lunch yet?' she asked, with affected casualness.

'Not yet.'

'Come and meet me in the park, by the Serpentine. We'll have a picnic!'

Outside my window it was a blustery day in late October, hardly picnic weather. 'All right. All right, I will,' I said, and then I knew. I knew why she wanted to meet. I hung up and sat for some time at my desk, not moving, but laughing quietly to myself. We would be parents. I would be a father – a husband *and* a father. It felt like some wonderful promotion. I told my colleagues that I'd be late back.

In Hyde Park, I saw her some way off, standing by the Serpentine, hands in pockets, collar raised. The grin that she struggled to suppress confirmed my suspicions and as I approached I felt such . . . it's a very broad term, 'love', so elastic in its definition as to be almost useless, but there is no other word, except perhaps adoration. Adoration would do too, at a push.

We kissed, briefly, casually. I had decided to play dumb. 'So. This is a nice surprise.'

'Let's walk a little, shall we?'

'I've not brought anything to eat.'

'Me neither. Let's just walk.' We walked. 'What time do you have to be back at the lab?' she said.

'No rush. Why?'

'Because there's something I wanted to tell you.'

'That sounds intriguing . . .' Perhaps I rubbed my chin, I can't recall. I've never been obliged to choose between science and a career on the stage.

'Douglas. I'm pregnant!'

And then there was no need to act, we just laughed, and hugged and kissed. She took my arm, and we walked around the Serpentine three, perhaps four times, talking, speculating, making plans until the day grew dark and the streetlamps came on. She would be a wonderful mother, I had no doubt, and I – well, I would do my best. The notion that what doesn't kill you makes you stronger is patently nonsense, but we had sailed close to disaster, my wife and I, and survived, and we were now about to embark on this next chapter with renewed zeal. We would not be apart again.

## 114. home-making

Some wag once remarked that married couples only have children so that they have something to talk about. A rather cynical view, I suppose, but it was certainly true that Connie's pregnancy led to something of a renaissance in our marriage. The highs and lows of the process are so well documented in film and television that they are scarcely worth recounting here, except to confirm that, yes, there were bouts of morning sickness, insomnia, aching feet and tempestuous mood swings. There were comical food cravings and times when the sheer strain of carrying that ever-growing load drove Connie into tearful rages. In the face of the irrational demands and sudden furies, I adopted the persona of an attentive butler, thick-skinned, uncomplaining and able, cooking careful meals, organising visitors, making tea. It suited me.

And pregnancy suited Connie, too, as she swelled and bloomed in magnificent ways. The smoky parties, the late nights and hangovers were set aside with surprising ease, almost relief, and now she was rarely without a bag of desiccated fruit or some awful juice of a pondweed green. That's not to say that she became pious or saintly about the condition. She was funny again, pretending irritation, fury sometimes at this new encumbrance. 'Look what you've done to me! Look!' We stayed at home now, hibernating through the winter into spring. Watched films and banal quiz shows. Lay on the sofa, reading. The spare room was finally acknowledged as the nursery and we equipped and decorated it in a defiantly unisex fashion, classical music playing on the stereo, proper grown-ups now. At night I pushed my thumbs into the hard soles of her aching feet. We were home-making, a dreary and pedestrian activity to anyone but us, and we were happy.

We returned to the hospital for our second scan with only a small amount of trepidation, just enough not to seem complacent. After all, we were healthy and responsible adults in a medically advanced country in the final years of the twentieth century. The chances of anything going wrong seemed vanishingly small and sure enough, there it was on the screen, a blurred comma of flesh and soft bone animated with those jerky movements suggestive of a stick puppet. Beautiful, we said. Objectively, of course, there is no such thing as a beautiful scan; it's a bad photocopy of a vertebrate that looks, frankly, like something you might find in an underground lake. But does any parent find this not beautiful? There was the heart, the size of a raspberry, pulsing away; there were the fingers. Does any parent ever shrug and refuse the printout? We held hands and laughed.

But the 'it' was troubling. Would we like to know the sex? Yes please, we said, and squinted at the image I couldn't see it myself, but apparently it was a girl. I would have a daughter, and although I had never expressed a preference, I must confess that I was secretly pleased. I had experienced, and was continuing to experience, the awkwardness of the father–son relationship, but didn't all daughters love their dads and vice versa? Probably there was a certain amount of relief, too; wouldn't our daughter look to Connie for advice and guidance? Wouldn't she be the role model and soul-mate, as well as the butt of the biggest rows? They'd swap clothes and confide and when adolescence came around, the doors would slam in Connie's face, not mine. As a father to a daughter, all I'd have to do was provide the lifts, the pocket money, the understanding ear and proud paternal hug at graduation. All I'd have to do was worry about her, and that was entirely within my abilities.

We took our smudged image home and stuck it on a pinboard, surrounded by Post-it notes with all the names we liked – or rather all the names Connie liked, my imagination balking at anything more esoteric than Emily, Charlotte, Jessica, Grace. Perversely, Connie settled on Jane, a name so ordinary that it was practically avant-garde. We rubbed the bump with oil. Connie stopped work and readied the house, I worked long hours on a new project, zebrafish now, and waited for the call.

And here, with some reluctance, I must return to that notion of time as a loop of celluloid. The first snip of the scissors came on London Bridge on the night I met my wife, but where was that second cut? While her affair had been traumatic, it would be worth reliving if only for the happiness of what came after, the winter and spring of her pregnancy during which our marriage once again made perfect sense.

But some things cannot be lived through twice and so, if asked, I think I'd like to make that other cut round about now please.

## 115. pompidou paris accordion cat amazing

Could there be a clearer indicator of the dizzying pace of technological change than the demise of the internet café? Once so space-age, so cutting-edge, portals to a world of knowledge and fantasy, until cheap wifi and the smart phone rendered them obsolete, and they became as quaint and anachronistic as the telegram office or the video rental outlet.

In Venice, only one internet café remained, situated in a gloomy little parade of shops near a housing estate in Cannaregio. Exhausted and made lame by my second circuit of the city I took refuge in its cool, dark interior, squeezing past a wall of telephone booths where Indians and Pakistanis, Arabs and Africans chattered urgently, to the computer bays where the poor and desperate joined the scammers, the blackmailers and stalkers, all of us hunched and furtive on swivel chairs leaking yellow foam in the unhealthy glow of the screens. Explosions and laser-blasts could be heard to my left where a nine-year-old boy was hammering his keyboard as aliens disintegrated all around, while to my right an earnest young man stared intently at a page of dense Arabic script. I smiled hello and turned to my computer. The console and keyboard were ancient and filthy, the dirty cream of old Bakelite, but I was exhausted and almost out of credit on my tablet and so I sat there, grateful, in the room that smelt of wet cardboard and instant coffee, and took my quest online.

Doubts had begun to assail me. I knew from Albie's call to the hotel that he and Cat had been heading this way, but what if they had changed their minds, or left already? In need of reassurance, I searched for

| accordion venice, | 🔍 |
|---|---|

| buskers venice, | 🔍 |
|---|---|

| cat playing accordion, | 🔍 |
|---|---|

| venice busker cat accordion, | 🔍 |
|---|---|

an alchemist, tossing ingredients into a cauldron in the vain hope of finding gold. I searched for

| cathy albie italy busker, | 🔍 |
|---|---|

| catherine venezia rock accordionist | 🔍 |
|---|---|

| italy accordion cat | 🔍 |
|---|---|

I saw things no man should ever see, but I did not see my son. Taking a more direct approach, I searched for Albie Petersen. Ever the contrarian, Albie was not a slave to social media and, besides, his accounts were locked. But his friends were not so cagey or discreet and I found that I could easily fill the screen with snaps of my son; at parties with a cigarette dangling blatantly from pouting lips, on stage with his terrible college band (I had been there but couldn't bear to listen, had sneaked out to check the car was locked, had stayed in the car). Here he was as a Nazi in *Cabaret* (I was working late that week) and here with a girlfriend that I vaguely remembered, the one before the one before, a lovely quiet girl, heartbroken now I imagined, my son her first love. Here he was lounging on some riverbank on an overcast day in some previous summer, his body bony and pale and visibly goose-bumped, then, in a series of consecutive snaps, arms and legs wheeling as he let go of a rope swing and plummeted into the river. I laughed at this, my neighbour glancing from my face to the screen, which I changed quickly, double-clicking on some of Albie's photographic work from an online exhibition: a dilapidated shed in an allotment, a close-up of tree bark, and a rather good portrait in high-contrast black and white of two elderly men on the same allotment, their faces extraordinarily gnarled and wrinkled, creased deeply like the bark, which was the point I suppose. I liked this one, and I resolved to tell him that I liked it if and when I found him.

I would never find him, I knew that now. The quest was absurd, a delusional attempt to salvage some dignity from this whole disastrous trip, to make amends for years of fumbling, mumbling incoherence. People travelling in Europe do not bump into each other, it's just not possible. If he returned, and surely he would return eventually, he would do so in his own time. The image that I'd cherished, that I would carry him back to my wife like a fireman emerging from a burning building, was a vain and self-indulgent fantasy. The only reason I remained in Europe was because I was too scared and humiliated to go home and face the future. I closed the page of images of Albie.

The YouTube searches remained open underneath. I would try one more time. I typed in *pompidou paris accordion cat street performer*, flicked though screen after screen of beat-boxing flautists, Siamese cats on piano keyboards and depressing clips of living statues, and there in the bleak, uncharted depths of the fourth page of search results, was Cat in an unseasonable velvet top hat, playing 'Psycho Killer' on the forecourt of the Pompidou. 'Yes!' I said out loud.

I let the video play, the four hundred and eighty-sixth person to do so, and read the prose beneath.

*Saw this gr8 busker wen in Paris. She great, she crazy buy her Cd Kat play rock accordion —styl!!!!!*

Underneath, another contributor was in a more critical mood:

*haha she sing like u speak English . . . i.e. wewy wewy painful where u lurn English dum boy hahaha*

The debate continued in Socratic form for several exchanges.

The video, I noted, was two years old. No matter. I had made a small breakthrough: Cat was a Kat.

Encouraged, I began my search again: *kat accordion cover version, kat street performer* and found her once again, sitting on a bed in a crowded, candlelit room. Melbourne, apparently. The video had been uploaded some six months before, had been viewed a modest forty-six times and consisted of a spirited rendition of 'Hey Jude', with the other party guests banging beer bottles together, playing the bongos, etc. The video was twenty-two minutes long and seemed unlikely to 'go viral'. Had I been immortal I might have watched it all, but there was no need because in the description I found:

*Our old friend Katherine 'Kat' Kilgour from Theatre Factory still singing the songs and doin' her thang. Love u Kat Babe, Holly*

Kat Kilgour. I had a surname, and not a Smith or Evans either. I searched again, striking a rich seam now, linking from one video to the next until I found what I'd been searching for.

In an Italianate square, in blazing sunlight, Kat and Albie perched on the steps of an ornate church, singing 'Homeward Bound', the old Simon and Garfunkel song. A strangely old-fashioned choice of song, as distant in time to my son as the Charleston was to me, but part of the very small cultural legacy that I had passed on to Albie. Connie had never cared for Simon and Garfunkel, thought them too middle-of-the-road, but as a small boy Albie had loved them, and on long car journeys we'd play the *Greatest Hits*, Albie and I singing along, much to Connie's irritation. Had he suggested the song to Kat, or vice versa? Did he even think of it as something that he'd taken from me? Did he want to come home?

'Too loud!' said the war-gaming boy to my left, and I realised that I had been singing along too. I apologised, pulled on a pair of greasy headphones and turned my attention back to the video, posted two days previously and viewed a modest three times. The description, while at least literate, provided no further assistance. 'Saw these guys on our tour of Italy and talked to them afterwards. She's called Kat Kilgour and she's really talented!!!' And what about Albie, hm? In truth the harmonies were experimental, the crowd small and indifferent. Still, I felt such pleasure in seeing him again. He looked well. Perhaps not 'well', exactly – skinny and hunched and none too fresh – but he looked exactly like a student backpacker should, and he was safe.

But where was he? I played the video once more, a detective looking for clues. The church, the café, the pigeons, the square, the tourists – it might have been anywhere in Italy. I freeze-framed, took screen grabs, zoomed in on Albie, his clothes, his face, looking for goodness knows what. I zoomed in on the faces of the few indifferent tourists, on the shop fronts and walls in case of street names, I let the video play and play again, grabbing shots at key moments until something drew my eye to a knot of people coming into frame in the final seconds, a man crouching at a café table to confer with a tourist, a striped T-shirt, a black hat with a ribbon.

A gondolier.

'Yes! Yes, yes, yes, yes, yes!'

## 116. the vivaldi experience

Taking full advantage of my online anonymity, I left my comment – 'You guys are excellent! The boy in particular! Please, please stay in Venice!' – then emailed myself a link to the page and hurried back to the *pensione*, hobbling but in high spirits. Tomorrow was the day that our pre-paid reservation at the hotel came in to force. Lured by the offer of free residency in a nice hotel, chosen for its comfort, convenience and romance, might not Albie take the room? Connie had been calling him from our home in England. Clean sheets, a shower, no parents, a chance to impress his girlfriend with one of her beloved buffet breakfasts? I felt certain he would come. All I would need to do was take a seat at a pavement café nearby and wait. What I would say, other than sorry and come home, remained a mystery, but I would have got something *right* for once.

Pausing at reception, I wrote a note on the back of a flyer for The Vivaldi Experience.

*Freja, apologies for my rudeness today. You must think me unhinged, and you are not the only one to do so. Please let me make amends by buying you dinner tonight, then perhaps I can explain a little too. If the idea does not appal you I am in room 56, the super-heated cupboard near the roof. And if I don't hear from you by eight p.m., it was extremely nice to meet you. I enjoyed our trip to the ACCaDEMia very much! Best wishes, Douglas*

Before I could reconsider, I handed it to the receptionist for the Danish lady travelling alone. Freja Kristensen? *Grazie mille.* Then I climbed the stairs stiffly and sat heavily on the bed. The treacherous running shoes were removed with a queasy sucking sound. Where was their promised comfort now? Despite my best efforts with bandages and plasters, my feet looked as if they'd been eaten by crabs. The blisters on the knuckles of my toes had burst, the new flesh rubbed raw, and on the soles of my feet dead skin hung down like tattered flags. Swelling rendered my other shoes, a pair of serviceable brown brogues, unwearable, and so I did my best to patch my wounds while I waited for my lady friend to call.

## 117. not a date

It was not a date, of course. We were merely two travellers taking temporary comfort in each other's company. But I realised, unwrapping a new shirt and combing my hair, that I had not eaten a meal with a woman other than my wife for perhaps twenty years. It was all very strange and I resolved to be extremely casual about the whole business, selecting in advance a small, unpretentious trattoria that I had noticed on my hike around the city; pleasant but functional and not too cluttered with red candles or gypsy violins.

Freja, on the other hand, seemed to have gone to some effort. She was waiting in the lobby, subtly but effectively made up and wearing a rather snug skirt and the kind of off-white satin shirt that one might really only term a 'blouse'. She looked fresh, healthy and tasteful, and yet I found myself instinctively wanting to do up an extra button, and I wondered if I might be the only man in the world to have dressed a woman with his eyes.

'Hi,' I said, pronouncing it 'haaaiii,' giving that difficult word a little Scandinavian twist to be more easily understood.

'Good evening, Douglas.'

'You look nice,' I said, silken-tongued.

'Thank you. I really do like those shoes. They're very striking and bright!'

'"Box-fresh" is the correct term, I believe.'

'Have you been playing basketball?'

'Actually, they were meant for walking, but they've attached themselves to my feet like some awful alien parasite and now they're the only thing I can wear.'

'I like them,' she said, placing her hand lightly on my forearm. 'You look very fly.'

'My skateboard is parked outside.' I took her arm and hobbled towards the door and out into the kind of warm, hazy evening which is sometimes labelled 'sultry'.

We headed east through the *sestiere* of Castello, the tip of the tail, walking the back streets and enjoying the feeling of belonging that the serious traveller enjoys when the day-trippers have returned to their coaches and cruise ships.

'You don't even need a map any more.'

'No, I'm almost a local.'

We emerged at the immense gates of the Arsenale, the walls crenellated like a toy fort. I'd read about this in the guidebook. 'The great innovation of the Venetians was to mass-produce ships in kit form, standardising all the parts. It was here that the shipbuilders of Venice amazed Henry IV of France by building an entire galleon—'

'—in the time it took him to eat his supper, and thus was the modern production line born,' said Freja. 'Except I think it was Henry III of France. We have the same guidebook.'

'God, what an old bore I am,' I said.

'Not at all, I'm the same. I think it's good to have a desire to educate. Perhaps it comes of having children. My husband, ex-husband and I, we used to drive our daughters to distraction, taking them to ruins and cemeteries and dusty old galleries. "Here is Ibsen's grave, here is the Sistine Chapel . . . Look! Look! Look!" when all they really wanted to do was go to the beach and flirt with boys. Now they're older they appreciate it, but at the time . . .'

'That's how we were meant to spend this summer. My wife and I were meant to be taking my son around all the great galleries of Europe.'

'And instead?'

'My son left a note and ran off with an accordionist. My wife is in England, thinking about leaving me.'

Freja laughed. 'I'm sorry, but *that* is a very bad holiday.'

'It has been both fun and harrowing.'

'What's left to go wrong, I wonder?'

'Are there sharks in this lagoon?'

'I shouldn't laugh. I'm sorry. No wonder you were so upset. I'll try not to add to your woes tonight.' Here she took my arm and at that precise moment, as if she had activated an alarm, my telephone rang.


## 118. tangled web

'Hello?'

'Hi there. Where are you?'

'Oh, out walking, walking. As usual.'

'No news, then.'

'Not yet.' To Freja I mouthed, *Sorry, one minute*, and indicated she should walk ahead. 'But I'm closing in.'

'What does that mean, closing in?'

'It means I have a good lead. The net is tightening!'

'You sound like a private detective.'

'I'm wearing a mackintosh as we speak. I'm not.'

'No. So – tell me, then.'

'You'll see.'

'You've heard from him? You've spoken to him?'

'You'll find out.'

'But why won't you tell me?'

'Trust me, I have material proof that he's fit and well.'

'Well, should I fly out to you?'

'No! No, I've told you, I'll bring him back.'

'Because it's been five days now, and I'd really like to know, Douglas.'

'I'd prefer to tell you when it's definite.'

There was a silence.

'I think you should come home.'

'I will when I've found him.'

'Except you're not really looking for him, are you?'

I felt an irrational moment of panic, absurdly turning my back on Freja, who was waiting patiently at the next bridge. 'I am! I'm out looking now.'

'That's not what I mean. I mean you're doing something else.'

*Should we turn left or right?* mimed Freja.

'I'm about to get something to eat. Can I call you back?' I said, and mouthed *one minute*.

'Oh. Okay. I'd hoped we could talk, but if you're too busy . . .'

'I'm sitting at a table, the food's about to arrive. Not the food, the menu – the menu's about to arrive.'

'You said you were walking.'

'I was, and now I'm sitting at a table. I hate talking on phones in restaurants, it's very rude. The waiter's glaring at me.' With this last detail I had overreached myself, because I could hear Connie frowning.

'Where are you exactly?'

'I'm in Castello, by the Arsenale. I'm sitting outside and the waiter's standing over me. I can send you a photo if you like.'

There was a pause that seemed to last an age, a lowering of her voice. 'I'm worried about you, Douglas. I think you might be—'

'Got to go,' I said and hung up. I'd never done this before, hung up on Connie. Then, to my amazement, I turned the phone off too, and limped quickly towards Freja.

'I'm sorry about that. Connie, my wife.'

'I thought, when the phone rang, you were going to leap into the canal.'

'It startled me, that's all. I need a drink. The restaurant's just here.' And we turned into a tiny campo. No carnival masks or postcards for sale here. Instead laundry hung between the buildings like celebratory bunting, televisions and radios played in first-floor rooms, and in the corner of the square was a small trattoria that, despite my best intentions, looked undeniably romantic.

'What do you think?'

'I think it looks perfect.'

## 119. daughters

We were seated outside in adjacent chairs, facing the square. The restaurant had no menu and instead we were brought glasses of prosecco by a small elderly man with suspiciously black hair, then small bowls of marinated squid and octopus and anchovies, sharp and oily and entirely delicious. As if to reassure each other of the platonic nature of the evening, Freja showed me pictures of her daughters on her telephone, two startlingly beautiful girls with very blue eyes, born a year apart, growing in montage form into straight-limbed, long-haired, white-teethed young women, the very embodiment of health and vigour, pictured against a varied background of windswept Atlantic beaches and Thai palm trees, the Sphinx, a glacier somewhere. With shrewd editing it might, I suppose, be possible to compile an upbeat slideshow of even the most grim and Dickensian of childhoods, but on the evidence of Freja's photo album her daughters had been particularly blessed. They seemed like the kind of healthy, wholesome family who'd be happy to share the same toothbrush. Of course she was far too nice a woman to gloat, but I couldn't help but be aware that while Freja was usually pictured in the embrace of her photogenic offspring, I could not recall a single photo of my son and me. Perhaps when he was a small child, but in the last eight, ten years? Never mind, here was a photograph of Anastasia Kristensen, swimming with dolphins; here was Babette Kristensen, volunteering in an African village. Here was our pasta, and more wine.

'Anastasia is a documentary-maker now. Babette is an

environmentalist. I'm very proud of them, as you can probably tell. I have an almost limitless capacity to bore people about them. I'll stop now before you slump forward into your linguine.'

'Not at all. They seem like lovely girls,' I said.

'They are,' she replied, returning the phone to her bag. 'Of course when they were younger they could be little bitches . . .' She put her hand to her mouth. 'I shouldn't say that even if it's true – but goodness, we fought! Thankfully those things get easier with time. One more . . .' She produced her phone again. 'I debated whether or not to show you this, you'll understand why . . .'

And here was Babette, twenty years old, sitting naked in a hospital chair, a newborn baby girl the colour of an aubergine at her breast, her hair sticking to her forehead with sweat. 'Yes, this year I actually became a grandmother. Can you believe it? I'm a *mormor* at fifty-two! Good God!' She shook her head and reached for her glass.

'Who is this here?' To the left of the chair stood a lean, distinguished-looking man, a Roman senator, absurdly handsome despite the foolish grin and surgical frock.

'That's my ex-husband.'

'He looks like a film star.'

'And is all too well aware of the fact, I'm afraid.'

'He has incredible eyes.'

'My downfall.'

'Wait – he was at the birth?'

'Yes, of course.'

'He saw his grandchild . . . come out?'

'Yes, yes, we both did.'

'That's very Scandinavian.'

Freja laughed and I peered once again. 'He really is a very handsome man.'

'That's where my daughters get their looks.'

'I'm not sure if that's entirely true,' I said obligingly, and Freja nudged me with her elbow. 'Are they friendly with their father?'

'Of course, they adore him. I repeatedly instruct them not to, but they insist on worshipping him.'

My son did not worship me, and that was fine. To be worshipped would have made me uncomfortable, likewise 'adored'. But 'friendly with', I could have lived with that. 'I always thought that daughters were more forgiving of their fathers,' I said. 'It always seems like an easier relationship than fathers and sons. I wonder why that is?'

'I suppose it's because you're freed of the obligation of being a role model. Or at least the comparison is less direct. Whereas with a son . . .'

'Perhaps. I'd never thought of that.' Had Albie ever aspired to be like me? In what respect? If I thought long enough, perhaps I'd come up with something, but now Freja was pouring wine.

'I feel the same about sons. I'd have loved a son. A handsome, rather old-fashioned boy who I could mould and dress up and then hate his girlfriends. Besides, you mustn't idolise girls. If you had a daughter, that would bring its own problems too.'

'I did have a daughter.'

'You did?'

'My wife and I. Our first child was a girl, Jane, but she died.'

'When?'

'Soon after she was born.'

A moment passed. Over the years I've noted that some people, when told we lost our baby, seem almost angry, as if we've played a trick on them. Others try to shrug it off, as if it doesn't really count, but thankfully this is rare. For the most part people are thoughtful and kind and when the situation arises, as it sometimes does, I have a facial expression I produce, a smile of sorts – Connie has one too – to reassure people that we are okay, and I produced it now.

'Douglas, I'm very sorry.'

'It was a long time ago. More than twenty years now.' *My daughter would have been twenty this year.*

'No, but still – it's the worst thing that can happen to a couple.'

'I didn't raise it to be dramatic, but Connie and I, we have a policy of never avoiding the subject either. We don't want it to be a secret, or something taboo. We want to be . . . straightforward about it.'

'I understand,' said Freja, but her eyes were reddening.

'Please, Freja, I don't want to spoil the evening . . .' *No, not twenty, nineteen years old – just. She'd be about to start her second year at university.*

'No, but still—'

'I don't want to cast a gloomy spell.' *Medicine, or architecture, I'd imagined. Or perhaps she'd be an actress, or an artist. I wouldn't mind . . .*

'So your son . . .'

'Albie is our only child, but our second child.'

'And is that why you're here? Because of your son?'

'That's right.'

'He's gone missing?'

'He's run away.'

'And he is . . . ?'

'Seventeen.'

'Ah!' She nodded, as if this explained everything. 'Is he sensible?'

I laughed. 'Not always. Rarely, in fact.'

'Well he is seventeen, why should he be?'

'I was very sensible at seventeen.'

Freja shook her head and laughed. 'I was not. Are you particularly close?'

'No. Quite the opposite. That's why I'm here.'

'Do you talk to each other?'

'Not really. Do you? With your daughters?'

'Of course. We talk about everything!'

'With my son and I, it's like a rather awkward chat show. Albie's this surly young pop star who doesn't want to be there. "So, how are things? What have you been up to? Any future plans?"'

'But if you don't talk to each other, that must be a worry.'

'It is. It is.'

'Perhaps we should change the subject. Except to say, I don't mean to underdo – is that a word? Underrate, underestimate your concern, but if he has access to money and a phone for emergencies—'

'He does—'

'And he's an adult, more or less. Why not just let him be?'

'I promised my wife I'd find him.'

'The wife you are separated from.'

'Not yet,' I said defensively. 'We're not separated yet. We're just not in the same city. We are . . . geographically separated.'

'I see.'

We sat quietly until our waiter had taken our plates away.

'Also, we argued, my son and I. Things were said and I'd like to make amends. In person. Does that sound insane?'

'Not at all. It sounds very noble. But if I had to apologise to my daughters for all the foolish things I've said to them, we would never talk about anything else. I think, as a parent, one has the right to make some mistakes, and to be forgiven for them. Don't you agree?'


## 120. daughter

Certainly, I felt guilty about Jane. Irrationally so, of course, but then guilt is rarely rational. We were assured, over and over again, that there was nothing we could have done, that the sepsis that killed our daughter was not a result of behaviour or lifestyle, was not present in the womb. Although she was a little premature, there was every reason to believe that she was healthy and well at birth. Because anger was preferable to guilt, I had searched for blame; the prenatal care, the postnatal care, the staff. The word 'sepsis' suggested infection – was that someone's fault? But it soon became clear that the staff were blameless – better than blameless, immaculate really – in their handling of the situation. It was one of those things that happens, they told us; very rarely, but it happens. Which was fine, but what were we meant to do with all that anger, all that guilt? Connie directed hers inwards. Was it the fault of some past behaviour, smoking or drinking, was it complacency on her part? She must have done something. Surely there couldn't be a punishment as harsh as this without some crime? No, we had done nothing wrong and there was nothing we could have done. It was one of those things that happens. That was all.

There had been no sense of danger at the birth. That had all gone well, the experience traumatic but thrilling, too, both familiar and entirely new. Connie's waters had broken in the night. At first neither of us could believe this – it was only the thirty-fourth week – but the sodden mattress was undeniable and we put our plan into action, driving to the hospital where we paced and waited, boredom alternating with elation and anxiety. The contractions began mid-morning and then things happened very quickly. Connie was as strong and ferocious as I knew she'd be, and by 11.58 a.m., Jane was with us, mewling and shouting, punching at the air with tiny fists, pedalling away, a shade over 4lbs but fierce; oh, she was a beauty, all the worry, anxiety and pain swept away by her perfection and the joy of it all. She was healthy and we could hold her as we'd hoped. There were photographs and private vows; I would do all I could to care for her and protect her from harm. Connie took her to her breast and though she didn't feed at first, all seemed well. There'd be no need for an incubator, just a careful eye. We returned to the ward.

Through the afternoon I sat by the bed and watched them sleep, Connie pale, exhausted and quite beautiful. Goodness knows why it should have come as a surprise, but I'd been shocked and stunned by the violence of the delivery room, the blood and sweat, the complete absence of delicacy. Had I found myself in that situation I'd have opted not just for gas and air, but full general anaesthetic and six months' convalescence. But nothing had ever come so naturally to Connie as giving birth, and I felt very proud. 'You were incredible,' I'd told her when she opened her eyes.

'Did I swear?' she said.

'A lot. I mean, a lot.'

'Good,' she smiled.

'But it all seemed so natural, too. You were like some . . . Viking washerwoman or something.'

'Thank you,' she said. 'Are you pleased with her? She's very small.'

'She's perfect. I'm delighted.'

'Me too.'

They wanted to keep both Jane and Connie in overnight – nothing to worry about, so we didn't worry. With some reluctance on Connie's part, it was suggested that I should go home and prepare for mother and baby's return and so I took that journey, surely one of the strangest journeys a man ever makes, back to the home that was exactly how we'd left it. There was something rather ritualistic about those few hours, preparation for something monumental, as if this would be the last time I'd ever be alone in my life. Moving in a daze, I washed up and tidied things away, stocked the fridge, organised the equipment just so. I fielded texts, made reassuring phone calls, mother and baby doing well. I made the bed with fresh sheets and when everything was in place, I spoke to Connie and went to sleep . . .

. . . and was woken by a call a little after four a.m., that awful hour. No need to panic – terrible words – but Baby Jane was a little listless. She was having some difficulty breathing and had been moved to a different ward. They had administered antibiotics and were confident this would help, but would I come to the hospital straight away? Best not to drive. I stumbled into clothes and out of the house, seizing on the conversation's positive elements – no need to panic – but unable to forget the phrase 'some difficulty breathing', because what could be more fundamental than the need to breathe? 'Breathe' and 'live', weren't they the same words? I ran down to Kilburn High Road, found a cab, hurled myself into it and out again, into the hospital, feet slapping on the floor as I ran to Connie's ward, saw the curtains drawn around her bed, heard her cries and I knew. I pulled the curtain to one side, saw her curled in a ball, her back to me – oh, Connie – and I knew.

Next morning they took us to a private room and let us spend some time with Jane, though I'd rather not go into that. Somehow I was able to take some photographs, some hand- and footprints too. We were advised, though this might feel strange, that we might be pleased to have them in the future, and we were. We said our goodbyes then we were sent home, never more empty-handed.

## 121. afterwards

And so, just as we had informed people of the successful birth, we set about withdrawing the good news. Word spread, of course, bad news moving faster than good, and before long friends and colleagues gathered around. All were kind, their condolences sincere and well intentioned and yet I found myself becoming surly and sharp when they employed absurd euphemisms for our daughter's death. No, she had not 'passed away'. 'Passed over', 'passed on', 'departed' were equally repellent to me, and neither had we 'lost her'; we were all too aware of where she was. That she had 'left us' implied willingness on her part, 'taken away' implied some purpose or destination, and so I snapped at well-meaning friends and they apologised because what else could they do? Debate the point? Of course I regret my intolerance now, because the instinct to soften the language is a decent and humane one. The term the doctor had used was 'collapse'. The collapse had come very quickly, he said, and I could comprehend that word. But if someone had told us that she had 'gone to a better place' then I might well have struck them. 'Torn away' – that might have fitted better. Torn or ripped away.

Anyway, my surliness was unpleasant and unreasonable and there was, I suspect, a sense that I was 'not taking it well'. Grief is sometimes compared to numbness, though to begin with that was very far from our experience. Numbness would have been welcome. Instead we felt flayed, tormented, furious that the world was apparently carrying on. Connie in particular was prone to terrible rage, though for the most part she kept this private or directed it at me where it could do no harm.

'People keep telling me I'm young,' she said, in the calm after one such explosion. 'They say that there's plenty of time and we can have another baby. But I didn't want another baby. I wanted this one.'

So we were not gracious, we were not wise. We did not learn anything. We were ugly and angry, red-eyed and snot-nosed and mad, and so we kept ourselves to ourselves. Friends wrote letters, which we read and were thankful for, and then threw away. What else were we to do? Put them on the mantelpiece, like Christmas cards? The overwrought emotionalism of some of Connie's friends was particularly hard to bear. Shall we come and see you, they asked in tearful, hugging voices. No, we're fine, we said, and resolved to let the phone ring on next time. We were dragged into the daylight for the funeral, a brief and tormenting affair – what stories could we tell, what fond anecdotes about a personality so unformed? – and it occurred to me once again that grief is as much about regret for what you've never had as sadness for what you've lost. Anyway, we got through it somehow. Connie's mother was there, a few of her close friends, my sister. My father said he would come if I wanted him there, but I did not. We returned home immediately after the ceremony, took off our funeral clothes and went to bed, and for the next week or so that was where we stayed. We would lie around and sleep during the day, eat poor meals without tasting, watch television with our eyes fixed a little to the side. By then we were numb. I've never sleepwalked, so can't confirm the similarity, but we sat and stood, walked and ate without really being alive.

Sometimes Connie would wake in the night in tears. The grief of someone we love is terrible to see but Connie's sobbing was entirely animal and abandoned, and I wanted more than anything to make it stop. So I'd hold her until she fell asleep again, or we'd give up on sleep and watch the window together – it was summer, and the days were cruelly long – and during those dawn hours I would repeat a solemn promise.

Of course the promises we make at such times are all too often nonsense; the athlete swears that he will win this race and comes in eighth, the child promises to play the piano piece perfectly and fumbles in the first bar. Hadn't I sworn, in the delivery room, that I would look after my daughter and make sure no harm ever came to her? My wife and I had exchanged vows that had been broken within six months. Be kinder, work harder, listen more, tidy up, do what's right; perpetual resolutions that always crumble when exposed to the light of day, and what was the point of one more broken vow?

Nevertheless, I made the promise to myself. I swore that to the best of my ability I would look after her from now on. I would answer the phone and I would never hang up on her. I would do everything I could to make her happy and certainly I would never, never leave her. A good husband. I would be a good husband and I would not let her down.

## 122. blue

Time passed. I returned to work and endured the sympathy, Connie stayed at home and sank into something that we hesitated to call 'depression', or perhaps it was simply grief. 'Blue' was our rather winsome euphemism: she was 'feeling blue'. I'd call her from the lab, knowing she was there and knowing that she would not pick up. On the rare occasions that she did answer, her replies would be mumbled and monosyllabic, or irritable, or angry, and I would find myself wishing that she'd let the phone go on ringing. 'You feeling blue?' 'Yes. A little blue.' I'd try and carry on with work, sick with anxiety, sit silent and unhearing in departmental meetings, then at night I'd climb the stairs to the flat, hear the television playing far too loud and I would hesitate, key in hand. There were times, I must confess, when I contemplated turning around, walking back downstairs and out to . . . anywhere, really, other than that room.

But I never did. Instead I'd take a deep breath before opening the door to find her in old clothes, eyes red, lying on the sofa. Sometimes a bottle of wine would have been opened, sometimes emptied, or I would find that some mania had seized her and that she had embarked on a purifying task – painting all the cupboards yellow, clearing out the loft – the project abandoned halfway through. I'd repair the damage as best I could, cook food, something healthy, then join her on the sofa.

Here, I wish I could transcribe some speech I made to bring her out of this awful state, something about coming back to life or learning to live again. Perhaps it would have ended with a flourish – I could have thrown open the windows, perhaps, or found some inspiration in nature. Perhaps a good enough speech might have brought about some 'closure'. I tried to compose it, many times, lying awake at night; poetical variations on banal ideas, about optimism or seizing the day, something about the seasons. But I am not a maker of speeches, I lack the eloquence and the imagination, and after twenty years we have not come close to experiencing anything as simple and neat as closure. Even if it were available, I'm not sure if closure is something we have ever craved. Stop remembering or caring? To what end?

But I did sit and wait with her through the great unhappiness. We returned to life eventually and our marriage as I think of it now began around that time. We straightened our backs and began to leave the house, to go to films and exhibitions together. Ate dinner afterwards, began to talk once more. We didn't really laugh, not to begin with. It was enough to be able to answer the phone. Some of our more frivolous friends fell away during our seclusion, but that was all right. Other friends had started families of their own, and were wary of flaunting their good fortune. We understood, and we were happy to stay away. We would live a smaller, simpler life from now on.

Still finding herself unable to paint, Connie changed careers. The commercial gallery had never really pleased or satisfied her, and instead she began a part-time course in arts administration, which she loved. Alongside, she found work in the museum, learning the ropes of the education department, which she runs today with such success. In the autumn, a year after the day that we walked round and round the Serpentine, the two of us took a sleeper train once more to Skye, a place with no particular significance except that it was somewhere we both loved and somewhere we might have taken Jane. We woke early one morning, walked from our hotel to the shore in a steady rain, and scattered her ashes there.

The few photographs we had were placed in a drawer in our bedroom and looked at now and then. Each year we would acknowledge the anniversary of her arrival and departure, and continue to do so now. Occasionally Connie speculates on an imaginary future for our daughter – what she might have been like, her interests and talents. She does so without sentiment, mawkishness or tears. There's almost an element of bravado in it – like holding her palm over a candle flame, she does it to show how strong she has become. But I have always disliked this speculation, at least out loud. I listen, but I keep such thoughts to myself.

The following May, in a hotel on rue Jacob in Paris, our son was conceived and eighteen years later, I went to find him and to bring him home.

## 123. geographical separation

Though I was unlikely to find him here, in a pleasant little restaurant in the back streets of Venice. In fact, I must confess, Albie had rather slipped my mind. I was having too nice a time, shoulder to shoulder with an attractive and flirtatious Dane, both of us a little drunk now and overwhelmed by the wonderful seafood pasta, cold white wine and fresh fish, displayed to us before and after grilling, something that has already made me feel irrationally guilty . . .

'Why?'

'Because they show you this beautiful silver thing from the sea and you turn it into a pile of bones, and the head stares up at you saying, "Look, look what you've done to me!"'

'Douglas, you are a very strange man.'

Then strawberries and some sweet, syrupy liqueur, then, with wild abandon, coffee. Coffee! At night-time on a weekday!

'I'm going to have to walk this off, I think,' said Freja.

'A good idea.' We paid the bill, quite reasonable for Venice, splitting it fifty-fifty. I lavishly tipped our waiter, who stood shaking our hands, nodding, nodding, standing on tiptoe to kiss Freja on the cheek, indicating in vociferous Italian that I was a very lucky man, very *fortunato*.

'Now I think he's saying I have a very beautiful wife.'

'I'm sure you do, it's just it is not me.'

'I don't know how to explain that.'

'Perhaps it's easier to let him think I am your wife,' said Freja, and so that's what we did.

We walked back to the fine wide street of Via Garibaldi, still busy with local families eating in the pavement restaurants, then turned into a tree-lined processional avenue between grand villas. We walked, and perhaps it was the wine or the beauty of the evening or the medicated plasters, but I was barely aware of the blisters on my toes or the torn skin on the soles of my feet. I told Freja about today's breakthrough and my plan to lie in wait outside the hotel tomorrow.

'And what if he doesn't come?'

'A free hotel in Venice without his mum and dad? I'm sure he'll come.'

'Okay, what if he does? What then?'

We walked on.

'I'll ask him to come for a drink. I'll apologise. I'll say we've missed him and that I hope things will be better in the future.'

But even as I announced the plan, I sensed its inherent implausibility. Who were these two characters, father and son, frankly discussing their emotions? We had barely had a relaxed conversation since 'cow goes moo' and now here we were chatting about feelings over beer. 'Who knows, perhaps if we can patch things up I can get Connie to fly over, and we can carry on with the Grand Tour. There's still Florence, Rome, Pompeii, Naples. He can bring his girlfriend along if he wants. If not, I'll take him back to England.'

'And if he doesn't want to go back?'

'Then I have a chloroformed handkerchief and some strong rope. I'll rent a car and drive back with him in the boot.' Freja laughed, I shrugged. 'If he wants to travel on without us, that's fine. At least we'll know he's safe and well.'

We were at the apex of a high bridge now, looking east towards the Lido. 'I almost wish that I could wait with you, although I'm not sure how we would explain that to him.'

'"Albie, meet my new friend Freja. Freja, this is Albie."'

'Yes, that might be tricky.'

'It might.'

'For no reason!'

'No. For no reason,' I said, though when I looked down, it seemed that she had taken my hand, and we walked like this back along the Riva degli Schiavoni.

'And where are you heading tomorrow?' I said.

'I'm catching the train to Florence. I have tickets for the Uffizi the day after. Three nights in Rome, then Pompeii, Herculaneum, Capri, Naples. Almost the same route as you. Then in two weeks' time I fly back to Copenhagen from Palermo.'

'The holiday of a lifetime.'

She laughed. 'I certainly hope I never have to do it again.'

'Has it been that bad?'

'No, no, no. I've seen wonderful, beautiful things. Look at this, now – it is extraordinary.' We scanned the horizon, from the Lido to Giudecca where an illuminated ocean liner, as gargantuan as some intergalactic cruiser, set off for the Adriatic. 'And the art and the buildings, the lakes and the mountains. Wonderful things I'll never see again, but for the first time I'm seeing these things alone. I keep opening my mouth, and realising there's no need. Of course, I tell myself it's healthy and good for the soul, but I'm not sure yet that we're meant to be alone. Humans, I mean. It feels too much like a test, like surviving in the wilderness. It's a good experience to have, one is pleased to have succeeded, but it's still not the best. I miss company. I miss my girls, and my granddaughter. I'll be glad to get back home and to hold them.' She exhaled suddenly, rolled her head and shoulders as if shrugging something off. 'This is the most I've spoken in three weeks. It must be the wine! I hope you don't mind.'

'Not in the least.' Soon we were back at the *pensione*, standing on the threshold, facing each other.

'Today has been the best time of my trip, the gallery and then tonight. I'm sorry it has come so late for both of us.'

'Me too.'

A moment passed.

'I hope the ceiling doesn't spin when I lie down,' she said.

'So do I.'

Another moment.

'Well!'

'Well . . .'

'We both have an early start tomorrow. We should go to bed.'

'Sadly so.'

I opened the door but Freja didn't move, and I closed it again. She laughed, shook her head, then in a rush said:

'I hate to use alcohol as an excuse for anything but I don't know if I'd have said this sober and perhaps, given your situation, you don't care for the idea, but I hate the thought of you in that awful little room, and if you wanted to join me, for tonight, in my room, nothing . . . amorous, not necessarily, just for warmth – well, not warmth, it's too hot for warmth – for company, just a safe port, safe harbour, is that correct? Well, if you feel you could do that without guilt or anxiety, then I would be most delighted.'

'Yes,' I said. 'I'd like that very much.' And so that was what we did.

## 124. wild nights, wild nights

Well, that was a mistake.

Despite clinical exhaustion I did not sleep at all that night, though not for the reasons one might expect. Caffeine, wine and a whirring mind kept me awake, much more so than any erotic fervour. In fact Freja was asleep on my shoulder within minutes, her breath smelling strongly of booze and an unfamiliar brand of toothpaste, and while she didn't snore exactly, there was a certain amount of snuffling and gurgling and the crackle of something catching in her throat. Modesty and self-consciousness required that we both wore T-shirts, which made us uncomfortably warm, and the pressure of even a single cotton sheet on my ruined feet kept me twitching and straining, and sure enough, as the hours ticked by, the undoubted pleasures of the evening shaded into discomfort, guilt and anxiety. With the best will in the world, it was hard to see how lying pinned beneath this woman would save my marriage, and I was acutely aware that in the pocket of my trousers, folded on the chair, my phone remained switched off. Had Connie called back? What if there was news? What if she needed me? Was she lying awake too? As the radio alarm ticked over from three to four a.m. I abandoned any hope of sleep, eased my shoulder from beneath Freja's head and retrieved my phone.

The glare of a screen at four in the morning is a more effective stimulant than any espresso and within moments I was entirely alert. There were no messages, no texts or emails. Seeking reassurance, with a sentimental desire to see my son's face animated and smiling, I opened the link to the video of them singing 'Homeward Bound' in that unknown Venetian square. Their performance was more appealing with the sound muted, and I even noted a foolish longing look between them that I'd missed before. 'Maybe you should let them go,' Freja had said. 'Let him be.'

Impossible. I typed in *kat kilgour* once again, followed one or two dead ends and then, on an image-sharing website, found a virtual, visual diary of her travels. Photographs, many, many photographs. Here were Kat and Albie on the Rialto Bridge, pouting, cheeks pressed together, offering up their foreheads to the phone's fish-eye lens in that pose that has become standard these days. Here was a moody shot of Albie, posturing with his cheek against the neck of his guitar in moody black and white, the caption 'lover and friend, Albie Petersen' and a poorly punctuated commentary beneath from KK's friends and fans – *gorgeous!!! back off bitch hes mine, two thumbs up, bring him to sydney, hes easy on the eye damn gurl he beautiful* – my strange pride battling with bemusement at this brazen new world that Albie occupied, where ratings were accorded to everything, including the sexual attractiveness of strangers, and where no opinion went unexpressed. No inhibitions, no repression. *I would!* said one remark. That's all, just *I would!* What had happened to loaded conversations and drunken, whispered confidences in back-street trattorias? Good God, I thought, how might I have fared in a world where people were free to say what they felt?

And now here was Albie in a bed somewhere, his bony torso exposed, cigarette dangling like a French film star, and more comments of a personal nature. I could, I thought, have added one of my own without fear of discovery; chipped in with 'smoking is NOT cool' and pasted in a jpeg of a diseased lung, but instead I moved on, skimming past a photo of Kat sleeping on a railway platform, and now standing in front of the Tower of Pisa, pushing it back into alignment and I laughed, actually laughed at the thought of Albie succumbing to the temptation of that picture before catching myself and thinking –

The Tower of Pisa. That's not right.

The Tower of Pisa is not in Venice. It's in . . . well, it's in Pisa.

I looked at the photograph's date. Today – yesterday. I swore at the f-ing Tower of f-ing Pisa – and put my hand to my mouth.

I flicked back to the previous photograph, Kat on the train platform. The sign above the bench – Bologna. The caption:

*Venice u killed us man. 2 many tourists. On the road again!*

I swore louder this time, causing Freja to shift and mumble

in her sleep. I felt the panic rise in my chest. Stay calm. Perhaps it was a day trip! Where was Pisa exactly? A traveller's guide to Italy sat on the top of Freja's packed case. Bologna sat in the centre of Italy's thigh, but Pisa was in . . . Tuscany? I was not just in the wrong city, I was on the wrong coast.

I skimmed forward to the Pisa photos, Albie looking surly and bored on the long promenade of the Arno, head resting awkwardly on his guitar case. *Albie on a downer. keep moving on, moving on. sometimes travelling is hard, man. bone-tired. need a place where we can lay our heads.* So come back to Reading then, you silly boy! Next, a night-time shot, a photo of Albie arguing with a *carabinieri*, Albie's face caught in a sneer, the officer's eyes shaded beneath his cap. 'That's a policeman, Albie!' I wanted to shout. 'Don't argue with a policeman!' *Moved on by fascists* was all that Kat could say on the subject. What would the next photo bring? Albie bleeding from a truncheon blow? No, a stray cat drinking from the cap of a water bottle. *Night night kitty*, said the caption. *Siena tomorrow!*

Tomorrow. That meant today, this morning, in Siena. The current time was eight minutes past four. Gathering my trousers up in my arms, dangling the evil shoes from my fingertips, I tiptoed to the door.

## 125. a letter to freja kristensen, posted beneath her door

*Dear Freja,*
*I believe this is called a 'French exit' – leaving without saying goodbye. I wonder if that is an idiom that you're aware of? You know all the others. It seems rather dramatic, I know, and possibly a little rude, and I do hope that you are not offended. But you looked so peaceful sleeping there and I did not want to wake you.*

*The reason for my hasty departure is that I have what we detectives call a 'hot lead' on my son's whereabouts and I need to travel the width of Italy before lunch. Who knows if I will make it in time, or if the trip will prove futile, but I feel an obligation to try. I hope that, as a parent yourself, you will understand.*

*My other reason for not waking you was that I wasn't sure what I would say, and felt I stood a better chance of successfully conveying my thoughts on paper, even at this early hour. I thought very hard about leaving a phone number or address at the top of this page, but to what end? I so enjoyed our conversation last night, but it also served to remind me why I am here in the first place, and certain promises and obligations that I carry with me.*

*So while it seems unlikely that we will ever meet again, this in no way reflects my warmth of feeling towards you, or my gratitude. You are an extremely interesting, intelligent and compassionate woman, with superb vocabulary. While I have no belief in fate or destiny, I was extremely lucky to have bumped into you at a difficult point in my journey. You are extremely good company and also, I might add, an extremely attractive woman, grandmother or no! Part of me would have enjoyed travelling on with you to Florence and Rome and Naples, though sadly this cannot be.*

*But I hope you enjoy the rest of your holiday and, looking to the future, I hope you find happiness, on your own or with someone new, and continue to take pleasure in your beautiful children and grandchildren. For my part, I will always remember the day we spent in each other's company, will always think of you fondly and with immense gratitude as well as, I suspect, a certain degree of regret.*

*With very best wishes,*
  *Douglas Petersen*

## 126. departure at dawn

Sunrise found the city abandoned. I hurried through silent streets and squares, encountering not a single soul until the Strada Nuova, where the office cleaners, the hotel workers and waiters on the early shift stumbled along, heads down, inured to the rosy light, the beauty of this place. My one thought now was to leave.

I caught the first train to Florence with three minutes to spare, scalding my hand with the two double espressos that I'd deemed essential to this journey, along with some kind of pastry, greasy as a bag of chips. I wiped my hands on a tiny napkin that disintegrated immediately, then we were out into the startling daylight, the train sliding gingerly along the causeway that connects Venice umbilically to the mainland. To my left, the strangest sight: cars.

The mainland suburbs of Venice were scrappy and dull and I set my alarm for two hours hence, and closed my eyes in the hope of sleep. But the four ill-considered shots of espresso put paid to this ambition and I found the words of my note to Freja running around my head. She would be waking now, finding the note beneath the door, reading it and feeling – what? Embarrassment? Regret? Irritation? Amusement at my misreading of events? Would she give a wry, wise smile as she placed it in the folds of her guidebook, or tear it smartly in two? Perhaps I should have said goodbye in person after all. A thought occurred.

Unlike with Albie, I knew exactly where Freja would be today. In two hours' time she would be sitting on this very train, looking out at parched suburban gardens, industrial estates and generic office blocks and, like me, regretting that second bottle of wine, and I might easily wait for her at the station in Florence, perhaps with a small gift of flowers. We could exchange a few words and an email address – 'let's keep in touch, just as friends' – and I could still make it to Siena by the afternoon.

Or, more fantastically, I might abandon my quest completely and stay with her for as long as that lasted. Hurl my phone from the train window into the lagoon, leave Albie to his fate, let my wife do what she wanted. Hadn't Connie always been the instinctive, passionate one? And hadn't I earnt the right, after all these years of diligence and reliability, to one last fit of selfish spontaneity?

But the trouble with living in the moment is that the moment passes. Impulse and spontaneity take no account of the longer term, of responsibilities and obligations, debts to be paid, promises to fulfil. I had lost sight of the people I cared for, and it was vital now that I turn my attention once again to the task in hand, rescuing my son and winning back my wife.

And so I decided to forget about Freja Kristensen, and continue with my journey.

part six

# TUSCANY

—

Richard suddenly saw his father as a young man, full of
ambitious plans for his son, and he wondered if he had ever
danced his child on his knee, hurried home from work to do
so; if he felt this fierce protectiveness.

It was one of the strangest ideas Richard had ever had,
and it made him uneasy.

Elizabeth Taylor, *The Soul of Kindness*

## 127. florence in thirty-six minutes flat

Thirty-six minutes. This was the time I had allowed to see the jewel of the Renaissance and still safely make my connection on to Siena. A challenge, I realised, but it would be fun, too, a chance to clear my head of Venice and the night before, and so I hopped from the train and deposited my bag in the *deposito bagagli*, a piece of Italian that sounded, frankly, made up. I set the alarm on my phone and strode out into the petroleum haze of the station square, past the shabby tourist shops and snack bars, the dubious hostels, multiple pharmacies and Bureaux de Change – who still needs a Bureau de Change, I wondered, in this age of the international cashpoint card? Never mind that, at the end of the street I glimpsed a sliver of the famous Duomo, startling in its scale and intricacy even at a distance, but there was no time, no time, eight minutes on the clock already, and so with one eye on the tourist information map, I strode to the right, past phone shops and stalls selling tacky leather goods under graceful arches, zigzagging to a great square – the Piazza della Signoria, my map told me – dominated by a crenellated fortress, the kind a child might make from a cardboard box and, to the right, a cluster of immense statues like the pieces from some deranged game of chess; gods, lions and dragons, warriors with raised swords and severed heads, another naked soldier dying extravagantly in his comrade's arms, screaming women, a naked, psychotic man with a truncheon clubbing a centaur to death and, watching over all of this surreal ultra-violence with fey distaste, Michelangelo's *David*. Fifteen minutes gone now, and my guidebook had informed me that this was only a reproduction so I noted the disproportionate size of the hands and walked on towards the Uffizi Gallery. It was not yet ten in the morning and already an immense queue of people stretched beneath the colonnade, fanning themselves with hotel maps while living statues of, incomprehensibly, the Statue of Liberty and an Egyptian pharaoh, stood on crates beneath the marble images of Giotto, Donatello and Pisano. Nineteen minutes gone, and now here was a woman in a pink body-stocking and a long blonde wig, balanced upon a papier-mâché clamshell for the amusement of the weary queue while tantalisingly, in the elegant galleries above our heads, was the real thing, hanging alongside Uccellos and Caravaggios and da Vincis, Titian's famous *Venus of Urbino* and three – three! – Rembrandt self-portraits. Connie had been here to the Uffizi as a student, had talked yearningly about returning – a little jewel, she said, very cool and beautiful – and like a smart traveller, I had pre-booked tickets for four days hence, and it occurred to me, as the timer showed nineteen minutes, that if this afternoon's reunion with Albie went well, we might still make our booking! Perhaps my son and I could travel around some Tuscan hill towns then rendezvous with Connie right here. 'They should call it the "Queue-ffizi!" I'd quip as we strolled past the hordes of less canny, less forward-thinking tourists. 'You pre-booked – great idea, Dad!' Albie would say, and standing in front of *Primavera* once again, Connie would take my hand. 'Thank you, Douglas!' she'd say, and all my care and preparation would be vindicated. No time to daydream, though – twenty minutes had gone now. I strode towards the river, hoping for a glimpse of the Ponte Vecchio, but now the alarm was sounding on my phone, meaning that I had fourteen minutes to return to the station and for the moment I would have to settle for seeing only the queue for the Uffizi, one thin slice of the great Duomo, an artificial *David*, a living statue *Venus*. Seen in twenty-two minutes, Florence was a Botticelli fridge magnet in a tan leather handbag, but never mind, we'd be back as a family. I retraced my steps and at twenty-nine minutes the station was in sight again. Breathless, sleep-deprived, perspiring quite heavily, I resolved to stop alternating strong coffee with alcohol and to rest on the Siena train, settling smugly into my seat on the 1010 with a comfortable three minutes to spare. I listened to the train announcement. Montelupo-Capraia, Empoli, Castelfiorentino, San Gimignano; even the names were picturesque. I would be in Siena by 1138, about the time that Albie would be getting out of bed. I closed my eyes, reclined my seat as far as it would go – the pleasures of European rolling stock! – and watched the outskirts of the city go by, feeling my eyelids growing heavy then realising, with a start, that I had left all of my belongings in the left-luggage office of Santa Maria Novella station.

## 128. the siena train

I had no change of clothes or footwear. I had no money, save the notes and coins in my pocket, twenty-three euros and eighty cents. No passport, no guidebook, no toothbrush nor razor, tablet or phone charger. I had my phone, of course, but because I had not slept in my own room last night the power stood at 18 per cent, and now suddenly here was a whole series of texts that Connie had sent, arriving all at once like a hail of stones:

> where are you? why did you hang up on me?
> you sounded strange I'm worried about you D. please call
> I'm not angry I'm worried. First egg now you.
> I'm coming out to find you. please just tell me where you
> are. tell me you are safe.
> please let me know you are safe and well.

I pressed reply then hesitated, no longer quite sure if I was.

## 129. a glass, full to the brim

Understandably, the months leading up to the due date were anxious, with Connie prone to all kinds of irrational fears about her health and her abilities. I did my best to reassure her that all would be well this time. Connie was determined, strong, able, brave; who could be better at this? But our confidence, our complacency had been cruelly exposed before and so we were cautious to the point of paranoia. Vitamins, oils and tonics, an organic diet, meditation, yoga – all played their part. Most of it was mumbo-jumbo, of course, based on the fallacious conviction that we – she – had done something wrong the last time, but it eased Connie's mind so I kept quiet. Still, there was less of the boisterous good humour of the first pregnancy. Imagine carrying a glass, full to the brim, around for thirty-six weeks without spilling a drop. Caution, care, a contrived and fragile serenity. A certain sadness, too.

But it's hard to stay sad or serene in the sweaty, bloody mess of that shocking business of birth. The first contractions came at two in the morning, the first but not the last time Albie would wake us at that hour. 'Tell me that it's going to be all right,' Connie demanded as we paced the delivery room, her fingernails digging deep into my palm. 'Of course it is,' I said, because what else could I say?

But it was all right, it was. For there to be another catastrophe would have been too cruel, and Albie came easily, almost before we knew it (though Connie may take a different view on this). By nine a.m. I was father to a son, and of course he was beautiful too. Even purple-faced and smeared with that nameless gunk, he was lovely – strong-featured, with his mother's black, black hair. As the frightening colour of his skin faded, as his features settled into repose and his curious eyes opened, a new word suggested itself: handsome. A handsome boy, as handsome as his sister had been beautiful. I held him through the morning while Connie slept, sitting up in a vinyl chair beside her bed, winter sun on his face and, God, I loved him. Had my own father held me like this? He was of the generation that had been encouraged to read magazines and smoke in the waiting room, offspring only presented to them when the mess and gore of birth had been swabbed away. I was old enough to recall my sister being brought home from hospital and the awkwardness with which he'd held her, how reluctant he had seemed, shifting his cigarette from one hand to another, keen to pass her on. Extraordinary to think he was a medical man, too; someone who should have handled flesh and blood with ease, especially his own. Well, I would not be like that, I decided. I would maintain an easy, relaxed demeanour around my son – good God, 'my son', I had a son – and we would be such good friends.

We transported him home with neurotic care, almost literally wrapped in cotton wool. The visitors who had come to sympathise now came to celebrate and we accepted the cards and gifts and congratulations, with their hint of consolation, with good grace. We listened to his crying in the night with weary relief. Connie's mother moved in to lend a hand, and my sister became a constant presence, regressing to coos and gurgles and knitting awful little cardigans, and I did what I was required to do, keeping the kettle on a rolling boil, tidying, cleaning and shopping, slipping once more into that persona of the endlessly capable butler, taking my turn to rise in the night and have Albie scream into my ear. I gave myself instructions. Remain positive, enthusiastic, loving and full of care. Keep a watchful eye and make sure no harm comes to either of them. More resolutions.

## 130. the caring professions

When Albie was sturdy enough, we drove below the speed limit to the small flat my father had moved to after my mother's death, pleasant enough when he'd arrived but now dark and rather bleak, with an ashtray smell and nothing in the fridge. Boxes remained unpacked, pictures were not yet hung, and it felt like a storeroom for a former life rather than a home for the future. Having retired early from his surgery, my father spent his days reading thrillers or watching old black-and-white movies in the afternoon, subsisting on instant coffee and cigarettes and occasional plates of baby-ish food – scrambled eggs, baked beans, packet soups; as a GP, he had always led by instruction rather than example.

He had never been a particularly vigorous man, but as soon as he opened the door it was clear he was not thriving alone. His teeth were furred and his skin pale and unevenly shaved with wiry hair sprouting on his cheeks, from his ears and the tip of his nose. For the first time in my life I was aware of being taller than him. Of course he smiled at his grandchild, cooed and remarked on the size of Albie's fingernails, his hair and eyes. 'He looks like you, Connie, thank God!' he said and laughed, but he was not at ease. He held his grandson as if assessing his weight, then passed him back and there it was again; the wariness, the discomfort.

But then he was never a natural candidate for the caring professions. As a GP, he tended to view all but the most serious of ailments as signs of carelessness or neglect, and I think he frightened many of his patients into good health. I remember once, on a family holiday to Anglesey, scraping my shin against a piece of corrugated iron, looking down and seeing the skin hanging there, perfectly white, like waxy paper in the moment before the blood began to flow, and I remember my father sighing at the sight, as if I'd taken the paintwork off the family car. The fact that it had been an accident was irrelevant. If I hadn't been playing, it wouldn't have happened. He issued sympathy with the same reluctance that he prescribed antibiotics.

I did not feel hard done by. My father was exactly as I expected dads to be: a professional man, able and confident and somewhat withdrawn, but serious about his obligations to provide materially for his family. Dads had favourite armchairs in which they sat like starship captains, issuing orders and receiving cups of tea and shouting at the news without fear of contradiction. Dads controlled the television, the telephone and thermostat, they decided mealtimes, bedtimes, holidays. Raised in an anarcho-socialist republic, Connie and her family were always bellowing and bawling at each other about music and politics, sex and digestion, but my own father and I never had anything that you might call an intimate conversation and I'm not entirely sure I ever wanted one. He taught me how to use a slide-rule and how to change a bicycle inner tube, but he was no more likely to embrace me than to break into a tap-dance.

That was a long, uncomfortable afternoon we spent with my father. I had such strutting pride in the new family we had made. *Look*, I wanted to say, *look, I have found this wonderful woman, or she has found me. We have experienced things, terrible things, but here we are holding hands, right here on your sofa. Look at the way I carry my son, the way I change nappies with confidence and ease! No offence, I am profoundly grateful, but I am not like you.*

Oh, the smugness and complacency of the new parent! See how *good* we are! Let us show you how it should be done! I'm sure my parents had wanted to teach their own parents similar lessons, and so on back into history and forward, too; I'm sure that some day Albie will be keen to settle some scores and give me some pointers as to where we – I – went wrong. But perhaps it's a delusion for each generation to think that they know better than their parents. If this were true, then parental wisdom would increase with time like the processing power of computer chips, refining over generations, and we'd now be living in some utopia of openness and understanding.

'Well, we'd best be going,' I told my dad that evening, refusing his offer of a night in the spare room, which was crammed with cardboard boxes, a single bulb overhead. 'I'll turn the radiator on,' he offered as an incentive. 'No, it's a long drive back,' I said, though we all knew that it wasn't. Perhaps I imagined this to ease my conscience, but he seemed relieved and turned the news back on before we left. *Goodbye, Dad! Goodbye! Albie, give Granddad a wave! Goodbye, we'll see you soon!*

My father died six weeks later. Of course I have no belief in an afterlife, least of all the one depicted in newspaper cartoons, but if he was looking down from some cloud on to the Siena train, he might, I suppose, be allowed one of his old favourite remarks:

*You see? You see? Not so bloody clever now!*


## 131. tartaric acid

I fell into something of a low.

It was not merely the loss of my belongings – they were, after all, perfectly safe and retrievable – but my increasing loss of control. It had been some time since I'd spoken to Connie. I missed hearing her voice but did not quite trust my own. I was sure Siena would mark some kind of turning point, and I would speak to her when there was good news. But if there was no good news, how could I go home?

At Empoli, I was joined at my table by a little boy in a striped vest, three years old, perhaps, travelling with his grandparents who

were large and jovial, full of proud smiles as they watched the boy
lay out the contents of a small bag of sweets, twelve artificially
coloured jellies, four red, eight blue, sprinkled with the tartaric
acid that causes them to fizz on the tongue. He counted them,
then counted them again. He divided them into rows and columns,
three by four, two by six, showing that instinctive pleasure in play
that seems to disappear as soon as we call it mathematics. He
licked the tip of his finger and dabbed at the sweet-sharp sugar
that had become detached, making a great show of choosing which
sweet to eat first. I watched him quite openly, perhaps a little too
openly for this day and age. He was aware of giving a performance
and when he finally settled on a red sweet, popped it into his
mouth and puckered his lips at the tartness of it, I laughed and
we both laughed together, his grandparents too, nodding, smiling.

He said something to me in burbling Italian. '*Inglese*,' I replied,
'*no parlo Italiano*,' and he nodded as if this made sense and slid
a blue sweet towards me, arm fully extended, and the gesture
seemed so generous and so familiar that I thought, *Oh God, it's
Albie. It's exactly how Albie used to be.*

## 132. the 'record' button

Because he really was a charming little boy, like a kid from a
comic, full of benign mischief. There were difficult days, of
course, particularly in the early months. Croup! He caught croup,
a disease designed by nature specifically to terrify parents, and
there were further panics to come, over mysterious rashes or
inexplicable tears, our nerves perpetually jangled from lack of
sleep. But we bore all of this gladly and with only the occasional
loss of composure, because hadn't we yearned for this disruption
in our lives? I returned to work, half regretful, half grateful for
some respite, then came home and did my bit to bathe and feed
him, and the days and weeks and months went by.

At some point around this time, he must have begun acquiring first memories. I hope so, anyway, because it's hard to imagine a child who was more adored and cared for by parents who, for the most part, got on incredibly well. The inability to control a child's recollections is a frustrating one. I know my own parents did their best to provide sun-dappled days of picnics and paddling pools, but mainly I remember advertising jingles, wet socks on radiators, inane TV theme tunes, arguments about wasted food. With my own son, there were times when I definitely thought 'remember this' – Albie toppling through the high grass of a summer meadow, the three of us lolling in bed on a winter Sunday or dancing around the kitchen to some silly song – wishing there was some way to press 'record', because the three of us were, for the most part, pretty good together, a family at last.

## 133. the scientific basis for unconditional love

We were sharing a bath one night, at a time when we did such things, Albie lying between his mother's legs, head resting on her belly, and I made an observation that, while all of us might sometimes covet other people's lives, their careers, their spouses (I coveted no one's spouse, but knew from experience that others coveted mine), it was extremely rare – unheard of, even, and certainly taboo – to prefer someone else's children to your own. Everyone thinks their own child is delightful, yet not all children are delightful, so why are parents unaffected by that? What is the reason for this fixed and unshakeable bond: neurological, sociological, genetic? Perhaps, I suggested, we're hard-wired to love our own children over others as a kind of survival mechanism, for the propagation of the species.

Connie frowned. 'You mean the love you feel for your child is not real, it's just science.'

'Not at all. It's real *because* it's science! The way you feel about friends or lovers or even siblings is dependent and conditional on their behaviour. With your children, that's irrelevant. It doesn't matter what they do. People with bratty kids don't love them less, do they?'

'No, they teach them not to be bratty.'

'And that's the difference – they stick with them and even if they don't succeed, even if they stay brats, they'd still give their life for them.'

'Albie's not bratty.'

'No, he's lovely. But everybody thinks their own children are lovely, even when they're not.'

'And they shouldn't?'

'Of course they should! But that's what people mean by "unconditional love".'

'Which apparently you think is a bad thing?'

'No—'

'Or an illusion, a "behavioural instinct".'

'No, I'm just . . . thinking aloud.'

We both went silent for a while. The bath was cooling now but getting out would have felt like conceding a point.

'What a stupid thing to say in front of Albie!'

I laughed. 'He's eighteen months old! He doesn't understand.'

'And I suppose you know that, too.'

'I was thinking aloud, that's all.'

'The eminent child psychologist,' she said, rising suddenly from the bath, Albie in her arms.

'I was thinking out loud! It was just a theory.'

'Well I don't need a *theory*, Douglas,' she said, wrapping him in a towel and bundling him away. My wife has always had a gift for effective exit lines. I lay alone in the bath for some time, feeling the water grow more tepid around me. *She's tired*, I thought, *it's nothing*, and sure enough the debate was forgotten almost instantly by everyone except me.

At least I presume she has forgotten it.

## 134. lego incident

But from the beginning there was never any doubt that she was better at it all, so much more competent, kind and patient, never bored in that dull old playground, never reaching for a newspaper, happy to watch the twentieth, twenty-first, twenty-second trip down the slide. Is there anything duller than pushing a swing? Yet she never seemed resentful – or only occasionally – of the hours and days and weeks that he consumed, the attention he demanded, the irrational tears, the trail of destruction and spilt paint and mashed carrot that he left behind, never repulsed or angered by the vomit that stained our new sofa, the poo that found its way into the cracks between the floorboards and is still there now, I expect, at some molecular level. As Albie got older, his devotion to his mother became more and more blatant and extreme. In early years this circumstance is so commonplace as to be barely worth acknowledging. Strain as he might, even the most fervent father lacks the ability to breast-feed, and the paternal bonding would come later, wouldn't it, over chemistry sets and model planes, camping trips and driving lessons? He would beat me at badminton and in return I'd show him how to make a battery out of a lemon. In the meantime, there seemed little to do, except wait patiently for the day we became close.

But increasingly I seemed to have a particular gift for upsetting him, standing awkwardly while he wriggled and writhed in my arms, waiting for Connie to relieve me. Without her there, we were both on edge. The journey from baby to toddler will involve a certain number of mishaps, but something about her absence made him tumble and trip so that even now there are scars and dents that Connie can point to and attribute to me. There, that's the coffee-table incident; that's the fall from the tree; that's the ceiling-fan affair. And always, always, his arms would stretch towards his mother on her return because he knew he would be safe.

All my best intentions seemed to backfire, and even my loving nicknames didn't stick. Connie invented Egg, as in Albie/albumen/egg white/Egg, a pleasing name that seemed to fit. Noting the somewhat simian way he clung to his mother's hip, I made a play for 'Monkey' but it didn't take, and I abandoned it after a week or two. Then there was the incident with the Lego, an episode that has since passed into Petersen folklore as an illustration of . . . I don't quite know what, because my behaviour always seemed entirely reasonable to me. Needless to say I was raised on Lego, which was a rather more rigorous and austere toy in my day but nevertheless something of a secret vice for me; that satisfying click, the symmetry, the neat tessellations. Maths, engineering, design – they were all there disguised as play, and so I looked forward to the day when Albie and I could sit shoulder to shoulder in front of a tea-tray, open the cellophane bag, turn to page one and build!

Yet Albie's technique just wasn't there. He seemed incapable of following the simplest instructions, happy instead to jam different-coloured pieces together at random, to chew the pieces so that they became unusable, gum them up with Plasticine, drop them behind the radiator, throw them at the wall. If I constructed something on his behalf – a police station say, or an elaborate spaceship – he would smash the toy to pieces within minutes and make instead some nameless, formless thing to shove down the back of the sofa. Set after set expired this way, a perfectly good toy turned into detritus for the vacuum cleaner.

One night, motivated entirely by a desire to give my son something lasting and permanent to play with, I waited until he and Connie were in bed, poured myself a large Scotch, mixed together some Araldite adhesive in a jam-jar lid, laid the instructions before me and carefully glued together a pirate ship, a troll castle and an ambulance. Now, instead of a box of expensive shingle, here were three terrific, long-lasting toys. I displayed them on the kitchen table and went to bed, anticipating much acclaim.

The tears and wailing that woke me the next morning were therefore something of a disappointment, and certainly quite out of proportion to my crimes. But look, I told Albie, now they'll last forever! Now they won't smash! But he doesn't want them to last forever, said Connie, consoling tearful Albie, he wants to smash them, that's the point! That's what's creative about them. That destruction could be creative seemed like one of those things artists say, but I let the point go and went off to the lab, sour and frustrated, the pleasures of Lego quite lost to us now. The offending articles were stashed away in a high cupboard, the story materialising years later as an anecdote at dinner, signifying . . . what, exactly? A lack of imagination on my part, a lack of creativity, I suppose. Lack of fun. Oh yes, they remembered *that*.

Anyway, the anecdote always seemed to get a big laugh, and as a father I have learnt to develop a thick skin and appreciate jokes at my expense. Nobody would ever have dared to laugh at my own father and this is progress, I suppose, of a sort.

## 135. siena

Certainly the boy on the Siena train found me engaging enough and by the time we arrived at my destination we were firm friends, nodding away at each other, nodding, nodding. I was grateful for the sweet he offered me and would gladly have gorged on all of them, because who knew when I would eat again? But we were pulling into Siena. *Ciao, ciao!* Say goodbye to the nice crazy man. I shook the sticky fingers of the boy's hand and stepped out into the brutal heat of a Tuscan noon.

The bus that shuttled into the old town was packed and I was aware of how smugly unencumbered I felt amidst the backpacks and suitcases, as free and light as a recently escaped lunatic. Now we were passing through a mediaeval gate, now disembarking, the suitcases rumbling behind me as I hurried ahead, through another gate and then, without any expectation, out into the bright light of an immense piazza, a fan divided into nine slim wedges like a peacock's tail or a tin of Scottish shortbread, radiating from an immense Gothic palace, the whole scene baked a terracotta red. Quite, quite overwhelming, and heartening too, because Siena was a walled town, compact and self-contained, and if Venice was a maze, this was a shoebox. The Piazza del Campo was inescapable, with a clear focal point at its base. Like ants beneath a magnifying glass, it would be impossible for Kat and Albie to avoid passing before me. Optimistic, alert, I chose a spot on the herringboned bricks about halfway down the slope, pulled my baseball cap down over my eyes and promptly fell asleep.

## 136. the reunion

I woke a little after three and swore so extravagantly that the tourists turned to stare. How could I have been so stupid? Struggling to my feet, I found that I could barely stand. In my exhaustion, my head had lolled to one side and the right side of my face and neck had the familiar tightness that precedes sunburn. I stumbled, then sat once again on the hot bricks. Three hours! Three hours in which I felt almost certain they had passed me by. I had a perfect image of Albie stepping over me, collapsed here like some drunk. My mouth was dry while my clothes dripped with perspiration – I had left a damp patch on the ground where the bricks had drawn the remaining moisture from my body – and my head throbbed with what surely must be sunstroke. Water, I must have water. I tried to stand again, resting on my toes a moment then staggering up the sides of the sun-baked terracotta bowl, like Lawrence of Arabia clambering up a dune.

In a kiosk at the edge of the square I paid an extortionate amount of money for two bottles of water, draining one and half of the other before stopping to take in my reflection in the mirrored wall. A vertical line divided the crimson half of my face and neck from the white, while across my forehead the shade of the baseball cap had created an equator. My face had been stencilled by the sun into something resembling the Danish flag. I touched the skin – the tenderness told me there was worse to come – and laughed, the kind of laughter that precedes great sobbing tears, and stepped out into the heat.

I felt faint, nauseous, irrational. Returning to the cauldron of the piazza was inconceivable, but there was no hotel room to lie down in and only twelve euros in my pocket, not even enough to get me back to Florence where my wallet and passport were even now accumulating fines. Instead I staggered through the crowds, water bottle in my hand, dizzy and deranged, clinging to the shade like a vampire, with scarcely a rational thought in my head, until the street opened up into a courtyard, the ornate candy-striped façade of the Duomo rising up vertically. A sudden clamour of bells from the *campanile* raised every eye to the sky and then, even louder than the church bells, I heard the celestial sound of Kat Kilgour playing 'Beat It' on her accordion.

I waited until the final chords before I stepped forward and threw my arms around her. 'Kat Kilgour!' I said, through cracked lips. 'I am so, so pleased to see you!'

'Jeez, Mr Petersen,' she said, recoiling a little. 'You look completely f***** up.'

Yes, it was an emotional reunion on my part, but I still wish the police hadn't got involved.

## 137. sweet child of mine

I'm loath to throw around terms like 'brutality'. It was all a misunderstanding, or perhaps an overreaction on their part, and mine too. If I'd been more level-headed I'd have handled the situation differently. Nevertheless . . .

'Kat, you have no idea what I've been through.'

I was undeniably pleased to see her, a great deal more than she was pleased to see me, because she was already launching into her next number, an anthemic 'Sweet Child of Mine'. It's a demanding vocal so I waited patiently until the instrumental, then:

'Kat, I need to see Albie. Is he with you?'

'Can't talk, Mr P.—'

'No, quite, but I need to know if he's all right. Maybe later?'

'Can't talk, Mr P.—'

'Oh. Okay. Okay. I'm sorry, you're playing your solo, but if I could just know where—'

'He's not here.'

'But nearby? Yes? Yes?' She began the next verse, and it seemed only fair that I should drop my coins into her bowler hat. 'If you could just point me in the right direction?' A five, a ten euro note followed, the last of my cash all gone. I began to search my pockets for more coins. 'Kat, I'll leave you alone, but I've travelled a very long way and . . .'

The song ended, but she embarked immediately on 'Riders on the Storm', and if she started that then she might never stop.

'Kat, I am actually paying you to stop playing!' I shouted, and here I put my hand into the bellows of the accordion, which was too much, I concede now. Certainly, Kat's response was violent, the song abandoned, a finger jabbed in my face.

'Do NOT touch, Mr P.! If your son wants to hide from you, then it's none of your business—'

'Well, it sort of is—'

'I know all too well what it's like to live with an oppressive, overbearing father—'

'*Oppressive?* I'm not oppressive.'

'. . . and even if your son's not my favourite person at the moment, I would never split on him. Never!'

'Not your favourite . . . why, have you argued?'

'I think that's a fair assessment.'

'Have you . . . have you split up?'

'Yes, we've split up! Try to conceal your glee, Mr P.'

'When?'

'Last night, if you must know.'

'So, so where is he? Where did he go? Kat, please tell me . . .' And here I put my hand on her arm, which was also a mistake.

'Get off me!' she shouted, and I began to sense the hostility of the small crowd who had so enjoyed 'Sweet Child of Mine'. 'I've told you, it is none of your business what Albie does and . . . oh, jeez.' She looked over my shoulder. 'Here we go again.'

It seemed our discussion had attracted the attention of two *carabinieri*, large, handsome men in pale blue short-sleeve shirts heading straight towards us. Kat knelt down and began hurriedly cramming her takings into the tight pockets of her cut-off jeans.

'Don't worry, I'll talk to them.'

'It's not you they're interested in, it's me.'

And sure enough, the police went straight for Kat, one on each side, speaking rapidly in urgent voices. A crowd was gathering around us now, and I heard mention of permits, of local regulations, Kat talking over them in a weary and impertinent tone – exactly the wrong tone, I thought, to adopt when speaking to armed officers. 'Yeah, I know, I need a permit . . . No, I don't have one, as you well know . . . Fine, okay, you've made your point, I'll pack up and be gone . . .' She bundled her accordion like a child to her chest and attempted to put her head down and slip away, but the larger of the policemen, broad, bullet-headed, placed one hand on her shoulder and reached for a notepad. 'How can I pay a fine if you won't let me earn any—? No, I will not empty my pockets! No! Get stuffed, you bastards! Get your hands off me!' And now the crowd was parting as the policemen marched Kat towards the car that would take her away, and with her all clues to Albie's whereabouts.

'No!' I said. 'No, no, no, no, you can't do this!' and I hurried after them.

I wish I could pretend that gallantry prompted me to inter-vene, rather than self-interest, but Kat was my last hope, my only link to Albie, and so I found myself squeezing between the policemen, placing my hand on an arm, trying to loosen the grip – not aggressively, I thought, but coaxingly. To an outsider, this might have resembled a scuffle, and it's true that I was not calm. 'Stay out of it, Mr P.!' shouted Kat over her shoulder, but I was attached now. 'That isn't necessary!' I was shouting. 'You're overreacting! No necessary, no overreact!' I was tugging on the larger policeman's forearm, noticing by the by that, like many bald men, he had extremely hairy arms and also a very elborate watch, four little dials on its face, like scuba divers wear and I wondered, as he spun me around and slipped and tightened one of those plastic ties around my wrists, the kind I use at home to tidy the cables behind the TV, if he went diving at weekends.

## 138. the jailbird

As a child I had sometimes wondered how I might fare in the prison environment. It was a concern that followed me into adulthood, and I came to the conclusion: not well. Of course, the situation was unlikely ever to arise. True, I had recently stolen a packet of Soft Mints from the newsagents in Munich airport, but surely this was beyond the jurisdiction of Italy's legal system, and besides, the evidence was long gone. So I felt reasonably calm as I sat at the desk of Siena's main police station. What, after all, was my crime?

Nevertheless, I seemed to cause quite a stir. Who was this mystery man? What kind of tourist has no passport or driving licence, no wallet, no money or keys or hotel reservations? Lack of ID, it seemed, marked me down as some sort of desperate character, which was accurate, though not in the way they imagined. I explained that all would be clear if I could just borrow some money and pop back to Firenze, and that I'd then be happy to pay any fine, my own and Kat's too, but no one seemed willing to offer up the fare and neither was I permitted to leave. A connection had been made between Kat and myself. Despite my protests, they insisted on calling her my girlfriend. I can only imagine how Kat must have felt about that.

Gradually, the desk staff lost interest, directing me to a chair in the waiting room and leaving me there. Kat was somewhere in the offices behind the desk and it seemed my punishment would be to wait for her, to wait and wait for hours on end, on hard plastic chairs, as a parade of tourists – legitimate tourists with even tans and passports – came in to report lost luggage, wallets, cameras, in order that they could claim insurance. Of course I would wait – what choice did I have? At least I was out of the sun.

But it was early evening by the time they finally reunited me with my 'girlfriend', demanding that she also take a seat and wait. Kat was unwilling at first to acknowledge my presence, but finally:

'Nice trainers, Mr P.'

'Thank you.'

'What happened to your face?'

'Hm? Oh, this. I fell asleep in the sun.'

'Looks sore.'

'It is. It is.'

'Did you tell them about me stealing that croissant from the breakfast buffet?'

I held my hands out to the side, palms upwards. 'Hey, I'm no stoolie,' I said, quite the comedian.

She smiled. 'You shouldn't have got involved back there.'

'They did overreact a little, I thought.'

'Occupational hazard. You're meant to have a permit, but it's a bureaucratic *nightmare*. Also, they know me here, I'm a bit of a repeat offender, so . . .'

'I was scared they were going to take you away.'

'Very noble of you, I'm sure.'

'I was thinking of myself, really.'

'You mustn't take this the wrong way, Mr P., but you don't smell too good.'

'No. No, I'm aware of that. I'd keep your distance if I were you.'

She smiled and moved one chair closer. 'I still can't tell you where he is.'

'But can you at least tell me he's okay?'

'Define "okay". He's a very troubled boy, your Albie.'

'Yes, clearly.'

'He's quite . . . dark.'

'I know that—'

'Very angry. Very, very angry. He has a lot of issues. A lot. With you, I mean. He talks about you a lot.'

'Does he?'

'And not in a good way.'

'Well, that's why I'm here. I wanted to make amends, Kat, for the scene . . . well, you were there.'

'That was cold, Mr P., really cold.'

'I'm aware of that. Which is why I need to see him.'

'It's not as easy as that; it goes a lot further back.'

'I'm sure it does.'

She narrowed her eyes at me. 'Did you really glue all his Lego bricks together?'

'*Some*. Not all, just some.'

'Did you tell him he was stupid?'

'Good God, no! Is that what he told you? That's not true.'

'He says he disappoints you.'

'And that's not true either—'

'That he feels like you're disappointed in him—'

'Absolutely not true!'

'He says you and Mrs P. might be splitting up.'

I was not able to deny this.

'Well, that . . . might be true, it's . . . up in the air. Did his mother tell him that?'

'He said there wasn't any need, you haven't got on for years. But yeah. Yeah, Mrs P. did tell him that.'

I felt a contraction in my chest. 'That we *were* splitting up, or that we *might* be?'

'That you might be.'

'Good, good—'

'But Albie thinks you will.'

'Oh.'

After a while, I managed: 'Well, relationships are never easy.'

My observation was a platitude at best, yet it seemed to strike Kat as a remarkable insight. 'You can say that again!' she said and started to cry and I found myself placing an arm around her shoulder while the officer at the desk looked on sympathetically. 'I really loved him, Mr P.'

'I'm sorry, Kat—'

'But we were arguing all the time.' She sniffed, laughed. 'He's a moody little bugger, isn't he?'

'He can be at times. What did you argue about?'

'Everything! Politics, sex—'

'O-kay—'

'Astrology! We even argued about astrology!'

'What exactly did he say?'

'He really went off on one – he said that it was bullshit to think planets could influence human characteristics and anyone who believed it was just dumb . . .'

'I'm so sorry to hear that,' I said and proudly thought *that's my boy.*

'He said I was too old for him. I'm only twenty-six, for God's sake! He said I was smothering him, he wanted some time by himself.'

Her head was on my shoulder now, my arm around her, and I consoled her for some time before making my move. 'Maybe, Kat, if I talked to him, I could put a word in?'

'What's the point, Mr P.? What's the bloody point?'

'Nevertheless, if you could just give me the name of the hotel?'

'He's not in a hotel.'

'A hostel, then.'

'He's not in a hostel, either.'

'So where is he, Kat?'

Kat sniffed and cleared her throat. Her nose was running and, rather unusually I thought, she wiped it on my bare arm, leaving a trail of tears and mucus that I could see glinting in the overhead light.

'Spain.'

'Spain?'

'Madrid.'

'Albie's in Madrid?'

'He said he'd had enough of churches, he wanted to see *Guernica*. There was a cheap flight, he'll be long gone by now.'

'Where is he in Madrid, Kat?'

'I have absolutely no idea.'

Albie was gone. This was neither right nor just, I thought. Because surely, surely you have to succeed, if you give everything you have?

But it seemed that this was not the case and I realised in that moment that I'd lost not just my son, but probably my wife too, and then it was Kat's turn to console me as I fell entirely to pieces.

## 139. the cell

I spent the night in a jail cell, though not in a bad way.

Perhaps my breaking down had something to do with it, but after hours of inactivity the staff now sprang into action and I was led away from Kat and taken to a back room where, once I'd calmed down, it was made clear through complicated mime that there would be no formal charges against me. But where would I go? As it was nearly midnight and I had no passport or money, I was shown to a cell by the desk sergeant with the slightly apologetic air of a hotel manager who really has nothing better left. The small windowless room smelt of a lemony disinfectant, reassuring in this context, with a mattress in blue vinyl that was deliciously cool to the touch. The stainless steel toilet had no seat and was closer to the bed than was ideal, and I was wary of the pillow, too. Prison pillows are different from other pillows. But perhaps if I wrapped it in my shirt and tried not to use the toilet, I'd be okay. After all, I had paid upwards of one hundred and forty euros for less comfortable rooms than this and the alternative, sleeping rough on the streets of Siena, held little appeal. So I accepted the bargain happily, on the proviso that the cell door be left ajar.

'*Porta aperta, sì?*'

'*Sì, porta aperta.*'

And then I was alone.

The great virtue of defeat, once accepted, is that it at least allows one to rest. Hope had kept me awake for too long, and now, untroubled by the fantasy of a happy ending, I was finally able to fall into a sleep that was remarkable for the total absence of dreams.

## 140. the list

'I don't think our son likes me very much,' I said to Connie one night in bed.

'Don't be ridiculous, Douglas. What makes you say that?'

'I don't know. The way he cries when you leave the room. Oh, also, he tells me.'

She laughed, and drew closer. 'He's going through a mummy phase. All boys, girls too, have it. In a few years' time you'll be his idol, you'll see.'

And so I waited to become his idol.

He started school, and was happy there I think, though often he'd be in bed when I got back from work. If he was asleep, I'd go and watch him, brush his hair back and kiss his forehead. I loved that smell on him, freshly bathed, Pears soap and strawberry toothpaste. If he was awake:

'Do you want me to read tonight?'

'No, I want Mummy to read.'

'Are you sure? Because I'd really like to read to—'

'Mummy! MUMMY!'

'Okay, I'll get Mummy,' I'd say, then on closing the door, 'You know you shouldn't go to bed with wet hair, Albie. You'll catch flu.' I'd say this, even though the science on the issue was dubious to say the least. Still I couldn't help myself, any more than, on holidays, I could resist telling him not to swim immediately after eating in case of cramps. What was it about water against skin that caused the intestines to suddenly spasm and contract? Why should that be? Didn't matter – it was one of those phrases on the list.

Because throughout my childhood and teenage years I had

been compiling a list of banal and irritating remarks that I swore I would never, ever make when I was a parent. All children make this list, and all lists are unique, though no doubt there is considerable overlap. *Don't touch that, it's dirty! Write your thank-you letters, or no more presents! How can you waste food when people are starving?* All through Albie's childhood, out they tumbled. *No more biscuits, you'll spoil your appetite! Tidy your room! It is WAY past your bedtime! Do NOT come downstairs again! Yes, you do have to have the lights off! What on earth are you afraid of? Don't cry! You're acting like a baby. I told you, stop crying. Do. Not. Cry!*

## 141. conversation while washing-up

'Can I ask you a question?'

'Go on.'

'At work, how many people do you know who can't tie their shoelaces?'

'None.'

'And how many adults do you know who can't use a knife or don't eat any vegetables at all?'

'Connie—'

'Or who talk about poo and wee at dinner, or leave the lids off felt-tips, or are afraid of the dark?'

'I realise the point you're making but—'

'So can we just assume that Albie will learn these things and that the time you spend constantly getting at him, which is all the time, is not well spent?'

'The point you're making doesn't stand.'

'Why not?'

'Because it's not about teaching him how to tie his laces or to eat broccoli or talk sensibly. It's about doing things properly; teaching him application, perseverance and discipline.'

'Discipline!'

'I'm teaching him that not everything in this life is easy or fun.'

'Yes,' Connie sighed and shook her head. 'You certainly are.'

Was I an authoritarian? Certainly less so than my own father, and never unreasonably so. Connie was of the school that thought a certain degree of cheekiness, irreverence, rebellion – the crayon on the wall, the unwanted cauliflower hidden in the shoe – should be treated with an indulgent nod, a wink, a ruffling of the hair. I wasn't like that, it was not in my nature or upbringing, and neither was I of the school that thought praise should be unearnt, or that 'I love you' should be tossed around with wild abandon, just another way of saying 'goodnight' or 'well done' or 'see you later', a clearing of the throat. I did love my son, of course I did, but not when he tried to set fire to things, not when he refused to do his maths homework, not when he spilt apple juice into my laptop, not when he whined because I'd turned off the TV. He would thank me in the long run, and if I did overstep the mark sometimes, if I did lose my temper, snarl when I should have forced a smile then, well, I was very, very tired.

## 142. opportunities

I was commuting by then, eating breakfast before sunrise and fighting against the tide of in-comers at Paddington as I travelled to my work as a project manager based in the research labs just outside Reading. A tube, a train, another train, a walk; then, at night-time, the same journey in reverse. Exhausting, brutal, that working day, and yet I had only myself to blame.

I had left academia. Shortly after Albie started school, I had been offered a new job in the private sector, working for a multi-national that you will have heard of, on the news or in documentaries, a huge global company with diverse interests in the world of pharmaceuticals and agrochemicals, a company that had, at times, in the past, perhaps not placed ethical considerations at the heart of its strategy.

But now here was this job proposal, brought to me by an old colleague with a tan and a sharp suit, and here was my family in a perfectly pleasant flat but with no savings, no pension and a hefty mortgage. Before Albie arrived I'd been employed on a series of short-term projects on reasonable but unspectacular pay and this had been enough for the cinema tickets and vodka and tonics that made up the greater part of our household budget. I had a fellowship now, with students working for me, and there seemed every chance that in a few years, I'd become a professor. But now, with nursery fees and endless new shoes, with Connie on a part-time salary from the museum, money was considerably tighter. There were other frustrations, too: long-term insecurity, administrative demands, the endless pressure to publish in 'high-impact' journals, the undignified scramble for funding. When I began to study science I had presumed, naïvely I suppose, that politicians would be falling over themselves to further human knowledge. Surely any government, irrespective of its political hue, could see that innovation in science and technology led to wealth and prosperity? True, not all research had an immediate commercial application, it was not all obviously 'translational', but who knew where a line of thought might lead? So many of the great breakthroughs had first been glimpsed out of the corner of an eye, and surely anything that added to the sum of human knowledge was valuable? More than valuable – essential.

Not if our funding was anything to go by. Increasingly we found ourselves scrabbling around for enough money to pay our research assistants the lowest possible wage. Apparently the nation's future lay not in innovation and development but in global finance and telesales, in the entertainment industry and coffee shops. Britain would lead the world in frothing milk and making period dramas.

And now here was this large multinational company, with its security and pension scheme and its salary commensurate to my achievements and qualifications, its well-equipped labs and the brightest, best graduates, and here was my family too. I felt – is this common among new fathers, I wonder? – a new-found obligation to provide, which all sounds very atavistic and primitive but there it is. Of course, I couldn't make the decision independently. Connie and I talked many nights until late. She had heard of my potential employers, had noted their name in the press and on the news, and while she never used the phrase out loud, it played on her lips: *sell-out*. Her response to big business was instinctive and emotional and, I thought, naïve, and in turn I rationalised the issues: surely it was only by working for a large organisation that you could make a meaningful change, and wasn't it better to be inside than out? Was profit really such a dirty word? And what about the financial security, the extra money? What about another room, a garden of our own, or a house near a much, much better school, outside London maybe? A studio for Connie – she could paint again! What about school fees?

Connie bridled. 'I don't want those things—'

'Not now, perhaps—'

'And don't pretend you're doing it for us!'

'But I am; if I accepted, I would be, to an extent . . .'

'The bottom line is I don't think you should make a decision based on money, that's all.'

Which is a noble sentiment, and a very Connie thing to say, Connie the nurturing artist. But substitute that chilly word 'money' for 'security' or 'safety', substitute 'money' for 'comfort' or 'peace of mind' or 'well-being', 'a good education' or 'travel' or simply 'a happy family'. Often – not always, but often – didn't they equate to the same thing?

'No,' said Connie. 'Not at all.'

'So what would you have me do? If it was up to you?'

'It isn't up to me. It's your job, your career—'

'But if it was up to you?'

'I wouldn't take the job. You'll lose your freedom. You'll be working for accountants, not for yourself. If you're not making money for them, they'll cut you off and you'll hate that, and it won't be fun. There'll be no joy in it. Find something better paid or more secure by all means, but I wouldn't take this job.'

I took the job.

She did not berate me for it, or very rarely, though Albie certainly would in years to come. But neither was she sympathetic if I struggled in at eight or nine or ten at night, and there was no doubt in my mind that I had slipped somewhat in her estimation. An awful feeling, that; sliding down the scree, scrabbling at the dust but unable to get a grip. That shine, the idealism I suppose, that had caught Connie's attention on the night we met, had faded. It couldn't last but still, I regretted its passing. Connie had always said I was at my most attractive when I talked about my work. 'The lights come on,' she had said. Now I'd have to find another way to make that happen.

## 143. a free man

A little before seven a.m. I was woken by a warder bearing an excellent cup of coffee. I had eaten nothing since the jelly sweet that I'd taken from the boy on the Siena train, and though the thick black liquid burned my mouth and made my stomach spasm, it was delicious. I sat on the edge of the cell bench, sipped from the plastic cup, rubbed my eyes and forced myself to acknowledge the full, all-encompassing hopelessness of my situation.

Grimly, I sketched out my retreat to London. I would walk down the hill to Siena station, find out the cost of a single ticket to Florence, and plead with the clerk – in English? – to take my wristwatch and phone as security for the train ticket. That accomplished, I'd retrieve my property in Florence, withdraw cash, return to Siena to buy back my watch and phone, then try and catch the next plane to London from Pisa. It was a dull and dispiriting plan, requiring some leniency on the part of the Italian Rail Service, but the alternative – phoning Connie and asking her to wire some money – was unacceptable. What did that mean, anyway, 'wiring money'? It was one of those things that people only did in films.

I switched on my telephone. Battery power stood at 2 per cent. Without considering what I would say, I decided to call home. I pictured Connie's phone on top of her pile of books, her sleeping figure, recalled the comforting scent of the sheets, and I imagined how things might have been had all gone to plan. Imagined the sound of a car on the driveway, Connie going to the window, seeing Albie and me stepping out of the taxi, Albie smiling a little shame-facedly, raising his hand to the bedroom window, me joining him, my arm around his shoulder. I imagined the tears of gratitude in Connie's eyes as she ran for the door. I had returned him safe and sound as I had promised. 'You found him! In all of Europe! Douglas, how did you do it? You clever, brilliant man—'

Back in the real world, Connie picked up. 'Hello?'

'Darling, it's me—'

'It's six in the morning, Douglas!'

'I know, I'm sorry, but the phone's about to die, and I wanted to tell you—'

I heard the rustle of sheets as she sat up in bed. 'Douglas, have you found him? Is he safe?'

'I lost him. I almost had him, almost, almost, but I lost him.'

A sigh. 'Oh, Douglas.'

'You mustn't worry, he's perfectly safe and well, I know that—'

'How can you know that?'

'I found Kat.'

'How on earth did you—?'

'It's a long story. My phone's about to run out. Anyway, I'm sorry, I failed.'

'Douglas, you didn't "fail".'

'Well, I didn't achieve my result, so yes, I did fail.'

'But at least we know he's safe. Where are you now? Are there people with you? Are you safe, are you well?'

'I'm in a hotel, in Siena.' I tapped the stainless-steel toilet with my toe. 'It's very nice.'

'Do you want me to come out?'

'No, no, I want to come home.'

'Good idea. Come home, Douglas. We'll wait for him together here.'

'I'll be back tonight, tomorrow at the latest.'

'I'll be waiting. And Douglas? At least you tried. I'm grateful—'

'Go back to sleep.'

'And when you come home—'

A bleep, and the phone died. I fastened my watch, placed the phone in my pocket, folded my blanket neatly on the bench and left my cell, closing the door behind me.

It was a bright, cool summer morning, fresh and clean. The police station lay in the modern outskirts of the town, beneath the city walls. I was about to walk down the hill towards the station when I heard music, the theme from *The Godfather*, played on the accordion.

Perched impertinently on the bonnet of a police car was Kat.

'Hey,' she said, offering her fist to bump. I obliged.

'Hello, Kat. What are you doing here?'

'Waiting for you. How was your first night behind bars?'

'Better than some hotels I've stayed in. I regret the tattoo, though.'

'What tattoo did you get, Mr P.?'

'Just gang-related stuff. Big dragon.'

'Your tan's evened out. On your face. You look less like a road sign.'

'Well, that's something, I suppose.' She smiled and time passed. 'Well, Kat, I should get going. Nice to meet—'

'Have you tried texting him, Mr P.?'

'Of course, and calling too. He said he'd ignore them all and he has.'

'Then send him one he can't ignore. Here, hold Steve.' Kat slid off the bonnet, handed me accordion-Steve then reached into her pocket and produced her mobile phone, tapping on it with her head down. 'I shouldn't do this. It's a betrayal of trust, Mr P., and I feel bad. Plus there's the cost to my personal dignity and integrity. But given that you've come this far . . .'

'What are you writing, Kat?'

'. . . and "send"! There. All done. Take a look.'

She held her phone out to me, and I read:

**Albie I need to talk to you about something. Urgent. Has to be in person so don't call me! Just meet me tomorrow eleven am on the steps of the prado, do not be late!!!! Love you still kat**

'There you go,' said Kat. 'I'm delivering him to you.'

'Good God,' I exclaimed. 'I don't know what to say.'

'No thanks required.'

'But . . . but doesn't the message sort of imply . . . ?'

'. . . that he's knocked me up? You do want him to be there, don't you?'

'Well, yes, but—'

She took the phone from my hands. 'I can always tell him I was kidding . . .'

'No, no, no, I think . . . let it be. But tomorrow morning? Can I get to Madrid for tomorrow?'

'You can if you run.'

I laughed, bundled the wheezing accordion back into her arms and with a certain wariness – we were neither of us daisy-fresh – embraced Kat, and began to trot across the car park before halting and turning back.

'Kat, I realise I'm pushing my luck, but the money I gave you yesterday – could I get it back? My wallet is in Florence, you see . . .'

She shook her head slowly and sighed, crouched and reached into her backpack.

'And maybe if I could borrow twenty, maybe thirty euros more? And your bank details, so I can return the money . . .'

I confess I made this offer in the expectation of her declining, but she took some time to write out her account numbers, including IBAN and SWIFT codes. I promised to make good my debts as soon as I returned, and then I was off, running down the hill, running, running, running towards Spain.

# part seven

# MADRID

—

There is no such thing as reproduction. When two people decide to have a baby, they engage in an act of production, and the widespread use of the word reproduction for this activity, with its implication that two people are but braiding themselves together, is at best a euphemism to comfort prospective parents before they get in over their heads.

Andrew Solomon, *Far From the Tree*

## 144. the glitter wars

Time being what it is, we got older. We thickened and sagged in ways that would have seemed implausible, comical even, to our younger selves, just as our son, before our eyes, began to elongate. We accumulated things; vast quantities of moulded plastic, picture books, scooters, tricycles, bicycles, shoes and clothes and coats and paraphernalia that no longer served a purpose but which we couldn't quite throw away. Connie and I entered our forties in quick succession, and though we suspected we'd never need a bottle steriliser or rocking horse again, we found we couldn't quite discard them, and now there was a piano, too, now a train set, a castle, a tangled box kite.

My new salary meant that the fridge seemed fuller, the wine tasted better and we bought a bigger car, took Albie on trips abroad and came back to the same small flat we'd bought together before we were married, cramped and tatty now. We ought to move house, we knew it, but the effort required was beyond me. Five years of commuting against the tide had begun to take their toll, and I was perpetually tired, perpetually stressed and bad-tempered, so that my nightly homecoming brought no pleasure to either Albie or Connie, or indeed myself.

Take, for example, the famous Glitter Wars that scarred the December of Albie's ninth year. Albie and Connie had been making Christmas cards at the kitchen table, heads close together in that way they had, Phil Spector's *Christmas Album* playing, the kind of home-spun artsy-craftsy activity that occupied their evenings while I struggled to stay awake on the 1957 into Paddington, self-medicating with a warm gin and tonic from the station buffet then another from the trolley, hurrying through the rain to a flat that felt too small and entering to no greeting, no loving kiss or filial hug, just a scene of utter disarray; music blaring, tissue-paper and cotton wool everywhere, poster paint daubed all over the table. Here were my son and wife in their own little self-contained world, laughing at a self-contained joke, and here was Albie shaking glitter onto PVA glue and the table, too, and the floor and onto his pyjamas. Anyone who has attempted to clean away large quantities of spilt glitter will know that it is a pernicious and vile substance, a kind of festive asbestos that clings to clothes and burrows into carpets, sticks to the skin and stays there, and now here were great snowdrifts of the awful stuff blowing across the table.

'What the hell is going on in here!' I said, I shouted. They noticed me now.

'We're making Christmas cards!' said Connie, still smiling. 'Look! Isn't this a beauty?' She held up one of Albie's efforts and a shower of gold and silver cascaded to the floor. 'Your son is an artist!'

'Look! Look what you're doing. It's going everywhere! For Christ's sake, Connie,' and I threw down my briefcase and went to the sink to dampen a cloth. 'Would it kill you to put news-paper down first?'

'It's glitter, Douglas,' she said, forcing a laugh. 'Because it's Christmas?'

'And I'll be picking it out of my food and brushing it off my clothes until July! Look at this paint! Paint and glue on the table. Is it washable? No, stupid question, of course, it isn't—' I stopped scrubbing, threw the cloth down. 'Look! Look, it's on my hands!' I held them up to the light, to show how brightly they sparkled. 'I've got to go into meetings like this. I have to do presentations! Look! How is anyone supposed to take me seriously when I'm covered in this bloody . . .' My son was staring at the table now, his brow creased, lips protruding. Here you are, my darling boy – some memories for you.

'Egg, can you go next door please?' said Connie.

He shifted off his seat. 'Sorry, Dad.'

'I like your Christmas card!' I said to his back, but it was too late now. Connie and I were left alone.

'Well, you can really suck the joy out of pretty much anything these days, can't you?' said Connie.

But I was not quite ready to apologise yet and the battle that followed, erupting in skirmishes over the remaining days and weeks leading up to Christmas, was too painful and unpleasant to recount in great detail here. The glitter, as predicted, found its way into clothes and hair and the grain of the kitchen furniture; its sparkle would catch my eye as I ate a solitary breakfast in the dark, and the silences, the sniping and bickering continued until Christmas.

If my own mother ever caught me pulling faces, pouting or sneering, she would tell me: if the wind changes direction, you'll stay that way. I was sceptical at the time, but as the years passed I was not so sure. My everyday face, the one I wore at rest or when alone, had set and hardened, and wasn't one I cared for much any more.

## 145. christmas

The day itself was always spent at Connie's parents, a noisy, boisterous and boozy affair, the tiny terraced house packed with a mind-boggling number of nephews and nieces, aunts and uncles, both Cypriots and Londoners and combinations of the two, the children ever-multiplying, everyone laughing and joking and arguing in a smoky room with the TV on. Later, there'd be ridiculous dancing, four generations trampling walnut shells and Quality Street underfoot. Once upon a time these Christmas Days had seemed like a refreshing change from the rather chilly and restrained affair I was used to from childhood, but since the loss of my parents the event had taken on a melancholy air for me. I was the stranger here, an elderly orphan, an appendix to someone else's family, and the discord between my wife and me served only to heighten my gloom. There was work at home in my briefcase – perhaps I could sneak off early and do that? No, only lemonade for me. No, thank you, I don't smoke. And no, thank you, I do not wish to conga.

Of course Albie loved it there, sipping creamy cocktails when no one was looking, flirting with his cousins, dancing on his uncles' shoulders, and so I sat and watched and waited. We returned home after midnight, Albie falling asleep in the back-seat, and I carried him up to our top-floor flat – the last year I'd be able to do this – and fell backwards on to our bed. The three of us lay together, too exhausted to undress, my son's breath hot and sweet on my cheek.

'Are you unhappy?' said Connie.

'No. No, just a little blue.' That silly word again.

'Maybe we need to make a change.'

'What kind of change?' I asked.

'Perhaps a change of scene. So that you're not tired all the time.'

'Leave London, you mean?'

'If that's what it's going to take. Maybe find a house in the country somewhere, so you can drive to work. Somewhere with a good state school nearby. What d'you think?'

What did I think? In truth, I didn't love the city any more. It didn't belong to us in the same way. I did not like explaining to Albie why there were bunches of flowers tied to the railings, or instructing him to avoid the vomit on the way to the shops on Saturday morning. I was bored of road works and building sites – when would they ever finish the place? Why couldn't they leave it alone? When I returned at night, the city seemed an unnerving and aggressive place; I could feel my grip tightening on the handle of my briefcase as I left the tube, keys clenched in my other fist. Every siren, every terrorist threat seemed more urgent and more personal. And yes, there was all the great art, the wonderful theatre, but when had Connie last been to the theatre?

Perhaps the countryside was the answer. Sentimental, perhaps, but wouldn't it be great for Albie to know the names of birds other than magpies and pigeons? When I was a child, on walks my mother would habitually name all the grasses, flowers, birds and trees we passed – *Quercus robur*, the oak, *Troglodytes troglodytes*, the wren. These were my warmest memories of her, and even now I can recall the binomial for all the common British birds, though I've yet to be asked. But Albie's knowledge of nature came from trips to the city farm, his sense of the seasons from changes in the central heating. Perhaps exposure to nature would make him less sullen, moody and resentful towards me. I imagined him racing off on a bicycle with fishing net and spotter's guide, all rosy-cheeked and tousle-haired, then returning at dusk, a jam-jar full of sticklebacks sloshing on the handlebars, the kind of childhood I'd longed for. A biologist in the making; not hard science, but a start.

It was much more difficult to imagine Connie outside London. She had been born here, studied and worked here. We had fallen in love and been married here, raised Albie here. London exhausted and maddened me, but Connie carried the city around with her; pubs and bars and restaurants, theatre foyers, city parks, the top deck of the 22, the 55, the 38. She was not averse to the countryside, but even in a Cornish cove or on a Yorkshire moor, it seemed as if she might lift an arm and hail a cab.

'Well?' she said.

'Sorry, I'm just trying to imagine you in a field on a wet Tuesday in February.'

'Yeah, me too.' She closed her eyes. 'Not easy, is it?'

'What about your work?'

'I'll commute for a change. Stay over at Fran's if I have to. We'll sort that bit out. The main thing is d'you think you could be happy there?'

I didn't answer, and she continued:

'I think you would be. Happier, I mean, or less stressed. Which means that we all would be. In the long run.' Albie shifted in his sleep and curled towards his mother. 'I'd like you to be happy again. And if that means a new life in a new town . . . village . . .'

'Okay. Let's think about it.'

'Okay.'

'I love you, Connie. You do know that.'

'I do. Happy Christmas, my darling.'

'Happy Christmas to you.'

## 146. the miracle of air travel

Madrid in August; the dry heat and dust of it. Flying over the great plains of central Spain that afternoon, peering down, I had never felt so far from the sea.

After the chaos of the last few days, the journey to Spain had been blissfully smooth, the 0732 train from Siena bringing me to Florence in a little under ninety minutes, the journey slow but pleasant past great vineyards and *zone industriale*, the pleasure heightened by the excellent sandwich that I gorged on like some kind of caveman, followed by, in quick succession, a banana, an apple, a wonderful orange, the juice dribbling down my chin. Unshaven and not yet bathed, I suspect there was something a little feral about me, hunched in a corner seat, sticky-faced. Certainly the commuters who joined at Empoli regarded me with wariness. I returned their stares. What did I care? Like some newly freed jailbird, I was out and back on the streets, and I slid down in my seat to dream of hot baths, new razor blades, clean white sheets, etc.

Then into Florence's rush hour, and an altercation with a staff member about the return of my property, conducted in over-enunciated English. *How can I pay charge for overnight storage when wallet is in bag? Return my property and I pay! The sign above says* 'assistenza alla clientela'. *I am* clientela – *why you not assist me?* Oh yes, I was quite the bad-ass now, quite the bad-ass.

By 0920 I was in possession of my passport, my wallet, my phone charger, my tablet. I hugged them to me, whole again. In the station café I found a corner near a socket and sucked up electricity and wifi like a swimmer coming up for air. No Iberia flights to Madrid from Firenze or Pisa, but a 1235 flight from Bologna. Where was Bologna? Depressingly it seemed that the Apennines stood between that flight and me. But wait – thirty-seven minutes, the timetable said. What kind of miraculous train was this? I could make it with time to spare. I purchased my Madrid flight online, a window seat, hand baggage only, and boarded the Bologna train. In the toilet I coated myself with deodorant stick as if papering a wall. I brushed my teeth, and have never enjoyed the sensation more.

The trick to crossing the Apennines was to burrow beneath them. Much of the journey took place in a remarkably long tunnel, emerging now and then into light as if curtains had been hurled open to a view of wooded mountainside against bright sky, then whisked shut again. Almost too soon we were in Bologna, one of those cites where the airport is disconcertingly close to the centre, so that you might comfortably walk there with your shopping. But I had learnt my lesson in Florence and took a taxi. My guidebook sang the city's praises, but the taxi skirted the old town on the northern ring road and what I saw was squat, modern and pleasant, with a fragment of an ancient wall in the centre of a roundabout then the dull warehouses of the airport. Never mind, we'd come here again another time. For the moment, I was happy to find myself in the terminal and checked in with an hour and fifteen minutes to spare. Air travel had never seemed so glamorous, so thrillingly efficient, so full of hope.

## 147. atlas

We took off on time and I craned to look out of the window like a child. Everything was sharp and clear, the air pure, no hint of cloud, and I noted how new this experience was for humankind, the ability to see the earth laid out like this, and how complacent we were about it. Why were people reading magazines when there was all of this to see? Here were the mountains that I'd burrowed beneath just two hours before, there was Corsica, crisply outlined, a mossy green on blue. Then the Mediterranean was left behind and the desert plain unrolled; a desert in Europe. Spain seemed vast to me. No wonder they had once filmed Westerns there. What did it look like at ground level, I wondered, and would I ever find out? Now that I knew my journey was almost complete, the ability to travel seemed exciting again. I was not sure that I wanted to go home, even if I could.

Then a motorway, suburbs and a great sprawling city very far from water. An airport terminal like the set of a science-fiction film and then out into the thick air of the Spanish afternoon and into a taxi, the motorway to the city half abandoned, passing unpopulated building sites and new apartment blocks, not a human being to be seen. Madrid was unexpected to me. I had no guidebooks or maps, no knowledge or expectations. A corner of Paris could only be Paris, likewise New York or Rome. Madrid was harder to pin down, the buildings that lined the wide avenues a curious mix of eighties office blocks, grand residential palaces, stylish apartment buildings, all compacted together. That European passion for pharmacies was much in evidence, and a great deal of the city seemed as seventies as a lava lamp, while other buildings were absurdly ornate and grand. If Connie had been with me, she'd have named that style. Baroque? Was that right? Neo-baroque?

'What is this?' I asked my taxi-driver, pointing to an intricately carved palace, the crystalline white of cake icing.

'Post office,' said the driver, and I tried to imagine anyone buying a book of stamps there. 'Over there,' he pointed through the trees of a formal park towards a peach-coloured neo-clas-sical building (Connie, is that right? Neo-classical?) 'this is the Prado. Very famous, very beautiful. Velázquez, Goya. You must go.'

'I am,' I said. 'I'm meeting my son there tomorrow.'

## 148. keys through the letterbox

In the summer before Albie started 'big school' we left the small, garden-less Kilburn flat where he'd grown up and moved to the country. I had tried hard to present the whole experience as 'an adventure', but Albie was unconvinced. Perhaps Connie was too, though at least she didn't pout and whine and sulk like Albie. 'I'll be bored,' he would say, declaring his intentions. 'I'm leaving all my friends behind!' he'd say. 'You'll make new ones,' we'd reply, as if friends could be replaced like old shoes.

For Connie, too, the departure was proving something of a wrench. Evenings and weekends had been given over to 'sorting things out', which meant throwing stuff away with a ruthlessness that bordered on anger; old notebooks and diaries, photographs, art-school projects, artists' materials.

'What about these paints? Can't you use these? Can't Albie?'

'No. That's why I'm throwing them away.'

Or I'd find her drawings in the recycling bin beneath bottles and cans, shake off the mess and hold them up. 'Why are you throwing this away? It's lovely.'

'It's awful. I'm embarrassed by it.'

'I love this picture. I remember it from when we met.'

'It's just nostalgia, Douglas. We're never going to hang it up. It's scrap paper, get rid of it.'

'Well, can I keep it?'

She sighed. 'Just keep it out of my sight.' I took her sketches and drawings, pinned some up at work and put the rest in my filing cabinet.

Much of Albie's childhood was discarded; some baby clothes, too, girls' clothes that we'd bought for our daughter and kept carefully folded in the back of a drawer, not out of mawkish sentimentality nor as some strange totem, but for practical reasons. What if we had another child, a girl maybe? For a while we had tried, but not now. It was all a little too late for that now.

Never mind, because here was change, here was an adventure, and so the Saturday after Albie's final term at junior school, the removal men came stomping up those stairs. Nearly fifteen years earlier, two young people had moved into that flat, all of our possessions easily contained in the back of a hired van. Now we were a family, with our own furniture and pictures in proper frames, bicycles and snorkels, guitars, a drum kit and an upright piano, dinner sets and cast-iron cookware and far too many possessions for what was effectively a student flat. The new owners were a young couple in their twenties, baby on the way. They seemed nice at the viewing. We left them a bottle of champagne in the centre of the wooden floor that we'd stripped and painted. While Albie waited in the car, Connie and I walked from room to room, closing the doors. There was no time to be sentimental with the removal van blocking the street outside.

'You ready?' I said.

'I suppose so,' she murmured, already descending the stairs.

I pulled the door shut and posted the keys through the letterbox.

## 149. an adventure

All along the Westway I kept up my babble about it being an adventure, how spacious and grand the new house, new *home*, would be, how nice it would be to have a garden in the summer. It would feel like undoing a belt after a large meal – finally, a chance to breathe! Albie and Connie remained silent. Along with the keys and the instructions for the boiler, we had left something intangible behind. We had been extraordinarily happy in that little flat, and also sadder than we had ever thought possible. Whatever lay ahead, it couldn't match those extremes.

We drove west under overcast skies. The city faded into suburbs, then industrial estates and fir plantations and before long we left the motorway, bounced off the outskirts of Reading, down lanes past fields of wheat and rape; pleasant countryside, though not quite the remote and picturesque idyll I recalled from visits with the estate agent. There seemed to be an awful lot of pylons, a lot of high hedges, cars passing by in quick succession, lorries too. Never mind. We followed the removal van into a gravel drive, our gravel drive, the house early twentieth century, mock-Tudor beams, the largest in the village! There was an excellent state school nearby, my desk was just twenty minutes' drive away, there were great rail links. An hour from London by road, too, on a good day. If you listened you could hear the M40! There was work to do, of course, just enough to fill our weekends, but we could be happy here, no doubt about it. On the front drive – with room for three more cars! – I draped my arms around my wife and son like a figure-skating coach. Look, in the trees – magpies, crows! We stood for a moment, then they broke free.

In the large family kitchen – flagstones, an Aga – I popped a bottle of champagne, pulled glasses from their newspaper and poured out an inch for Egg, and the three of us toasted new beginnings. But after we had placed the boxes in each room and the removal men had left, it became clear that a miscalculation had been made. Try as we might, the three of us could never fill this place. There weren't enough pictures for the walls or books for the shelves. Even with Albie's drum kit and guitar, we couldn't make enough noise to make these high rooms seem occupied. I had intended the house to symbolise prosperity and maturity, a haven of rural calm with good rail links to the chaos of the city. But it felt – and would always feel, I suppose – like a half-empty doll's house with not quite enough dolls.

Later that evening, I found Connie standing silently in a small gabled bedroom at the top of the house. The wallpaper was old-fashioned, flowered and marked with doodles, little biro-ed ants and felt-tip butterflies drawn on to the stems and petals of the roses. I knew Connie well enough to guess her thoughts, though we chose not to acknowledge them out loud.

'I thought this room could be your studio. Lovely light! You could paint again. Yes?'

She rested her head on my shoulder but said nothing.

We bought a dog.

## 150. schweppes!

I did not tell Connie of my whereabouts. In Siena, I had told her to expect me home the following day, and wouldn't it be better to phone her with Albie by my side? *I'm not at Heathrow, I'm in Madrid! It's a long story. Wait a minute, I have someone here to speak to you . . .* That was the plan, and so I was absurdly cheerful and optimistic that night, my mood lifted by the lavish hotel suite – a suite! Two rooms! – that I had booked on a whim and at a surprisingly reasonable price. At the marble and gold reception desk there seemed to be some doubt that this rather shabby, worn-out solitary guest could afford such decadence. No luggage? Were there any other guests with me? No, I was all alone, but there was a sofa-bed for Albie. Only if he wanted it, of course.

The room – no, the *suite* – was all white marble and cream leather, a dream of modern living from 1973. Closing the door, I set about repairing the damage of the last few days. I eased my partially sunburnt self into the cool onyx bath, washed my hair, shaved, and dressed the wounds on my feet. I put on the last of my clean clothes and sent the others to be laundered. In the shopping streets below I found a department store and bought a new shirt, a tie, some trousers and, back in my room, laid them out on a chair as if preparing for a job interview. So giddy and excited was I that I broke the central guiding principle of my life and took vodka and tonic from the mini-bar then, dizzy with decadence, the peanuts too, and like some modern-day Caligula sat on the balcony and watched the traffic on the Gran Vía fourteen floors below. At the junction ahead of me stood a fine modern building, a rounded wedge – art deco, Connie, is that right? – with a huge neon sign on its top floor, and as evening fell I caught the moment when the neon sput-tered into life, exclaiming *Schweppes!* against a rainbow back-ground, so that the street resembled a milder, more laid-back Times Square.

The Spaniards, I knew, had a reputation for late dining and I contemplated taking a 'disco nap', as Albie would put it, then setting out to explore. But the bed was so large and comfortable, the sheets cool and white and of such a high thread count, that I found myself lowering the mechanical shutters and settling down at nine fifteen. Plenty of time for tapas tomorrow, when I'd see my son again. I fell asleep, lulled by the most wonderful, unshakeable faith in the future.

## 151. the future

There has never been a shortage of topics to keep me awake at night, but as a teenager I was especially haunted by the prospect of nuclear war. The public information films intended to educate and reassure the populace sent everyone, us children in particular, into a frenzy of morbid fantasy and I was convinced that at some point, whether in Washington, Peking or Moscow, a button would be pressed – I imagined an actual button, large and red, like the stop button on an escalator – and soon my mother and father and I would be hunting for mutant rats in the smouldering remains of Ipswich city centre. There'd be no more 'don't touch that, it's dirty' in the post-apocalyptic Petersen family cave. The only question would be: do we eat Douglas or Karen first? So worried was I by this prospect that, unusually, I confessed my night terrors to my father. 'Well, if it does happen, you won't have time to do anything about it. Three minutes of panic and then you'll be crispy bacon!' he reassured me. Given three minutes' warning, what would we say to one another, my family and I? I imagined my father rushing to turn off the central heating.

Rightly or wrongly, that specific fear has faded. But the anxiety has not passed and now the face that I imagine in that future wasteland is not my own, but Albie's.

Over the years I have read many, many books about the future, my 'we're all doomed' books, as Connie liked to call them. 'All the books you read are either about how grim the past was or how gruesome the future will be. It might not be that way, Douglas. Things might turn out all right.' But these were well-researched, plausible studies, their conclusions highly persuasive, and I could become quite voluble on the subject.

Take, for instance, the fate of the middle-class, into which

Albie and I were born and to which Connie now belongs, albeit with some protest. In book after book I read that the middle-class are doomed. Globalisation and technology have already cut a swathe through previously secure professions, and 3D printing technology will soon wipe out the last of the manufacturing industries. The internet won't replace those jobs, and what place for the middle-classes if twelve people can run a giant corporation? I'm no communist firebrand, but even the most rabid free-marketeer would concede that market-forces capitalism, instead of spreading wealth and security throughout the population, has grotesquely magnified the gulf between rich and poor, forcing a global workforce into dangerous, unregulated, insecure low-paid labour while rewarding only a tiny elite of businessmen and technocrats. So-called 'secure' professions seem less and less so; first it was the miners and the ship- and steel-workers, soon it will be the bank clerks, the librarians, the teachers, the shop-owners, the supermarket check-out staff. The scientists might survive if it's the right type of science, but where do all the taxi-drivers in the world go when the taxis drive themselves? How do they feed their children or heat their homes and what happens when frustration turns to anger? Throw in terrorism, the seemingly insoluble problem of religious funda-mentalism, the rise of the extreme right-wing, under-employed youth and the under-pensioned elderly, fragile and corrupt banking systems, the inadequacy of the health and care systems to cope with vast numbers of the sick and old, the environmental repercussions of unprecedented factory-farming, the battle for finite resources of food, water, gas and oil, the changing course of the Gulf Stream, destruction of the biosphere and the statistical probability of a global pandemic, and there really is no reason why anyone should sleep soundly ever again.

By the time Albie is my age I will be long gone, or, best-case scenario, barricaded into my living module with enough rations to see out my days. But outside, I imagine vast, unregulated factories where workers count themselves lucky to toil through eighteen-hour days for less than a living wage before pulling on their gas masks to fight their way through the unemployed masses who are bartering with the mutated chickens and old tin-cans that they use for currency, those lucky workers returning to tiny, overcrowded shacks in a vast megalopolis where a tree is never seen, the air is thick with police drones, where car-bomb explosions, typhoons and freak hailstorms are so commonplace as to barely be remarked upon. Meanwhile, in literally gilded towers miles above the carcinogenic smog, the privileged 1 per cent of businessmen, celebrities and entrepreneurs look down through bullet-proof windows, accept cocktails in strange glasses from the robot waiters hovering nearby and laugh their tinkling laughs and somewhere, down there in that hellish, stewing mess of violence, poverty and desperation, is my son, Albie Petersen, a wandering minstrel with his guitar and his keen interest in photography, still refusing to wear a decent coat.

## 152. heritability

'So what you're saying,' said Connie, looking up from her novel, 'is that the future, basically, is going to be a bit like *Mad Max*?'

'Not exactly. But it might have elements of that.'

'So *Mad Max*, it's like a documentary, really—'

'All I mean is the future world might not be as hospitable as the one that you and I grew up in. That dream of progress is dead. Our parents imagined holiday camps on the moon. We . . . we have to get used to a different notion of the future.'

'And you want Albie to choose his GCSEs based on this *Mad Max*-like vision of the future.'

'Don't tease me. I want him to do subjects that are useful and practical; I want him to do something that will get him a job.'

'You want him to be up in the gilded tower. You want him to have a robot butler.'

'I want him to be successful,' I said. 'Is that a strange ambition for my son?'

'Our son.'

'Our son.'

At that time, Albie was not doing well. Instead of providing a sense of calm, the countryside enraged him. He showed no interest in learning the binomial names for the common British birds, and the frogspawn I procured for him held no appeal. He missed his friends, the cinema, the top deck of buses; he missed eating chips on the swings in the playground. But wasn't the countryside one wonderful giant playground? Apparently not. Albie went for walks with great reluctance, glaring at warblers, kicking the heads off flowers as he passed. If he could have burnt the countryside down, he would have. At school his grades were consistently poor, as were reports of his behaviour. He did not work, he did not concentrate, sometimes he didn't even turn up. Connie, though concerned, took all this in her stride, but I was angered and shocked by it. I had not expected obedience to be genetic but neither had I anticipated these calls from the headmaster's office, these letters home. My own son took me by surprise. He was not what I had expected, was not like me at all. Most hurtfully of all, he seemed to take a perverse pride in this.

I didn't lose my temper, or only every now and then, and I was not disappointed by *him*, only by his *behaviour*, a semantic distinction that was probably lost on a thirteen-year-old boy. He was smart, sharp, he had a good brain, he just required some structure and application. I assessed the key areas requiring attention, took the matter in hand, and despite my fatigue I'd spend evenings and weekends with him at the kitchen table, working through chemistry, physics and mathematics in what I hoped was a supportive fatherly manner, Connie hovering nearby like a boxing referee.

'How can you not do long division, Albie? It's pretty basic stuff.'

'I can do it, just not in the same way.'

'So you write down four and you carry the three over.'

'That's the bit we don't do any more, the carrying-the-three bit.'

'But that *is* long division. That's what long division is!'

'Not now it isn't. They do it differently.'

'There's only one way to divide, Albie, and this is it.'

'It isn't!'

'So show me! Show me some other magical way to divide . . .'

The pen would hover on the paper then be tossed across the table. 'Why can't we just use a calculator?'

I'm not proud to say that a number of those evenings of supportive coaching ended in raised voices and red eyes; the majority of them, perhaps. On one occasion he even punched a hole in his bedroom wall. Not a supporting wall, of course, just a plasterboard partition, but I was shocked nonetheless, especially when I paused to consider that he must have been imagining my face.

But I would not give up on him, I was sure of that. Each night we'd work, then argue. I'd patch things up as best I could and then lie in bed, kept awake by a vision of a boy of Albie's age, Chinese or South Korean, sitting up late and working away at his algebra, his organic chemistry, his computer code; this boy against whom my own son would some day compete for his livelihood.

## 153. colouring in

My son's faltering progress corresponded with a further cooling in our relationship. The little physical rapport we'd once shared, the tickling, the holding of hands, melted away with our growing self-consciousness, and I was surprised how much I missed it, especially the holding hands. I'd never been much of a wrestler, always too anxious about cracked skulls and sprained wrists, but now even a simple arm around the shoulder was shrugged away with a wince or a grunt. Bedroom and bathroom doors were locked and now instead of telling my son to go to bed at the weekend, I began to say goodnight and to leave the two of them downstairs on the sofa, Albie's head in Connie's lap or vice versa. *Goodnight, everyone! I said goodnight! Goodnight! Goodnight!*

I had been bracing myself for Albie's adolescence, but its arrival felt like the outbreak of a long-simmering civil war. We argued frequently. One example will be enough. I was making the case for why science and maths might make better qualifications than drama and art. A banal discussion, I know, the kind that every family has, but Connie was away in London, which made the topic dangerous.

'My point is this,' I said. 'Put an average member of the general public in a room with paintbrushes or a camera, give them a stage or a pen and paper and they'll achieve something. It might be inept or ugly or untutored, or it might show potential, or it might even reveal some hidden talent but everyone, anyone can knock up a painting or a poem or photo or whatever. Put someone in a room with a centrifuge, a selection of lab equipment, some chemicals and they'll produce nothing, nothing worthwhile whatsoever, just . . . mud pies. That's because science is methodical, it demands rigour, application and study. It's more difficult. It just is. It is.'

'So – what, you think, because you're a scientist, you're smarter than other people?'

'In my field, yes! And so I should be! That's what I studied for, that's why I stayed up late for ten years. To be good at it.'

'So if I drop a subject I hate and don't understand, you'll think less of me?'

'I'll think you didn't persevere. I'll think you gave up too soon.'

'You'll think I took the easy option?'

'Maybe—'

'Bit of a coward—'

'I didn't say that. Why are you twisting words like—?'

'For doing what I'm good at, rather than what *you're* good at?'

'No, for doing what's easy instead of what's hard. It's good to be challenged, to have your mind stretched.'

'So what I *can* do, anyone can do? There's nothing special about it.'

'There might be, but that doesn't mean you'll earn a living. Success comes to those who work hard and stick at things that are difficult. And I want you to be a success.'

'Like you?'

He said this with something of a sneer, and I felt a little twist of anger. 'The future is . . . well, it's terrifying, Albie, you have no idea, and I want you to be well prepared for it. I want you to have skills and information that will enable you to thrive and succeed and be happy in the future. And I'm afraid that spending all day colouring in does not count.'

'So, to summarise,' he said, blinking quickly now, 'what you're saying, basically, is that I should be shit-scared—'

'Albie!'

'And base my decisions on fear, because basically I've got no talent.'

'No, you may well have a talent, but it's a talent that is shared by millions of other people. Millions! That's all.'

And perhaps that was a poor choice of words. Perhaps this example does not present me in the best light, I would concede that. But as to the accusation that I wanted him to be something he was not? Well, yes, of course I did. Because what is a parent *for* if not to shape their child?

## 154. how a father should be

Connie and I also argued. Raising Albie accentuated the differences between us, differences that had seemed merely entertaining in the carefree days before parenthood. She was, to my mind, absurdly informal and laissez-faire. To take an analogy from botany, she imagined a child as an unopened flower; a parent had a responsibility to provide light and water, but also to stand back and watch. 'He can do anything he wants,' she said, 'as long as he's happy and cool.' In contrast, I saw no reason why the flower should not be bracketed to a bamboo stick, pruned, exposed to artificial light; if it made for a stronger, more resilient plant, why not? Of course Connie cajoled and encouraged him and made him do his homework, but still she felt that his natural qualities and talents would make themselves known unaided. I did not believe in natural talents. For me, nothing had ever come naturally, not even science. I had been obliged to work hard, often with my parents standing at either shoulder, and saw no reason why Albie shouldn't too.

And Albie could be maddening, quite maddening; self-pitying, irresponsible, lazy, and was I really so oppressive and joyless, so short-tempered and ill-humoured? I'd meet other boys' dads at school events, sports days and fundraising barbecues, note their avuncular ease, their joshing tone, like football managers coaxing a promising young player. I'd watch them for clues.

Albie's best friend Ryan's father was a farm-worker, handsome, stubbled, frequently topless for no good reason, always smelling of beer and engine oil. Mike was a widower, bringing up Ryan in a shabby bungalow at the edge of the village, and Albie became infatuated with this pair, would go there after school to play violent video games in a house where the curtains were perpetually closed and the weekly shop came from the petrol station. I went to pick Albie up one night, edging past the caravan, the dismantled cars and motorbikes and barking dogs to find Mike with his shirt off, sitting in a deckchair and smoking something other than tobacco.

'Hello, Mike! Any sign of Albie?'

He raised a can in greeting. 'Last I saw he was on the roof.'

'Okay. On the roof?'

'Up there. They're doing target practice.'

'Oh. Okay. They have a gun?'

'Only my old air rifle.'

On cue I felt movement in the air near my ear as a pellet pinged off the cement mixer and ricocheted into the unmown grass. I looked up in time to see Albie's grinning face disappearing behind the guttering. 'What can I say?' said Mike. 'Boys'll be boys.'

Ryan's house became a kind of paradise that summer, Ryan's dad a kind of god. He let them drive the van, climb towering trees, go night-fishing; he'd drive them to quarries, the two of them bouncing around in an open-bed truck, and hurl them off high rocks into the black water. The rustier and sharper an object, the more exposed the wires and blades, the more suitable a toy for the boys to play with. They welded! He let them weld! Mike never sat Ryan down to patiently explain the periodic table; there were no 'school nights' in Mike's domain. Oh no, life with Mike was just one long burning mattress. 'I think Albie's spending too much time at Ryan's,' I said, after one more revision session disintegrated into tears, bribes and acrimony. 'We can't ban him,' said Connie. 'Forbidding it will just make it more appealing.' This was a notion that I found alien. When my father forbade something, it became forbidden, not appealing.

Sometimes Mike would drop Albie home at some ungodly hour and he and Connie would stand in the front garden talking, talking. 'He's very charming,' she'd say, flushing slightly on her return. 'He's sparky, he's got a twinkle. I think it's admirable, the way he brings up Ryan on his own.'

Admirable! What was admirable about letting your kid run wild, with no thought to his future? What about my work, the years of late-night study that had been required to get me there? Albie had no desire to come and see the lab and meet my colleagues. If anything, he had a vague contempt for it, part of a growing 'political' consciousness that he refused to debate with me. 'What does Ryan's dad do, exactly?' I'd ask. Albie didn't know, but he knew about the girls, scarcely more than teenagers, that Ryan's dad brought back from the pub. He knew about the roll of banknotes that Mike kept, squeezed into the pocket of his greasy jeans.


## 155. rumble in the gymnasium

A showdown was inevitable, and it came at the school's annual Parents' and Teachers' Quiz, part of the never-ending jamboree of social events to raise funds for a new theatre (because it's always a new theatre that's needed, or a pottery kiln or a piano, never a new centrifuge or fume cupboard).

I like to think I'm not too bad at quizzes. I know things, facts, equations – it's the way my mind works, always has been, and not just science, either. As a teenager I was entranced by the *Guinness Book of Records*, and memorised great chunks of it. Temperature of the sun, speed of the cheetah, length of a diplodocus, these facts were my party trick, though they rarely came up at parties. Never mind, because while some knowledge had faded, certain key elements – highest mountains, deepest oceans, speeds of light and sound, pi to many places, flags of the world – were as indelible as tattoos. Connie would be there to cover art and culture, and I think that the Petersens felt quietly confident as we entered the sports hall.

'Sorry, no spouses on the same team!' said Mrs Whitehead, who had told me that very week that Albie lacked basic numeracy skills. 'Oi! Connie! Over here!' shouted Mike, resplendent in a boiler suit unzipped to the navel and I noted how, suddenly giddy, Connie practically skipped across the hall to join his team. Albie went to sit with Ryan on the benches, and I cast around for a prospective team, settling on a shuffling band of lone parents loitering by the door as if about to bolt. Not the most prepossessing group of contestants, but never mind. I raised my hand to Albie and allowed myself to imagine the conversation in class the next day. 'Your dad was on fire last night!' 'He carried that team. Your dad, he knows his stuff!' I understand, perhaps more than anyone, that intelligence is not the quality a son most values in a father – Mike, as far as I could tell, was as stupid as a wall – but it would do no harm for Albie to see me win at something, and in a public forum too. We were offered bottled beers and a selection of snacks and took our place at our trestle table.

Few activities in life are more unpleasant to me than the task of deciding an amusing name for a quiz team. I have undergone surgical procedures that were less painful. Why couldn't we be 'red' or 'blue' or 'green' team? After long deliberation it was decided, for reasons I can't bring myself to recall, that we would be the Kranium Krusherz and that I would be captain or, presumably, kaptain. Mike and Connie's team were called Mobiles at the Ready, which got a laugh but made me anxious, because that kind of anarchy is just intolerable to me. I pushed it out of my mind and thought about deepest lakes, longest rivers, highest peaks. A whistle of feedback and we began.

Of course the quiz was a travesty of what I understand by 'general knowledge'. The music questions were skewed heavily towards the current pop scene, the sports questions almost entirely towards football, the news and current affairs were trivial and tabloid in nature, there was nothing at all on science or geography, inventions or mental arithmetic. We did what we could but Mike's team, the aforementioned Mobiles at the Ready, were a tight little huddle of whispers and giggles, Mike and Connie head to head at its centre. 'Yes!' they hissed to each other. 'Well done! Write it down!' It seemed that Mike was not as dim as I'd imagined, at least with regard to song lyrics and celebrity tattoos, and Connie's hand gripped his forearm tight. 'Yes, Mike, yes! You're brilliant!'

Elsewhere other teams were cheating in a supposedly light-hearted way – you could hear the tap-tap-tap of tiny keyboards, phones bleeping in their pockets, and as the evening progressed my indignation increased, magnified by the effect of the bottles of beer we were encouraged to buy in aid of the theatre fund. Our chances dwindled. I slumped in my stackable chair.

'And now,' said the quizmaster, 'our penultimate round, flags of the world!'

Finally! I sat up straight. While the other teams scratched their heads I ticked them all off and showed both thumbs to Albie, who was distracted and didn't see me. Then, I couldn't quite believe it, name the rivers, name the lakes! I rallied our team, the correct answers accumulated, and it was time for marking.

We swapped papers with Mike and Connie's team and I watched as they laughed and jeered at our answers on pop music. In turn, I shook my head at their suggestions for the flags. Venezuela? Oh, Mike, I'm sorry, no. I remained rigorously fair in our marking, but in general the process was sloppy and ill-conceived. Was it one point for a bonus, or two? Eventually our team's papers were returned with a smug grin from Mike, and immediately I noticed several errors. Clearly there had been some spiteful marking down, points lost for writing USSR instead of Russia, when in fact USSR was the more accurate answer. Too late, though, because our scores had been noted and now the results were being announced.

Sixth, fifth, fourth, third. In second place – the Kranium Krusherz. Mike and Connie's team had beaten us by two points. I watched Mike and Connie embrace to cheers and applause, and on the benches, too, Ryan and Albie were clenching their fists and whooping in that simian way.

But I remained concerned. One point for each bonus question, when we had given them two? Nothing for the USSR? Mentally I calculated our correct score, calculated it again. There was no denying, we'd been cheated of victory, and I felt I had no choice but to cross to the quizmaster and make the case for a recount.

For a while, audience and contestants seemed confused. Was the evening over? Not quite yet, not until I'd consulted with Albie's head of year, Mr O'Connell, pointing out the discrepancies in the marking.

Mr O'Connell placed his hand over the microphone. 'Are you sure you want to do this?'

'Yes. I think so. Yes.'

By now the hall had taken on the grim and solemn air of a war crimes tribunal. I'd hoped my intervention would be taken in the light-hearted spirit I'd intended, but parents were shaking their heads and pulling on their coats, and still the recount continued until, after what seemed an age, justice prevailed and it was announced to the half-empty hall that our Kranium Krusherz had lived up to their name and won by half a point!

I looked to my son. He did not cheer. He did not punch the air. He sat on the bench gripping his hair with his hands while Ryan draped an arm around his shoulder. In silence, my fellow Krusherz divided up the spoils, £10 worth of vouchers to spend at the local garden centre, and we walked out to the school car park.

'Congratulations, Doug,' said Mike, standing by his Transit van with a grin. 'You showed us who's boss!' Then to my son, with a hateful wink: 'Your dad, he's practically a genius!' In times of old, we'd have just gone at each other with clubs and rocks. Perhaps that would have been better.

Anyway, the three of us drove home in silence. 'For as long as I'm alive I never, ever want to talk about this evening again,' said Connie quietly as she unlocked the front door. And Albie? He went upstairs to his room without a word, contemplating, I suppose, just how very clever his father was. 'Goodnight, son. See you tomorrow!' Standing at the bottom of the stairs, I watched him go and thought, not for the first or the last time, what an awful feeling it is to reach out for something and find your hand is grasping, grasping at the air.

## 156. rendezvous

Sweating, shaking, I woke with a start. The blackout blinds had done their job all too well and I was locked in a black box at the bottom of the ocean. I fumbled for the switch at the side of the bed and the metal shutters juddered apart, letting in a blinding morning sun bright enough for midday. I squinted at my watch – a little before seven. Madrid. I was in Madrid, on my way to see my son. Plenty of time to make the rendezvous. I lay back in bed to let my heart rate normalise, but the damp sheets had gone cold and so I padded to the window, saw the blue sky, the early-morning traffic on the Gran Vía, the bright new day. I showered at length and got dressed in my brand new clothes.

At breakfast, I ate a great deal of delicious ham and clumpy scrambled eggs and read the news back home on my tablet, missing the old sense of isolation that foreign travel used to bring. 'Abroad' seemed so much further away then, isolated from the British media, but here it was, all online, the usual mixture of rage, gossip, corruption, violence and bad weather. Good God, no wonder Albie had run away. Wary of souring my mood, I researched a little about Madrid instead, looking up the Wikipedia entry on Picasso's *Guernica* in case Albie and I made it there later. The steps of the Prado at eleven. Still not yet eight. I decided to go for a walk.

I rather liked Madrid; grandly ornamental in places, noisily, messily commercial in others, scruffy and unpretentious, like a fine old building covered in stickers and graffiti; no wonder Albie had headed here. Perhaps I was mistaken, but there was a sense that ordinary people lived here, right in the centre of the city, a possibility long lost to the citizens of London or Paris. Although I only had the hotel's complimentary map to guide me, I had covered some ground by nine forty-five, at which point I made my way to the Prado.

Like shoppers at the January sales, a small group of tourists was already waiting for the doors to open, visibly excited at the prospect of all that art, and I joined the queue and tried not to worry. 'What will you say when you see him?' I had been suppressing Freja's question, yet I remained fuzzy-headed about the answer, with only a jumble of apologies and justifications in mind. Along with self-reproach, resentment lurked too, that the holiday – potentially our last holiday – had been hijacked by Albie's disappearance. Not a word from him, not one word! Did he want us to worry? Clearly he did, but would it really have hurt him to pick up the phone? Did he really care so little for our peace of mind? The voice in my head was becoming increasingly indignant, and it was vital that I stay calm and conciliatory. In an attempt to find some repose, I shuffled into the Prado to settle a question that had been troubling me for some time.

## 157. *the garden of earthly delights*

'Is it Prah-do or Pray-doh?' I asked the lady at the ticket desk. I'd been alternating the two in my head, and was pleased to confirm that it was the former. 'Prah-do,' I said to myself, trying it out. 'Prah-do. Prah-do.'

Immediately, I could tell this museum was something special. Here was Bosch's *The Garden of Earthly Delights*, a picture that I'd been enthralled by as a child for its lunatic detail. In the flesh, it was as much an object as a painting, a large wooden box that unfolded to reveal the painting and called to mind the gatefold album sleeves of certain progressive rock bands that I'd enjoyed in the 1970s. Here, on the left panel, were Adam and Eve, so vivid and sharp that they might have been painted yesterday, and here was heaven, populated by innumerable nude figures, pot-bellied like children, clambering over giant strawberries or riding on the backs of finches, and here was hell on the right, perverse and nightmarish, lit by bonfires on which those same tiny pot-bellied figures were the fuel. A sword embedded in a neck, a feather quill between disembodied ears, a sinister giant, fused with a pig, fused with a tree. A non-academic word, I know, but it was 'trippy', the kind of thrillingly horrible picture that a teenage boy would love and I hoped that, once he'd accepted my apology, Albie and I would return this way and absorb all the psychedelic detail.

No time now. I headed upstairs past El Grecos and Riberas to a spectacular room, a startling collection of portraits of moustachioed aristocrats, the Hapsburgs painted by Velázquez. One face recurred throughout, lantern-jawed and moist-lipped, here as a self-conscious, pink-cheeked teenage prince in brand new armour, here dressed absurdly as a fancy-dress hunter, now a sad, spaniel-faced monarch in late middle age. I wondered how he'd responded to the paintings, if Philip IV had squirmed the way we all do when we catch sight of our true likeness. 'I wonder, Signor Diego, if there's any way to make my chin a little smaller?'

These portraits were extraordinary enough, but dominating the whole room was a painting the like of which I'd never seen before, of a small girl, perhaps four or five years old, encased in a stiff satin dress as wide as a table at the hips, very strange on a child. *Las Meninas*, it was called, which means *The Maids of Honour*, and sure enough the princess was surrounded by courtiers, a nun, a finely dressed female dwarf and a small boy, or perhaps he was another dwarf, prodding a dog with his foot. To the left, a painter with a comically Spanish moustache – a likeness, I supposed, of Velázquez himself – stood in front of a huge canvas, facing out as if he was painting not the little girl but the viewer, specifically me, Douglas Timothy Petersen, the illusion so convincing that I wanted to crane around the canvas to see what he'd made of my nose. A mirror on the back wall showed two other figures, the girl's parents I guessed, Mariana and Philip IV, the large-chinned gentleman on the wall to my left. Despite being distant and blurred, it seemed that they were the true subject of the artist's portrait, but nevertheless the artist, the little girl, the female dwarf all seemed to stare out of the painting at me with such level intensity that I began to feel rather self-conscious, and confused, too, as to how a painting could have so many subjects: the little princess, the ladies in waiting, the artist, the royal couple, and me. It was as disorientating as the moment when you step between two mirrors and see infinite versions of yourself stretching into, well, infinity. Clearly there was 'a lot going on' in this painting too, and I'd return with Albie soon.

I returned to the central atrium, ducking in and out of rooms, glimpsing wonderful things. I would have returned to the front steps and waited there, had I not seen a sign for something called the Black Paintings, which sounded intriguing in a rather Hammer-horror kind of way.

## 158. francisco goya

The canvases in question were in a gloomy room in the basement of the gallery, as if they were some dark family secret, and one glimpse at them revealed why. They weren't even canvases, but murals painted directly on to the walls of a house by Goya and clearly the work of a deeply disturbed man. In one, a grinning woman raised a knife ready to hack off someone's head, in another a circle of grotesque women sat around Satan, manifested in the form of a monstrous goat. Up to their knees in some filthy bog, two men stood smashing at each other's bloodied heads with cudgels. A drowning dog's sad-eyed head peeked out of quicksand. Even the innocent scenarios – women laughing, two old men eating soup – seemed crammed with fear and spite, but the worst was still to come. In some sort of cave a mad giant tore at the flesh of a corpse with his teeth. The picture was called *Saturn Devouring His Son*, though this god was nothing like the handsome figures I'd seen in France and Italy. He seemed deranged, his body old, sagging and grey, with a look of such terrible self-loathing in his horrible black eyes . . .

I heard a ringing in my ears, felt a tightening in my chest and a sensation of such dread and anxiety that I was forced to hurry from the room, wishing that I had never seen the painting, that it had remained on the walls of some remote, derelict house. I am not a superstitious man, but there was something of the occult about the pictures. With only ten minutes to go before my rendezvous, I felt I needed some sort of antidote and I hurried back upstairs, along the gallery's main corridor, looking left and right for a calm spot in which to rest and gather my thoughts. On my right was the Velázquez room and I thought that I might sit for a moment in front of the small girl in *Las Meninas*, to clear my head.

But the gallery had become a great deal busier since I'd first arrived, and the picture was now concealed behind a party of tourists. Nevertheless I sat and attempted to regain my composure, pressing my fingers against my eyes so that it took me a moment to sense a presence, look up and see my son standing right in front of me, saying those words that every father longs to hear.

'Jesus Christ, Dad, why can't you just leave me alone?'

## 159. paseo del prado

'Hello, Albie. It's me!'

'I can see that, Dad.'

'I've been looking for you everywhere. It's good to see you. I—'

'Where's Kat?'

'Kat's not coming, Albie.'

'She's not coming? She sent me a text.'

'Yes, I was there.'

'Why isn't she coming?'

'Well, Albie, to be honest, she was never coming.'

'I don't understand. She tricked me?'

'No, she didn't *trick* you—'

'What, you tricked me?'

'Not tricked, she helped, Kat helped. Me find you.'

'But I didn't want you to find me.'

'No, I realise that. But your mother was worried and I wanted to—'

'If I'd wanted you to find me, I'd have told you where I was.'

'Nevertheless, we've been worried about you, your mother and I—'

'But the text message, I thought . . . I thought that Kat was pregnant!'

'Yes, you might have got that impression . . .'

'I thought I was going to be a dad!'

'Yes, that was sort of implied. Sorry about that.'

'Do you know what that feels like?'

'I do, as a matter of fact.'

'I'm seventeen! I've been going nuts!'

'Yes, I can see how that might have come as a bit of a shock.'

'Was that your idea?'

'No!'

'Whose fucking idea was it, then, Dad?'

'Hey, Albie, that's enough!' People were staring now, the museum guard poised to approach. 'Maybe we should go somewhere else . . .'

It seemed Albie had already thought of this because he was loping off at quite some speed, head down against the tide of tourists who were suddenly flooding the atrium. I did my best to follow, throwing out '*scusi*'s and '*por favor*'s until we were outside, the light unnaturally bright now, the heat quite shocking as we tumbled down the steps and headed for the tree-lined avenue that skirts the museum.

'It would really be a lot easier to explain if we could sit down.'

'What's to explain? I wanted to be alone to think and you wouldn't allow it.'

'We were worried!'

'You were worried because you don't trust me. You've never trusted me—'

'We simply wanted to know where you were and that you were safe, that's not unusual. Would you prefer we didn't care?'

'You always say that, Dad! Right after you've been screaming and shouting at me and jabbing your finger, it's always because we care! "We care!" you say while you're pressing the pillow down on my face!'

'There's no need to be melodramatic, Albie! When have I ever . . . ? Albie . . .' He was pretty nimble on his feet, and I was having difficulty speaking now. 'Please, can we . . . this would be a whole lot easier if we could . . .' I stopped, hands on my knees, hoping that he would not disappear. I glanced up, and he was there, kicking at the path with his heel.

'I wanted . . . to apologise . . . for what I said in Amsterdam . . .'

'What *did* you say in Amsterdam, Dad?' he asked, and I realised my son had no intention of making it easy for me.

'I'm sure you can remember, Albie.'

'But just to make sure . . .'

Perspiration was dripping from my forehead onto the footpath. I saw the drops hit the ground, counted them, one, two, three. 'I said I was . . . embarrassed by you. And I wanted to say that I'm not. I think your behaviour was over the top, I think there was no need to start a fight, but I didn't express myself very well and I wanted to apologise. In person. For that. And for other times when I may have overreacted. I've been under a lot of strain recently . . . at work and, well, at home too and . . . Anyway. No excuses. I'm sorry.' I straightened up. 'Do you accept my apology?'

'No.'

'I see. May I ask why?'

'Because I don't think you should apologise for what you really think.'

'What do I really think, Albie?'

'That I am an embarrassment.'

'How can you say that, Albie? I care about you very, very much. I'm sorry if that's not always been clear, but surely you can see—'

'Everything you do, Dad, everything you say to me, there's this . . . contempt, this constant stream of dislike and irritation—'

'Is there? I don't think there is—'

'Belittling me and criticising me—'

'Oh, Albie, that's not true. You're my boy, my dear boy—'

'Christ, it's like I'm not even your favourite child!'

'What do you mean, Albie?'

He inhaled sharply through his nose, his features bunching up, the face he used to make as a small boy when trying not to cry. 'I've seen the photos you've got stashed away. I've seen you and Mum look at them longingly.'

'They're not stashed away, Albie. We've shown them to you.'

'And don't you think that's weird?'

'Not at all! Not in the least. We've always been honest about your sister. She isn't some secret – that would be awful. We loved Jane when she was born, and then we loved you too, just as much.'

'Except she never fucked up, did she? She never embarrassed you in public or fucked up at school. She got to be perfect, whereas me, your stupid fucked-up son—'

And here I must admit I laughed. Not maliciously, but at the melodrama of it all, the adolescent self-pity. 'Albie, come on, you're just feeling sorry for yourself—'

'Don't laugh at me! Don't! Can't you see, everything you do shows how stupid you think I am!'

'I don't think you're stupid—'

'You've told me I am! You've told me! To my face.'

'Have I?'

'Yeah, you have, Dad! You have!'

And I suppose I might have told him that, maybe once or twice.

I closed my eyes. I suddenly felt very tired and very sad and very far away from home. The futility of this whole expedition seemed suddenly overwhelming. I had told myself that it was not too late, that there was still time to make amends for the raised voices and bared teeth, the indifference and thoughtless remarks. I had regrets, certainly, about things I'd said, things I'd done, but behind it all there had always been . . . wasn't it obvious that there had always been . . .

I sat heavily on a stone bench. An old man on a bench.

'Are you all right?' asked Albie.

'I am. I'm fine. I'm just . . . very, very tired. It's been a very long journey.'

He came to stand in front of me. 'What are you wearing on your feet?'

351

I stuck a foot out, turned it from side to side. 'You like them?'

'You look ridiculous.'

'Yes, I'm aware of that. Albie, Egg, will you sit a minute? Just a minute, then you can go.' He looked left, then right, already planning his escape. 'I won't follow you this time. I swear.'

He sat down.

'I don't know what I can say to you, Albie. I had hoped the words would just come, but I don't seem to have made a very good job of expressing myself. I hope you know I have regrets, things I shouldn't have said. Or things I should have said but didn't, which is often worse. I hope you have some regrets too. You haven't always made it easy for us, Albie.'

He hunched his shoulders. 'No. I know.'

'The state of your room, it's as if you do it deliberately to annoy me.'

'I do,' he said, and laughed. 'Still. You can have it back now.'

'You're still going to college then? In October?'

'Are you going to talk me out of it?'

'Of course not. If that's what you want to do with your life—'

'Well I am.'

'Good. Good. I'm pleased you're going. I mean not pleased you're leaving home, but pleased—'

'I get it.'

'Your mother's terrified of what it will be like without you.'

'I know.'

'So much so that she's thinking about leaving too. Leaving me. But you've always been close, so I expect you knew that.'

'I did.'

'She told you?'

He shrugged. 'I sort of guessed.'

'Do you mind?'

He shrugged again. 'She doesn't seem very happy.'

'No, she doesn't, does she? She doesn't. Well, I've been trying to address that. I had hoped that we'd have fun together this summer, our last summer, all of us together. I'd hoped to change her mind. Perhaps I tried too hard. I'll find out soon enough. Anyway. I'm sorry for what I said to you. It's not what I believe. Whatever I might have said, I'm very proud of you, though I might not show it, and I know that you'll do great things in the future. You're my boy, and I'd hate for you to go off into the world without knowing that we will miss you and will want you to be safe and happy and that we love you. Not just your mum, you know how much your mother loves you. But me too. I love you too, Albie. There. I think that's really what I came to say. So now you can go. Do whatever you want, as long as it's safe. I won't follow you any more. I'll just sit here for a while. Sit here and rest.'

## 160. museo reina sofia

Later that afternoon, we went to see *Guernica*. We had both calmed down by then and while still not quite at ease – would we ever be at ease? – we were at least more comfortable in our silence. As we walked around the Museo Reina Sofia, I stole little sideways glances. He was, as far as I could tell, wearing the same clothes that he'd worn in Amsterdam: the stained T-shirt that showed his bony chest, jeans that cried out for a belt, sandals on his blackened feet. His vestigial beard was scraggy and unhygienic, hair lank and unwashed and he seemed very thin. In other words, nothing much had changed, and I was pleased.

We found ourselves in front of *Guernica*. I found the picture very striking, much larger than I expected and moving in a way that I had not associated with more abstract works (goodness, Connie, listen to me!). I would have liked to take in the picture quietly, but I allowed Albie to talk me through the historical context and significance of the work, insights he had clearly garnered from the same Wikipedia entry that I had read at breakfast. I watched him as he spoke. He talked a great deal, pointing out things that were obvious to anyone with even a passing knowledge of art. Wanting to educate me, I suppose. In fact he was rather boring on the subject, but I kept quiet and took comfort in that old saying about fallen apples and their distance from trees.

In a commuter café opposite the Atocha station we had *churros con chocolate*. The overhead lights blazed off the zinc tabletops, greasy discarded napkins littered the floor. It seemed entirely the wrong time of day and year to be eating deep-fried extruded batter dipped in thick hot chocolate, but it was pleasant to be out of the midday sun's atomic heat. Albie assured me that this was what everyone did here and, despite the café being empty, I chose not to contradict him.

'Where are you staying?'

'I'm in this hostel.'

'What's it like?'

He shrugged. 'It's a hostel.'

'I've never stayed in a hostel.'

'What, a seasoned inter-railer like you?'

'What's it like?'

He laughed. 'It's grim. Hostile. It's a hostile hostel.'

'I have a suite in a hotel on the Gran Vía.'

'A suite? What are you, some oligarch?'

'I know. It's all very sumptuous.'

'I hope you're not drinking from the mini-bar, Dad.'

'Albie, I'm not *mad*. Anyway, the point is there's a spare room that might be more comfortable. A fold-out sofa-bed. While you decide where you want to go next.'

He paused to concentrate on wiping the sugar from his stubble beard. 'Are you not eating your *churros*?'

I pushed the plate towards him. 'How do you eat so much and stay so skinny?'

He rolled his bony shoulders and posted another doughnut into his mouth. 'Nervous energy, I s'pose.'

'Yes, I know something about that.'

## 161. clever man

We fetched his things and returned to the hotel late in the afternoon, and I lay on the bed while Albie showered for an absurdly long time. I had not checked my phone for twenty-four hours, and with some dread I turned it on to find a selection of texts from Connie, the impatience spiralling into irritation.

**When are you home? Can't wait to see you.**

**Information please. Are you alive?**

**Are you back today, tomorrow, ever?**

**Frantic here. Douglas, please just call.**

There was a voicemail, too, from my sister, and I played it back with the phone some distance from my ear.

'Why aren't you answering your phone? You always answer your phone. Douglas, it's Karen. What the hell is going on? Connie's frantic. She says you're wandering round Europe looking for Albie. She made me swear I wouldn't tell you this but she thinks you've had some sort of nervous breakdown. Or a midlife crisis. Or both!' Karen sighed and I smiled. 'Give it up, Douglas. Albie will come home when he wants to. Anyway, call me. Do it, D. That's an order!'

Albie was standing in the doorway, wrapped in the hotel dressing gown, demonstrating that unique ability he has to shower for twenty minutes and still look dirty.

'Can I borrow your razor to shave?'

'Please do.'

'Who was on the phone?'

'Your Auntie Karen.'

'I thought I heard shouting.'

'I'm going to call your mother, Albie. Will you speak to her?'

''Course.'

'Now?'

He hesitated a moment. 'Okay.'

I dialled immediately and waited. 'Hello?' said Connie.

'Hello, darling.'

'Douglas, you're meant to be home! I was expecting you this morning. Are you at the airport?'

'No, no, I didn't catch the plane.'

'You're still in Italy?'

'Actually, I'm in Madrid.'

'What are you doing in . . . ?' She paused, gathered herself and continued in the kind of voice used to persuade people down off ledges. 'Douglas, we agreed it was time to come home . . .' I tried not to laugh.

'Connie? Connie, can you hold on for one moment? I've got someone here who wants to speak to you.'

I held the phone out. Albie hesitated then took it from my hand. '*Hola*,' he said, and closed the door.

I picked up a Spanish magazine with that exact same title, and stared at pictures of unfamiliar celebrities. I looked through the magazine once, twice. Connie and Albie spoke for so long that my sense of triumph was tempered by a growing anxiety about the cost of the call, and I thought about interrupting the conversation and asking Connie to call us back. But as I looked through the gap in the door to the other room, I noticed that Albie was somewhat red-eyed, which would mean that Connie was crying too and so not in the mood to discuss international call rates. I also noted that, true to form, Albie had managed to use all eight of the hotel towels, large and small, and to distribute them around the room, including one on a lampshade where it might easily burst into flames. Deep breath. Let it pass. Let the burning towels pass. I looked through the magazine a third time, and then a hand poked through the bedroom door and waggled the phone at me.

'Pick up the towels, please, Egg,' I said, taking the phone.

'"You treat this place like a hotel!"' said Albie, and closed the door.

I waited a moment then put the phone to my ear. 'Hello?'

Silence.

'Hello, Connie?'

I could hear her breathing.

. . .

. . .

'Connie, are you there?'

'Clever man,' she said, and hung up the phone.

## 162. in chueca

I do not know what Connie said to Albie in that call, but later, much later, as we ordered more drinks in a *taberna* in Madrid's gay district at some ungodly hour in the morning, I tentatively raised the subject of future plans. The bar was dark, wood-panelled, packed with noisy and attractive madrileños drinking – was it sherry? vermouth? – with Serrano ham and anchovies and oily chorizo.

'This is delicious!' I shouted, wiping grease off my chin. 'But I'm worried that they don't eat enough vegetables. As a nation, I mean.'

'I'm leaving tomorrow!' Albie shouted back. 'For Barcelona! First thing!'

I tried to hide my disappointment. In truth, I had not entirely abandoned the idea of Connie joining us and us all returning to the Grand Tour, perhaps retracing our steps to Florence. Our hotel reservations were still in place, and those tickets for the Uffizi . . .

'Oh. Okay. That's a shame. I thought we'd go back to—'

'You could come with me!'

The room really was very noisy and I asked him to repeat himself. He put his mouth to my ear:

'D'you want to come with me?'

'Where?'

'To Barcelona. Just for a night or two.'

'I've never been to Barcelona.'

'No, that's why I asked.'

'Barcelona?'

'It's on the sea.'

'I know where Barcelona is, Egg.'

'I thought it would be good to swim in the sea.'

'I'd like that.'

'You can even-up your tan. Colour in your left side.'

'Does that still show?'

'A little.'

I laughed.

'Okay. Okay! We'll go. We'll swim in the sea.'

part eight

# BARCELONA

—

'It's nothing to come to Europe,' she said to Isabel; 'it doesn't seem to me one needs so many reasons for that. It is something to stay at home; this is much more important.'

Henry James, *The Portrait of a Lady*

## 163. running towards the sea

It was with some relief that I discovered Barcelona had almost
no art galleries at all.

That wasn't quite true, of course. There was a Picasso Museum
and a Miró Museum and perhaps I should dip a toe into the
world of abstract, non-representational art after so many Old
Masters. But there was no single monolithic institution like the
Louvre or Prado and so no pressure. Instead Barcelona offered
us an opportunity to 'hang out'. For a day or so. We'd hang
out. Just . . . hang out.

This was the extent of Albie's itinerary, and he had already
showed admirable organisational ability in getting us to Madrid's
Atocha station in time for the nine thirty train. Quite a sight,
the Atocha station, more like a botanical garden hothouse than
a conventional transport hub, with a vast jungle of tropical
plants filling the central atrium, and I would have appreciated
it more had I not been suffering from the most appalling hang-
over of my life.

Our night in Chueca had turned into what Albie referred to
as a 'big one'. We had stayed in that particular bar for many
hours, sitting on high stools, eating wonderful food from the
edge of my comfort zone; fishy pastes, squid, chopped octopus
and fried hot green peppers, all of it very salty and dehydrating,
which caused us to drink even more vermouth – I'd developed
quite a taste for vermouth – which in turn allowed us to chat
happily with strangers about Spain, the recession and the euro,
Angela Merkel and the legacy of Franco, all the usual bar-room
chat. Albie, amicably drunk, kept introducing me to strangers
as 'my dad, the famous scientist' and then drifting off elsewhere,
but everyone was very friendly and it was refreshing to have

actual conversations with people of another nation, rather than just buying tickets or ordering food. Anyway, the evening went very well – so well, in fact, that we stepped from the bar into a hazy dawn, birds singing in the Plaza de Chueca. I associated dawn with anxiety and insomnia, but the partygoers and clubbers we passed on their way home all seemed in high spirits. *¡Buenos Días! ¡Hola!* It was all very open and friendly, and we decided that we liked Madrid, and Chueca in particular, very much. It was only some months later, when Albie announced to Connie and me that he was gay and in a serious relationship with a fellow student, that I realised this night out had been his first heavy hint. I had missed it at the time. I'd just thought he was being terrifically sociable.

Four hours later we were hurrying across the station concourse, nausea rising, the taste of vermouth and paprika stale in my mouth. Albie's constitution being stronger than mine, he took my elbow and helped me onto the train. Once out of Madrid we passed through the same terrain that I had flown across two days before, but I only glimpsed it through fluttering eyelids, sleeping all the way to the coast, waking to find that Albie had already booked a twin room in a large modern hotel right on the beach. 'I've put it on your card. Hope you don't mind.' I did not mind.

## 164. barceloneta

The hotel was one of those up-to-date establishments that have barely changed since 2003 – modular furniture in beige leather, large-screen TVs and a great deal of bamboo.

'Well. This is all very smart!' I said, taking the left-hand bed.

'You're sure you don't want your own room?'

'In case you cramp my style? I think we'll be okay.' I stepped out onto the balcony: a view of the Mediterranean and, across a four-lane road, a beach that seemed as densely packed as any city shopping street.

'So would you like to get something to eat, Dad? Or shall we go straight to the beach?' He really was being extremely accommodating, unnaturally so, and I put this down to his telephone conversation with Connie the previous day. *Look after your old dad. Be nice to him for a day or so, then send him home*, that kind of thing. He was acting under strict instructions, and it would not last, but for the moment I decided to enjoy this new companionability. We were neither of us being our usual selves, and perhaps this was for the best. I rolled up my trouser legs, grabbed a towel from the bathroom and, in the hotel lobby's gift shop, I purchased some trunks from the limited range, peach-toned Speedos two sizes too small, and we set out for the beach.

I have always found beaches to be uniquely hostile environments. Greasy and gritty, too bright to read, too hot and uncomfortable to sleep, the lack of shade frankly alarming, the lack of decent public toilets, too – unless of course you count the sea, as all too many swimmers do. On a crowded beach, even the bluest ocean takes on the quality of a stranger's bathwater, and this really was a very crowded beach, the concrete and fumes and cranes overhead giving it the quality of an unusually lax building site. Young Barcelona was handsome, muscular, cocky and deeply tanned, and there were bare breasts, too, though both Albie and I made a very big deal about not making this a big deal. 'It's nothing like Walberswick, is it?' I observed, all nonchalant as a group of barely-dressed girls settled nearby, and we both agreed that it was nothing like Walberswick.

The mutant trainers had been abandoned in Madrid and I was singularly lacking in beachwear, so I untied the laces of my brogues and performed the contortions required to pull on the offensive trunks beneath a towel, a fiddly procedure that recalled tying up the end of a balloon, then lay somewhat self-consciously on the hot sand. For all his enthusiasm for the sea, Albie seemed reluctant to swim, but the afternoon heat was like a salamander grill. I was becoming aware of my scalp's vulnerability and when I could not bear it any longer, I sat, up sprayed my head with sunblock and said, 'Egg, can I borrow your goggles?'

## 165. *pelagia noctiluca*

The water near the shore was cloudy with suntan lotion, greasy as the sink after a Sunday roast and dense with people standing still, bemused, hands on hips, as if trying to recall where they'd put their keys. Fish darted between our shins, but this close to the shore they were drab and unhealthy looking, scavengers feeding off God knows what. I waded out further, and as the coastal shelf deepened, the water cleared and turned a startling blue and I began to enjoy myself once more. I settled Albie's goggles on my eyes and dived, and immediately the last of the previous night's vermouth was washed away. I am a strong and confident swimmer and before long I was pretty much on my own, looking back towards the city, its radio towers and cranes and cable cars, and the hazy hills beyond. How strange to have stumbled, clambered and barged all over Europe and only now to have reached the ocean. From here Barcelona looked fine, handsome and modern, and I looked forward to exploring it with my son. Somewhere in that mass of bodies on the beach he was safe and well. The journey had reached its natural end and in two or three days' time, I'd return to Connie and make my case, whatever that was. Don't worry about it now. I closed my eyes, rolled onto my back and turned my face to the afternoon sun.

What happened next remains something of a blur, though I distinctly recall the shock of the first sting on the bridge of my foot, an extraordinarily painful sensation like being slashed with a blade. The cause should have been obvious, but my first idea was that I'd kicked against broken glass and it was only when

I immersed my head in the water, saw the sand far, far below and all around me the pink and blue clouds of jellyfish – a swarm, there really was no other word – that I realised the trouble I was in. I tried to steady my breath and reassure myself that, if I took my time, it should be perfectly possible to pick my way through these mines and reach the shore. But had there really been so many? I inhaled, and sank beneath the water once again, and blurted out the air. It was as if I were the first witness to some alien invasion, a beach landing, and here I was far, far behind enemy lines, an impression underscored by a sharp pain in the small of my back like the blow of a whip. I reached around, felt something as soft as sodden paper tissue and then the sting of the whip once more, on my wrist this time. Bobbing up, I examined the wound, which was already raised in a lurid pink, the outline of the tentacles quite clearly branded on the skin. I swore and tried not to move but my stillness caused me to dip underwater once again, vertically, like a fisherman's float, inhaling when I should have exhaled as I saw another of the vile creatures just inches from my face as if deliberately intimidating me. Absurdly, I punched it because nothing hurts a jellyfish more, nothing affronts their sense of dignity, than an underwater punch in the face. Escaping a sting, I pushed backwards and steadied myself, staying afloat by swirling my hands and feet in little circles. I scanned the surface of the ocean. The nearest swimmer was some fifty yards away, and as I watched he too yelped with pain and began to pound towards the shore, and I was alone.

I opened my mouth to shout. Perhaps I should call for help, but that word, 'help', stuck in my throat. It suddenly seemed like such a silly word. 'Help!' Who really cried for help? What a cliché! And what was 'help' in Spanish, anyway – or should it be Catalan? Would 'aidez-moi!' be any good? Did French people, drowning, feel silly shouting 'aidez-moi!' and even if someone was close enough to hear, how could they possibly help me, surrounded as I was? They would have to hoist me out by helicopter, a great gelatinous mass of these monsters dangling from my pale legs. 'Sorry!', that's what I should shout. 'Sorry! Sorry for being so bloody foolish!'

I looked to the shore, trying to find Albie there, but I was too far away, bobbing uselessly, the pain in my foot and back and arm refusing to fade and now I was underwater again, eyes squeezed tight this time, no longer wanting to know what was around me, and now another blow of the whip, on my shoulder this time and I thought, oh God, I'm going to die here, I'm going to drown, pass out with the toxic shock of innumerable stings and slip below the surface. I was sure that I'd die, surer than I've ever been, and then I laughed to myself, because it would be such a ridiculous death – would make the British papers, probably – and then I remembered my swimwear, uncomfortably close to flesh tone, and a 30-inch waist when they really should have been 34, 36 even, and I thought, please God, don't let them find my dead body in these 30-inch bathers; I don't want Connie to identify me in these children's bathers. *Yes, that's my husband, but the bathers, they belong to someone else.* Perhaps they'd have to bury me in them. 'Oh, Christ,' I said out loud, and laughed again, a spluttering laugh through a mouthful of seawater. 'Oh, Christ, Connie, I'm sorry.' Quite consciously I conjured up an image of her face, the one I always think of, taken from a photograph, which sounds sentimental I know, but I think we are allowed to be sentimental at such times. So there it is. I thought of Connie, Albie too, our little family, I took another breath and swam with all my might towards the shore, attempting as best I could to skim across the surface of the water.

### 166. *medusa, medusa*

My exit from the ocean was even less elegant than my entrance, as I staggered ashore like some shipwreck victim, hunched on all fours in the shallows in the midst of someone's volleyball game. In my panic I had misjudged my direction and had come to land one hundred yards or so from Albie, and there was no one there to help me to my feet or ask what was wrong. So while I knelt and caught my breath, the volleyball game resumed over my head.

When finally I felt that I could walk, I began to search for Albie. The sun was brutally hot as if focused through a magnifying glass. At least the water had been cooling; out in the open I felt grilled. Even the movement of air across the stings was painful, and neither was I alone in my distress. Now word had spread along the beach and I heard the word '*medusa, medusa*' follow me as I searched for Albie once more.

I found him eventually, sound asleep.

'Albie! Albie, wake up.'

'Da-ad!' he growled, shielding his eyes against the light. 'What's up?'

'I got jumped. By some jellyfish.'

He sat up. 'In the water?'

'No, on the land. They took my keys and wallet.'

'You're shaking.'

'Because it hurts, Albie, it really, really hurts.'

When he saw my discomfort, Albie sprang into action, immediately lunging for his phone and Googling 'jellyfish sting' while I sheltered beneath a towel, wincing at its contact with the stings.

'I'm not going to have to wee on you, am I? Because that'd just be too Freudian and weird. That's fifty years of therapy, right there.'

'I think the urine thing is a myth.'

He referred to his phone. 'It is! It is a myth! In fact, it says here you've got to just pick off any tentacles and stinging sacs and take a lot of painkillers. Where are you going?'

I pulled on my shirt wincing, an awful nausea creeping up on me. 'I'm going to lie down in the room. I have some paracetamol in my bag.'

'Okay, I'll come with you.'

'No, you stay here.'

'I want to—'

'Seriously, Albie, you have a nice time. I'm only going to sleep it off. Don't swim. And what SP factor are you using, by the way?'

'Factor eight.'

'You're insane. Look where the sun is! You need SPF30 at least.'

'Dad, I think I'm old enough to decide—'

'Here . . .' I tossed him the lotion. 'Don't forget the tops of your ears. I'll see you back at the hotel.' With shoes and trousers in my hand, arms held out to the side, I picked my way through the crowd and stumbled back to the hotel.

I was inappropriately dressed for the crowded lobby, but did not care. By the time I reached my room, the nausea had increased, though the pain had eased somewhat and would soon seem almost negligible in comparison with the series of heart attacks that hit me in quick succession, like blows against my sternum from some mighty sledgehammer, the first swiping me to the floor and knocking all the breath from my body.

## 167. under the wardrobe

There's an old twist in the horror stories that I secretly enjoyed as a child, where it's revealed that the central character has been dead all along. I've seen this twist in films, too, and, quite apart from the assumptions it makes about consciousness and the afterlife, it has always struck me as a cheap trick. So I should say straight away that I did not die, nor was I invited to walk towards any white light.

The fact is, my son saved my life. Whether through guilt or concern, he had been unable to relax on the beach and so had followed on a few minutes behind, entering the room to find my feet protruding from between the two single beds. The pain had spread through my chest, into my arms, neck and jaw, and I was breathing with some difficulty, panicking too because, until Egg arrived, I saw no possibility of rescue and was obliged simply to lie there on the hardwood floor, pinned down as if by some immense old wardrobe, contemplating the ball of fluff beneath the bed, my son's discarded socks and trainers and towels just beyond and then, miraculously, my son's blessed filthy feet in the doorway.

'Dad? What are you playing at?'

'Come here, please, Albie.'

He clambered over the bed, looking down at me crammed unhappily against the bedside table, and I explained what I thought had happened. He did not Google 'heart attack'. Instead he picked up the phone and called reception, adopting a sensible and clear tone that I had not heard before; admirably calm, just how I'd have done things. When he was sure that help was on its way, he stood astride me, wriggling his hands into my armpits and attempting to bring me into a sitting position. But I was wedged securely, too weak to assist, and so instead he squeezed in beside me on the floor between the beds and held my hand while we waited.

'You see?' he said, after a while. 'I told you those trunks were too tight.'

I winced. 'Don't make me laugh, Albie.'

'Are you in pain?'

'Yes. Yes, I am.'

'I'm sorry.'

'Aspirin would help.'

'Do we have any?'

'We have paracetamol.'

'Will that help, Dad?'

'Don't think so.'

'Okay. Let's just lie still, then.'

Some time passed, perhaps three, four minutes, and though I tried to remain calm I could not help considering that my own father had probably found himself in this position too, alone in that flat without anyone to lie there or make silly jokes. Without anyone? Without me. 'His heart basically exploded,' the doctor had said with inappropriate relish. I felt another spasm in my chest and winced.

'You okay?'

'I'm fine.'

'Keep breathing, Dad.'

'I intend to.'

Time passed, but barely.

'What happens if you lose consciousness?'

'Perhaps we should talk about something else, Egg.'

'Sorry.'

'If I lose consciousness, that will be cardiac arrest. You'll have to do CPR.'

'The kiss-of-life thing?'

'I think so.'

'Oh, Christ. Don't lose consciousness, will you?'

'I'm trying hard not to.'

'Good.'

'Do you know how to do CPR, Egg?'

'No. I'll Google it. Perhaps I should do that now.'

I laughed again. If anything was going to kill me, it would be the sight of Albie desperately reading up on CPR. 'No. Just lie here with me. I'm going to be fine. This is all going to be fine.' Albie exhaled slowly, squeezed my hand and rubbed my knuckles with his thumb. A shame, I thought, to regain this intimacy at such a cost.

'Albie—'

'Dad, you shouldn't really talk, you know.'

'I know—'

'It's all going to be fine.'

'I know, but if I'm not fine. If I'm not . . .'

Some people, I imagine, would have welcomed this opportunity to make some definitive, final statement to the world, and various formulations ran through my head. But they all seemed rather fraught and melodramatic, and so instead we lay there, still and silent, wedged between the beds, holding hands and waiting for the ambulance to arrive.

## 168. *ataque al corazón*

I can't speak highly enough of the Spanish health system. The paramedics were no-nonsense and rather 'macho' in a reassuring way, and I was scooped up in their hairy arms and taken a short distance to the local hospital where, after tests and X-rays and the administering of blood-thinning medication, it was explained by a Dr Yolanda Jimenez, in good, clear English, that I would be subject to an operation. Immediately I imagined the buzzing of surgical saws and my rib-cage being cracked open like a lobster shell, but the doctor explained that the procedure would be much more localised than that. A tube would be inserted into my thigh under local anaesthetic, passing, somewhat improbably, all the way up into my heart, allowing the artery to be widened and a stent to be left in its place. I pictured pipe-cleaners, dental floss, an unravelled wire coat hanger. The operation would take place the next morning.

'Well, that doesn't sound so bad,' I said cheerily after the doctor had left. In truth, I did not relish the prospect of a catheter being inserted into my thigh and probing its way past my internal organs, but I did not want Albie to worry. 'If they go too far, presumably it comes out of my ear!' I said and he forced a smile.

Albie returned to the hotel to bring me a change of clothes. The obscene trunks were discarded and we were transferred to a ward to spend the night. I wish I could report some unique Barcelona atmosphere, with everyone promenading down the corridors and eating octopus off cocktail sticks until dawn. It was as anxious and depressing as any hospital ward in the world, but with the oaths, groans and sobbing cries in a different accent. Albie, who had never been inside a hospital since his birth, looked shaken. 'Dad, if this is all some elaborate ruse to stop me smoking, then it's worked.'

'Well, that's something, I suppose. Albie, you can leave me here if you want.'

'What, and go and party?'

'At least go back to the hotel. You can't sleep in a chair.'

'I'll go later. Now we need to phone Mum.'

'I know.'

'Do you want to do it, or shall I?'

'I'll talk to her, then pass her on to you.'

So I called her and next day, by the time the procedure was complete and I was waking from a sedative-assisted sleep, my wife was by my side.


## 169. her face

Connie lay, somewhat awkwardly, half on, half off the hospital bed, her fantastic face close to mine.

'How are you?'

'I'm fine! A little sore, a little bruised.'

'I thought it was keyhole surgery.'

'More Chubb than Yale.'

'Are you in pain? Shall I get off you?'

'No, no, I like having you here. Don't move. I'm sorry if I stink.' I had not bathed properly since the Mediterranean and was painfully aware of staleness of both breath and body.

'Christ, I don't care. Shows you're alive. How was the . . . ?'

'A little uncomfortable. A pressure in the chest, as if someone's got their finger inside you somehow—'

'Bloody hell, Douglas!'

'I'm fine. I'm sorry you had to come all this way.'

'Well, I was thinking maybe just let it go, let him go through surgery by himself, but there was nothing on TV, so – here I am.' Her hand was on my cheek now. 'Look at this crazy beard. You look like you've been shipwrecked or something.'

'I've missed you.'

'Oh God, I've missed you too.' She was crying now, and perhaps I was too. 'Let's do exactly this same holiday next year, shall we?'

'Exactly like this. Don't change a thing. I want it to be exactly like this every year.'

'Holiday of a lifetime.'

'Holiday of a lifetime.'

## 170. pillow

After the angiogram, and with the angioplasty considered a success, it was decided that the heart attack was 'not serious'. It had certainly felt serious enough as I'd lain sprawled on the floor between those beds, but I did not quibble because the good news was that I could leave the hospital after one more night and, with the correct medication, would be allowed on a plane back to England in ten days or so.

Taking control with admirable efficiency, Connie and Albie found an apartment. This would be more comfortable and less claustrophobic than a hotel and so we filled in medical forms, scheduled various tests, and then took a taxi to Eixample, a bourgeois residential area full of rather grand apartment blocks. Ours was a pleasant, quiet, book-lined place on the first floor – not too many stairs – the home of an absent academic, with a balcony at the rear and places to walk nearby. There were Gaudí buildings and restaurants, the Sagrada Família was seven blocks away; all very civilised and ruinously expensive, too, but, perhaps for the first time in my life, I was able to point out the value of comprehensive travel insurance. We would not worry about expense. It was important that I did not worry about anything at all.

There's a kind of luxury in convalescence, and I was carried from place to place with great care and attention like an old vase. Albie in particular was terrifically attentive and interested as if, up until now, he'd thought mortality was a myth. Some months later I discovered that my admission into hospital had been the subject of a series of verité-style photographs; stark, black-and-white high-contrast images of my gawping face while sleeping, extreme close-ups of the various heart monitors affixed to my chest, the cannula piercing my skin. To the teenager all disasters are a rite of passage, but I was happy, at long last, to have provided him with some inspiration. At least he had some photos of me now.

Once it became clear that I would not be dying any time soon, Albie lost interest. Connie and I encouraged him to leave us on our own and his relief was palpable. His college friends were meeting up in Ibiza before heading off in all kinds of directions, and he flew out to join them, with a store of dramatic stories to tell. Perhaps he embellished the truth; perhaps he'd administered CPR. Perhaps a part of him wondered how it might have felt if I hadn't pulled through, who knows. The crisis had been mine, but I was happy for him to receive his share of attention and acclaim. I was proud of him.

What happened to Albie in Ibiza that summer I will never know, which is exactly how it should be. He contacted us daily to assure us of his safety and his happiness, which was all we asked, and for the moment my dear wife and I were alone once more.

## 171. *homage to catalonia*

Perhaps it sounds perverse, but I count my convalescence in Barcelona as among the happiest times of our marriage.

I would sleep late, with no thought of an alarm clock, while Connie sat on the balcony, with oranges and tea reading a book. When we were ready we would take a walk, perhaps down to La Boqueria, the food market that we both loved, where I would drink fruit juice but no coffee, no booze. There was much talk of my having to adopt a Mediterranean diet from now on, a gruesome notion in Berkshire but no chore whatsoever while we were here. We bought bread, olives and fruit from our favourite stalls and walked on.

The Ramblas was a little too touristic for us residents, so usually we would strike left or right into the back streets of Raval or the Gothic Quarter, taking frequent breaks in cafés. In a little English-language bookshop in Gràcia, Connie had found a copy of Orwell's *Homage to Catalonia* and a history of the Spanish Civil War, and we would sit in the shade to read and drink fresh orange juice. In the late afternoon we'd doze, then in courtyard restaurants we'd eat early in the evening like the other tourists, resisting with some regret the chorizo, the fried squid, the cold beer, then walk slowly, very slowly, home to bed and rest.

One morning we took a taxi to the Joan Miró Foundation high above the city, which sent Connie into paroxysms but left me unsure and feeling that I still had some way to go as far as abstract art was concerned. Then a wonderful cable car from the Parc de Montjuïc to the sea, high over the harbour, over cranes and swimming pools, warehouses and motorways, over the decks of ocean liners and container ships. You see over there?

There's the Sagrada Família, and there's the hotel where I held hands with my son and thought that I would die. The cable car lowered us gently from the mountain to the sea, and this was how my time in Barcelona felt; as if I'd been lifted up and carried with great care and affection. It was almost like early childhood, and therefore could not last forever. At some point my head would strike the door jamb, and I'd be jerked back into the real world and the consequences of my condition; the anxieties, the tests and procedures, the implications for my lifestyle and career.

But for the time being Connie and I were as harmonious and content and interested in each other, as in love, for want of a better phrase, as we had ever been. Clearly the key to having a long and successful marriage would be to have a non-lethal heart attack every three months or so for the next forty years. If I could only pull off that trick, then we might just be all right.

One night, lying in the large, cool bed I asked:

'Do you think we can have sex again at some point? I mean without me clutching at my chest and dropping dead on top of you?'

'Actually, I looked that up.'

'You did?'

'I did. They recommend four weeks, but I think it's okay as long as I do all the work and you don't get excited.'

'No change there then.'

She laughed, which pleased me hugely.

'I think we'll be all right, don't you?' I said.

'That's what I thought too,' said Connie, and we were. We were all right.


## 172. home

After a week or so, we were quite the Barcelonese, if that is the word; no maps, no guidebooks, no more itineraries. We even picked up a few words of Catalan. *¡Bona tarda! ¡Si us plau!* Every few days we'd make our way to the hospital and sit comfortably in Spanish waiting rooms until finally I was given the all-clear and passed back into the care of the National Health Service. It was safe for me to travel. We could go home.

'Well. That's good news,' I said.

'Isn't it?' said Connie.

Nevertheless, it was with some reluctance that we packed our bags and I watched uselessly as Connie carried the suitcases to the taxi. We held hands in the cab and looked out of either window. We held hands on the plane, too, Connie's index finger along my wrist as if surreptitiously checking my pulse. The effort of achieving an entirely stress-free journey produced its own anxieties, and we neither of us spoke much. I took the window seat, my forehead resting on the glass.

The sun was shining down on all of Europe that day, and I looked out over Spain and the Mediterranean and then France's great green centre. England rolled around to meet us; the white cliffs, the motorways, the orderly fields of corn and wheat and oilseed rape, the dull English towns with their ring roads and superstores, their high streets and roundabouts. At Heathrow we were greeted by Fran, who was full of jokes and uncharacteristic concern, and we were driven home to our door. 'You okay getting out of the car?' 'You okay getting up the stairs?' 'You allowed a cup of coffee?' This attentiveness soon became quite maddening, the guiding hand on the elbow, the tilt of the head and caring tone of voice, like a terrible glimpse of a geriatric life that I'd assumed was thirty or more years away, and I resolved to do everything within my power to get well. No, more than well, to become healthier and stronger than I'd been before, something that I have gone some way to achieving in the year that has passed since then. The doctors are very pleased with me now. I ride my bicycle down country lanes. I play a kind of badminton with friends, always doubles, though with less of the ferocity of old. I jog sporadically and self-consciously, unsure of what to do with my hands. The prognosis is good.

But I'm leaping ahead. I made a fuss of Mr Jones and submitted to having my face licked. I watched uselessly as Connie carried the cases upstairs. I helped unpack, restoring everything to its usual place – the toothbrush to its holder, the passport to its drawer. Fran left at last and we were alone in the house once more, experiencing that mixture of sadness and pleasure that accompanies return after a long time away; the pile of unopened mail, toast and tea, the sound of a radio, motes of dust in the air. On the hall table, a great pile of unread newspapers described events that we never knew had taken place.

'You forgot to cancel the papers,' I said, filling the recycling bin in one go.

'I had other things on my mind!' said Connie, with some irritation. 'I thought you were dying. Remember?'

We took Mr Jones out for a walk, the usual route, up the hill and back. It was cooler than August had any right to be. There was a suggestion of autumn in the air, that hint of a change in season acting as a tap upon my shoulder. 'I wish I'd brought a coat,' I said as we walked slowly, arm in arm along the lane.

'Do you want me to go back for it?'

'Connie, I don't want you to—'

'I'll run back. Won't take me a minute . . .'

'I don't think you should leave me.'

I spoke for some time about all we had been through. I had been thinking a great deal about where things had gone wrong, and how they might change in the future. Perhaps we might move back to London, or at least find a little place there, and spend the weekends in the city. Move to a smaller house, in the proper countryside. Go out more. Travel further afield. We talked about fresh starts and we talked about our shared past, nearly twenty-five years of it, about our daughter and our son, how we had got through all of that together and how close it had made us. Inseparable, I said, because I found the idea of life without her quite unthinkable, unthinkable in the truest sense; I could not picture a future without her by my side, and I passionately believed that we could and would be happier together than apart. I wanted us to grow old together. The idea of doing so alone, and of dying alone, it was – well, that word again – it was unthinkable, and not just unthinkable, monstrous, frightening. I'd had a glimpse of it and had felt such terror. 'So I don't think you should leave. Things will be better. There are only good things ahead of us from now on, and I will make you happy again, I swear.'

Despite the chill of the evening, we lay down in the long grass on the side of the hill. Connie kissed me, and laid her head on my shoulder and we stayed like this for quite some time, the sound of the M40 a little way off. 'We'll see,' she said after a while. 'There's no rush. We'll see. Let's wait and see how things turn out.'

When we'd set out on our journey I had vowed that I would win her back. But it seemed that I could not fulfil my vow and despite, or perhaps because of my best efforts, I could not make her happy again, or as happy as she wanted to be. The following January, two weeks shy of twenty-five years together, we embraced and said goodbye and began our lives apart.

# part nine

# ENGLAND, AGAIN

—

Home is so sad. It stays as it was left,
Shaped to the comfort of the last to go
As if to win them back. Instead, bereft
Of anyone to please, it withers so,
Having no heart to put aside the theft

And turn again to what it started as,
A joyous shot at how things ought to be,
Long fallen wide. You can see how it was:
Look at the pictures and the cutlery.
The music in the piano stool. That vase.

Philip Larkin, 'Home is so Sad'

## 173. points of view

Here is the same story as you might have heard it, told from alternative points of view.

A young boy grows up with a mother whom he idolises and a father he can barely believe is his own. They argue a great deal, and when not arguing they are often silent. While good-intentioned, the father lacks imagination, emotional intelligence or empathy or some such stuff. Consequently the parents' marriage is full of tension and unspoken resentment, and the boy longs to escape. Like many teenagers, he is a little preten-tious and irresponsible, and is keen to get on with life and find out who he really *is*. But first he must endure a long, dull holiday walking around various dusty old museums, watching his parents bickering, then making peace, then bickering again. He meets a girl, a rebel who has run away from home, and who shares his views on Art! Politics! Life! When his father insults him publicly, the boy runs away with the girl, ignoring his parents' anxious calls and living on the money they make from busking. But the adventure sours. The girl has feelings for him that he is unable to reciprocate despite his best efforts. A question he has carried in the back of his mind for years now demands to be answered and so he flees to a city where he knows no one and asks: just who the hell *am* I? His father, guilt-ridden, tracks him down. An uneasy truce is established, and made firm when he manages to save his father's life – actually *save his life* – in a Barcelona hotel room. Having completed this rite of passage, the charis-matic, complex and unconventional young man leaves his grateful parents and sets off on his own. Who knows what adventures will come his way on this road through, etc., etc., etc.

I believe such stories are called coming-of-age stories. I can see the appeal of that mixture of idealism, cynicism, narcissism and self-righteousness, with some sex and drugs thrown in. It's not really my thing, perhaps because I've never understood that 'who am I?' question. Even as a teenager I always knew who I was, even if I didn't much care for the answer. But I can see that Albie's concerns were somewhat greater than my own. I can see how that story might have been of interest to some.

If not, how about this one?

A young artist – beautiful, witty, a little insecure – leads a wild and irresponsible life with her temperamental but talented boyfriend. They argue violently and break up for the last time and soon after, at a party, she meets another man, a scientist this time, passably attractive, a little conventional perhaps, but nice enough, and they begin a relationship. This man is reliable, intelligent and clearly adores her, and they fall in love. But when he asks her to marry him she hesitates. What about her work, what about the passion and unpredictability of her earlier life? Pushing these doubts aside, she says yes. They marry and for a while they are happy. But their first child dies and their second child is a source of tension. Questions arise in her mind. What about her ambitions as a painter? What about her old life? Her husband is loyal and decent and loves her very much, but her days are now provincial and dull and when the time is right, she summons up all her courage, wakes him in the night and announces her intention to leave. He is heartbroken, of course, and his heartbreak causes her some sadness too. Life alone is difficult for both of them. He asks her to return and she is tempted.

But despite its occasional loneliness there is something thrilling about her new life in a little London flat, about starting to paint again. She resists her husband's pleas. He gets to keep the dog.

She is fifty-two years old, uncertain of the future but happy to be alone.

But then – and here comes the late twist – one night at an old friend's party in London she meets her former lover. He is not the wild, arrogant artist that he used to be. Now he makes an erratic living as a car mechanic, living out on the North Yorkshire moors, still painting brilliantly in his spare time but chastened by his past, the boozing and sleeping around, and full of regret and humility.

But despite the paunch and thinning hair, the artist is still handsome and charismatic. The mutual attraction is still there, even with her thicker waist, the grey in her hair. That same night they fall into bed with each other and, soon after, fall back in love. The woman finds happiness again, and just in time.

This was what I found so hard at first, that Connie and Angelo's story was so much better than my own. I imagine them telling it to people at the kind of parties that they go to now. 'How did you two meet?' the strangers ask, noting the intensity with which they cling to each other, how they still kiss and hold hands like lovers half their age, and they take it in turns to tell how they met thirty years ago, how they married other people but returned like comets on a long trajectory or some such silly-arsed nonsense 'Oh,' the listeners sigh, 'what a lovely story, how romantic,' and meanwhile all those intervening years, all that we went through together, our *marriage*, is contained within parentheses.

# 174. technically

'It's a little more complicated than that, Douglas,' Connie told me. 'We're feeling our way. We're . . . seeing what happens. He says he's changed, but no one changes that much, do they? Even if they want to.' I agreed; no, they did not. 'Anyway, I wanted to tell you. I thought you ought to know straight away. I like to think you'll tell me too. If and when you meet someone. Which I hope you will.'

The occasion was our lunch in London in June, one of the regular meetings we had promised to have when negotiating our separation. We are not divorced and may not be for some time, though I suppose that will happen some day. For the moment, technically, we are still husband and wife. Technically. 'I'm not in any hurry to change that. Are you?' she'd said. No, I was not in any hurry.

The restaurant was in Soho, Spanish-themed for old times' sake, and so fashionable that we had to queue for some time to get in. Queuing, it seems, is also fashionable now. You're meant to feel honoured, and grateful for your seat, and I wonder how long it will be before they ask you to wash up, too. Anyway, we drank wine while waiting in the queue, took our seats – benches, in fact – between couples much younger than us, and it was all very civilised, very pleasant. Anyone watching would have thought that we were a long-time married couple, enjoying our day in the city, which I suppose is more or less what we were; comfortable, familiar, touching across the table, the difference being that soon Connie would be returning to her basement in Kennington and I'd be on the train back to Oxford.

'How is your flat?' asked Connie, hoping for some reassurance, I suppose. 'Is it comfortable? Have you met anyone? Are you happy there?' Please say yes.

## 175. possessions

I had moved to a small but comfortable garden flat on the outskirts of Oxford. Our old family home would be too large and depressing for me to live in on my own. Neither did I relish the prospect of spending my evenings showing prospective buyers around the attractive kitchen, the many light and spacious bedrooms, perfect for a growing family. So a flat was rented while we waited for the house to sell. Conscious of my father's experience, I had made sure that the place was welcoming and cheerful. There was a spare room for when Albie came to stay, a small garden, river walks and friends nearby. Work was forty-five minutes away. There were moments – wet weekday nights or three p.m. on a Sunday afternoon – when an awful sadness overtook the place, finding its way into the corners of each room like some sort of creeping gas, and I would have to pack Mr Jones in the car and go for a brisk walk, but for the most part I was happy enough. Reduced to essentials, it transpired that I needed fewer possessions than I'd thought, and I liked the order and simplicity of this life. Like Darwin's cabin on the *Beagle*, everything was in its place. I worked late. I cooked simple, health-conscious meals. Watched whatever I wanted on television. I exercised. Read. I walked Mr Jones and ran the dishwasher just twice a week.

## 176. good friday

On the first warm day of the year, Connie had driven a hired van from London to the family house ('Can you manage?' 'Of course I can manage.' 'Should I get the train to London and drive the van?' 'Douglas – I can manage!') and we spent that long Easter weekend disentangling our mingled lives. We had invited Albie along, too, promising him that it would not be a grim and acrimonious affair, that there would be almost a carnival atmosphere! But he said that he was busy, photographing the back of people's heads or something, I expect. When I phoned to ask what we should do with all his stuff, his old artwork, his childhood toys, he said, 'Burn it. Burn it all.' Connie and I laughed about this a great deal. We donned rubber gloves to clear his room and, finding a stinking old trainer or an ancient pair of pants, we'd chant, 'Burn it! Burn it all!'

We didn't actually burn anything, that would have felt a little melodramatic, but nevertheless that Easter weekend had the air of a rather melancholy ritual. Five piles were made in separate rooms; one for Connie, one for myself, to dump, to sell, to give to charity, and it was interesting to note how easily everything we owned fell into one of those categories. We did our best to keep the mood upbeat. Connie had made a compilation of new music that she'd discovered – she was listening to music again – and on Saturday we drank wine and ate simple food that did not require many pans. There were chocolate eggs on Sunday morning and later that afternoon, smudge-faced from the dust and cobwebs in the attic, Connie and I went to bed and made love for the last time. I won't say much except to mention that thankfully there was nothing sombre about it. In fact, there was a certain amount of laughter, and warmth and affection. Fondness, I suppose. Afterwards we lay for a long time in that bare room, saying nothing, slept for a while in each other's arms, then woke, got dressed and went downstairs to empty the kitchen cupboards.

## 177. easter sunday

At other times that weekend had the quality of an archaeological dig, the relics getting dustier and shabbier as we sifted further back. Most items were easy to allocate. Connie and I had always had different tastes and although they had converged to an extent over the years, there was rarely any question of what was mine and what was hers. In the early days of our relationship we had bombarded each other with gifts of favourite books and music – or rather Connie had bombarded me – and it seemed churlish now to snatch those items back. And so I kept the John Coltrane CDs and the Kafka short stories, the Baudelaire poems and the Jacques Brel on vinyl, even though I have no record player and would not play it if I did. I was happy to keep them all, because they were the making of us. On the front page of Rimbaud's poetry I found 'Happy Valentine's Day, you wonderful man. I love you very much, signed ???' I showed it to Connie.

'Did you send this?'

She laughed and shook her head. 'Not me.'

I placed the book in my pile, knowing that I would never read it and never throw it away.

Only a few items presented a dilemma. In an old 35mm film canister – artefact of ancient times – we found ten or twelve little yellow chips of ivory. Albie's milk teeth, the ones he hadn't swallowed or lost in the playground. In truth, they were unpleasant, slightly macabre objects, something you might wrinkle your nose at in the Egyptian rooms of a museum, but throwing them away didn't seem right either. Should we take six each? It was all slightly ridiculous, haggling over milk teeth. 'You have them,' I said. So Connie got the milk teeth.

But the photographs were a predicament. We had the negatives, of course, but, even more than the VHS tapes and the audiocassettes, photographic negatives seem like the relics of an ancient civilisation and we threw most of them away. The slim wallet of photos of our daughter went to Connie, and she assured me that she would make good copies for me as soon as she could, a promise she has since fulfilled. With all the other, pre-digital photos, we sat on the floor and dealt them into piles like playing cards, discarding the dull and out of focus, making a stack of the best, the ones that we would both like copies of. Here we were at all those endless parties and weddings, thumbs up in the rain on the Isle of Skye, here was Venice in the rain again, here was Albie on his mother's breast. The process was agonisingly slow, each photo leading us down another avenue of nostalgia. Whatever happened to so-and-so? God, d'you remember that car? Here I was, putting up shelves in the Kilburn flat, smooth-cheeked and impossibly young, and here was Connie on our wedding day.

'That awful dress – what was I thinking of?'

'I think you look wonderful.'

'Look at you in that suit. Very nineties.'

'You do want copies of these, don't you?'

'Of course I do!'

Here was Albie learning to swim on other holidays, here blowing out candles at two, three, four and five. Here he was in a hammock curled up on my chest, asleep. Here were Christmas mornings, school sports days and happier Easters than this one. After a while I found it all too much. From an evolutionary point of view, most emotions – fear, desire, anger – serve some practical purpose, but nostalgia is a useless, futile thing because it is a longing for something that is permanently lost, and I felt its futility now. Rather sourly, I tossed the remaining photos onto the floor, swore and told her she could keep them all. She mumbled something about making copies, and put them in the 'Connie' pile. I slept in a separate room that night.

## 178. easter monday

Bank Holiday Mondays are depressing at the best of times, and the following day was bleak and sour. By lunchtime Connie had loaded up the Transit van. It was barely half full.

'Do you want me to drive you back?'

'I can drive.'

'The motorway will be horrible. I can drive with you and catch the train tonight.'

'Douglas, I'll be fine. I'll see you in London. Next week. I'll choose a restaurant.' We had a deal. Lunch, once a month. No exceptions. Like a therapist or a social worker, she was very strict about these meetings. She wanted to keep an eye on me, I suppose.

'Drive carefully. Use the wing mirrors.'

'I will.'

A moment passed.

'I found that hard,' I said.

'Me too. But it could have been much harder, Douglas.'

'I suppose so.'

'Nothing got smashed against the wall, nothing got torn in two.'

'No.'

'Thank you, Douglas.'

'What for?'

'For not hating me.'

In truth there had been times when I had hated her, in the wrenching and tearing of the previous months, but not then. We kissed goodbye and after she had gone, crunching through the gears on the drive, I went back into the house once more to rinse the mugs, pack the kettle, turn off the gas and water. I loaded up the boot and backseat of my car then walked from room to room, closed the windows and doors for the last time, and noted how empty an empty house can feel. For all the difficulties we had faced there, I had never wanted us to leave and yet here I was closing the front door and posting the keys through the letterbox. There was no reason for me to return, and this felt like defeat and so I felt ashamed.

## 179. amicable

But the lunches in London in April and May were pleasant and light-hearted enough. I had said that life without her by my side was inconceivable and now I was being coaxed into conceiving of a future where we might be friends. Patently, she was happy to be back in the city. The flat in Kennington was tiny, but she didn't mind. She was seeing friends, going to exhibitions, even painting again, and I had to admit that this new life suited her. There was a glow about her, a spark, a quick wit and a vague disreputability that recalled the Connie I'd first met, and this made me both happy and a little sad, because while it was pleasing to see her come back to life, it was harsh to be revealed as the encumbrance to her spirits. So we strove to be cheerful and amicable, and succeeded for the most part, at least until our lunch in June, when she told me about Angelo.

'Was there any overlap? Tell me.'

'No—'

'You'd not been in touch at all?'

'Not until three weeks ago.'

'You swear?'

'Is this really the most important thing?'

'If he's the reason our marriage ended, then yes!'

'He isn't the reason, you know that.'

'Well he must be feeling pretty pleased with himself, I expect.'

'Why?'

'Well, because he won after all!'

'Fuck off, Douglas!'

'Connie!'

'Well, really, how dare you! I'm not some fucking trophy for you and Angelo to tussle over. And he hasn't "won" me, either! We're seeing each other. We're taking things slowly. I thought you had the right to know—'

But I was standing now, searching for my wallet.

'Don't storm out! Don't be melodramatic, please.'

'Connie, I can understand why you'd want this break-up to be pain-free, but it isn't. All right? You can't . . . rip something apart like this and expect not to cause any pain.'

'You're really walking out?'

'Yes, I am, yes.'

'Well, sit down for a minute. We'll get the bill and I'll walk out with you.'

'I don't want you to walk out with—'

'If we're going to storm out, then we'll storm out together.'

I sat down. In silence we split the bill then walked from Soho back towards Paddington, both of us grim-faced and silent until, on Marylebone High Street, she suddenly took my arm. 'You remember when I had that fling?'

'With the guy at work?'

'Angus.'

'Angus. Christ, you're not seeing him as well, are you?'

'Don't make me push you in front of a car, Douglas. That man, he was an idiot, that's not the point. The point is when you threw me out – quite right too – and gave me that ultimatum,

I thought about it for a long, long time. I was dizzy with the fact of being someone's wife. I'd never thought I'd be anyone's wife and I wondered, should I go back? Was it a mistake to get married?'

'Well, clearly it was!'

'No it was not! Don't you see?' She was angry now, holding on to both my arms and forcing me to face her. 'It was not a mistake! That's the whole point. It was not! I have never thought that it was a mistake, never ever, and I have never regretted it since and I never will. Meeting you and marrying you, that was by far the best thing I ever did. You rescued me, and more than once, because when Jane died I wanted to die too, and the only reason I didn't was because you were there. *You*. You are a wonderful man, Douglas, you are, and you have no idea how much I love you and loved being married to you. You made me laugh and taught me things and you made me happy, and now you'll be my wonderful, brilliant ex-husband. We have a wonderful son who is exactly as maddening and absurd as an eighteen-year-old boy should be, and he's our son, *ours*, mine and *yours* now. And the fact that you and I didn't last forever, well, you have to stop thinking of that as failure or defeat. It feels awful now, I know, but this is not the end of your world, Douglas. It is not. It is *not*.'

Well, it was all very emotional, more emotional than a public conversation should be in my opinion, so we stepped into a bar and spent the afternoon there, laughing and crying in turn. Much, much later we parted, friends again, and exchanged various affectionate texts on the journey back. I arrived home a little after nine p.m., the flat cool and quiet, Mr Jones waiting for me at the door. He would need a walk but I suddenly felt very weary and, still wearing my coat, without even turning on the lights, I sat heavily on the sofa.

I took in the familiar possessions in the unfamiliar room, the pictures and posters that I'd not yet got around to hanging, the fading light at the window, the carpet I would not have chosen, the blank TV, too prominent by far.

After several minutes of silence, the telephone rang, the landline, a sound so unusual that it startled me, and I felt strangely nervous about answering.

'Hello?'

'Dad?'

'Albie, you frightened me.'

'It's only just gone nine.'

'No, I mean the landline, I'm not used to it.'

'I thought you preferred it to the mobile?'

'I do, it's just, well, I'm not used to it.'

'So – d'you want me to call the mobile?'

'No, this is good. Is anything wrong?'

'No, nothing's *wrong*, I just wanted a chat, s'all.'

*He has spoken to his mother*, I thought. *She has told him, 'Phone your dad.'* 'Well, how are you? How's college?'

'S'cool.'

'What are you working on?'

And he told me about his projects in great, incomprehensible detail, with that blameless egotism he has – all answers, no questions – and we had a perfectly nice conversation, clocking in at a mighty eleven and a half minutes, a new international world record for a phone call between father and son. While we spoke I warmed up last night's rather good soup, then I said goodbye to Albie and ate it standing up. I took Mr Jones for a walk.

Then, closing the door, finding myself quite cheerful and content, and noting that I was still not remotely sleepy, I did something that I'd been privately contemplating for some time. I sat at my computer, opened a new window and I typed the following words . . .

180. freja kristensen dentist copenhagen

# acknowledgements

I'd like to thank Hannah Macdonald, Michael McCoy, Roanna Benn, Damian Barr and Elizabeth Kilgarriff for their advice and encouragement. Also Paula Alexandre, Rhiannon Rose White, Malcolm Logan, Sadie Holland, Natalie Doherty, Dr Claire Isaac, Alison Moulding, Grenville Fox, Jane Brook and Andrew Shennan for their expertise. Any errors are all mine.

I'm grateful to Jonny Geller, Kirsten Foster and all at Curtis Brown, my editor Nick Sayers, Laura Macdougall, Emma Knight, Auriol Bishop and all the team at Hodder & Stoughton. Also Amber Burlinson, Ayse Tashkiran, Sophie Heawood and, in particular, Erica Stewart and Sands, the stillbirth and neonatal death charity (https://www.uk-sands.org/).

Ernst Gombrich's *The Story of Art* was a great help, as were Wikipedia and Google Maps, and I discovered Nathaniel Hawthorne's letter to Sophie Peabody in Evan S. Connell's fine novel, *Mr Bridge*. The epigraph from *Far From The Tree* is reprinted by permission of The Random House Group, Lorrie Moore and Philip Larkin by permission of Faber, Penelope Fitzgerald by permission of 4th Estate and Elizabeth Taylor by permission of Virago, an imprint of Little, Brown Book Group. While I've done my best to make Douglas' journey accurate, I've sometimes made minor adjustments to reality. For instance, it is not possible to see the Prado from the Plaza de Cibeles, and neither is there a bench in front of Las Meninas.

Finally, love and gratitude is due to Hannah Weaver for her patience and humour, her encouragement and inspiration.

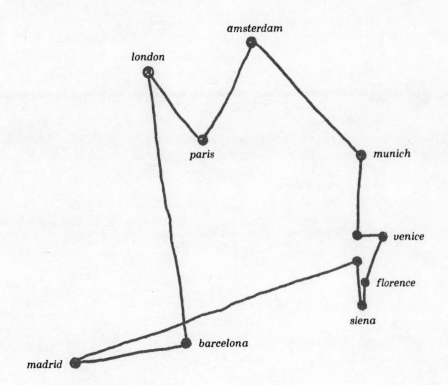

# The Grand Tour

**PARIS** — *Louvre*

**Musée d'Orsay**

Botticelli, fresco
  – *Venus and the Three Graces*
  *Presenting Gifts to a Young Woman*
Uccello – *The Battle of San Romano*
Arcimboldo – *L'Automne*
da Vinci – *Mona Lisa*
Titian – *The Pastoral Concert*
Piero della Francesca – *Portrait of Sigismondo Pandolfo Malesta*
Gericault – *The Raft of the Medusa*

Courbet – *L'Origine du Monde*

**MUNICH** — *Alte Pinakothek*

**VENICE** — *Accademia*

**FLORENCE** — *Uffizi Gallery*

Bruegel
  – *Das Schlaraffenland*
Durer
Raphael
Rembrandt

Veronese
  – *The Feast in the*
  *House of Levi*
Carpaccio, mural
  – *The Legend of Saint Ursula*

Titian – *Venus of Urbino*
Rembrandt – self portraits
Botticelli – *Primavera*

**AMSTERDAM**

*Rijksmuseum*

*Rembrandt House Museum*

*Van Gogh Museum*

Rembrandt
– *Self Portrait as the Apostle Paul*
– *The Night Watch*
Vermeer
– *The Milkmaid*

Van Gogh – *Sunflowers*

**MADRID**

*Museo del Prado*

*Museo Reina Sofía*

**BARCELONA**

Bosch
– *The Garden of Earthly Delights*
Velazquez
– *Las Meninas*
Goya
– *Saturn Devouring His Son*

Picasso
– *Guernica*

# Follow the journey of *Us* at

'I need some fresh air. Goodnight.
Goodnight. I'll find my own way home.'